UNTAMED
HIGHLANDER

DONNA GRANT

St. Martin's Paperbacks

This is a work of fiction. All of the characters, organizations, and events portrayed in this novel are either products of the author's imagination or are used fictitiously.

UNTAMED HIGHLANDER

Copyright © 2011 by Donna Grant.
Excerpt from *Shadow Highlander* copyright © 2011 by Donna Grant.

All rights reserved.

For information address St. Martin's Press, 175 Fifth Avenue, New York, NY 10010.

ISBN: 978-0-312-53347-2

Printed in the United States of America

St. Martin's Paperbacks edition / May 2011

St. Martin's Paperbacks are published by St. Martin's Press, 175 Fifth Avenue, New York, NY 10010.

10 9 8 7 6 5 4 3 2 1

To the incredible Jennifer Haymore.
Your strength, positive attitude, and dedication
to your family while struggling with breast cancer
inspires me. Never give up. And know
we are here for you. Always.

UNTAMED
HIGHLANDER

ONE

Cairn Toul Mountain
Summer 1603

Hayden Campbell swore viciously as he turned over yet another frozen body on the rocky slope.

"This one is dead," Fallon MacLeod yelled from his position farther up the mountain.

"They're all dead." Hayden blew out a breath that puffed around him, ignoring the frigid temperatures and steady snowfall. Though he felt the cold it didn't bother him because he wasn't quite human.

He was a Warrior, an immortal with an archaic god inside him that gave him powers and immeasurable strength— among other things.

Hayden rubbed the ice from his eyelashes as his gaze wandered over the snow-covered slope and the numerous dead Druids. "We should have returned sooner."

Fallon, another Warrior, walked toward him with heavy footsteps, his green eyes grave. "Aye, we should have, but my concern was for Quinn. We scarcely got him and Marcail out of this cursed mountain in time as it was."

"I ken." Hayden gazed at the hated mound of rock. He had always loved looking at the great mountains, but being locked in Cairn Toul for too many decades and forced to watch the evil that grew there took away the pleasure the mountains had once given him. "Damn Deirdre."

Deirdre, the one who began it all, was finally dead. She was a Druid, but from a sect who gave their blood and souls to *diabhul,* the Devil, for the use of black magic. She was, or had been, a *drough.*

There was another set of Druids, the *mie,* who used the pure magic born in all Druids to bond with nature and harness the natural power that came to all of them. The *mie* used their magic to heal and aid those in need, not to destroy as the *drough* and Deirdre did.

But Hayden and the other Warriors had defeated her. It had cost many lives, however. Too many lives.

Hundreds of Druids had been imprisoned in the mountain for Deirdre to drain their blood and harvest their magic to add to her own. No one knew how old Deirdre was, but if Hayden could believe the rumors, she had lived for nearly a thousand years, going back to the time just after Rome was driven from the land by Warriors.

The Warriors had been made thanks to both the *drough* and *mie* in response to the cries of the Celts for help, and Hayden couldn't fault the Druids. Rome had been slowly suffocating Britain, ending all that made Britain great. And the Celts had been unable to defeat them.

The Druids had done what they could for Britain. They had no idea the primeval gods they called up from Hell would refuse to leave the men they took control of.

The gods were so potent the Druids couldn't remove them. The only thing the Druids could do was bind the gods inside the men after Rome had been defeated and departed Britain's shores.

And so the gods moved from generation to generation through the bloodline and into the strongest warriors. Until Deirdre found the MacLeods and unbound their god.

Deirdre's reign of evil had lasted far longer than Hayden liked to think about. Deirdre might have been powerful, but even a *drough* could be killed.

Hayden grinned, reliving the moment Deirdre's neck had been crushed by another Warrior and Hayden had engulfed her in fire.

"What are you smiling at?" Fallon asked, breaking into Hayden's thoughts.

Fallon was leader of their group of Warriors. They had banded together to fight Deirdre and the wickedness she spawned. Though they had expected it would take years, Deirdre had changed everything when she took the youngest MacLeod brother, Quinn, captive. That's when they had taken the fight to Deirdre.

"The fact Deirdre is dead," Hayden explained. "Everything we've been fighting against all these years is over. Gone."

Fallon smiled and slapped him on the shoulder. "It's a wonderful feeling, isn't it? Now all we have to worry about is having the Druids find the spell to bind our gods once more. Then we can live as mortal men."

Binding the gods was all Fallon, Lucan, and Quinn spoke about. But the MacLeod brothers had wives, so they yearned to have their gods gone from their lives.

Hayden, on the other hand, wasn't sure he wanted to be mortal again. He was too powerless that way.

"I'm going to look on the other side of the mountain," Fallon said. "Maybe we'll find someone alive."

"I think the ones who could make it out of the mountain did. It was the weather that killed them."

Fallon blew out a ragged breath and clenched his jaw. "We should look inside the mountain, then. Some might have been too afraid to leave."

They both turned to the door that stood ajar amid the

rock as if waiting for them to enter its wicked domain. All Druids were gifted with a certain power. Deirdre's had been moving stone. She had instructed the mountain to shift and form so that she had a palace inside it, shielded from the world.

Hidden from all.

Countless Druids had died heinously, and many a Highlander had been brought to her to have his god unbound. If he didn't house a god, he was killed.

Even now Hayden could smell the stench of death and iniquity that permeated from the mountain, could still feel the helplessness which had weighed heavily on his shoulders while he had been locked in one of the various prisons.

But he had been one of the lucky ones. Hayden had broken free and escaped, determined to fight Deirdre and her bid to rule the world.

"Why would anyone stay inside that place?" Hayden murmured as unease rippled down his spine. He fisted his hands and forced himself to stand still and not give into the urge to turn away from the malevolent mountain.

Fallon scratched his jaw, his gaze thoughtful. "I doona know, but it's worth a look. We freed these people, and it's our responsibility to make sure they return to their homes."

Hayden considered Fallon's words. "They may not want our help. We are, after all, Warriors. They might not be able to tell the difference between us and the Warriors who allied themselves to Deirdre."

"True. But I must look either way. I wasna held longer than a few days in the mountain so it doesn't hold the memories for me as it does for you."

Hayden might not want to go into Cairn Toul, but he would. "I'm not afraid."

Fallon put his hand on Hayden's shoulder and looked

into his eyes. "I would never think that, my friend. I would not torment you, though." He dropped his arm and smiled. "Besides, I want to return to Larena as quickly as I can. You give a final look over the mountain while I go inside."

Before Hayden could object Fallon was gone. He used the power his god gave him to "jump" inside the mountain in the blink of an eye. Fallon couldn't jump somewhere he had never been before, but the use of his power had saved them countless times.

They all had different powers. For Hayden, Ouraneon, the god of massacre which was inside him, gave him the ability to call up and control fire. There were other differences as well. Each god favored a color, so every Warrior transformed to that color when he released his god.

Yet, for all their differences, there was a great deal they had in common, like strength, speed, enhanced senses, as well as deadly claws and sharp fangs. The most disturbing, though, was that their eyes changed to the same color as their god.

It had taken Hayden a long time to get used to that. He hadn't seen his own eyes, but he could imagine how he looked when the whites of his eyes disappeared and his entire eye turned red.

As much as Hayden had rebelled and fought the god within him, that same god allowed him to defeat Deirdre. With Deirdre dead and his family massacred by a *drough* sent by Deirdre, there was nothing in this world for Hayden to do.

For so many years he had roamed Scotland, watching the world change around him while he hunted *droughs*. Deirdre had taunted him that she had sent a *drough* to kill his family as she tortured him day after day. So he fought against Deirdre while seeking his vengeance on the *droughs*.

Now there was no place for him in this new world.
There was no place for him anywhere.

He continued his wandering of the mountain, looking
for anyone who might still be alive, as he thought of what
his next move might be. He had stayed in Scotland because of Deirdre and his revenge, but maybe he would
travel and see the different countries others spoke about.

Hayden leaned against a boulder and raked his hand
through his damp hair. The snowfall had begun to grow
more dense, the flakes thicker and heavier, but it didn't
hamper his superior eyesight. They stuck to his eyelashes
and covered everything in a blinding white blanket.

Hours went by with Hayden locating nothing but more
dead. The fact they were most likely Druids only made the
findings more difficult to bear. Druids might have magic,
but they were susceptible to the elements as any human
was, and thanks to Deirdre's affinity for killing them, the
Druids were becoming more and more scarce.

A shout from Fallon let Hayden know it was time to
return to MacLeod Castle. As Hayden began to turn away
something caught his eye.

He paused and narrowed his gaze when a gust of wind
lifted a lock of long, black hair in the snow. Though Hayden
knew the woman was most likely dead, he hurried to her
anyway, hopeful he would leave the mountain with at least
one alive. He spotted the pool of bright red blood in the
snow that gave him hope she was still alive.

"Fallon," he barked while scraping away the flurries
and ice from around the small, much too slim body.

The woman was lying on her stomach, an arm bent with
her hand near her face and matted ebony hair obscuring
her features. Her fingers were slim as they dug into the
snow as if she had tried to crawl away.

Hayden could only imagine the pain she had been put through, the heartache Deirdre had given her. He held his breath as he put a finger beneath her nose and felt a soft stirring of air.

At least they would leave the cursed mountain with one life. He reached for her and paused again. He didn't want to hurt her, but it had been so long since he had been gentle, he wasn't sure he knew how. All he knew was battle and death.

Maybe he should allow Fallon care for her. But as soon as the thought went through his mind, Hayden rejected it. He found her, he would see to her. He didn't know why, he just knew that it was important to him.

Hayden blew out a breath and slowly, firmly placed his hands on the woman's body before he tenderly turned her over. Her arm fell to the side, lifeless and still. Disquiet settled in his gut like a stone.

He shifted so that he leaned over her, shielding her from the onslaught of snow. Once he had her in his arms, Hayden brushed the hair from her face to see her incredibly long black lashes spiked with frozen snow.

He felt something shift inside him when he saw her face was pale as death, but even beneath the scratches, dried blood, and ice he could see her beauty, her timeless allure.

She had high cheekbones and a small, pert nose. Her brows were as black as the midnight sky and arched over her eyes. Her lips were full, sensual, and her neck long and lean.

But it was her cream-colored skin, so flawless and perfect, that made him reach out and stroke her cheek with the back of his finger.

A shock of something primitive and urgent went through

his body like a bolt of lightning. He couldn't take his eyes from her, couldn't stop touching her.

Her body struggled for breath, struggled for life, proving she was a fighter. Even with the elements taking the breath from her one heartbeat at a time, she didn't give up.

Something inside him broke at that moment. He hadn't been able to save his family or the many Druids on Cairn Toul, but he would save this woman, whoever she was.

A feeling of protectiveness wound through him. It had been so long since he'd felt protective of anyone or anything that he almost hadn't recognized the emotion. Now that he did, however, it grew stronger the longer he held her in his arms.

He would make sure she survived. He would ensure she was protected at all times. It wouldn't make up for the lives of his family or the Druids, but he had to do it.

Hayden found himself wishing she'd open her eyes so he could see them. He wanted to give his oath to her right then, for her to know he would fight with her. Instead, she lay unconscious in his arms.

His vow would have to wait, but nothing could stop him from pledging himself to her.

"Does she live?" Fallon asked.

Hayden glanced up, startled to find Fallon near when he hadn't heard him approach. That wasn't like Hayden, but then again, he had never held such a lovely woman in his arms before, especially one who needed him as she did. "Just. She's bleeding badly, though I cannot tell where she is wounded."

"Judging by the blood on your hand, I would say somewhere on her back."

Hayden looked at the hand holding her and grimaced. He doubted they had much time to save her. For the first

time in . . . ages . . . the need to defend, to shield someone consumed him, drove him. "She's shivering."

"Then let's get her out of here," Fallon said.

Hayden lifted her small frame in his arms. She was
light, but through her clothes he could feel the sumptuous
curves that proclaimed her a woman. He gave a nod to
Fallon and waited. Fallon laid his hand on Hayden's arm,
and in a blink they were standing in the great hall of
MacLeod Castle.

"God's teeth!" someone yelled at their sudden appearance in the castle.

"Sonya!" Fallon bellowed.

The hall swarmed with Warriors, but Hayden only had
eyes for the woman. He wanted, nay needed, her to survive,
and was surprised to find himself praying—something he
hadn't done since before his family's murder. He decided
then and there he would protect her with his life.

He felt the warm stickiness of her blood as it traveled
from his hand down his arm to his elbow to drop on the
stone floor. Her breathing was ragged, her body so still he
would think her dead if he didn't see her chest rising and
falling, slowly but surely.

"Sonya, hurry!" Hayden shouted. The thought of holding another dead body in his arms made Hayden's heart
quicken with dread.

Death surrounded him, always had, most likely always
would. But now, he wanted life for this small woman,
whoever she was.

There was a whooshing sound as Broc landed in the
great hall, Sonya in his arms. Broc folded his large, sleek
indigo wings against him as he set Sonya on her feet and
pushed his god down and returned to normal.

Sonya said not a word as she rushed to Hayden. The

single, thick braid holding her fiery hair hung down her back with small tendrils curling about her face.

"Put her on the table," Sonya instructed him.

Hayden didn't want to relinquish his hold on the woman, but he knew he had no choice if he wanted her to survive. He glanced at her, at her parted lips and ethereal face. "She's cold."

"And I'll get her warm as soon as I heal her," Sonya told him, her amber eyes meeting his gaze. "Let me heal her, Hayden."

Quinn took a step toward the table. "Broc—"

"I know," Broc answered.

Hayden looked between the two Warriors to find their gazes locked on the female in his arms. There was something in their tone, something he should recognize, but he couldn't focus on anything but the woman.

He forced his attention back to Sonya. "I think the wound is on her back."

"Then lay her on her stomach," Sonya said as she pushed up the sleeves of her gown.

"I'll help," said Lucan's wife, Cara.

Hayden glanced down at Cara. They'd had their differences, and in some ways still did since Cara carried *drough* blood in her veins. She might never have undergone the ritual, but it was enough that Hayden had wanted to see her dead.

It was only out of respect for the MacLeods that Hayden left Cara alone. Still, it rankled him to have her near. Evil bred evil, it was just a matter of time before it took Cara.

The next thing Hayden knew, the other two women of the castle, Marcail and Larena, were also there. All but Larena were Druids. Larena was the only female Warrior, and she had the distinction of being Fallon's wife.

Matter of fact, the only female who wasn't mated to a MacLeod was Sonya, and Hayden had seen the way Broc watched the Druid when he thought no one was looking.

"I need her gown cut," Sonya said.

Hayden didn't hesitate to allow a red claw to lengthen from his fingertip. He sliced the woman's gown with one swipe, and when the gown fell open to reveal the female's back, the entire hall sucked in a breath. Hayden's gut clenched and his blood turned to ice.

"Holy hell," Quinn murmured and rubbed a hand over his mouth.

There were no words as Hayden stared at the scars that crisscrossed the slender back of the woman on the table. Whoever this female was, she had suffered greatly and horrifically. And often. If he felt protective of her before, it was nothing compared to what arose in him then.

He would find who did this to her, find them and make them suffer as they had made her suffer. Then he would kill them.

However, it was the wound on her shoulder which drew Hayden's gaze. "What happened to her?"

Sonya leaned close and poked at the bleeding injury. "Looks like a blade of some sort. I need to clean it to be sure what happened, but from what I can see I think the weapon pierced her skin, and then was dragged from her shoulder down her back to her shoulder blade."

In an instant a bowl of water was placed next to Sonya. She wrung out a cloth and began to clean the woman's wound. Agonizing moments later, Sonya lifted her head, her lips compressed in a tight line.

"There's magic involved in this wound. I cannot tell if it caused the wound or only made it fester."

Lucan and Fallon moved to stand on either side of Quinn, who was at the woman's feet. Broc had also shifted closer to Sonya. It was then Hayden looked around the hall and noticed every Warrior at MacLeod Castle now ogled the female.

Hayden's gaze swung to Quinn to find the youngest MacLeod watching him with sharp, pale green eyes. Before he could ask Quinn why he was staring, the woman let out a low moan full of suffering and agony.

Sonya stilled. A heartbeat later she tossed down the cloth and lifted her hands over the woman's wound, palm down, fingers splayed. Sonya's eyes closed, and Hayden could feel her magic fill the hall as she began to heal the wound.

Cara and Marcail soon joined their magic with Sonya's, but nothing they did seemed to assist the healing. The woman let out a scream and tried to jerk from the table.

Hayden held her down, careful not to touch her wound, but the more magic the Druids used, the worse the woman became. Frustration welled up within Hayden while he watched helplessly as the woman suffered.

"What are you doing to her?" he demanded of Sonya.

The Druid's amber eyes snapped open to glare at him. Sonya reached over and took Cara's and Marcail's arms and lowered them. As soon as they did the woman stopped her movements and laid still and quiet.

It was like she had died. Yet Hayden could still see the breath leaving her body, could still see the blood flow from the wound.

"Something isn't right," Sonya said.

Marcail shook her head, her rows of tiny, sable braids on the crown of her head moving against her cheek. "It was almost as if she fought against our magic."

"What could possibly do that?" Cara asked. Her mahogany eyes sought out Sonya, but Sonya didn't answer.

Instead, Sonya moved aside the tangled mass of ebony

locks from the woman's neck. With slow movements, she tugged at the thin leather strap until she found what she was looking for.

Hayden took one look at the Demon's Kiss dangling from Sonya's fingers and felt the same betrayal and fury he had on the night of his family's murder.

TWO

"Easy, Hayden," Quinn said.

Hayden swiveled his head to the MacLeods. An icy feeling of dread consumed him as he looked at the brothers. "You knew, didn't you? You knew who she was, what she is?"

"Aye," Quinn answered. "Before you condemn Isla, know that Deirdre kept her sister and niece prisoners in Cairn Toul."

But all Hayden could think about was the Demon's Kiss around Isla's neck. It was but a small silver vial. However, it held the first drops of a Druid's blood after they completed the ritual of a *drough* to serve *diabhul*.

A *drough*. The very thing Hayden had scoured Scotland to kill.

Druids were born with pure magic, magic which was all that was good and right. But there were some who wanted more magic than a *mie* had. Those Druids turned against all the good inside them and become *droughs*.

Hayden glanced down at Isla, the woman he had been willing to vow to protect. Her face was turned toward him with scratches on her cheek and forehead. How could he have ever wanted to shield her?

"She's *drough*." Hayden spat the word as if it was the

vilest thing he had ever encountered, and next to Deirdre, it was.

Droughs deserved only death. Anything so immoral shouldn't be allowed to walk the earth.

Broc folded his arms across his chest. "You doona know Isla, Hayden."

"I know all I need to know."

"Enough!" Fallon bellowed before a full blown argument could ensue. "Sonya, can you use Isla's Demon's Kiss to heal her wound? I'd like to speak with her."

Hayden fisted his hands in an effort not to jerk the vial out of Sonya's hands and toss it away forever. The blood in the vial could heal a *drough* of its wounds instantly, or kill a Warrior. There was something about a *drough*'s blood that was poison to a Warrior.

As if Sonya knew what he was thinking, she clutched the vial in her hand and stared at him. Hayden didn't want to harm Sonya, so he could only watch as she uncorked the vial and tilted the small silver bottle over Isla's wound.

Only nothing came out.

"It's empty." Sonya lifted her eyes first to Quinn, and then looked at Broc. "There's nothing left."

Lucan ran a hand down his face and blew out a harsh breath. "Look at her scars. I say she had cause to use her Demon's Kiss many times before."

"There's not that much in the vials," Cara said, fingering her own Demon's Kiss around her neck.

Hayden had to remind himself Cara wasn't a *drough*, that it was her mother's necklace she wore. The element which had sent him killing all *droughs* after his family's murder raged within him again. There was a *drough* on the table and another with *drough* blood around her neck. He could kill them both in a matter of moments.

But if he did he'd lose the first home he'd had since his own. He'd lose the men he called friends, brothers. He lowered his eyes to Isla's midnight locks and tried to calm the anger raging through him.

"Heal her, Sonya," Fallon ordered. "Regardless that she served Deirdre and is a *drough*, I willna allow her to die in my castle."

Hayden had seen enough. He might have found Isla and brought her to the castle, but he wouldn't stay and help them to mend her. Once the evil was inside a *drough*, it was always there.

He started to turn away when Isla stiffened and let out a tortured scream that made even Hayden jerk in response. Her body began to shake on the table and blood poured from her wound.

"What's happening?" Fallon asked.

Sonya shrugged, a look of confusion and helplessness on her face. "I have no idea."

"Let me," Galen said. The dark blond Warrior walked to the head of the table and placed his hand on Isla's skull. Almost immediately he snatched his hand back with a hiss, his face losing all color.

He paused for just a moment before he flattened his lips. "Hold her."

Quinn grabbed Isla's ankles. "What did you see?"

Galen shook his head and once more placed his hand on Isla's head.

Broc, Quinn, Fallon, and Lucan all had hold of Isla. Only Hayden refused to touch her. He started to move aside so another Warrior could help when Galen put his other hand on Hayden's head.

In a blink, Hayden could see images projected in his mind of Isla being beaten and whipped by Deirdre in ways that would have most men begging for their lives.

Deirdre was vicious in her torture, her laughter ringing inside Hayden's mind as she slashed Isla's back over and over again, leaving Isla soaked in blood.

Isla withstood it all, her body moving with the impact of the hits, her face never showing any emotion, not even when the cuts penetrated muscle to the bone.

Hayden then saw Deirdre with her hand above Isla's chest and a black cloud rushing over Isla to engulf her. The cloud suffocated Isla, tearing at her soul and making her see people being ripped apart, their terrified screams echoing in Isla's mind.

The images brought Hayden to his knees only to come level with a pair of the most amazing ice-blue eyes which were staring at him.

"End this," Isla whispered. "Please, take my head."

Not knowing if it was real or not, Hayden pushed Galen's hand from his head, but Isla still gazed at him.

"Please," she begged hoarsely, her eyes beseeching him. "You must kill me now."

It was what Hayden should do. She was a *drough*, and *droughs* must die. But no matter how she pleaded with her mesmerizing blue eyes, Hayden couldn't bring himself to do it.

Was it because of what Galen had shown him, or because of the soft pleading in her voice? Whatever it was, Hayden knew he couldn't be the one to end her life.

Sonya once more tried to heal Isla, and this time Hayden grasped Isla's arm when she tried to move away. Isla fought them with all her might, but she was weakened from her injury. The mix of worry and dread in Hayden's stomach only grew the more magic Sonya poured into Isla.

Isla screamed words Hayden didn't understand, they were so garbled with pain. No matter how they held her, she fought to get away.

Time stretched into eternity and the hall was flooded with magic before Isla's eyes finally closed as she fell back into unconsciousness. Hayden was surprised to find her hand holding onto his arm in a death grip, her broken nails cut into the skin of his forearm.

"Do you still want to kill her?" Galen asked, his tone clipped, angry. "After you saw what was in her mind, do you still think she deserves to die?"

Hayden didn't bother to answer. He wasn't sure if he could. His need to protect warred with the feelings that demanded justice for his family's death. What he was going to do in the end, he hadn't decided yet.

A glance at Isla's shoulder showed the wound had mended, but not as it should have. It no longer gaped and oozed blood, but it wasn't fully healed either.

"Isla fought Sonya's magic," Broc said into the silence.

Quinn shook his head. "Why would she do that?"

"She asked me to kill her," Hayden said, still kneeling so his face was even with Isla's. He tried to look away, but was held captivated by her haunting beauty. He was more than troubled by her request. Troubled and disturbed because he'd seen the earnestness of her appeal on her eyes. Why would she want to die? "She told me she needed to die, to end it."

"We heard her," Fallon said. He sighed and looked to Larena. "Do we have a spare chamber?"

Hayden climbed to his feet. Since Deirdre had destroyed the cottages they had built, everyone was housed in the castle with no room to spare. "Give her mine," Hayden said before he changed his mind.

He rolled his eyes when everyone just stared at him. "She canna stay on the table, and all the chambers are full."

Fallon gave a small nod. "See it done."

Hayden watched as Sonya motioned to Broc, who gently rolled Isla onto her back and lifted her in his arms. Hayden didn't take pleasure in the fact that he wanted to be the one who carried Isla.

That the need to hit Broc for daring to touch her had Hayden rising to his feet with his hand fisted. It was ridiculous. She was a *drough*.

"Are you all right?"

Hayden turned to find his closest friend, Logan, beside him. Logan was the one who kept everyone laughing. He was always ready with a jest and a smile. But there was no smile on his face now, only concern reflected in his hazel eyes.

"Aye, my friend," Hayden lied. He tried to keep from looking at Broc carrying Isla, but failed. Hayden hated the war going on inside of himself. It should be easy. Isla was *drough*, and because of that she should die.

Why then couldn't Hayden bring himself to kill her?

Logan moved to stand in front of him. "What did you see when Galen put his hand on your head?"

The other Warriors moved closer around Hayden. All of them, it seemed, wanted to know the answer. He swallowed and tried to form the words, but couldn't. Even after everything he had witnessed in his one hundred and eighty years of immortality, what he had seen in Isla's mind horrified him.

To see that torment done to a man was one thing, but to know it had been done to a woman, a woman who was supposed to be cherished and protected by the men of her family, sickened him.

"Horrors unlike you could possibly imagine," Galen answered when Hayden couldn't. "Isla suffered greatly, and repeatedly, at Deirdre's hand, of that Hayden and I can attest to."

Lucan leaned on the table and drummed his fingers. "Yet she served Deirdre."

"Did she?" Quinn asked. His brow furrowed and he crossed his arms over his chest. "I'm not so sure. There were times I thought she might have been trying to help me in Cairn Toul. The way she spoke sometimes, as if her words held double meaning, as if she had been trying to tell me something."

There was a snort from the back of the hall. Hayden turned to find one of the twins, Duncan, with his long brown hair, standing against the wall whittling a piece of wood.

"Let's not forget," Quinn ignored Duncan and continued. "We all saw Isla's sister in the blue flames, bound and used by Deirdre. Though none of you saw her, there is Isla's niece who Deirdre used her magic to keep as a child."

Fallon walked to Larena's side and put his arm around his wife's shoulders. "I went inside the mountain to look for survivors who might not have left. I found a child. She was dead, the dagger still sticking from her stomach."

"Though I wish no child death, Deirdre had corrupted her," Quinn said. "It's probably better that she is dead."

Larena licked her lips and glanced at Fallon. "What now? Once Isla is healed, what do we do with her?"

"Keep her as a prisoner as she did all of us," Duncan said.

Before Duncan could say more, his twin, Ian, put a hand on his shoulder. "It wasn't Isla who captured us. That was Deirdre, and she's dead."

"I won't allow her to be a prisoner," Larena said before Duncan could argue with his twin.

Fallon shook his head. "Nay, we willna imprison Isla. We'll heal her and send her on her way."

Hayden tried to get the vision of Isla's hauntingly beautiful ice-blue eyes out of his mind, but he couldn't. He wanted to see her again, to make sure he hadn't been mistaken of their color. And her vulnerability.

"What happened at Cairn Toul?" Lucan asked Hayden and Fallon.

Hayden lowered himself on a bench with his back against the table and listened with half an ear as Fallon told the others what occurred during their search of the mountain.

"And then I brought them here," Fallon finished. "The rest you know."

Quinn blew out a long breath. "I had hoped you wouldn't find anyone, that all had managed to get away, but I fully expected them to be alive if anyone was still at the mountain."

"It was too cold," Hayden said, remembering how the strands of Isla's ebony hair had been frozen.

While the MacLeod brothers gathered close together and spoke in whispers, Hayden lifted a brow when Galen and Logan sat on either side of him.

Hayden wasn't the type of man who wanted—or needed—company. If anything, he desired to be alone with his thoughts, particularly those that warred within him now. It was how he had lived for so long, that even being at MacLeod Castle with the other Warriors sometimes got to him and had him leaving the castle.

He never went far, but just being by himself always helped.

"I willna apologize for giving you a glimpse into Isla's mind," Galen said after a lull of silence.

Hayden shrugged. "I didn't ask for an apology."

Logan cocked his head to the side and narrowed his eyes. "You didn't see your face when you discovered she was *drough*. For a moment, I thought you would kill her where she lay."

Did they think him such a monster? Hayden drew in a tired breath. He supposed he was such a beast. He couldn't deny the urge to kill her had passed through his mind or that he still considered it. She had asked it of him, after all.

How could he ignore the fact she was *drough* when it was a *drough* who had slaughtered his family—every one of them?

"I don't murder people," Hayden said. "I give the *droughs* a fair chance at battle before I kill them."

Logan leaned forward until his elbows rested on his knees. "I wouldna blame you for wanting to kill her. As you said, she's a *drough*. And I know why you hate them so."

He was one of the few who Hayden had confided in, one of the few who knew why Hayden's hatred went so deep. Deirdre had taken something from every Warrior, so Hayden didn't expect special treatment for the grudge he carried.

Galen rose to his feet. "I don't know your reasons, Hayden, but I can guess. If you ever want to have a future you must let go of the past."

Once Galen had walked away, Logan turned his head to Hayden. "Would you be sitting here if Isla wasn't a *drough*?"

Hayden raised a brow. "What?"

"It's a simple enough question. I saw how protective of her you were. I'll ask again. Would you be sitting here if Isla wasn't a *drough*?"

Hayden shook his head, unable to deny the answer.

"I didna think so." Logan sat up and rubbed his hands on his thighs. "Arran said she was pretty."

Arran would know, too. He, Ian, and Duncan had been

locked in Deirdre's mountain together with Quinn. The four Warriors had formed a tight bond during those awful weeks in the Pit.

Hayden had just thought his torment was over with Deirdre's death, but the presence of a *drough*, even one who might have been forced to serve Deirdre, put his sanity to the test.

THREE

Hayden stayed in the corner of his chamber. He'd told himself to stay away, that he didn't care about Isla, but his curiosity about her had swayed him. And Fallon had requested his presence. Why, Hayden wasn't so sure.

He watched Isla thrash on the bed, her black hair tangled about her head and face. She burned with fever. Her body was flushed and sweat glistened on her skin, but he had a suspicion that's not what made her mumble incoherently in her sleep, fear and dread visible on her oval face.

"I don't understand," Cara said from beside Lucan, their hands joined together. "Why didn't our magic heal her? I've seen Sonya heal more serious wounds."

Sonya shifted her thick braid over her shoulder, her gaze on Isla. "She fought our magic. It's like she doesn't want to be healed."

"She did ask Hayden to kill her," Fallon said.

Marcail sat beside the bed and wiped Isla's brow once more with a damp cloth. "Regardless, she is in much pain. I can sense the terror within her."

Hayden saw Quinn start toward his wife, but he wasn't quick enough. Marcail put her hand on Isla and right before their eyes they saw the stiffness leave Isla's body in the space of a heartbeat.

"Marcail, damn you," Quinn said as he knelt and caught his wife against him as she crumpled to the side.

Before Marcail could answer, she leaned over and emptied her stomach in a bucket. When she finished and Quinn turned her in his arms, Marcail's face was ashen and sweat beaded her brow.

Isla had begged for death and fought the healing, but still Marcail had used her magic and pulled the emotions within Isla into her own body. It was Marcail's gift as a Druid. She could take others' emotions into herself, though the greater the emotion the more it made Marcail ill.

Quinn held Marcail gently as the effects rushed through her body. "Why?" Quinn asked his wife.

"I could help her. Why wouldn't I? She didn't hurt us in Deirdre's mountain, Quinn. Not once did she ever harm us."

"How bad is it?"

Marcail visibly swallowed and closed her eyes. "Awful. I've never felt anything so ghastly in my life. Not even when I took Duncan's pain from him. I don't know how Isla is still alive."

Hayden saw the slight movement on the bed and elbowed Fallon. "She moves."

Isla knew it was a dream, but she didn't care. She was with her sister, Lavena, once more. And in Isla's arms was the most beautiful little girl alive—Grania, her niece.

The thick woods of her home surrounded Isla in their comfort and beauty. As a Druid she loved nature, and the closer she was to it the stronger her magic became.

The sky was clear and the birds loud as they flew from branch to branch while their songs filled the air. The smell of pine and oak, of fern and heather mixed together to bring the familiar smell of the forest to her. Isla could stay in the area forever.

But as always the beautiful day turned black and grim with the arrival of the mercenaries. Grania's laughter turned into shrieks of panic as she was jerked from Isla's arms.

Isla fought to get to her niece but the men were too strong, laughing through her struggles. Lavena yelled at Isla to get Grania, but Isla could do nothing against the strong arms that held her.

She managed to get free and tried to reach Grania, but a meaty fist slammed into her face, stopping Isla in her tracks. Then the men separated the three of them. Dread filled Isla. Not for herself but for her sister and Grania.

The dream changed again, turning darker and even more sinister as she was delivered into hell—Deirdre's lair in the mountain. Thick black smoke surrounded her, the evil palpable as it began to drown her in the vapor.

And then, the dream was gone. For a moment Isla did nothing but lay there, unsure of what had happened. She didn't know where she was. The anguish of her dreams had vanished. The terror of it all, however, still filled her.

Of a sudden, she recalled the solemn black eyes which had stared at her as she begged for death. Obviously the blond man hadn't carried out her wishes.

Isla tried to swallow and felt her raw throat rebel at the effort. Her body burned with the ravages of a fever and her skin itched from sweating, but at least she was out of the snow and ice.

Between one heartbeat and the next she realized she wasn't alone. She cracked open her eyes to find herself staring at Fallon and Lucan MacLeod as they stood at the foot of the bed.

Isla threw off the covers and dashed toward the door she spotted to her left. Instant, agonizing pain tore through her, but she had withstood far worse in her years at Cairn Toul and she pushed through the weighty mantle of pain.

She had to get away from them, away from everyone, before it was too late! She had taken only a few steps before a big blond stepped in front of the doorway, effectively blocking her escape.

She skidded to a halt, her body aching with each breath. With frantic hands Isla clawed at the strands of hair that clung to her sweat-covered face so she could better see. Her gaze scanned the chamber to find five men and three women watching her, but her gaze returned to the blond giant.

He stood silently, almost at ease, but she wasn't fooled. He had the look of a Warrior, battle-hardened and ready for anything. At any moment.

"Let me leave," she demanded of the chamber at large.

"Isla, you're injured."

She blinked and focused her vision on the man who spoke. "Broc?" Could the winged Warrior actually have sided with the MacLeods? Somehow she wasn't surprised.

"Aye. It's me." His voice was soft, as if he were talking to a half-wit. "You need to rest."

Isla shook her head, and then instantly regretted it as the chamber spun. She stepped back and ran into a wall. Her stomach churned, and she sunk her fingers into the stones to help keep herself standing. Her body was weak, and she didn't know how long she could stand before what little strength she had was depleted.

"You have to let me go," she panted. "Now. You have no idea what you've done by bringing me here."

Fallon MacLeod stepped forward, his dark brown hair pulled in a queue at the back of his neck. He looked like the natural leader that he was. "Deirdre is dead, Isla. There is nothing for you to fear anymore."

Isla couldn't control the bubble of laughter that welled up inside her. She clamped a hand over her mouth and blinked back the sudden rush of tears. She shook her head and lowered her hand. "She's not dead."

"She is," Lucan said.

Quinn nodded. "Listen to my brothers, Isla, for they're correct. I saw Deirdre die with my own eyes."

Isla briefly wondered why Marcail, who was on Quinn's lap, looked ill, but the need to leave was too great for her to think of anything else. "Deirdre isn't dead."

A red-headed female with sharp amber eyes took a step toward Isla. "You have a fever, and your wound festers. Allow your body to recover. You will then see we speak the truth."

Isla knew it was pointless to argue with them. As much as she didn't want to say the words, she had to. "Stop it!" she yelled. "I'm not addled. I know Deirdre better than any of you. She isn't dead, because if she was, I would be as well. We are linked through her black magic."

The MacLeods shared a look, but it was Broc's furrowed brow that told her he might understand what she was trying to say. Even the blond giant's brow puckered at her words.

"Broc, I'm speaking true," Isla said. He had to trust her so she could leave. "Deirdre isn't dead. You have to believe me."

Fallon shook his head. "I doona understand this. We saw Deirdre's neck snap, and Hayden set her on fire."

Isla didn't know who Hayden was and didn't care. "Deirdre cannot be killed by a broken neck or being burned."

"Stay here and heal," Quinn said again. "If you leave now you'll die."

"If only that were true," Isla murmured, tired to her soul. She saw the hulking blond glance away from her and she took that moment to dart toward him, intent on escaping under his arm.

She wasn't quick enough, however. As she reached him, his arms wrapped around her like iron manacles and dragged her against his hard chest. Her injury throbbed and her bones felt as if they would crush any moment under the impact of his strength. She looked up into the same black eyes she had seen before.

His face was a mask of anger, but flickering in the dark depths of his eyes, Isla saw a glimmer of emotion, as if he battled within himself over something.

Her hands had come to rest against his chest to push away, but beneath her palms was a solid wall of hard, un-yielding muscle which wouldn't be budged.

For a moment, she had the insane urge to run her hands over his chest, to feel all that sinew moving beneath her fingertips. She lost herself in the black pits of his eyes, wondering what it would feel like to stop fighting him and lay her head on his thick shoulder, to relinquish the need to stay strong and allow him to carry her burdens for a bit.

She had seen striking men before, but there was something about the man holding her that was different, special. It could be the hardness of his black eyes or the way his blond brows slashed over those eyes giving him a harsh, sinister look.

It could be the strong jaw and chin and hollowed cheeks or the way his blond hair fell haphazardly around his face and shoulders, as if he raked his hands through it often.

Whatever it was that held her it urged her not to fight him, to give into the new and wondrous sensations his touch caused. Her eyes dropped to his lips. What would it be like to press her mouth against his? She had never kissed a man before, never wanted to.

What was it about this man? How was he connected to the MacLeods? And what was wrong with her? Had her wound affected her thinking and her body?

All too soon she remembered where she was, and why she needed to leave.

"You should have taken my head as I asked," she told him.

His wide, firm lips compressed into a tight line. She knew she should fight him, but she was held transfixed by the handsome face staring back at her.

"Nay." That one word was said with finality, his deep voice laced with an edge.

Though she couldn't see much of his body, the way he held her effortlessly against him told her all she needed to know about his strength. The fact he was a Warrior was a given.

She also noticed while the others wore tunic and breeches, this Warrior wore a kilt of blue, green, and white with a saffron shirt beneath it that did nothing to hide his chest corded with muscles, muscles her hands itched to caress.

"Please," she tried again, disturbed to her soul at her reaction to this man. "Let me leave. You're all in terrible danger if I stay."

His gaze flickered over her shoulder, and that's when Isla heard the chant.

"Nay!" she screamed and tried to wrench out of the Warrior's arms. "Do not make me slumber!"

The last thing she wanted to do was go back to sleep and be tormented by her nightmares once more. There was no chance for her to fight the magic, though, not in her damaged state. She tried to beg the Warrior once more, but the sleeping chant took her before she could.

Hayden looked down at the woman in his arms. Isla's ice-blue eyes had gone wild when she'd heard Sonya's chant, her fingers digging into his shoulders.

Now, Isla's eyes were closed, her head resting back

against his arm. He could still hear her soft, velvet voice beseeching him to allow her leave the castle, could still feel the heat of her gaze as she looked over his face.

Had she liked what she saw? He didn't want to care . . . but he was strangely curious. He'd never had trouble enticing women into his bed before. Yet there had been no emotion on Isla's face as she looked her fill of him.

"What did you do to her?" Hayden demanded of Sonya.

Sonya lifted a shoulder. "I put her to sleep. She was becoming irate, and she needs to heal."

"She was giving us information. And you didn't see the fear in her eyes. She didna want to sleep."

"Sleep will heal her."

"I don't think so," Marcail said. "If what I took from her happens when she sleeps, it's no wonder she became so agitated when she heard the chant. She'll be back in that same distress once again."

Hayden lifted Isla's small body in his arms. They had taken her dirty, damaged gown and replaced it with a plain white chemise which was much too thin. Much too revealing. Even now Hayden could make out Isla's small, pert breasts and her dark nipples. Most of the dirt from Isla's face, arms, and chest was gone leaving only creamy skin he had glimpsed on Cairn Toul.

Skin he once more longed to caress.

To Hayden's surprise, he found his body reacting to the soft curves beneath the simple linen. He knew the feel of her breasts pressed against him. He knew the feel of her small hands on his chest. He knew the slender curves that tantalized and teased his body.

And saints help him, he knew the way her lips parted softly, beckoning him to taste her, as she looked at him. He didn't want to respond to Isla, but it seemed his body was not his own where she was concerned.

Hayden glared at Sonya instead of moving toward the bed. He wanted to know why Isla thought Deirdre was alive, but it would have to wait. And he'd have to wait for another look into her startling ice-blue eyes.

"I'm sorry," Sonya said. "I thought it would be better if she rested."

Fallon rubbed his eyes with his thumb and forefinger. "You didn't know. How long will she sleep?"

"It differs."

Hayden silently cursed. Isla might be a *drough*, but he couldn't forget the fear in her eyes. Whatever it was Marcail took from Isla earlier was enough to frighten the *drough* so that she clung to him, a stranger, someone who prevented her from leaving.

It took a moment for Hayden to realize Lucan was standing beside him, a dark brow raised in question. Lucan's sea green eyes watched him carefully.

"What is it?" Hayden inquired.

"I asked if you planned to hold her the entire time she slept or lay her down?"

Hayden blew out a breath and walked to the bed. He glanced at Marcail to find the Druid studying him as he lay Isla down. Hayden pulled the covers over Isla and turned to leave.

"Was she telling the truth?" Fallon asked.

Hayden stopped and turned to face the others. "She's determined to either leave or have herself killed. All you have to do is look into her eyes to see she believes what she is speaking about Deirdre. Whether it's the truth or not, I cannot say."

Fallon nodded.

"I'm inclined to believe her," Quinn said. "Deirdre showed me Isla's sister and niece. She used them to keep Isla doing what she wanted."

Broc leaned a hand against the stone wall and dropped his head back so he looked at the ceiling. "Isla kept to herself except when Deirdre would send for her. Even then, she held all emotion from her face. The fear we saw just now was real." He lowered his head and looked at Fallon. "And that worries me."

"We all know how powerful Deirdre had gotten," Lucan said. "What if Isla is telling the truth? What if Deirdre isn't dead?"

Marcail moaned and buried her head in Quinn's neck. "God help us all."

"Then where is Deirdre?" Fallon asked.

Though Hayden hated to have to ask it, he knew he had to. "Did you find her body in the mountain?"

Fallon shook his head. "Nothing."

"Holy hell," Quinn mumbled and held onto Marcail tighter.

Hayden found his gaze on Isla, her pallor matching that of the linens. She would know where Deirdre was.

And Hayden intended to ensure she told them everything.

Dunmore kicked at the log in the hearth, sending sparks flying into the air, before he reclined in his chair. A moment later the log broke in half with a loud crack.

He had retreated to the cottage he kept close to Cairn Toul so he could get to Deirdre easily when she needed him. He still couldn't believe she was gone. She had given him plenty of coin for his work, but to know that he was doing something for someone as great as she had brought meaning to his life.

Ever since he had found her as a lad of just sixteen summers, he had known Deirdre would do great things. It had never entered his mind that she would be killed. By the MacLeods. She was the greatest *drough* to ever live. It should never have happened.

"I'm not dead, Dunmore."

Dunmore sat up in his chair and looked around his cottage as he reached for his sword that lay beside him. He was alone just as he had been a moment before. But the voice had come from inside his head.

"You're not hearing things. My body was destroyed, as well as most of my wyrran. My magic is regenerating my body even as we speak. I will have a form once more, Dunmore. Until then, there is something I need you to do."

It never entered Dunmore's mind that the voice in his head wasn't Deirdre. He had seen what her magic could do, and he knew she had lived for a thousand years. She was the goddess she claimed to be.

"How can I serve?" he asked.

Deirdre chuckled. *"My wyrran are cleaning my mountain. I need you to get to Cairn Toul quickly. I've a need for a Druid. The MacLeods will pay for ruining my empire."*

"I will see it done," Dunmore vowed and leapt to his feet.

FOUR

Hayden closed the door to his chamber behind him as he stepped out into the hallway with Fallon, Lucan, and Broc.

"You haven't said much," Lucan said to him. "What are your thoughts?"

Hayden crossed his arms over his chest. "Regardless of whether or not Deirdre held Isla against her will, Isla is *drough*. A *drough* is evil. Do you really want something evil in the castle?"

"I'll make sure Isla doesn't do anything," Broc spoke up. "But she is injured and needs to heal. If we send her out now she'll die."

Fallon shook his head. "Not if we believe her. She said she cannot die, just as Deirdre cannot die. Did you hear of anything like that while under Deirdre's service, Broc?"

"Nay," Broc said. "There were times when Isla didn't act herself. As a Warrior I had to interact with other Warriors, but Isla was always by herself unless Deirdre had need of her. Isla had no one in that cursed mountain."

Hayden didn't want to feel a connection with the *drough*, but hearing that she preferred to be alone made it impossible. "So what do we do?"

"I would think Quinn would fight to have Isla removed since Marcail is carrying his child, but I saw the determination on Marcail's face," Lucan said. "She wants Isla to stay. At least for now."

The door opened and Cara walked from the chamber straight to Lucan's side. "Marcail is trying to take Isla's emotions again, but Quinn is preventing it. Whatever holds Isla in its grip while she dreams is . . . horrific."

Lucan kissed her forehead and pulled her against him. "What do you feel about Isla and what she told us regarding Deirdre?"

Cara tucked a curl of chestnut hair behind her ear and raised her dark eyes to her husband. "I believe her, Lucan. As much as I don't want to, I believe her."

"Then Deirdre isna dead," Broc said into the silence and shook his head sadly. "I thought her wicked ways had ended."

Hayden heard someone approach and turned to find Arran. Arran was one of the three Warriors who had united with Quinn while he was locked in Cairn Toul.

He didn't know much about Arran, but Hayden liked the Warrior. The more Warriors they had on their side, the better. Especially now if Deirdre truly wasn't gone as they had thought.

Arran stopped beside Hayden and pushed his dark brown hair from his face with a swift movement of his hand. "What is going on?"

"First," Fallon said, "I'd like your thoughts on Isla. You dealt with her in the mountain."

Arran shrugged as his gaze scanned the small crowd. "She came to the Pit on occasion, but she never harmed us and rarely spoke to us. She would come to ask who wanted to pledge themselves to Deirdre. Other than that, we didn't see her."

Broc raised a blond brow. "Do you think Quinn and I lied?"

"Nay," Lucan answered for Fallon. "We just like to get opinions. We're not sure what we're dealing with now."

"And what is it exactly that we're dealing with?" Arran asked.

Hayden met Arran's gaze. "Isla says Deirdre isn't dead."

"How is that possible?"

"They're connected somehow," Hayden explained. "Deirdre used her black magic."

Arran leaned his head back against the wall and sighed. "Just when I thought it was over."

"So you believe her?" Fallon asked.

Arran laughed, though no mirth was in the sound. "After the things I witnessed in that mountain, it wouldn't surprise me. I always thought Deirdre died too easily."

"I did wonder about that as well," Lucan admitted. "I just thought we managed to get the upper hand."

Broc leaned a hand on the stone wall and shook his head. "If Deirdre isn't dead, then we can expect her to come after us."

"Maybe she already has," Arran said. "If Isla is linked to her, maybe Isla is her weapon."

"Nay." The response was instant for Hayden. He didn't think too hard on how he knew, though. "Isla wants to leave. She's begged us to let her go. That wasn't an act."

Lucan rubbed a hand down his face. "I agree with Hayden. Deirdre wouldn't have any idea that we'd return to the mountain to look for prisoners. So Isla being found by Hayden couldna have been planned."

"Aye," Fallon said. "My worry is the danger Isla said we were in."

Arran cursed. "Because if she's linked to Deirdre, Deirdre can use her at any time."

Hayden began to wonder if he should have killed Isla when he'd had the chance.

* * *

The next time Isla opened her eyes it was to find the chamber dark with only a candle to chase away the shadows. She had no idea how much time had passed, but she knew she had to get her strength back to evade another sleeping chant.

Just thinking of reliving that dream over and over again made her skin crawl. She was awake now, and she intended to stay that way for quite a while.

"We're not going to hurt you."

The soft, feminine voice came from her right. Isla turned her head and found Marcail watching her with those unusual turquoise eyes.

"By keeping me here, you are hurting yourselves," Isla told her.

Marcail glanced down at her hands. "Why is that?"

"You don't believe me about Deirdre." Isla had never imagined they would doubt her.

"Please understand they saw her die."

Isla sighed and sat up. She pulled her legs to her chest and rested her chin on her knees. She wanted nothing more than food and a bath, but it would have to wait. At least her body didn't hurt as much as it had earlier.

"I never asked to be brought here."

Marcail smiled. "Nay, you didn't. You did, however, fight our magic. Why?"

"Because the weaker I am the more difficult it is for Deirdre to use me."

"I see." Marcail's hand went to her stomach with a telltale sigh.

"You are carrying Quinn's child, are you not?"

Marcail nodded slowly, her face draining of color. "I am. I thought we were safe from Deirdre and the evil she spawned."

The thought of Deirdre harming another innocent child made Isla seethe with anger. Too many had been hurt already. Before she could think better of it, she said, "There is something I can do to help you."

"What?"

The eagerness in Marcail's gaze pulled at Isla. "I can shield the castle for a time to make it more difficult for Deirdre to find me."

"Therefore more difficult to find us."

"Precisely. As soon as I leave, however, the shield will no longer work."

Marcail fingered the gold band wrapped around one of her braids. "Why would you offer such a thing? You were with Deirdre."

"I was never *with* Deirdre. I did what I had to do to keep my sister and niece alive. They are both dead now, so there's no reason not to fight Deirdre."

Marcail rose and walked to the foot of the bed. "I need to tell the others what you've told me."

Isla nodded, expecting no less.

"I shall have food and a bath sent up immediately."

Isla couldn't remember a time when someone had been kind to her simply because they wanted to. It had been so many years since she was Isla, daughter of the village baker, that her old life seemed like a figment of her imagination.

"I would very much appreciate it."

Marcail stopped at the door and gave her a small smile. "Trust us, Isla. We're only trying to help."

Isla waited until Marcail was gone before she dropped her head into her hands. Alone with her thoughts, she felt the tears prick her eyes as she realized she was truly alone in the world for the first time in over five hundred years.

She might not have spoken with her sister or seen much of her niece, but they had always been there in one form or another. Now, with Lavena no longer sustained by Deirdre's blue flames, and Grania dead by Isla's own hand—albeit by accident—there was no one.

Marcail had told her to trust them. If only Isla could, but she had seen what trusting someone could do. She had trusted Deirdre not to kill her sister. Instead, Deirdre had put Lavena into the magical blue flames where she'd never be able to leave again.

Trust wasn't something Isla could give anyone. Not now. Not ever.

Yet, she couldn't stop the need to help Marcail and her unborn child. Isla hadn't been able to prevent Deirdre from taking Grania, but Isla would do everything within her power to protect Marcail.

And what power Isla had now. She had only thought she had magic when she was a simple *mie*. The magic had been pure, but it hadn't been strong.

Deirdre was the one that made her turn *drough*. Isla had fought it for as long as she could, but when Grania's life had been threatened, Isla had given in and completed the ritual.

She shuddered just thinking about seeing and feeling the evil that had taken hold of her when she had said the words and cut her wrists. Her fingers absently rubbed the scars, scars that told the world who and what she was.

The malice had tried to take control of her, and sometimes it actually had. There were times, however, when she'd gained the upper hand. Each time got progressively easier until Isla was able to keep the evil tamped down.

Until Deirdre would use her magic.

There was a light knock on the door before it opened and Arran brought in a tray of food. She looked at the tall

Warrior. Gone was the haggard expression on his face and the white skin of his god, and in its place was someone content. And it showed by his confidence and ease.

Arran had been one of the Warriors Deirdre had wanted in her bed. Isla could understand why, with Arran's dark good looks and sinewy body.

"Hello," he said as he placed the tray on the bed.

Isla licked her lips. "Hello."

"Are you in pain?"

She was surprised by the question. How could she answer? She'd been in constant pain for centuries.

"Your wound," he said. "Does it pain you?"

"Only a little. It is nothing."

He nodded and backed away. "Your bath will be brought up shortly."

Isla reached for the bread, her stomach rumbling with hunger. "Thank you."

She didn't hear Arran leave as she closed her eyes and savored the taste of fresh-baked bread as it filled her mouth. The venison was next, and then the wine.

Isla didn't think she had ever been so hungry. It had been days since she'd eaten, but she could survive even starvation as she had learned before.

It was while she was finishing her meal that a wooden tub was brought into her chamber and filled with steaming water. She couldn't wait to get into the bath and scrub off the sweat and grime that coated her skin.

It was more Warriors who brought the water. So far she had seen no servants. Did the MacLeods not have any, or were they keeping them away from Isla?

She didn't know the Warriors' names, but she did think she recognized one of them. It was his steely gray eyes that watched her carefully, as if he searched for something.

Isla ignored him, and as soon as they were gone, she

jumped from the bed. In one movement she had the chemise off and one leg already in the bath.

She lowered herself into the tub with a sigh. Though she longed to relax in the water, she didn't know how long she had before someone came to fetch her. So she reached for the soap and began to scrub.

With her hair clean and dripping over the side, Isla washed her body twice. She was just rinsing off when the door opened and the blond giant with black eyes filled the doorway.

She paused, one arm lifted and water cascading down her chest. The look in his eyes as he stared at her caused her stomach to flip and her heart to race. His hot gaze raked her, leaving her struggling for breath and trying to understand how one look could do that to her.

He opened his mouth, and then shut it only to open it again. "I dinna know you were in the middle of bathing."

"I'm nearly finished."

His gaze never wavered. She lowered her arm and waited for him to continue.

After a moment he turned his head away. "I'm to escort you to the great hall. I have a gown for you. Cara said it might be a wee big."

Isla watched a small bundle sail through the air from his fist and land on the bed.

"I'll wait in the hall." He left and shut the door before she could say anything.

Isla's heart pounded in her chest. No man had seen her naked before. The water had covered her, but still. She was without clothes. Why then did the prospect of him seeing her give her a little thrill? Had she lost part of her wits on Cairn Toul as well as her soul?

As she finished rinsing and rose to dry off, she thought

she had seen something flash in his eyes, some emotion she had never seen before.

She wished she knew the Warrior's name. After all, she had begged him to kill her. He could have at least given her his name.

Isla reached for the gown and found undergarments, a new chemise, stockings, and shoes. She hurried to dress, afraid the big Warrior would return before she was finished.

The shoes were too big and kept falling off her feet, so Isla decided not to wear them. The gown was of simple design, but in a pretty lavender color that conformed to her curves in a becoming way. It was so long she had to lift it to be able to walk, and the sleeves had to be rolled up. All in all, it was of decent fit.

She found a comb on the table beside the bed and hurried to brush out the tangles. It took longer than she expected, and her hair was still wet when she went to the door.

As soon as she opened it she found the Warrior standing across the hall, his arms crossed over his muscular chest. His dark gaze looked her up and down before he pushed off the wall.

"How is your wound?"

His voice was rough and deep and made her pulse jump. "It's healing."

"They are going to have questions for you. Many questions."

"I have no doubt. I have survived much worse than an inquisition."

"I know."

It was the way he said it, as if he had witnessed her tortures himself. It gave her pause and made her wonder just who he was. And why he had such an effect on her. "Who are you?"

His gaze lowered to the ground for a moment before he looked into her eyes. "Hayden Campbell."

"Well, Hayden Campbell, I have the answers everyone wants. Shall you take me to the great hall?"

He gave a quick nod of his head and turned. His strides were long, making Isla have to hurry to catch up with him. She had always hated being so short. She had to crane her neck to look at everyone, especially this giant called Hayden.

Isla's foot caught on the hem of her gown, causing her to trip. In less than a heartbeat Hayden was beside her, his arms like bands of steel, wrapped around her to steady her. Instantly, her blood turned to fire and her heart leapt to her throat.

She lifted her eyes to see his face breaths from hers. A scent of spice and woods filled her. Isla could make out the shadow of a beard, and no matter how hard she looked, she couldn't find his pupils in his onyx eyes.

"I tripped," she explained when she got her breath back. "The gown is a bit long."

He released her so quickly Isla had to reach for the wall to balance herself. She lifted her hem and gave him a nod. "I won't stumble again."

Without another word Hayden resumed walking, though Isla soon took note that he had shortened his stride. For her?

Surely not.

FIVE

Hayden fisted his hands, then flexed them in an effort to rid his skin of the feel of Isla. Of her warm, soft, all-too-alluring skin.

He had heard her sharp intake of breath and turned to see her falling. With the powers his god gave him, it took but a blink to reach her to prevent the fall.

Ever since he had walked in on her bath he had been rattled, his senses attuned to her in a way that left him hot and aroused.

He had seen nothing of her body other than her slim shoulder, graceful neck, and lean arms. But it was more than enough to make his balls tighten. Her black hair, wet and slicked back from her freshly scrubbed face, would haunt him for eternity as would her eyes that had grown large and round when she spotted him.

When he had found her on Cairn Toul he had known she was pretty, but he hadn't known she was breathtakingly so. Without the grime and blood covering her, he could hardly take his eyes from her.

His body had reacted quickly to the sight of her bare flesh covered with droplets of water. He had grown instantly—and shockingly—hard. He had made sure to keep his distance until she had nearly fallen. And that had put him face to face with her.

He inhaled and smelled her scent of snow and wild pansies which beckoned him closer. Tempted him, charmed him.

Ensnared him.

Once more her soft, alluring body was pressed against him, teasing him, enticing him to touch and kiss her. The irresistible yearning to take her mouth left him shaking with a hunger that threatened to devour him.

But he had to remember who she was, *what* she was, and that a *drough* had viciously killed his family.

As he walked her to the great hall he was careful to keep his pace sedate and his stride short. He didn't need her falling again. Not because he cared whether she hurt herself, but because he couldn't touch her again. If he did, he was likely to give into the crushing desire to taste her lips.

When they turned to descend to the hall, he felt her pause behind him. He glanced over his shoulder and saw her taking in the people waiting for her.

There were twelve Warriors now, including him. With the MacLeod wives and Sonya, it was a crowd of sixteen that awaited her.

Hayden was impressed to see her lift her head high as she walked down the stairs and followed him to the chair the others had set aside for her. The chair was centered between the two long tables so that it faced them and the others could see her. She remained standing, however, the excessive material of her gown pooling like a lavender sea at her feet.

"We have some questions based on what you've told us and Marcail," Fallon said from his place at the head of the table.

Isla clasped her hands in front of her and waited. No emotion showed on her face. Hayden didn't know if she was nervous or excited. She was a master at hiding her feelings.

"And I will answer those questions," Isla said.

Quinn motioned to the chair. "Please, sit and make yourself comfortable."

Isla lowered herself into the chair. Hayden noticed her feet didn't quite touch the floor. She sat with her back straight and her gaze level. Waiting.

"Do you wish for something to eat or drink?" Lucan asked.

"Nay," Isla said. "I'm ready to begin."

Hayden met Fallon's gaze for a moment. Hayden was the only one of the Warriors not sitting at the table, but then again he was content to be apart from the others.

"All right. Is Deirdre dead?" Fallon asked.

Isla shook her head. "She is very much alive."

"I burned her body," Hayden said.

Isla's ice-blue gaze swung to him. "As I tried to explain earlier, there is nothing that can kill Deirdre. She has had a thousand years to perfect her black magic, ensuring that she never dies."

"Nothing can kill her?" Arran asked.

Isla's head turned back to the group. "She took great pains in showing us all the ways someone might kill her, and every time it failed. Her body might be gone, but she's still here."

"How do you know?" Larena asked.

For the first time Hayden saw a spark of emotion. Isla's gaze shifted to the floor, and he could have sworn she shivered.

"I've felt her trying to communicate with me in my mind a few times," Isla said. "I was too weak from my wound for her to be able to control me."

Quinn steepled his hands. "How is Deirdre going to continue without a body?"

"Her magic. I don't think any of you understand just

how powerful she is. She can generate another body for herself. It will take some time, but she will do it."

"How much time?"

Isla shrugged. "Weeks. Months if we're lucky."

Lucan raked a hand through his hair. "Saints help us."

"Tell us of your and Deirdre's connection," Fallon urged.

Isla would rather not, but they deserved the truth. They needed to know just how dangerous she was to them so they would let her go. She took in a deep breath and felt Hayden's gaze on her once again.

He stood to the side of her, watching. Always watching. It should unnerve her, but there was something comforting and secure in his gaze. Something hot and provocative that awoke an emotion inside herself she had never felt before.

The others—and there were many others—were across from her with various expressions from dismay to anger to concern to pity. She couldn't blame them. The Warriors had assumed they'd killed Deirdre.

If only that had been the case.

"It might be better if I start at the beginning," she said. "There is much I think will help you all understand why your gods were unbound."

Fallon nodded in agreement.

Isla licked her lips and pulled up the memories of that fateful day so many centuries ago. "I lived in a small, obscure village made up strictly of Druids. We saw very few outsiders, and when they did come, they came for our wisdom and healing."

"You were a *mie*," Cara said.

"Aye. My father was the village baker. We lived simply, as did everyone in the village. It was a beautiful place next to a loch and surrounded by a thick forest. I went into the forest daily to gather herbs, but one day everything changed."

Lucan set aside his goblet after taking a long drink. "What happened?"

"I was with my sister and niece. Grania was just three summers and the joy of my life. I was holding her while Lavena picked some herbs when the wyrran and men appeared. The men weren't Warriors, but they had strength like nothing I had ever seen."

Isla's stomach churned each time she relived that fateful day. "Grania was pulled from my arms. Lavena and I were then bound and taken to Cairn Toul. Deirdre had wanted Lavena because of her ability to see into the future, because Deirdre was searching for someone."

"Who?" Quinn asked.

"The MacLeod Warrior."

Isla waited for that to sink in as the brothers looked at each other. She glanced at Hayden to find his gaze narrowed on her as if he didn't believe a word she said. In his place, she probably wouldn't believe her either. But what good would it do for her to lie now? The truth was better for everyone.

Fallon was the first to turn back to her. "Explain yourself."

"Deirdre had found scrolls hidden in her village. One scroll was the spell to unbind your gods, and in that scroll was one name. MacLeod."

"Why our clan?" Lucan asked.

Isla shrugged. "That I cannot answer. But tell me this. Did men go missing from your clan about once every generation? Were they your strongest warriors?"

"Aye," Fallon replied softly.

"That was Deirdre. She was trying to find the one who housed the god."

Quinn snorted in disgust. "When that didn't work she brought your sister to her."

"She did. My sister was able to see parts of the future. I was an added bonus, and with both me and Grania in Deirdre's control, Lavena didn't have much of a choice. My sister tried to fight Deirdre, but . . . Deirdre has her ways."

Isla broke off, remembering when Deirdre had Lavena raped in an effort to break her. She could still hear her sister's screams, still remember the blood and the way the man had enjoyed Lavena fighting him. Just recalling that awful experience made Isla want to gag.

Something touched her hand. Isla looked down to find Marcail and a goblet full of wine. Marcail's eyes were filled with sorrow, and a part of Isla broke in that moment. No one knew of this story besides Deirdre. And no one had ever felt compassion for Isla before.

"Go on," Marcail said before she returned to Quinn's side.

Isla took a drink of the wine, letting it slide down her throat and burn her stomach as it settled there. "Lavena finally broke. Neither of us realized just what Deirdre wanted from her until it was too late. We thought Lavena would try to call up the future, but Deirdre put her in the blue flames, magical flames that would keep Lavena alive but unable to function on her own, where she remained until a few days ago."

"How long was she in there?" Lucan asked.

Isla looked into the goblet and the red liquid. "Five hundred years."

Sound filled the hall as everyone began talking at once. There was only one that was silent. Her watcher, Hayden.

Fallon banged his empty goblet on the table. "Quiet. I want to hear the rest of this." He turned to Isla. "Go on."

"Lavena's gift of seeing the future couldn't be called up at will. It would come to her sporadically. In the blue flames Deirdre was able to add her black magic with Lavena's to help channel specific things, namely finding the MacLeod who had the god.

"It took Lavena about a year before she saw what Deirdre wanted. In her vision Lavena said it wasn't one MacLeod, but three. Three brothers, to be exact, who shared the god. The three would be the strongest of their clan. After that, Deirdre had only to watch and wait."

Quinn rubbed his jaw and sighed. "That's when she attacked our clan."

"And then captured you. She didn't expect your escape, though. You were lucky."

"How did she find the rest of us?" Hayden asked.

Isla fidgeted with the goblet. "Through my sister, of course. Deirdre had her seeking anything to do with the gods as she built her army. At the time Druids were plentiful. Her wyrran hunted them mercilessly, and as they grew scarcer, Deirdre used the spring equinox to find more.

"It was only recently that Deirdre had Lavena also searching for more Druids. It's how she found Marcail."

Lucan rose and began to pace, his agitation clear. Cara eventually took his hand and pulled him back down beside her. Despite everything the MacLeod brothers had been through, each of them had a woman who obviously loved him.

"What happened to you in the mountain?" Lucan asked.

Isla rubbed her fingers on the rim of the goblet. This part of the telling was going to be the most difficult. "Deirdre was going to kill me and claim my magic, but for some reason she changed her mind. She wanted to utilize me as she had Lavena so she set about using the same tactics to break me. They didn't work."

Duncan braced his hands on the table and slowly rose. Isla watched as his lips lifted in a sneer. He hated her, and he had every right to despise her.

"You evidently broke, though. What did she offer you? Power?" Duncan demanded.

It was Duncan's twin, Ian, who jerked Duncan back down on the bench. The only way to tell the twins apart was that Duncan's dark hair hung down his back and Ian's was cropped close to his head.

To Isla's surprise, Hayden had moved away from his position when Duncan had risen. It was only after Duncan had resumed his seat that Hayden once again leaned against the wall as if he were leisurely listening to a story.

Hayden's response baffled Isla. The blond Warrior clearly didn't like her, but why would he then act like he was going to defend her?

"Isla?" Quinn urged.

She sighed and nodded. "Deirdre threatened to kill Grania if I didn't do as she asked."

Fallon raised a brow. "And what did she ask of you?"

"To become a *drough*."

"Which you did," Lucan said. "When did the mind connection take place?"

"A few months later. Deirdre expected that once I became *drough* that she could control me, that the evil would make me more susceptible to her cause."

Fallon shook his head in confusion. "I doona understand. Didn't the evil do exactly that?"

"It tried, but since I performed the *drough* ceremony under duress, I wasn't giving my soul completely to the evil. In withholding a part of myself, I was able to gain control of the malice within me."

Isla saw the doubt on the faces before her, and though

they might not believe, she had battled the evil every day for centuries. She knew the truth.

"I managed to fool Deirdre for a time, but then I began to question her. She began to doubt me."

Fallon tapped a finger on the arm of his chair. "How have you been alive for five hundred years?"

Isla swallowed, her throat dry and raw. She knew what she was about to tell the group would surprise them. "Deirdre managed to link her mind with mine, thereby controlling me."

"What happens when she does that?" Lucan asked.

"There is pain as if my head is splitting open. Then, I hear Deirdre's voice in my mind commanding me to carry out some order. I'm powerless to fight against it no matter how many times I try."

Quinn frowned. "What exactly does she want you to do?"

"To kill."

SIX

Isla knew her statement shocked them. "As soon as the command is given, I lose control of my body. I have no memory of what takes place while Deirdre has control. She cannot hold me for long, though, as it requires a tremendous amount of magic."

Once again the hall erupted in sound as they talked amongst themselves about her revelation. She imagined it was worrisome, and it was the reason she couldn't stay.

Fallon raised his hand and quiet once more reigned. "Have you ever gotten control during one of these . . . outings?"

"Once," Isla said, barely hiding the shudder that wracked her. "Only once."

The silence that followed was deafening. Isla didn't like to think of the time Deirdre's control had slipped. It had been horrifying. To see for herself just how vicious and gruesome she was at killing had left Isla physically ill. She had retched long after there was anything left in her stomach.

Isla licked her lips. "I cannot stop Deirdre from taking control of me. It's the reason I need to leave immediately. For every moment I am here I put all of you in danger."

"But you could help us."

Isla looked at the female. She recognized the Druid with the fiery hair as the one who had put the sleeping chant on her. The *mie's* magic was strong, very strong. "Who are you?"

"Sonya."

"You would risk everyone's lives on the chance that I could help you, Sonya?" Isla asked.

"The information you could give us about Deirdre will help us. Knowledge is power."

Marcail chose that moment to speak up. "And what of the shielding you told me about?"

Isla regretted telling Marcail of her ability. Staying at the castle was the last thing Isla needed to do. She stood, the cool stones penetrating her stockings. "You don't understand. None of you understand."

"We do," Broc said as he also rose and walked towards her. "You know things about Deirdre's magic that we don't. Think what we could do to her with our combined knowledge."

Isla looked at Marcail, the Druid's hand once more on her stomach. Another child's life was in the balance. But was it worth the risk for Isla to stay?

The answer was a resounding nay.

"I'm sorry, but I cannot. It will take another day for my body to heal the wound, and then I must go."

"Go where?" Fallon asked.

Isla shrugged. "Does it matter? I will go far away from here, away from anyone and everyone so I can no longer be used to harm people. Had Hayden taken my head as I asked, none of you would be in jeopardy."

Duncan slammed his hand on the table. "You canna really expect us to believe you want to die."

She looked into the Warrior's brown eyes that were full

of anger and vengeance. "There is nothing I want more. I'm tired of being used, tired of having no control over my destiny, my life. I want it to end."

"And the only way to do that is to take your head?" Quinn asked.

Isla nodded and swallowed the lump that had grown in her throat. "Just as a Warrior can only die by taking his head, my life will not come to an end unless Deirdre dies or my head is severed from my body."

"Holy hell," Quinn mumbled and blew out a harsh breath.

Isla then thought about the last thing Deirdre had been researching. Maybe if she told the MacLeods it would be enough for them to turn their attention away from her. Isla could use her powers against them. They were Warriors and therefore strong with their gods' powers, but she was a *drough* with five hundred years of perfecting her magic. She would be a force to be reckoned with, but she'd rather not hurt anyone at MacLeod Castle. They were good people trying to do the right thing.

She walked to the table and sat down the wine she had barely touched. "Deirdre prided herself on her knowledge of Druids and magic. She knew there were those among the Druids who plotted their revenge and gave magic to items that could hamper her powers."

Isla ignored the stares and walked around the great hall. Hayden had shifted from his place against the wall and moved toward her. Did he think she meant to flee? That would come in time, but not yet.

"What are you speaking of, woman?" Hayden demanded. His voice was hard and laced with impatience and a bit of doubt. But the way he watched her, with intent and hunger, made her heart race.

"Objects actually. They are hidden all over Scotland.

Some that could hinder Deirdre's magic, others she could turn so that they gave her even more power."

Lucan groaned. "Just what we need. Deirdre more powerful than she already is."

Isla stopped when she stood in front of Hayden. She had to tilt her head back just to look into his face, and what a handsome face it was. She found herself reaching up to trace his wide lips, but caught herself in time, tucking her hair behind her ear to hide what she had been about.

If she wasn't who she was and things were different, she might actually think of flirting with him.

As soon as the thought filled her mind she disregarded it. Thinking such thoughts wasn't for her. Her path had already been set, and there would be no altering it.

"How do you know of these . . . objects?" Hayden asked.

She gazed into his eyes, eyes so black she couldn't see his pupils. Hayden wasn't a man who bent for anyone or anything. He was a man shaped by his life just as she was, so Isla understood his gruffness.

"Long ago when I was but a child there were stories of some powerful Druid tribes who had relics passed down to each high priestess. Every generation, the Druids of the village would pour their magic into these relics."

Hayden's brow furrowed. "Why would they do such a thing?"

"After what happened with the release of the gods and being unable to remove the gods from the men, the Druids sought to find another way to protect Britain. They believed if an object had enough magic that it could keep us safe."

"And did it?"

Isla briefly closed her eyes. "It was never put to the test. With Deirdre pursuing them and the Christians wanting them dead, the Druids had to bury these objects and hide. The locations were supposedly passed down through the ages."

"Aye," Sonya voice interrupted. "I've heard such tales from the Druids that raised me. They themselves did not have such a relic, but they retold the stories nonetheless."

Fallon looked from Sonya to Isla. "Do either of you know where one of these relics is buried?"

"Not exactly," Isla said. "I discovered what Deirdre was looking for when she began to ask me questions about those tales. So, I asked a few questions of my own."

She paused then and looked back at Hayden. "I'm not sure how much I believe of what she told me next."

"Why?" Hayden asked.

"Because she lies."

"True enough," Quinn said. "But tell us what she told you."

Isla made her feet move away from Hayden. Being so near him unsettled her, made her think of only him, of how it felt to have his arms around her. There was something about the giant that set her off balance, and around these Warriors Isla needed to keep her focus.

She walked back to the chair she had sat in and looked at the group of Warriors and Druids who watched her. "Deirdre told me that my sister had given her a clue as to where to find the one object that could kill her."

"What?" Fallon bellowed. "And you're just now telling us?"

"I was going to find it myself," Isla hurried to say. "However, I realize now I would never get to it before Deirdre finds me. Once I woke up here, I knew if anyone could find the object, it was one of you."

A Warrior with black hair cut short rose to his feet. She looked into his gray eyes for the second time that day, and it was then she remembered who he was. Ramsey MacDonald.

"Ramsey," she whispered.

So many Warriors had been in and out of the mountain that Isla couldn't remember them all, but a few stood out. Ramsey was just such a Warrior. He and Broc had been inseparable while they'd been prisoners. Then one day Ramsey had escaped and Broc had given his allegiance to Deirdre. Isla now wondered if that allegiance had ever been genuine.

"You know me?" Ramsey asked as he walked toward her.

She felt a presence beside her, and somehow wasn't surprised to find Hayden had moved near her. "I remember you from when you were held prisoner. Deirdre wanted you on her side desperately. She knew your god held great power."

Ramsey cocked his head to the side as he regarded her. "Galen tells us that you were tortured at Deirdre's hand."

Isla was thankful her hand rested on the chair, for her knees nearly buckled. She forced her breathing to remain calm. "And who is Galen?"

"Me," said a tall Warrior with dark blond hair and deep blue eyes. "I have the power to read minds. I saw into yours when Hayden and Fallon brought you back to the castle."

Her gut twisted and knotted viciously. To know someone had witnessed the things she had been through left her shaking and cold. "You had no right."

Galen lifted a shoulder in a shrug. "You were fighting Sonya's healing. We needed to know why."

"And so you shared my private hell with everyone?"

"Isla," Broc said. "Galen told us because he thought it was proof enough for us to trust you."

She forced a laugh to keep her anger in check. "So, again, my tortures are evidence enough for you to believe me?"

"When I was in the mountain," Quinn said, "you walked past me in the corridor and I saw blood dripping from your hand. What happened?"

Isla took a step back and slammed into a wall of muscle.

"Easy," Hayden's deep voice whispered.

Just knowing it was him behind her gave her a measure of calm, but it didn't stop the humiliation of them knowing what she had been through. Repeatedly.

With no other choice, Isla smothered her emotions and kept the anger from her voice even as her heart hammered wildly in her chest. "Since you know everything else, there's no reason not to speak of it. I was punished for disobeying Deirdre."

"How?" Hayden promoted.

"I . . ." The knot in Isla's stomach tightened as she recalled her last punishment from Deirdre. Isla had taken too long in gaining Phelan's blood for Deirdre. The Warrior's blood would heal anything, but in Deirdre it only strengthened her evil. "I hesitated to bleed a Warrior. So, I was punished."

It was too much. Recalling Phelan and the disgust in his eyes for her made her ill. She had kept her dreams and thoughts to herself these last five centuries. To know her mind had been invaded, for whatever reason, was a violation she couldn't stomach.

Isla needed some time to herself. She spun away from Hayden and walked to the door as if she wasn't hurting and silently screaming inside. No one stopped her as she opened the door and stepped into the bailey.

* * *

Hayden held up a hand when Marcail and Broc went to follow her. "Give her some time. She feels as though she's been invaded."

Galen set his jaw, his unreadable gaze on the door. "She was. By me."

"And if she tries to run away?" Fallon asked.

Hayden lifted a shoulder in a shrug. "Then Broc can find her."

Ramsey raised a black brow and asked, "Why do you care about her, Hayden? She is a *drough*."

Hayden glared at Ramsey, hating him for daring to speak the very thoughts he himself had. He was having a difficult enough time dealing with his need to kill *and* protect Isla. He didn't need the others to know what was going on inside him.

"We need all the information, don't we? After that, if she still wants to die, I see no reason not to give her what she wants."

"You cannot be serious?" Cara said, her voice rising in outrage.

Hayden glanced at Cara and shrugged. "Why not? Isla has as much as admitted about the evil inside her. Do you want it infecting this castle? Marcail's child? Think about that."

While he thought about why he continued to want to protect Isla. Damn, this was not good. Not good at all.

"I'll make sure she doesna leave the castle," Hayden said.

"As will I," Logan announced and stood.

Together they took the stairs to the battlements. Hayden intended to give Isla the time alone she needed. Besides, he didn't have anything to say to her.

Logan didn't utter a word as they walked onto the

battlements. They quickly found Isla wandering the bailey as if she were lost in thought.

"Do you believe her?" Logan asked. "About the objects or relics or whatever? Do you think they are really out there?"

Hayden's gaze followed Isla. Her black hair was drying as it flowed freely about her shoulders and down to her waist thick, glossy, and straight. Her head was bent forward and her hair shielded her face. He wondered what she was thinking.

The admission that they knew of her torture had surprised her. She hadn't liked that they knew. As to if he believed her, he wasn't sure.

"She could be telling the truth," he answered. "I can see Deirdre wanting to keep under lock and key anything that could help—or hurt—her magic. If she had the objects, no one else could use them against her."

Logan nodded his head, his brown hair falling into his eyes. "I believe her. She was forced to turn *drough* against her will. Why wouldn't she want Deirdre dead?"

"Unless she's as good a liar as Deirdre is."

Logan snorted. "You're the one who said you looked into her eyes and knew she spoke the truth about Deirdre being alive. Look into her eyes again."

That was the problem. Hayden had done just that. He didn't want to find Isla attractive. He didn't want to inhale her scent of snow and wild pansies again. But damn him if he didn't yearn to do both.

What was next? Would he want to kiss her? Bed her? Surely not? Not even her beauty could get him past his aversion to *droughs*. He knew in the depths of his heart his yearning couldn't continue.

"She handles herself well," Logan said. "Despite the questions and stares, she didn't act frightened."

Hayden shrugged. "I'm sure she learned that trait while with Deirdre. Deirdre feeds on weakness, Logan. You know that."

"Exactly. Isla is a strong woman to have endured everything she has. What kind of torture did Deirdre put her through?"

"You doona want to know." And Hayden wasn't going to tell him. If Isla wanted Logan to know, then she could tell him what she suffered.

Until then, Hayden would keep what he knew to himself.

SEVEN

Isla walked the perimeter of the bailey and seethed. How could she have allowed herself to become so agitated in front of so many? She had worked decades to be able to hide every emotion only to have everything shredded with just a few words.

Something had changed, and she didn't like it. She had endured as long as she had by surviving on her wits and ability to hide her feelings. All of that was ruined if she couldn't control herself around these Warriors.

Isla paused and leaned against the stone wall. It was then she noticed the sky above her. Her breath rushed past her lips as she realized she could stay out in the sunshine for as long as she wanted.

Deirdre had liked to keep Isla deep in the mountain away from the sun and fresh air that *mies* thrived on. Isla had fought her need to escape Cairn Toul many times. As a *drough*, she shouldn't crave light.

"It takes some getting used to."

Isla's heart jumped at the sound of Broc's voice. She hadn't heard him approach. He must have flown. Those wings of his did come in handy. "What takes getting used to?"

"The freedom. The absence of evil. Deirdre's hold."

"Ah, but I have none of those things. I'm still *drough*. That evil will always be in me."

Broc clasped his hands behind his back and shrugged. "I think there's an argument that you aren't *drough*."

Isla didn't want to have this conversation. Not now. Not ever. "May I leave the castle?"

"Why?"

"I would like to see the sea."

Broc started to answer her when the castle door opened and Cara leaned her head out. "It's time for supper. Hurry before Galen eats it all," she said with a grin.

Broc rolled his eyes and turned on his heel. "Are you coming?" he asked over his shoulder.

Surprisingly, Isla found that she was hungry again. She pushed off the wall and started to follow Broc when movement out of the corner of her eye caught her attention. On the battlements were two Warriors watching her. Hayden and another man with brown hair. So, the MacLeods must not trust her, not that she could blame them.

Which meant she would probably not be allowed to leave the castle. She could if she wanted to use her magic, and she would if they continued to hold her against her will. They had until nightfall. After that, she was gone.

Isla didn't know what she expected when she returned to the hall, but it wasn't to see the great and feared Warriors laughing and talking while food was being passed around.

It was so different than Deirdre's Warriors who gorged themselves, acting more like animals instead of the men they were.

"You look surprised," Quinn said as he walked from the kitchens, a pitcher in his hands.

"I am," Isla said.

Quinn studied the group a moment. "It's not the same hall I grew up in, but these men and women are my family now, my clan."

"After everything that has happened to you, how can you be so pleased with your life?"

"A good woman's love can change even the angriest of men," he said with an easy grin. "And I had my brothers. I grew tired of holding all that rage. It was exhausting. Love, on the other hand, can give you strength when you think you have no more, and hope when there is none."

Isla turned her head to find his pale green eyes watching her. "And your god? Your immortality?"

He blew out a breath. "I battle with the knowledge that if my god cannot be bound once more that I will one day bury my wife. Every time I think of it my stomach sours, but one day with Marcail is worth more than never having her."

"I never expected such words from you, Quinn. Your brothers maybe, but not you."

Quinn chuckled. "I'm not the same man I was. I let go of the past. You might want to try that."

"Enough talking," Larena said with a wink as she came toward them.

Isla watched with awe and a little jealousy at the way Larena walked with such confidence. Not even being in a tunic and breeches seemed to daunt Larena, or anyone at the castle for that matter.

The female Warrior stopped and smiled down at Isla. Larena was stunning with her golden hair and smoky blue eyes. Combined with her long legs encased in the tight fitting breeches, it was no wonder Fallon couldn't take his eyes off his elegant wife.

"I don't think we've been properly introduced. I'm Larena MacLeod."

Isla nodded. "Fallon's wife. Aye, I heard Deirdre speak

your name many times over the past few months. I applaud you for eluding her. She was eager to have you on her side."

Larena rolled her eyes. "Deirdre always wants what isn't hers. And though I would love to take the credit for evading her, I had help. Now come and sit. There's plenty of room. Just elbow the men out of the way."

Isla didn't want to sit. She couldn't remember the last time she had shared a meal with anyone. Trepidation filled her. Maybe she should have declined the invitation to join them.

She stared at the two tables placed together to make one long one. There was one chair at the head of the table that Fallon reclined in, a smile on his face as he listened to something Lucan said.

Cara placed loaves of bread at various spots on the table, and Galen was quick to grab one which he kept all to himself. Cara shook her head with a smile and motioned to the empty space beside Galen. "Isla, you can sit here."

Isla stepped over the bench and sank down beside Galen. He was deep in conversation with Ramsey, who sat across from him. Across from Isla sat Marcail and on Marcail's right was Quinn.

Cara sat beside Isla with a sigh. "We're going to need to add more tables if any more Warriors arrive."

Marcail nodded. "Or Druids."

Isla sat with her hands in her lap as the trenchers were passed around the table and everyone grabbed what they wanted. To her shock, Galen speared several slices of meat and put them on her plate.

"You need to eat," he said by way of explanation.

After that, Isla took what she wanted. Conversation filled the hall, easing her muscles and lightening her mood. The food was delicious, but it was everything else that made her long for her village and the laughter she used to share around her family's table.

Quinn had suggested she let go of the past, but if she did what would she have? Nothing.

"Isla," Fallon called. "Is Galen keeping his fingers from your trencher? He has a habit of stealing food."

Galen grunted as he finished drinking and set down his goblet. "I doona take food from a lady, Fallon. However, if she's full, I'll be more than happy to finish her meal."

Everyone laughed, and Isla found herself grinning as well. When was the last time she smiled, truly smiled? And then her gaze clashed with eyes as black as midnight. Her heart skipped a beat as she returned Hayden's stare, lost in the darkness of his gaze.

She had the insane urge to go to him, to sit beside him and . . . what? What did she want him to do?

Too many things. None of which I can allow.

It was only when Logan nudged him that Hayden looked away from her. Isla didn't understand the disappointment that rose within her. Hayden was a dangerous man, a reckless Warrior. She needed to stay as far away from him as she could.

Why then did she find she wanted to be near him?

She looked down at her trencher to see she had eaten nearly everything. For a few heartbeats, she had forgotten who she was and where she had been. She had lived in the moment, and it had been glorious.

"Hayden willna hurt you," Galen leaned over and whispered.

She looked into Galen's dark blue eyes and saw his sincerity. "I do not fear Hayden or any Warrior."

He smiled and nodded. "Nay, I doona believe you do. Does it bother you that Hayden watches you?"

"I gather he doesn't trust me."

Galen shrugged and bit into the bread. "It goes deeper than that. He doesna care for *droughs*."

"I hadn't noticed," she replied with sarcasm.

Galen laughed, causing many to look their way. "You have wit, Isla. I don't think you should keep it all bottled inside you. Listen to what the MacLeods have to say. We can help."

If only that were the truth.

All too soon the meal was over. The men rose and left the hall while the MacLeod brothers and a few Warriors remained.

Isla helped the women clear the table. The act of cleaning was not one she had done in ages, but she had never minded it. She and her sister had shared many a good time of washing clothes or the dishes.

With five of them cleaning it didn't take long before it was finished. Isla was going to return to her chamber to get ready to leave, but when she entered the hall, Quinn called her over.

The brothers hadn't moved from their seats at the table, and their wives resumed their places beside their husbands. Broc, Sonya, and Galen were also present.

"We'd like to speak with you some more," Lucan said. "Would you please sit with us?"

A few more moments wouldn't matter. Besides, she was curious as to what they would say to her. "All right," Isla said as she lowered herself onto the bench.

She lifted her gaze to the stairwell and the open wall of the corridor above. A man stood there. A man with obsidian eyes and fair hair. A man who watched her constantly.

Somehow, she was glad to know Hayden was there, even if he didn't like what she was. It was odd, and she couldn't explain it, but there it was.

"First," Fallon said and leaned his forearms on the table, "I wanted to apologize for letting the others know what Galen discovered when he read your mind. But please understand he didn't do it maliciously."

Galen shook his head. "I already told her I did it because we needed to know why she fought Sonya's healing. I told them she was tortured, but I didn't tell them specifics."

"I fought the healing because I wanted and needed to stay weak," Isla said. She was relieved to know Galen hadn't seen everything, or if he did, he wisely kept it to himself.

Cara nodded. "To fight against Deirdre's hold."

Quinn blew out a breath. "Finding you has given us an advantage over Deirdre. You know so much, Isla. You could help us fight her."

"And I would," she told them. "If I'd had a choice, I would never have stayed with Deirdre, never have become *drough*, and I would have helped you. But I will be more of a hindrance than anything else."

"You mentioned artifacts," Fallon said. "Are you sure of what you heard?"

"Of course," she replied. "I would not lie."

Sonya raised her fiery brows. "Then why haven't you told us where to locate it?"

Isla turned to the *mie* and held her gaze for several long moments before she looked back at Fallon, dismissing Sonya from her mind. "I don't have an exact location, but an area. It is with a group of Druids so it shouldn't be too difficult to find."

"And you'll share that with us? Freely?" Lucan asked.

Isla almost smiled. She had shocked them. Good. "All that I ask is that once I give you the information I'm allowed to leave."

Marcail frowned. "But you aren't a prisoner."

Isla lifted a shoulder. "I would disagree. I'm healing and my magic is strong again. I can force my way out of the castle, but I'd rather not. You are everyone's only hope of ending Deirdre for good, and I don't wish to harm any of you."

"I believe Isla speaks the truth," Galen said.

Broc folded his arms over his chest. "As do I."

After a nod from both Quinn and Lucan, Fallon said, "Give us as much detail as you can. There's no reason for us not to investigate this. If it's real and we reach it before Deirdre, we'll be that much stronger against her."

"Tell me one thing," Lucan said. "Why haven't you gotten the artifact yourself?"

"I had to guard myself constantly with Deirdre. She didn't allow me outside the mountain unless I was carrying out her orders, and most of those times she was in control of my mind. When would I have had time to find the Druids and convince them to give me the artifact?"

Lucan grunted. "True enough."

"The Druids are deep in the mountains," Isla answered Fallon. "Near Loch Awe in the region of Argyll. The last I heard, they had made their home in one of the dense forests."

Galen ran a hand down his face. "It'll take days to search around the loch."

"Not if I go," Broc said.

Isla knew it would take Broc no time to find the Druids. After all, his power from the god inside him was to track down anyone, anywhere. It was a power Deirdre had used often.

"Nay," Lucan said. "I think I have somewhere else we could use you."

Broc clenched his jaw. "More important than finding these Druids so they can tell us where the artifact is?"

Lucan nodded, a slow smile pulling at his lips. "I think you'll like this better."

"I doubt it. What is it?"

"Aye," Quinn said. "Tell all of us, brother."

Lucan threw a piece of bread at Quinn who ducked to avoid it. "Because there's no way of knowing if the Druids will even give us the artifact, I think we might be better using your talents to track down the one person we need to locate, Broc."

"Deirdre," Larena whispered, as if the realization just came to her.

Lucan nodded. "Aye. Are you up for it, Broc?"

"You know I am," Broc replied, his lips twisted in a snarl.

"Good. Verra good," Fallon said. "And good thinking on finding Deirdre, Lucan."

Isla licked her lips and looked at Broc. "You might find it more difficult to find Deirdre than you expect. She won't have a body, not yet anyway. You'll have to search for her essence."

Broc stood and glanced at Sonya. "I'll find her. I'll leave now."

"Wait," Quinn said. "We need to discuss this with the others as well. They should know what we plan."

Isla didn't think she could be more surprised by the MacLeod brothers, but the longer she was in the castle, the more they astonished her.

"I'll go after the Druids and the artifact," Galen said.

Fallon gave a slow nod. "I want at least one other Warrior with you."

The men then rose and started out of the castle. Isla raised her gaze to search for Hayden, but he was gone as well. Which left Isla alone with the women.

"We'd like to talk to you a moment," Marcail said. "We want to help."

"There's nothing you can do," Isla said. "I've already told you that."

Larena leaned forward in her chair. "Maybe there is."

"How?"

Cara shifted around so that she faced Isla. "We were talking as we finished cooking. What if one of the artifacts can, in some way, sever the link Deirdre has with you? Sonya told us they are very powerful."

It was too heady of a proposition for Isla to even consider. "Deirdre never mentioned anything."

"Why would she?" Sonya asked. "It was to Deirdre's benefit to know you would always be under her control one way or another. If any of the relics can hinder Deirdre's magic, why couldn't it sever her link with you as well?"

It was true, and Isla hated it. "I only know of the one artifact. That won't do us any good."

"Unless we learn of others," Larena said. "You've helped us, Isla. Give us a chance to help you."

She looked at each one. "Why are you doing this? You don't know me."

"Because you didn't harm us when you could have," Marcail said. "I watched you while I was in the Pit. I knew you didn't want to be there."

Isla folded her hands in her lap and tried to calm herself and the hope growing inside her. "I didn't harm you, but I didn't help either."

"Would you have?" Larena asked. "If we hadn't shown up? Would you have helped Quinn?"

Isla slowly shook her head. "I wouldn't chance my sister or niece being harmed."

Cara glanced at the others. "And now? Would you help us?"

Isla knew it was time to make a decision, one that could do more harm than good. But the thought of being rid of Deirdre controlling her was one she couldn't ignore or pass up.

"I will help you."

EIGHT

Hayden listened to Fallon as he explained the plan with half an ear. He'd heard it all in the great hall. Besides, Hayden's attention was on Isla, or the lack of said female. Why hadn't she and the women come into the bailey with the others?

Were the women treating her kindly? And why the hell did he even care?

"Shite," he murmured.

Logan looked over at him, his hazel eyes seeing too much. "Something wrong?"

Hayden blew out a breath. "Nothing I cannot handle."

Night was taking the sky, turning the world dark—and for some, dangerous. Hayden unleashed his god long enough to light the torches around the bailey. Though the Warriors didn't need the light, the women did.

He glanced down at his hand to find his skin and claws red. At one time the sight had frightened him, but he'd gotten used to it soon enough. With barely a thought, Hayden tamped down his god until his skin had returned to normal and his claws disappeared.

"Galen is going to find the Druids," Fallon said to them. "We need another Warrior. Who wants to accompany him?"

Hayden needed to get away from Isla before he did something unwise, like kiss her. Which he could not do. She was a *drough*. Evil to the core.

He opened his mouth, ready to tell Fallon he would go, but another voice beat him to it.

"I'll do it," Logan said.

Fallon acknowledged Logan with a brisk nod. "Logan and Galen will set off at dawn."

Hayden snapped his mouth shut and stopped Logan when he would have walked away. "Why are you going?"

Logan shrugged, but wouldn't meet Hayden's gaze. "They needed another Warrior."

"Aye, and there are plenty of us who could have gone."

Logan slapped Hayden on the back, a too-bright smile on his face. "Never fear, my friend. I'll return soon enough. You willna have time to miss me for verra long."

Hayden threw up his hands in exasperation as Logan walked away to speak to Galen. Logan never took anything seriously. Everything was one big jest to him.

Although Hayden had noticed a decided lack of laughter lately with Logan. It wasn't obvious to those who didn't really know him, but he and Hayden were as close as brothers.

They knew each other's secrets. Or at least Hayden knew most of Logan's secrets. There had always been a part of Logan that he kept to himself. Not that Hayden could fault him. Sometimes secrets were best kept hidden. Even from oneself.

Logan was always ready for a fight, as any Warrior was. But the eagerness in which he volunteered, the obvious need he had to get away from the castle, surprised and worried Hayden.

Something was wrong with his friend, and with Logan leaving, Hayden couldn't help him.

Quinn walked up beside Hayden. "I expected you to volunteer to go with Galen."

"I was, but Logan wanted to go. He needs some time away from the castle."

Quinn raised a dark brow, clearly not believing Hayden. "The women are going to try and convince Isla to stay permanently. Is that going to be a problem?"

"You mean am I going to kill her?" Hayden asked. He didn't know whether to be annoyed or impressed that they bothered to ask him. In the end, he was irritated.

"Aye."

Hayden glanced at Logan to find his friend watching him. Could he refrain from killing Isla? That would be much easier than not kissing her. "I willna harm her unless she tries to hurt someone else."

"Fair enough." Quinn crossed his arms over his chest. "Isla may be our only hope of stopping Deirdre."

"I have no doubt Isla can tell us things about Deirdre we doona know, but you are asking all of us to trust a *drough*."

Quinn thought that over as he stared into the darkening sky. "Aye, we are. Need I remind you that she was turned against her will?"

"Or she's just a verra good liar."

Quinn laughed then and dropped his arms. "There's nothing I can say that will ease your discomfort of having her here. You've trusted me and my brothers before. Trust us now, Hayden."

"I do." Hayden replied without hesitation. The MacLeods had proven themselves time and again. There was no reason not to trust them.

The castle door opened and five women moved onto the castle steps, the torches lighting them in a red-orange glow. All but Isla descended to the bailey.

"Three hundred years without a woman in this castle,"

Quinn said. "I thought Lucan had gone daft when he brought Cara inside. I was the foolish one. How much difference a woman makes to a man's life."

"Women complicate things," Hayden said, unable to take his gaze from Isla. Even in her too-big gown she drew his gaze. Her ice-blue eyes looked not at the people in the bailey, but to the distance. He wondered what she was thinking.

Quinn just shook his head with a smile. "Whenever you find that one woman you cannot live without, then you can tell me how she causes difficulties."

Hayden didn't have any illusions about finding such a woman. He wasn't dense enough to allow himself to have feelings for a female, not while he was immortal. Why would he do that to himself or to her? It was unnecessary.

Everyone grew quiet as Isla closed her eyes. Wind began to move though the bailey with more force than normal, whipping through the torches causing the flames to spurt. The gusts swirled and coiled around Isla, causing her black locks to lift away from her and float on the breeze. The breeze caught the fabric of her gown and molded it to her body.

Hayden tried to swallow past the lump of desire that welled inside him at the sight of Isla's breasts and small waist. He saw her nipples pucker and bead in the wind, straining against the gown. His cock swelled and thickened, and he was eager to cup those breasts himself, to feel their weight as he buried himself deep inside her.

He was so involved in his body's reaction to her that it took a moment to realize it was magic he felt swirling around him. And not just any magic—Isla's. He'd never felt magic so enthralling, so erotic. He swayed and glanced around to see if anyone else was as affected, but it seemed he was the only one.

Her hands turned, palms up as she slowly lifted her arms out to her sides. Hayden started toward her, fearful that she would hurt them all with her magic. But a hand on his arm halted him. He looked to find Quinn holding him.

"She's helping us. Remember?" Quinn reminded him.

It took everything Hayden had to remain in place, to not jerk Isla out of the bailey to stop her magic and to kiss her. Quinn removed his hand, but Lucan had moved to Hayden's other side.

Hayden already had one home destroyed, he didn't want that to happen to another. He only wanted to protect those he considered his family, but they refused to see past the allure Isla brought. But if she harmed any of them, Hayden would destroy her regardless of the way his body yearned for her.

Isla's hands continued upward until her palms faced together over her head. The wind swirled around her angrily. Magic, her magic, invaded everything.

It was heady and dangerous, and Hayden hated to admit how much he enjoyed the feel of it. He'd felt magic before, but nothing as strong and seductive as Isla's.

There was a loud boom with the vanishing of the wind, and they saw the magic, nothing but a dull light in a small ring, shoot from Isla's hands straight up over them high in the sky. The ring ballooned out covering the castle and even the village only to disappear into the ground.

Isla licked her lips and focused her eyes on those around her. "The castle and village are now shielded with my magic. Deirdre knows where the castle is located. She will send others to try and find it. They won't be able to see it, but they'll know it's here."

"So we're safe from other Warriors and wyrran?" Marcail asked.

"For as long as I am here, and as long as my magic is

strong, the shield will last," Isla said. "To Deirdre's eyes, the castle, and all its occupants, will have disappeared. If you walk out of the shield, you will be spotted."

"Won't she know you helped us?" Lucan asked.

A niggle of worry moved in Hayden's gut when Isla glanced away from Lucan.

"Aye." Her voice was calm. Too calm.

She was troubled, and Hayden knew she had every right to be. He looked at Quinn. "You've gotten your wish, but I wonder just how much more Deirdre will bring to us now that we have her greatest weapon."

"We doona plan to find out," Quinn replied. "We're hoping one of the artifacts will be able to sever that link between Isla and Deirdre."

So that's what they told Isla to gain her cooperation. Hope was a powerful sentiment, and one that could conquer almost anything.

The urge to protect Isla once again assaulted Hayden. What was wrong with him? She didn't need protection. She was a *drough* with more magic than any Druid at the castle. If anything, Hayden needed to guard everyone else.

"You're playing with fire," Hayden told Quinn. "What do you think will happen when none of the artifacts help to break the bond?"

"And what if it does?" Quinn sighed and looked around the bailey. "We have something to fight for, Hayden, and I'll do whatever it takes to make sure everyone here is safe. Taking risks is part of this game, and though I'd rather not, sometimes there isn't a choice."

Hayden knew that all too well. He found himself turning to Isla once more. To his surprise she was staring at him. Her face gave nothing away, but in the depths of her ice-blue eyes, he saw pain . . . and hope.

NINE

Isla didn't know why she found herself staring at Hayden. His obvious dislike for her should have made her keep her distance.

Instead, she found him fascinating. Addictive.

Captivating.

He was a proud man, a loyal Warrior. He was the tallest among them, standing head and shoulders above the others. But it was more than just his height that made him stand out. It was his manner, his attitude of "I can do anything and you can't stop me."

Isla imagined he could do anything he set his mind to. Men like Hayden were few.

She allowed herself to look him over at her leisure as he spoke with Quinn. While Quinn and the other Warriors were well formed, Hayden's arms and shoulders bulged with muscles.

The way the material of his kilt hung over his left shoulder only accentuated the shapely form of his upper body. His wide chest narrowed into a vee, and his kilt wrapped lean hips.

He stood with his feet shoulder width apart, his arms crossed over his chest, and his jaw set. A Warrior waiting to defend those he cared for.

Isla had gotten a glimpse of a muscular thigh when

Hayden bent over earlier. She had to wonder if there was a place on his body that wasn't corded with muscle.

And then his black eyes turned to her.

She almost took a step back. She held her stance and returned his stare. He might intrigue her, but he also stirred a measure of fear. She wasn't sure why, but there was something about him that seemed almost . . . familiar. It quickly faded as her blood heated under his intense gaze.

"Thank you," Fallon said, drawing her attention—and her gaze—from Hayden.

Isla bowed her head as she faced the leader. "I don't know how long the shield will last once Deirdre realizes what I've done. She will try to use me, but the shield will make it difficult for her magic, now dimmed, to penetrate."

"But it could happen?" Cara asked.

As much as Isla wanted to lie to them, she knew she couldn't. "Aye." She then turned to Fallon. "The shield won't keep Deirdre out forever. She will eventually find me. When that happens, you must kill me."

"Isla," Fallon began.

She shook her head. "Your word, Fallon MacLeod. If you do not give me your word, I will leave now. I won't endanger everyone here."

Fallon closed his eyes and let out a ragged sigh. When he opened his eyes, she saw the resolve there.

"You have my word," Fallon pledged. "I pray it does not come to that. The more people we have to fight Deirdre the better."

Isla didn't bother to state her argument against her being able to fight Deirdre again. It had been said enough. "Let us hope you are correct, laird."

He smiled at her use of his title. "I never thought to hear anyone call me that. I thank you."

"May I leave the castle?"

"Of course."

Marcail stepped forward and took Isla's hand. She was surprised the Druid would so easily touch her.

"Thank you," Marcail said. "You didn't have to stay or shield us."

Isla forced a smile. "Thank me when it's over."

She wasn't used to people being so pleasant to her. It was a welcome reprieve, but after five centuries with nothing but evil surrounding her, Isla wasn't sure how to act.

Isla extracted her hand and walked down the steps to the bailey. The Warriors parted for her as she continued to the gatehouse and the gate that stood ajar. The light from the many torches danced on the ground and played at her feet.

She felt Hayden's eyes on her, and knew if she turned her head she would find him watching her. But she wouldn't turn. He might see the confusion inside her and think it a weakness.

It is a weakness.

A failing she had to hide. Whenever she was perplexed she tended to make the wrong choices, and these Druids and Warriors had asked for her help. She didn't want to think she had made the wrong decision to help them, but deep down, she feared she had.

Once she was through the gate, Isla turned toward the cliffs. She didn't stop until she reached the edge. A look down showed her just how high up they were as the razorbills found their nests for the night in the walls of rock.

She lifted her face to the sky and the setting sun and basked in its remaining warmth and light. The smell of the salt on the wind tickled her nose, but it was the sound of the sea as the waves rolled in that calmed her racing heart.

Isla opened her eyes and looked at the sea as it stretched

far into the horizon and beyond. The gray and brown rock of the cliffs clashed beautifully with the dark blue waters and bright green grass beneath her feet. It was almost as if she had entered another world, a world she had thought dead to her.

It was the flap of wings that alerted her she was no longer alone. "Hello, Broc."

He chuckled as he landed and folded his mighty wings behind him. "I should have known you would sense me."

"I should have known I wouldn't be allowed to be alone," she said and turned to face him. His indigo skin shown in the sinking sun, and his Warrior eyes, eyes the same color as his skin, measured her. She had always wanted to ask if their eyesight changed when the god took over since the color took over their entire eye.

His brow furrowed at her words. He swiped at an errant strand of his fair hair caught in the wind and blowing in his eyes. "No one sent me. I came to see how you were before I left."

"They don't trust me, do they? Not that I blame them. I am *drough*."

"Did you lie to us about what happened to you?"

Isla almost rolled her eyes. "Of course not."

"Then they believe you, and they trust you enough to ask you to stay. Give them a chance."

A chance. She probably shouldn't, but she was. "Deirdre will sense you coming. Be careful."

He looked at the castle over his shoulder. Isla saw a long figure standing on the battlements watching them. Sonya. Isla wondered if the Druid knew of Broc's feelings, and if Sonya returned those feelings.

"I will return," Broc promised. He turned back to Isla and smiled, showing his fangs. "They will take care of you here. They are good people."

"I know." She just hoped they didn't pay the ultimate price for taking her in.

With a single nod, his leathery wings unfolded. A moment later, he was soaring in the sky with only breeches covering his body.

She was going to miss having Broc at the castle. He was the only one she really knew, her only ally. And now he was gone.

Isla stood on the edge of the cliffs, the breeze buffeting her, and for the first time in ages she let her mind drift back to the days before Deirdre when Grania had still been an innocent child and Lavena hadn't been locked in the blue flames.

Isla waited for the stabbing pain that always came when she thought of her sister and niece, yet there was nothing but a hollow ache of regret for what could have been.

"Farewell, Lavena. May you find the peace you long sought," Isla whispered into the wind. "Grania, my dear sweet Grania, may the purity that made you so special as a child return to you in death. Forgive me, both of you."

Hayden flipped a dagger end over end as he leaned against a cottage. Rebuilding the village had begun again, but that's not why he was there. His target stood on the cliffs, her gaze never wavering from the sea.

What was it about the water that held Isla so? She hadn't moved from her spot since she had walked there after supper. Night had fallen and still she stood.

Arran walked from one of the cottages and dusted off his hands as he came toward Hayden. "What do you think she's doing?"

Hayden shrugged and sheathed the dagger at his hip. "I doona know."

"She's as still as a stone. Larena said to leave her be, but Quinn thinks we should bring her inside."

"Leave her," Hayden said.

"I told you he'd say that," Ian said with a chuckle.

Hayden glanced at Ian and his close cut hair. "Where is your twin?"

The smile on Ian's face dropped. "Are you worried he'll hurt Isla?"

Anger sliced through Hayden so quickly he almost didn't tamp down his god in time to stop the transformation. "Did Isla ever harm either of you?"

"You know she didn't," Ian answered.

"Then why does he hate her so? You were the one who was tortured, not Duncan."

Arran dropped his gaze to stare at the ground while Ian looked down the center road of the village.

Ian clenched his jaw. "Duncan blames himself for what happened to me."

"Do you blame him?" Hayden wanted to know.

Ian shook his head. "Never. The only ones I do blame are Deirdre and William."

"And William is dead," Arran said.

The men exchanged looks, smiles of satisfaction on their faces.

Hayden pushed away from the cottage wall and looked once more at Isla. "I understand your brother's anger, Ian. He needs something and someone to blame. Deirdre hasn't been found yet, and until he's seen her, that anger will transfer to Isla."

"Why not Broc as well?" Arran asked.

Ian took in a long breath. "Because Broc fought with us. No one saw Isla. I'll talk to him, Hayden."

"It willna do any good," Hayden said. "He needs time and proof that Deirdre is alive."

There was a loud crash in one of the nearby cottages followed by a bellow, then a curse, the voice belonging to Camdyn. Hayden waited for Camdyn to exit the cottage, and when he did the Warrior was covered in ash.

Hayden bit the inside of his mouth so he wouldn't smile at the sight before him.

Arran let out a bark of laughter while Ian quickly turned away to hide his own smile.

"Damned beam," Camdyn cursed and began brushing the ash from his long black hair. "It cracked in two before I had time to brace it. The fire took more of it than I first thought."

Hayden couldn't stop the smile this time. "You don't say?"

"Verra funny, Hayden," Camdyn said. "Next time you be the one to go check the sturdiness of the cottages."

"Another complete rebuild?" Hayden asked.

Camdyn nodded. "I'm afraid so. The fire didn't take the entire cottage, but the initial structure is so damaged that it would be better if it was rebuilt."

Hayden made a mental note, adding the tally for how many cottages could be salvaged.

"Is that Isla still out there?" Camdyn asked.

Arran nodded. "It seems Malcolm will have company tonight."

Hayden didn't need to look far down the edge of the cliffs to find Larena's cousin and the only human male at the castle—Malcolm Monroe.

He had risked his own life in helping Larena stay hidden from Deirdre. Deirdre had taken a special interest in Larena as a female Warrior.

Everyone had hoped Deirdre would forget Malcolm's involvement, but she hadn't. Her Warriors had attacked and nearly killed him. Broc had found him in time to kill

Malcolm's attackers, but not in time to save Malcolm's arm from being ruined.

Not even Sonya's magic could heal Malcolm's arm. The slashes on Malcolm's face had healed quickly, but they left scars he would bear forever. Hayden thought them a badge of courage, but he knew Malcolm didn't agree.

With Malcolm's right arm all but useless, he felt less than a man. Malcolm was next in line to be laird of the Monroe clan, but he declined to return to his people. As much as Hayden hated to admit it, the clan wouldn't accept Malcolm as he was now.

Which was why Fallon had made room for Malcolm among them. Hayden liked him, though Malcolm kept to himself, rarely talking to anyone. Malcolm walked the cliffs at night, a lone soul among the rocky outcroppings.

Except now, Isla was there as well.

"Would you have killed her?"

Hayden jerked his head to find Duncan beside him and the others gone. The twin stared at him with cold brown eyes. "What are you talking about?"

"When Isla asked you to take her head. Were you going to do it?"

"Would you have done it?"

Duncan nodded. "Aye."

That was Hayden's thought as well. He still didn't understand why he'd hesitated.

"Answer me," Duncan demanded.

"The pain that sits in your gut and festers willna ever go away, Duncan, no matter how many people you kill."

Duncan snorted. "And how would you know?"

Hayden faced the twin and caught his gaze. "I know. You can blame everyone you want, but the blame lies with only one person."

"Me."

"Nay. Deirdre. Would you blame Ian if it had been you taken?"

Duncan's face contorted. "Nay."

"Then doona fault yourself. There will be plenty of chances to fight Deirdre in the coming days. Save your anger for her."

"Is that what you've done? Saved your anger for her?"

Hayden shook his head. "I did the opposite, though I wish I'd had someone tell me what I've shared with you. I let my rage fester inside me until I've become a monster in every sense of the word. Is that what you want to become? Is that what you want Ian to see every time he looks into your face?"

Duncan sighed and ran a hand through his long hair. "He suffered, and I could do nothing. Even when we shared the same pain, Marcail took that from me in her effort to help."

"At least your brother is alive."

"And yours isn't?"

Hayden had said too much already. It wasn't like him to give out advice, but he saw the road Duncan was headed down since he had traveled that same path himself. It wasn't an easy one.

But then what path ever was?

"Hayden?" Duncan said.

"Nay, but it doesna matter," Hayden replied. "It was a long time ago."

Too damn long, yet it felt as if no time had passed since discovering his family murdered.

TEN

Hayden watched Isla from the village long past midnight. Not once did she move or utter a single sound. Duncan and the others had since returned to the castle, but Hayden didn't want to leave Isla alone.

Not that she was alone. Malcolm continued his stroll along the cliffs, though he gave Isla a wide berth. She seemed not to notice him, but Hayden imagined she detected every detail down to the smallest one.

Hours ticked by and still Hayden stayed just to see how long it would take before Isla crumpled to the ground. But the longer he watched her, the more he began to realize there was more to Isla than he initially thought.

When the first rays of sun peeked over the horizon he started toward her. He didn't know why, and though he told himself to turn away, his feet still took him to the petite *drough*.

He stopped several paces behind, and to the side of, her and surveyed the scene before him. MacLeod Castle was beautiful, but it was the sea and the cliffs that truly made the place spectacular. It was no wonder Isla had stood there all night.

So much had happened since Hayden had come to the castle that he hadn't bothered to look at it as Isla had done.

"You've watched me all night," Isla said. "Were you afraid I might jump?"

"It didn't cross my mind until now. Are you?"

She chuckled, the sound soft and sensual. "It wouldn't kill me, so why put myself through the pain?"

"How do you know you willna die? Have you tried jumping to your death before?"

She turned her head and stared at him with those intense ice-blue eyes. "I've died many times, Hayden. I lost count of the times I perished on that mountain freezing to death before I was brought here."

Hayden wasn't sure he believed her. The only ones he knew that could happen to were Warriors, and she most certainly wasn't a Warrior.

She cocked her head at him. "You don't believe me."

Hayden moved until he was even with her. "I'm not sure what I believe."

"Shall I prove it to you?"

"There's no need."

"Really?" Her eyes narrowed at him. "I think you'll continue to doubt me until I prove it to you."

Hayden looked away. "I believe you. All right? Now enough."

No sooner had the words left his mouth than he felt something touch his side where the dagger was. He looked down to find his blade gone and in Isla's small hand.

"You cannot kill me."

Isla rolled her eyes. "I know that. I'm not dim-witted, Hayden. I'm going to prove to you that I'm as immortal as you."

He took a step to her when he saw her raise the weapon and point the blade at her stomach. He stretched his fingers, readying to snatch the blade from her hand. "Enough, Isla."

She smiled, her eyes grave and serious. The next instant

she plunged the dagger into her abdomen. Hayden barely caught her before she hit the ground. Her hands fell to her sides as her eyes fluttered close.

"God's teeth," Hayden murmured as blood poured from the wound.

Memories of finding his family thus surged through his mind. He watched helplessly as Isla's blood, her life force, continued to gush through the wound.

The sound of feet running toward him didn't cause Hayden to raise his eyes from Isla. He could only stare at her dead body. Hayden, despite the god inside him, couldn't stop someone from dying. And it was being proven to him once again.

Hayden found himself trembling. The last time he held someone like this it was his younger brother. It brought back too many memories long buried, memories of helplessness and anger better left alone.

"Isla," Hayden said and shook her though he knew it was useless.

Her beautiful eyes were closed and her lips parted as if she slept, but Hayden knew she did more than sleep. She was dead.

"What happened?" Quinn demanded as he skidded to a halt beside him.

Hayden swallowed and reached for the dagger. He didn't like the way his hand shook as he wrapped his fingers around the pommel. He sucked in a breath and pulled the blade out of her with one jerk of his hand before he tossed it aside.

"She said she wanted to prove to me that she was immortal. She took my dagger and . . ."

"I know," Quinn said softly. "I saw that part. Tell me you don't have any open wounds, Hayden. Her *drough* blood can kill you."

Hayden shook his head in answer. He couldn't take his eyes from her face or the blood that coated her lavender gown. "I've no wounds."

"Check," Quinn demanded.

Hayden tore his gaze from Isla's face and glared at the youngest MacLeod. "I'm not the one lying here with a wound in my belly. Worry about Isla!"

As soon as the words were out of his mouth, Hayden turned his attention back to Isla. He shook her again, the panic clawing at his insides—just as it had all those years earlier when he'd found his family.

"Holy hell," Quinn murmured. "What has she done?"

"Isla," Hayden murmured. "Isla!"

Isla gasped as the first breath filled her lungs. Her eyes flew open to find Hayden leaning over her, his gaze filled with agonized worry.

That concern, however, quickly turned to irritation.

"I told you I was immortal," she said. She swallowed, hating the lump of anxiety in her stomach. There had been an instant when she'd first opened her eyes that she'd glimpsed such distress on Hayden's face that it left her breathless.

His lips compressed into a tight line, his face once more set in its rigid lines. "I should kill you again for scaring me so."

"So you didn't believe I couldn't be killed."

"Isla," he warned, his voice low and deep.

She had pushed him too far. Before she could utter an apology, Hayden stood and lifted her on her feet. She hadn't realized until that time she had been in his arms. Again.

How was it that she always seemed to end up there? And why did she enjoy it so?

"I think you've proved your point, Isla," Quinn said.

She hadn't noticed they weren't alone. Isla glanced at Quinn. "I do not like being doubted."

"We can see that," Hayden ground out.

Quinn rubbed his jaw. "So the only way for you to be killed is by beheading? Just like us?"

"Or Deirdre can kill me," she said. "She threatened it often enough."

"Because of her link to you?" Hayden asked.

Isla nodded. "At least that's what she told me."

"You doona believe her?"

Isla smoothed her hands over the front of her gown, the gown borrowed from Cara that was now ruined. She should have had a thought for it before she acted so rashly. It was so unlike her, yet it had felt good.

"Deirdre isn't all knowing. She likes to pretend that she is, but she isn't. It will take her some time to realize I'm not dead. Right now, she's trying to build up her magic to create another body."

"Will she look the same?" Quinn asked.

"Without a doubt."

Hayden fisted hands covered in her blood. He glanced down at them, and she saw what looked like pain and anger. Memories maybe? It troubled him, whatever it was.

Quinn's gaze narrowed on her before he looked at Hayden. "The morning meal is being prepared."

"Thank you." Isla couldn't move, not with Hayden's black gaze on her.

He waited until Quinn had departed before he asked, "What were you doing out here all night?"

"Deirdre rarely allowed me out of the mountain, and when she did it was for short periods. This time, I was able to do what I wanted. Do you have any idea how long it's been since I've seen the sun rise or set? Yet I was able to watch both."

She tried not to fidget when Hayden's eyes turned to the now healed wound in her stomach. Isla put her hand over the small hole in her gown. "I shouldn't have done it. I'm sorry."

"Don't," he said. "I doubted you, and you proved that I was mistaken. There is nothing to apologize for."

He surprised her, and few people did that.

"Come," Hayden said and turned to motion to the castle. "Quinn came because Marcail is worried about you."

But Isla hesitated. She had been shown kindness at MacLeod Castle, and in return she had ruined the gown given to her. She glanced down at the gown, wondering what she would tell Cara.

"Doona fash yourself over it," Hayden said as if reading her mind. "The women will be glad I was proven wrong. I'm sure there is another gown waiting for you even now."

She hoped Hayden was right, but if he wasn't, she deserved their anger.

By the time she and Hayden entered the great hall everyone was seated and eating. The only one missing was Broc. Though she had never considered Broc a friend, he was someone she knew and she missed him.

No one said anything about her ruined gown. Hayden had managed to wash the blood from his hands before sitting down.

There were so many men that she didn't know, and Isla hoped she was able to put names to the faces staring at her. Maybe she would ask one of the women later.

Fallon caught her gaze. "I had Ramsey draw a map of the Loch Awe area since he has been there. Do you know which side of the loch the Druids are hiding on?"

Isla finished chewing and swallowing before she reached for the parchment Ramsey held out for her. She was amazed at the intricate drawing. "You are very good."

Ramsey bowed his head. "Thank you. It has been several decades since I have been to the area, so I drew it all from what memory I have."

"I've never been," Isla said. "However, based on what Deirdre told me of the area, this matches it."

"Good," Lucan said.

Isla pulled the map closer as she struggled to remember if Deirdre said where the artifact was. A forest, yes, but there were many forests along the loch. If Galen and Logan had to search both sides, they could be gone a very long time.

"It's all right if you don't know," Cara whispered from beside her.

Isla glanced at the Druid. Cara was pretty with her dark eyes and hair, a perfect match for Lucan. "Give me a moment."

Isla then put her hand over the map and closed her eyes. She focused all of her magic to the map of Loch Awe and searched for the presence of Druids.

With her eyes still shut, she moved her hand over the parchment, stopping occasionally when she thought she felt something. And then . . . something stirred. Magic.

Her eyes flew open. "Here," she said and pointed with her finger. "The Druids will be in this area."

Galen leaned over and looked at the map before raising his blue eyes to her. "How did you do that?"

"My magic."

"Amazing," Ramsey said.

Isla knew the truth, though. It was the black magic that made her magic strong and allowed her to use it as *mies* could not. Similar to Deirdre, but different because Isla didn't rely on evil to strengthen her magic. She relied on her *mie* magic.

Fallon stood then. "Galen, Logan, you have your course."

When Logan stood, so did Hayden, who sat beside him. They clasped forearms. No words were needed. They were friends, brothers, parting ways for a mission that could end in failure and death.

When Galen was about to stand, Isla put her hand on his arm to stop him. "The Druids are fearful and hiding. They will use magic to keep others from finding them. You could easily overlook them."

"How do I find them then?"

"Trust your instincts. And once you do find them, they will not easily open up to you."

Sonya leaned forward and nodded. "Isla is correct. The Druids won't trust strangers, especially Warriors. Do your best not to show them exactly what you are."

Galen let out a sigh. "Logan, we have our work cut out for us."

"Then we best go," Logan replied with a smile.

Isla rose with Galen and walked to the door with everyone.

"Godspeed," Fallon said as Logan and Galen faced the small crowd.

Galen glanced at Logan. "We'll be back as quickly as we can."

"Bring the Druids if you can talk them into it," Cara said. "They'll be safer here."

"We'll do what we can," Logan promised.

After a round of farewells, the two Warriors departed. Isla ducked away from the others, intending to return to her chamber and change gowns.

Only when she turned the corner someone was in the chamber. She paused at the door, surprised to find Hayden digging through a chest at the foot of the bed.

He paused and lifted his head, blond hair falling over his face. He regarded her a moment, then went back to looking in the chest. "I'll be finished in a moment."

Finished? And when the realization came, she grew uncomfortable. "This is your chamber?"

"Aye," he said without looking up. "There were no empty ones, and I doona use mine."

"I cannot stay here," she said.

He straightened then. "And where will you stay? Will you sleep in the great hall?"

Isla hadn't thought that far ahead, but she couldn't keep Hayden out of his own chambers.

"I'll be fine," he said. "I'll use Logan's chamber while he's gone."

Isla clasped her hands behind her back. "You don't like me, yet you allow me to use your chamber?"

Hayden closed the lid and straightened. He walked to her and didn't stop until he stood in front of her. "I never said I didn't like you."

"You didn't have to. It's clear how you feel about *droughs*."

Hayden took in a deep breath and slowly let it out. "There is much your magic can do, Druid, but unless you possess Galen's power to read minds, you have no idea what I do or doona like."

And with that he was gone.

For long moments Isla didn't move. She looked at the chamber, the bed with new eyes. It was Hayden's. He had slept in the bed, dressed in the chamber.

She was going to have to find somewhere else to stay. Being in Hayden's bed would be too much. Already she found herself searching him out among the Warriors.

Isla stepped into the chamber and closed and bolted the door. She stripped off the ruined gown, thankful to find another lying across the bed.

She hurried to change, trying her best not to think of Hayden. And failing miserably.

ELEVEN

Hayden told himself he didn't care that Isla was in his chamber, that her body was covered by the same linens that had touched him.

But as soon as he had walked into his chamber, he had smelled her. The snow and wild pansy scent filled the room, reminding him of ice-blue eyes and midnight hair, of lush lips and creamy skin. Of an exquisite body and pert breasts.

The blood had rushed to his cock in less than a blink. He had tried to ignore it by searching his chest for another shirt, one that wasn't stained with Isla's blood.

Which brought him back to when he had thought her dead just an hour before. That fear had clawed at his insides just as it had when he'd found his family.

Worse, he didn't want to feel for Isla. He tried to tell himself that he didn't, but he knew the truth of it in his bones.

He had found her on that Godforsaken mountain and carried her back to the castle. He had seen in his mind her torture, had listened to her beg him for death. How could he not care?

How did he dare?

It seemed his feelings weren't as dead as he imagined. And that could be a very bad thing.

He'd been so lost in thought he hadn't heard Isla until

she had spoken from the doorway. He knew he couldn't stay in the same chamber alone with her. She was too much of a temptation, an enticement he didn't want, not when he didn't understand his body's reaction to her.

To get away, he had to pass her. And that had nearly done him in.

She wasn't afraid of him. That in itself made her more appealing. Dangerously so.

The urge to touch her skin, to feel its warmth, had pushed him closer to her. The desire to taste her lips, to sample the essence that was hers alone had overwhelmed him. The need to feel her against him, to have her breasts pressed against his chest had pushed him to the point of breaking.

He had two choices: give in to his desires. Or leave.

He'd left, and even now as he strode to Logan's chamber he regretted it. Hayden wondered what she would have done had he pulled her into his arms.

Would she have fought him? Given no reaction? Or would he have seen another side of Isla, a passionate side wild and eager to break free?

It was better that he never knew the answer to that question.

Hayden stood in Logan's chamber for several heartbeats before he jerked off his saffron shirt and tossed it on the bed. There was work to do in the village. Exactly what he needed to forget about Isla and the allure she offered.

Isla was amazed at how the new gown fit her to perfection. The sapphire color of the gown was beautiful in its simplicity. She couldn't remember the last time she had felt pretty.

She wondered what Hayden would think of the gown, and then she wondered why she cared.

Isla walked from the chamber in search of the women. She wasn't surprised to find Cara outside the kitchen tending to a garden. Cara was leaning over a plant, her hands hovering around it as she put her face close. The plants grew lush and bountiful from her pure magic.

And despite herself, Isla was jealous. She had once had that pure magic running through her. It might not be as powerful as black magic, but there was nothing like the feel of untainted magic running through a body.

"You found the gown," Cara said as she glanced up. "How does it fit? I didn't know your exact measurements, so I just guessed. Let me know if I need to alter anything."

"It fits wonderfully. Thank you."

Cara leaned back on her knees and dusted off her hands before rising. "I love the feel of the earth. Lucan says I spend more time with my plants than I do with him."

Isla returned Cara's smile, envy spiking through her once more. "The earth strengthens your magic. It's no wonder you find it hard to resist."

"That's the same thing Sonya said." Cara picked her way through the garden and walked to Isla. "Is something wrong?"

Isla was hesitant to ask. The MacLeods had sheltered her, helped to heal her, fed her, and clothed her. She didn't want to sound ungrateful. "Is there somewhere else I can sleep?"

"Did Hayden say something to you?"

Isla shook her head. "Not at all. I just . . . I can sleep in one of the cottages."

"Have you seen the cottages?" Cara asked with a sheepish smile. "The wyrran destroyed most of them. They aren't fit to house anyone."

"I can make do," Isla insisted. "I don't like the idea of putting anyone out of their chamber."

Cara gave her a wry smile. "There's no need to explain. I understand. There is one place you might like. In the north tower there is a chamber at the top. It isn't large, and it's empty."

"That would be perfect."

"Consider it done, then," Cara said. "Lucan is finishing a bed today that was supposed to go in one of the cottages. I'll have him bring it up to the tower."

Isla licked her lips, unsure if a simple thank you would be enough. "I appreciate everything, Cara."

Cara waved away her words. "No need to thank me. You are part of us now, one of the family."

"There you are," Marcail said as she strolled from the bailey. "I've been looking for you, Isla. I thought you might want to take a walk with me."

Cara nodded and shooed Isla away. "Aye, go with Marcail and learn about the castle. I'm sure you have many questions."

Isla soon found herself with Marcail at the top of the battlements staring down at the bailey where the men were gathered.

Hayden was easy to spot because of his height and golden locks. But there were many others she didn't know.

"To think it all started with just the MacLeods," Marcail said. "Now look at what has been created."

"There are many I do not know."

Marcail chuckled. "It was the same with me. I'm still getting to know them all. You know the MacLeods, obviously."

"Aye. And Broc," Isla said. "I've met Logan, Galen, and Ramsey as well."

Marcail leaned up on tiptop for a moment. "Logan is the happy one, the one who keeps everyone laughing. Galen is the one with the endless stomach."

"I learned that already." Isla couldn't help but grin as she recalled the way the others teased Galen.

Marcail smiled at her. "That's right, you have. Now, Ramsey, he's the quiet one. You never know what he's thinking, but when he does speak, it's usually in everyone's best interest to listen."

"I see."

"You also know Arran, and the twins, Ian and Duncan, right?"

Isla nodded.

"Then there's Camdyn and Malcolm. Have you met either of them?"

"Nay."

Marcail pointed to a Warrior in a bold red, black, and blue kilt. He had long black hair and stood almost as imposingly as Hayden. "That's Camdyn. He tends to keep to himself, though he is easy enough to get along with."

"And Malcolm?"

Marcail grimaced and looked away from the Warriors. "He is Larena's cousin."

"He's not a Warrior?"

"Nay."

Isla remembered a man walking the cliffs the previous night. His face was scarred, though it didn't distract from his good looks. "Is he the one with the scars on his face?"

"And a right arm he cannot use."

"What happened to him?"

"Deirdre's Warriors," Marcail answered with a sigh. "Sonya has a gift for healing, but she wasn't able to restore the use of his arm."

Isla understood why Malcolm roamed the cliffs then.

"And then of course there's Hayden," Marcail said.

"Tell me about him."

"You mean besides that he has a hatred for *droughs*

that goes beyond anything I've ever seen?" Marcail shuddered. "Watch yourself around him."

Isla shrugged and found her gaze on Hayden once more as he walked through the gates toward the village. "I'm not afraid of him."

Marcail studied her a moment. "I don't think you are. He was the one who found you on the mountain."

"Was he?" Now that was something she hadn't expected. "If he hates *droughs* so much, why didn't he kill me as I asked him to do?"

"Only Hayden can answer that," Marcail said. "We all expected him to do it."

Interesting. Very interesting.

Isla was taken on a tour of the castle. She hadn't seen it destroyed, but she remembered the gleeful rejoicing Deirdre had done when she'd made Isla watch as the MacLeods discovered what had happened.

It had made Isla physically sick to think of all the innocents that had been killed that day. Looking at the castle now, Isla was glad to see that something good was once more making a home among the old stones of Mac-Leod Castle.

After the tour Isla went with Marcail to the kitchen where Cara, Sonya, and Larena were already getting the noon meal ready.

"With these Warriors, we barely have enough food," Sonya said.

Larena grinned. "At least with Galen gone for a few days we'll have some left over."

"Larena!" Cara cried and tossed flour at her.

Isla found herself smiling at their antics and the way the women interacted, as if they had been lifelong friends. They had come from different paths of life, but they had all found common ground with each other.

They made the best of their lives despite the war that raged around them. They kept laughter and love and light among them, a testament to the Druid magic that filled the castle.

"You have flour on your face, Larena," Sonya said with a chuckle.

Marcail rolled her eyes. "It just gives Fallon a reason to kiss her."

"As if you have any right to talk," Larena said with a knowing grin. "You and Quinn run off every chance you get."

Sonya grinned. "And they think no one notices."

Marcail shrugged away their comments, but Isla saw the satisfied smile on her face. "What can I say? I'm irresistible."

Cara snorted. "More like the MacLeod brothers are insatiable."

Larena, Cara, and Marcail all busted out laughing, nodding their heads in agreement.

Isla felt a pang of remorse as she recalled the times she and her sister had shared such laughter. These women might not be bound by blood, but they were bound by family, and sometimes that could be stronger.

Sonya rolled her eyes at them as she continued to knead the dough. "I think I'm the only one with a sane thought around here."

Marcail and Cara exchanged a look. Larena just shook her head.

"So," Marcail said and turned to Isla. "Can you cook? Or are you like me and hopeless when it comes to preparing food?"

Memories of baking sweets with her family filled Isla's mind. "I used to be fairly good, but it has been a very long time."

"What's your specialty?" Larena asked.

Isla glanced at the expectant faces around her. "My father was a baker. I learned early on many of his recipes."

Cara clapped her flour-covered hands. "Wonderful. Do you remember any of them? Another set of hands in the kitchen would be a tremendous help."

Being needed as she was at that moment left Isla breathless. These women didn't seem to care that she had spent the last five hundred years immersed with evil.

"I'll see if I can recall any," Isla said. "I cannot promise that anything I prepare will be edible, however."

Sonya set aside the dough and leaned her hands on the work table. "I don't think the men taste half of what they eat, they cram it down so fast."

"Only so Galen doesn't get it," Cara joked.

Larena scratched her chin with the back of her hand. "Poor Galen. Everyone teases him so."

The hours flew by as Isla stayed in the kitchen and listened to the conversation. Occasionally she would speak, but mostly she listened. There was much laughter, much teasing, and obvious love between all of them.

And to have been included brought a longing to Isla she didn't want to feel.

The hope swelling within her, the inclusion in the MacLeod "family," and her fascination with Hayden could only spell one thing: disaster.

TWELVE

The day passed in a blur for Isla. She was so occupied with making herself useful to the others she didn't realize how fast the day was going until supper arrived.

With three of their members gone, the tables seemed to lack something. Hayden was one of four others who decided to continue to work on the cottages instead of stopping to eat.

Isla hated to admit that she missed being able to look at him. It was shameful, her need to gaze upon him and his sculpted body.

It wasn't as if she hadn't seen her fair share of handsome men, but with Hayden it was more than just his good looking face. It was him, the man. His manner.

It was a good thing she had never encountered Hayden while in Cairn Toul. If Deirdre ever discovered Isla's interest in Hayden . . . Isla shuddered just thinking about it.

When they finished cleaning the table Isla looked up to find Cara smiling at her.

"Are you ready to see your new chamber?" Cara asked.

Lucan walked up behind her and put his hands on Cara's shoulders. "She's wanted to show you ever since I brought the bed up."

"I would love to see it," Isla said.

Cara hurried to the steps with Lucan not far behind her.

Isla followed them both up the stairs to the second-floor corridor.

"It isn't much," Cara explained as she glanced back over her shoulder at Isla. "I can get more furniture to the tower soon."

"It will be perfect," Isla said, hoping it soothed Cara's anxiety.

Lucan smiled at his wife, the love shining in his eyes for the world to see.

When they reached the entrance to the tower after many twists and turns, Isla looked up the winding staircase.

"It's a beautiful view," Lucan said. "Cara was right to pick this tower."

Cara wrinkled her nose. "It never occurred to me to make the towers into chambers before. That gives us three more chambers if need be."

Lucan laughed and motioned Isla forward. "Your new chamber awaits."

Isla licked her lips and placed her foot on the first step. The stairs coiled high above her, nearly making her dizzy. She reached the top and opened the door to find a round chamber with the bed opposite the window and a small table beside the bed. There was a lone chair and a chest for her clothes.

"It isn't much, I know. I'm mending a tapestry I found that I can hang above the bed," Cara said, her voice low and sorrowful.

Isla turned and looked at her. "This is perfect, Cara. Thank you. I need nothing else."

Cara's smile was blinding as joy swept over her face. "I have a couple of other gowns I'm mending to fit you."

"You do too much."

"We take care of ours," Lucan said and wrapped an arm around Cara's shoulders.

Isla nodded, her throat thick with emotion. She didn't have the words anyway.

"We'll leave you now," Lucan said. "Let us know if you need anything."

Once alone, Isla turned to face her chamber. She ran her hand over the comb and hand mirror that had been placed on the bedside table.

She lowered herself onto her bed and just sat there. This was her chamber, not one loaned to her, but hers while she was at the castle. She hoped her stay would be a long one, but Isla feared Deirdre would gain her powers sooner than expected.

But until then, Isla had found a home. Her first true home in over five centuries.

It was dark and well past supper when Hayden made his way to the castle. He didn't see Isla in the hall or the kitchens where he stopped to grab cold meat and bread.

He didn't like that he searched for her, but he couldn't prevent the concern for where she was and what she was doing. She might be trying to harm the others, or at least that was the excuse he used for his feelings. She hadn't been on the cliffs, that he knew since he had searched. She had to be somewhere in the castle.

Hayden finished his meal and made his way to his chamber. He would just check on Isla to make sure she didn't need anything. Then he would take a swim in the sea to wash the sweat and grime from his body and try to get some rest.

He knocked, but there was no soft, feminine voice that answered him. In fact, there was no voice at all.

Hayden cracked open the door and looked inside to find the chamber empty. He went to his chest to find a new shirt, and somehow knew Isla had removed herself from the room.

He didn't understand the anger that surged through him. Shouldn't he be glad she was gone? Why then did he want her in his bed?

Determined to forget about Isla, Hayden went to his window. He had always felt if the god chose him and gave him powers, why not use them? This was one of those times.

Hayden watched the long scarlet claws extend from his fingers. They were the same deep shade of red as his skin, the same color as his Warrior eyes.

Immense, and terrible, power swept through him as it did every time he called up his god. But his god was part of him now, had been part of him for almost two hundred years. Would most likely be a part of him from now until the day his head was severed from his body.

Without another thought he jumped from his window. The fall from his chamber to the beach below was a long one, the wind howling past his ears.

Hayden landed in a crouch on top of a large boulder and pushed his god back down. He quickly stripped before he jumped to the rocky sand and waded into the cool water.

He walked until the water reached his waist before he dove under. It didn't take him long to wash and return to shore. With the castle built on the cliffs, not many walked the steep path down to the beach, which gave Hayden the privacy he wanted.

Although with his powers, he could get to any beach along the cliffs he wanted. He'd only seen one other place accessible to humans, but it wasn't near the castle. Most likely it was used by the MacClures, who had claimed the MacLeod lands and feared the castle.

Hayden looked up at the inky sky and the stars winking back at him. The half moon hung low, its light spilling across the sea. He had always loved looking at the moon, but tonight the midnight sky reminded him of long black hair.

With a sigh Hayden dressed and knew he wouldn't rest until he had found Isla and made sure she wasn't getting into anything. She hadn't left the area because he could still feel the magic of her shield.

He could simply ask someone, but then they would know of his interest. Or they would think the worst, that he was trying to kill her. Neither was something he wanted to deal with. So he would find her himself.

Hayden once more released his god to bound back up the cliffs to the castle. The easiest way for him to find Isla was to look through the windows.

He began with the chambers he knew were vacant—Broc's, Logan's, and Galen's. He didn't find her, but more importantly he didn't smell her scent, which meant she hadn't been in the chambers.

Hayden leapt atop the battlements to think of where he would search next when he saw a light coming from the north tower.

He didn't hesitate to work his way to the tower window, and when he looked inside there was the minx in question combing her long locks with slow, sure strokes.

Hayden should have left and returned to his own chamber. He should have ignored the lure of Isla's snow and wild pansy scent. He should have fought against the desire that roared to life in his body and demanded he sample her.

But he did none of those things.

Instead, he tamped down his god and landed without a sound inside the tower. He took a step toward the bed when Isla's hand paused and lowered the comb. She turned her head toward him. Without a word she stood and faced him.

He wanted to see fear in her ice-blue depths, anything to shake the fiery need running rampant through him. Fear, it seemed, wasn't an emotion Isla felt.

Knowing it was wrong, knowing he needed to leave, he walked toward her, each step fueling his desire until he had to touch her or go up in flames from the heat of it.

She retreated only two steps. Maybe a part of her feared him after all. It was what he wanted. Why then did it irk him?

Her scent surrounded him, lulled him. Excited him. If he didn't touch her, he knew he'd explode with the force of his desire. Unable to stop himself, he lifted his left hand and cupped her face.

She tilted her face into his hand, her gaze curious and seeking. He wondered what she saw when she looked at him. Did she see the monster he had become? Did it repulse her as he dreaded it might?

All thoughts vanished as he lost himself in the depths of her stunning ice-blue eyes. The world melted away leaving just the two of them and a passion he was unable to resist.

His thumb brushed her lips, aching to touch more. He bit back a groan as his cock swelled and his hunger consumed him. By the saints, he didn't understand this need riding him or why it had to be Isla that brought it out. No woman had ever done this to him.

But he couldn't ignore it any more than he could try and stop his heart from beating.

He wouldn't kiss her. He couldn't. Even though he fought against the yearning to taste her, to touch her, to claim her, he found his head dipping toward Isla's captivating lips.

As a last resort, Hayden placed a hand on the wall to help keep his distance from Isla's tempting, decadent mouth. It didn't work, not when he saw her lips part as if she wanted his kiss.

It was his undoing.

With his heart pounding and blood drumming in his ears, the scorching need filling him was too much for Hayden to fight. Even with his claws sunk into the stone near Isla's head, he couldn't distance himself from her, couldn't rein back his desire.

His head dipped closer. He inhaled, her scent filling his nose and his body. His rod thickened, wanting, needing to pull her soft curves against him and grind against her.

Her eyes softened, the ice-blue depths darkening with passion. Hayden was so close to her he could see the circle of darker blue that ringed her irises.

Coming ever closer, Hayden's hand slid from her cheek to her neck and his fingers plunged into the silky softness of her black locks. His hand cupped the back of her head as his gaze fell to her mouth.

Their lips were nearly touching. He could feel her warm breath fan over him, teasing him. He inhaled her scent deep within his lungs and knew he had lost the fight as soon as he had entered the tower.

He should have been angry, but all Hayden could feel was the lust that burned his veins. He would have her kiss. He would taste her sweet nectar and get the hunger for her out of his blood once and for all.

At least that's what he hoped would happen.

Just as he was about to place his lips atop hers and assuage his desires, his ears picked up a sound coming from the stairway.

Damn.

But it broke the hold over him. It was all Hayden needed to move away from her.

He allowed himself one last glance at Isla. It nearly broke him when he saw her eyes closed and her lips parted, waiting for him. There was no doubt she wanted his kiss.

Hayden turned and leapt out the tower window before he gave caution to the wind and took his kiss. He slid into the shadows as silent as the darkness. He wanted to know who her visitor was and if Isla would tell them he had been in her chamber.

His body ached for release, release that he wanted with Isla. His head dropped back against the stones of the tower as he let out a ragged sigh of regret and anger. He had almost kissed a *drough*.

What was worse is that he knew he would kiss her. Whatever drew him to Isla could not be severed. And God help him, but he didn't know if he wanted it to.

One moment Isla's hands were resting on Hayden's waist, his lips about to kiss her, and the next he was gone. As if he had been nothing more than a figment of her imagination. But she knew otherwise.

She could still smell a spicy woodsy scent. It reminded her of the forests where she was born. It was that scent that had told her he was in the tower.

It had surprised her that he had come looking for her. Then she had seen the desire in his eyes, desire she had never expected to see.

His touch had been gentle, almost reverent. What had torn her heart apart was the turmoil that showed too plainly on his face. He wanted her, but he didn't want to want her.

She understood him all too well.

Isla jumped when there was a soft knock at her door.

So maybe that's why Hayden had left before he'd kissed her. Had he heard the approach of someone?

He didn't want to be seen with you.

She wanted to deny it, but she knew the truth of her subconscious. And it hurt far more than she would have liked.

Isla walked to the door, her knees shaking from a mixture of passion and resentment. She opened it to find Larena.

Larena's smiled dropped when she got a look at Isla's face. "Is everything all right?"

Isla opened the door wider and motioned Larena inside. "Everything is wonderful. Why?"

"For a moment there you looked . . ." Larena paused and must have reconsidered her words. "I came to see if you needed anything."

Isla smiled and shook her head. "I have more than I need."

"Cara was quite pleased with herself getting this set up for you. It will get cold in here during the winter without a hearth."

"I will make do."

Larena studied her a moment. "Aye, I think you will. You're a strong woman, Isla. You've endured much more than we can ever imagine, haven't you?"

Isla didn't answer her, she couldn't. Her nightmares and tortures that she suffered were for her alone. They weren't to be shared with anyone.

"You will survive this," Larena continued. "This and anything else that comes your way. Would you like to know why?"

Isla couldn't help but ask, "Why?"

"Because you're a survivor. I'm glad you are here with us. Please know if you ever need anything, you can come to me."

"Thank you." Isla had said those two words more in the last two days than she had in the last five hundred years.

Larena walked to the door, but paused as she made to leave. "You've been on your own for a long time, trusting no one. I understand how that feels." She turned to look at Isla. "It took me a while to understand everyone here accepted me as I was."

"You don't have evil inside you."

Larena smiled sadly. "I do. Every one of us with a god has evil."

Isla swallowed and turned her head away. "You didn't have a choice, Larena. The god chose you."

"And Deirdre chose you. She threatened your family. Do not believe what you did was out of cowardice, Isla. It took a tremendous amount of courage to become a *drough*, knowing what you would become and who you would serve. That is what sets you apart from others."

Isla looked into Larena's smoky blue eyes. "And the things I've done? Shall I blame them on Deirdre as well?"

Larena glanced away, but not before Isla saw the distress pass over her face. "I wish I could take away those burdens, but I think even if I could you wouldn't allow me."

"You're correct. They are mine to bear."

"And how long will you carry them? When will you forgive yourself?"

"Never." Isla didn't deserve forgiveness. Not for the things she had done, regardless of the reasons.

"I hope you change your mind. Sleep well," Larena said and closed the door behind her as she left.

Isla wanted to hit something, anything to get the rage that had been building inside of her out. But she'd clamped down on her emotions for too long to do anything other than seethe quietly.

Everyone here was too welcoming, too understanding. They wanted to help her, but nothing and no one could help her.

No matter how hard she tried to rein in her scattered emotions, she couldn't get a handle on them. They overwhelmed her, mocking her, taunting her until Isla punched the stone wall before she broke apart.

Tears stung the backs of her eyes as her bones shattered from the impact. Blood seeped from her sliced knuckles, and she could do nothing other than look at them.

She collapsed onto the bed and curled onto her side. She held her broken hand softly, her heart breaking for the person she had become, the fiend she had vowed she would control.

The tears she knew she should cry wouldn't come. They never did.

THIRTEEN

Hayden watched Isla from the window. It disturbed him to see her lose control so harshly. He would never have expected it of her, though he should have after seeing some of her tortures himself. She restrained herself too tightly, and if she didn't watch it, she would fracture. Already she was on the verge.

He had almost returned to his chamber when he saw that it was Larena, but something had told him to stay, and he was glad he had. He had learned much from their conversation. Too much, maybe.

Isla wouldn't welcome him now, and he wouldn't know what to say to her anyway. Hayden jumped from the tower and made his way back to his chamber. Isla needed to be alone, and so did he. Except all he could think about as he lay in his bed was Isla, the way she made him yearn, and the words she had spoken to Larena.

There was no question Isla was lonely. Everyone at sometime felt loneliness, but Hayden suspected Isla's went much deeper.

He didn't like that he could relate to her or understand her. It was enough that he desired her. If he didn't watch it, he'd find himself in her bed much sooner than he'd like.

And what's wrong with that? Everyone has accepted her.

That was true enough. It made it too damn easy to convince himself it was all right to want her. But the memory of finding his family dead prevented even that.

Hayden bent an arm behind his head and stared at the ceiling of his chamber. Even in the darkness the powers from his god allowed him to see perfectly.

He knew sleep wouldn't come, not when he could still smell Isla in his chamber, still feel her breath on his cheek and her curves in his arms.

It was enough to tempt a saint, and Hayden most assuredly wasn't a saint.

Dunmore guided his horse as close to the entrance of Deirdre's mountain as he could amid the rocks. The creature was surefooted, but with the snow and ice, even Dunmore knew it was time to go it on foot.

He slid off his mount's back and dropped the reins. The horse wouldn't go far, not in the snowstorm.

Dunmore hated the creak in his bones as he climbed ever higher. It just proved he was getting old too fast. How much longer would Deirdre continue to turn to him for help before she realized he wasn't as fit as he used to be? He didn't imagine it would be much longer.

But right now she needed him. He would see that he did as she requested. After that, there would be no stopping Deirdre. Maybe then she would grant him the ultimate gift of immortality and youth.

Dunmore didn't bother to try and shield his face with his hands. The snow was coming down too quickly and too thick. He ducked his head and trudged forward.

It wasn't long before he heard the telltale shrieks of the wyrran. The undersized, hairless creatures were efficient and deadly, even if he couldn't stand to look at them with their mouthful of sharp teeth that lips couldn't close over.

Deirdre had created the creatures with her will and black magic, fashioning them to serve her and her alone. Three wyrran waited for him by the entrance into the mountain.

He nodded to the wyrran and stepped into the mountain. Once he was through the stone door, it closed behind him. Dunmore walked down the steps and narrow corridor before he turned into a wider hallway. He followed it down until he came to what Deirdre likened to a great hall.

The cavern was huge and shadowy. A massive chandelier with hundreds of candles hung from the ceiling, shedding minute light throughout. Below him, their faces tilted to him, were the wyrran that had survived the MacLeods' attack on Cairn Toul.

Dunmore leaned on the stone railing and took a deep breath. He would make sure he was essential to Deirdre so that she couldn't toss him aside. "We have much work to do. Our mistress had called to us. The ones who dared to defy her, who dared to think they could defeat her will pay. With their lives."

The wyrran shrieked their fury and glee at his words.

He held up a hand to quiet them. "But first, we must collect more Druids and find the Warriors who thought they could escape. We must move quickly and quietly over the land. Our first target is a Druid. Deirdre must have a sacrifice to have her body returned."

The wyrran began to howl and rock back and forth, eager to be on their way.

"We'll split into two groups. Half of you stay here and continue to ready the mountain for Deirdre. The other half come with me. We have Druid to hunt."

As Dunmore turned on his heel to leave, he felt something brush against him.

"Very well done, Dunmore."

"Mistress." He paused and waited for Deirdre to say more. He missed seeing her. She was the most beautiful thing he had ever seen. Her white hair that hung to the floor and white eyes were spectacular to behold. He'd take her for his own if she'd have him.

"You have rallied my wyrran. Let us hope you return with a Druid as quickly."

Dunmore bowed his head. "I will see it done."

"You will be rewarded. I give you my word."

"Anything for you," he whispered. But she was already gone. He felt her loss as keenly as his old bones felt the cold.

He would prove himself to her if it was the last thing he did. He owed her at least that.

Quinn never expected to find Lucan sitting in the great hall in the middle of the night. The fact his brother was staring off in thought told Quinn all he needed to know.

"Couldn't sleep?" he asked.

Lucan raised startled sea green eyes. "Nay. Neither can Fallon. He went to find something to eat."

Quinn slid onto the bench at the table across from Lucan. "What's kept you up?"

"Isla."

"You think she's lying?"

Lucan shook his head, the twin braids at his temples swinging. "Not at all. I fear she's telling us the truth, the entire ugly mess of it."

"Not that we wish otherwise," Fallon said as he entered through the kitchen. He had a goblet in his hand that Quinn knew was filled with water since Fallon had given up his need for wine.

"She's verra powerful," Quinn said. "Nothing that compares to Deirdre, but I could feel Isla's magic. And it's strong."

Lucan nodded. "I think we all felt it. The fact that she has battled the evil within her allows her to use that power for good."

"But how long will she have control?" Fallon asked. "Deirdre will gain back her power. It's simply a matter of time, and when she does she will bring her full wrath upon us and use Isla as well."

Quinn blew out a breath. "If we can sever the link Deirdre has with Isla, we'll be in a much better position."

"That's a big if, little brother," Lucan said. "We tempted Isla to stay on the chance that an artifact could break that link. I hope we weren't wrong."

Fallon ran his finger on the edge of the goblet. "It was a chance we took. Isla knows that as well. We need her here. Her shielding could help out tremendously, and with the Warriors we have, if something happens, we can kill Isla if we have to."

Quinn hoped it didn't come to that. "Isla is as much a victim as we are. If this artifact Galen and Logan seek cannot help her, maybe the Druids who guard it will be able to lead us to another."

"I don't know," Lucan said. "So much is stacked against us. Deirdre will be looking for the artifact as well. We aren't even sure what this artifact does."

"And we wouldna even know of it if Isla hadn't told us. We owe her this," Quinn stated.

Fallon looked at Quinn. "No one said we wouldn't try to help Isla. We will do all we can. We have more Warriors now, and another Druid. If you count Isla, we have a lot of added magic. Everything hinges on gaining the upper hand on Deirdre before she regains all her powers."

"I wish we knew where the other artifacts were," Lucan said. "We could send several Warriors after them."

Fallon leaned back in his chair and drank deeply. "I'm just happy there's a chance we can keep one out of Deirdre's hands. It's not much, but it's something."

"We need more," Lucan murmured.

Quinn puffed out his cheeks with air. Deirdre was always a step ahead of them. It didn't bode well for the outcome of the world.

"Did your women kick you out of your beds?" Hayden asked as he descended the stairs.

Fallon chuckled. "Larena is probably even now searching for me."

Hayden rolled his eyes as he took a seat near Quinn and grimaced. "Enough. I doona need to hear of your prowess in bed."

Quinn saw a ghost of a smile on the big blond's face, but it was fleeting. "Actually, we're discussing Isla."

"What about her?" Hayden demanded, his gaze hard and steady.

Was it Quinn's imagination or had Hayden become defensive?

"We're talking about what could happen if none of the artifacts help Isla," Lucan said.

Fallon set his goblet on the table and ran a hand down his face. "The simple truth is we want to keep everyone safe. If it was just Warriors here, I doona think we'd be as concerned."

"But there are Druids," Quinn said. "Isla's magic far succeeds even Sonya's."

Hayden looked from one to the other of them. They wanted something from him, and he feared he knew exactly what it was. "You want a Warrior to stay with her at all times, someone who will know if she's acting differently and put a stop to her before it's too late."

"Something like that, aye," Fallon said. He leaned forward and put his elbows on the table. "We don't want Isla to feel as if she's a prisoner."

"Having a Warrior follow her everywhere will make it seem that way. Why not have someone watch her discreetly?"

Lucan raised a dark brow. "Are you volunteering?"

Hayden threw up his hands. He knew he should never have sat down with the brothers. "Nay. Leave me out of it. Everyone already believes I'll kill her."

"And you won't?" Quinn asked.

Hayden wasn't fooled by the quiet tone of the youngest MacLeod. Quinn was sometimes too intelligent for his own good. "You asked me to trust in your decision. I'm doing just that."

"I think you'd be the best person," Lucan said. "I'm serious, Hayden. You aren't biased by her story or feel sorry for her. You feel nothing."

Oh, Hayden felt something all right, but it wasn't something he wanted to experience. Or let the brothers know about. "I'd rather you ask someone else."

"We'd talk to Broc, but he's on a mission." Fallon shrugged. "If you really doona want to do this, we will find someone else."

Hayden clenched his jaw. He didn't want anyone spying on Isla, not when he did it himself anyway. "Fine," he grumbled. "I'll do it. You trust me enough not to kill her?"

"Aye," Quinn said. "I saw how protective of her you were when you carried her into this hall. That wouldn't have changed had you never discovered she was a *drough*."

"Maybe. Maybe not," Hayden quipped. "We'll never know, now will we?"

The smile on Quinn's lips was slow and knowing. "Maybe. Maybe not."

Hayden held Quinn's gaze. Was his desire for Isla so obvious that Quinn had seen it? Surely not.

Quinn slapped his hands on the table and stood. "I think it's time I returned to my bed and my wife."

Fallon nodded and followed Quinn from the hall, leaving Lucan alone with Hayden.

"I would have thought spying on Isla would be what you wanted," Lucan said.

Hayden rubbed his tired eyes with his thumb and forefinger. Did everyone see his attraction for Isla? "I'd rather be out hunting and killing Deirdre's Warriors."

"We all would. Quinn said you were fine, but I wonder if having a *drough* here is too much for you. Not that I would blame you."

"It's not like she's the *drough* who killed my family," Hayden said. "She's helping us against Deirdre. For now, that's good enough. If she turns on any of us, I'll be the first to strike her down."

Lucan twisted his lips in a grimace. "I hope it doesn't come to that. The women have taken a liking to Isla."

"For everyone's sake, I hope it all works out as we hope. But what are the odds?"

"Not very good, I'm afraid."

Hayden nodded, hating to hear his own thoughts said aloud. "Unfortunately, I agree."

"Why didn't you go with Galen, if you don't mind me asking?"

"Logan needed to go," Hayden answered. "Though I would have liked to track down those Druids and the artifact myself."

"Is something wrong with Logan?"

"Something is wrong with all of us. You know that better than anyone."

Lucan snorted. "Aye, I do. Is there anything we can do for him?"

"You did. You let him go with Galen."

Lucan rubbed his chin and shifted in his seat, a question in his sea-green eyes.

"Just spit it out," Hayden said with a sigh.

"What do you mean?"

"You want to ask me something. Just ask it. If I don't want to answer it, I willna."

Lucan laughed and shook his head. "I always did like your forthrightness."

"Some would call it rudeness."

"Maybe." Lucan chuckled again. "That would be Ramsey that called you rude. Correct?"

Hayden grinned. "Correct. Now ask your question."

The smile vanished, replaced by a grim face. "You mentioned a *drough* killed your family."

Hayden glanced at his hands. If he wanted to call MacLeod Castle home, and he truly trusted the brothers, there was no use in keeping what happened to his family from them. He didn't like speaking about his past, but he considered these men close enough that he could share his past with them. "So I did."

"I didna know, Hayden. You don't need to say more."

But Hayden thought he should. After all, the MacLeods had given him a new home. "I think I do. You wish to know what happened?"

"If you're willing to tell it," Lucan said.

"I had been wounded after a battle with a rival clan. The wound wouldn't kill me, but I was in bad shape and needed to rest. I knew it was only a matter of time before my clan found me, so I settled in a grove of trees and bound my wounds."

He paused and took a breath, unable to look at anything but his hands in front of him. "I awoke to feel pain unlike anything I'd ever known before. There was a woman before me, a woman with unnatural white hair and eyes that speared my heart with fear."

"Deirdre," Lucan said.

Hayden nodded. "Once the pain had ended and I didn't feel as if my bones were going to pop out of my skin, I heard her laughing. I knew I had to get away, so I jumped up and ran. I never looked back, never stopped. Something told me I had to get to my family. When I did, I found them . . ." He cleared his throat twice before he could get out the words. "They were dead. My mother, my father, and my brother. All dead, all viciously killed."

"What happened next?" Lucan asked.

"I barely had time to register what had happened before wyrran and other Warriors surrounded me. I was knocked unconscious, and when I awoke I was in Cairn Toul with Deirdre standing over me. She was angry that I had dared to run and wanted to punish me. She used her hair to flay the skin from my back, all the while taunting me with how she had sent a *drough* to kill my family. I had lost everything, so I latched onto the only thing I could. Hatred and vengeance."

"It explains your loathing of *droughs*. We all wondered, and I knew it had to be something terrible for you to hate Cara so. I am sorry, Hayden."

"I doona hate Cara, I hate that she has *drough* blood in her veins and around her neck. We all had terrible things happen to us." Hayden shrugged, uncomfortable talking about something that still haunted him. "Your clan was murdered. So was my family."

"Thank you for telling me." Lucan rose to his feet and walked around the table to clasp Hayden on the shoulder. "We may not be of the same blood, but we are brothers. Every Warrior here is my brethren. Doona carry your burdens alone. They will eventually bury you."

Hayden waited until Lucan was at the top of the stairs before he whispered, "It's too late, Lucan. They already have buried me."

FOURTEEN

Isla left the tower hours before dawn. She had rested as much as she could, but she refused to allow herself to fall into a deep sleep where the nightmares awaited her.

While she had sat in her new chamber, she had let her mind wander over memories of the bakery and her father's favorite recipes.

It wasn't long before she decided to see what the kitchens at MacLeod Castle offered. There was nothing else for her to do, and she needed something to occupy her time before she went daft thinking of the near kiss Hayden had given her.

To Isla's surprise, she found all she needed to make her father's delicious custard pastry. Isla was glad she was alone as she tried to find her way in the kitchen again. It had been ages since she had cooked or even been in a kitchen. It took her longer than she'd have liked to get her bearings, but once she did, everything came back to her in a rush as if she hadn't spent five centuries away.

She was so immersed in her cooking she didn't see the sun rise or notice when others joined her.

"It smells wonderful," Marcail said as she moved to the opposite side of the large work table. "What are you baking?"

Isla glanced up and smiled. She ducked her head and

rubbed her nose on her shoulder since her hands were covered in flour. "Custard pastries. They were my mother's favorite."

"I cannot wait to try one."

Cara walked into the kitchen and inhaled. "The entire castle smells delicious. Who is responsible, and what are we going to eat?"

"It's Isla," Marcail said. "She's baking custard pastries."

Cara closed her eyes and groaned before licking her lips. "It's been years since I've had a custard pastry. How long until they're ready?"

Isla looked from one to the other, apprehension weighing like a stone in her stomach. What if the pastry didn't taste good? She couldn't bear to be embarrassed. "Soon," she answered.

"What are you making now?" Marcail asked and leaned close to take a look.

"Pudding."

Cara licked her lips. "I'm starving already. How long have you been down here?"

Isla shrugged and continued to stir the pudding in the bowl. "I don't know. A while, I suppose."

"Well before dawn," said a deep, masculine voice. A voice that sent tingles of awareness through Isla to settle between her legs. A voice she was beginning to recognize all too clearly.

She raised her gaze to find Hayden standing in the doorway with Larena and Fallon. His black eyes watched her closely. Searching. Seeking. All Isla could think about was the feel of his hard body next to hers and how he had nearly kissed her.

"I couldn't sleep. I decided to make myself useful." Isla continued to mix the pudding and did her best to look away from Hayden.

"I have a feeling my stomach will thank you," Fallon said. "But you needn't have done all this."

Isla didn't bother to answer him. She kept her focus on the pudding and making sure she eliminated all the lumps so it would be as smooth as her father's used to be.

The women began to gather items for the morning meal, their conversation filling the quiet. Isla didn't need to look up to know Hayden and Fallon were still in the kitchen. Nor did she need to check to see if Hayden's eyes were on her. She felt his hot gaze as surely as she felt the heat from the ovens.

Larena suddenly laughed and said, "Galen is going to be sorry he missed this."

Isla set aside the bowl and went to check the pastries. A glance into the ovens confirmed they were indeed ready. She removed them and set the steamy sweets out to cool.

Hayden walked up beside her. She looked at the pastries seeing the many mistakes she had made, mistakes her father would have scolded her for. Next time she would do better.

"They look and smell tasty," Hayden said. "When can I try one?"

"Let them cool first. They're too hot."

His nearness did crazy things to her body. She almost reached out to touch him, to stroke the hard sinew and bronzed skin. Isla managed to stop herself at the last moment and fisted her hands.

"You didn't have to sleep in the tower," he murmured. "My chamber was yours to use."

Isla swallowed, glad her back was to the others. "It wasn't right of me to take your chamber when there was another place for me to stay."

"The tower suits you, I think."

She looked at him then and found it difficult to breathe.

His black eyes were on her, desire smoldering in their depths, the same desire she had seen in his eyes the previous night when he had nearly kissed her. "Does it?"

"Aye. It gives you the distance you need from others."

"What makes you think that?"

He lifted a massive shoulder. "It's not difficult to discern. You kept to yourself in Cairn Toul. It only makes sense that you would want your privacy here as well."

"You think you know me?"

He leaned down so that his mouth was next to her ear. "I think I know you better than most."

Hayden turned on his heel and left the kitchen without another word. Isla let out a breath she hadn't known she'd been holding. Without Hayden in the kitchen, she was able to relax and once more focus on the pudding.

She went back to the work table and the pudding. She needed to shift her attention to other things besides Hayden and what he did to her.

Yet she found herself missing his dark gaze, his silent stares, and commanding manner. She missed his scent of woods and spices. In any other setting he would be a leader in his own right.

Thinking of him made her recall his appearance in her chamber. Why had he come? Was it to scare her? Talk to her? Or kiss her?

Isla wanted to ask him, but she was too afraid of the answer. It was better if she forgot about the near kiss. Besides, Hayden was the wrong man for her to be attracted to. He was wrong in so many ways.

Why then do you want his kiss?

Isla sighed, because there was no easy answer. It was true she wanted his kiss. She wanted . . . too much. There were things that could never be hers, and the quicker she realized that the better for everyone. Especially herself.

By the time she set aside the pudding, she was exhausted, but in a pleasant way. It felt appropriate to be baking once more and immersed in the kitchens. She wasn't sure how anything would taste, but it was a start.

The morning meal was more jovial than the previous evening, but even Isla could tell something bothered the MacLeod brothers.

Sonya was quiet, withdrawn, and that's when Isla realized they were worried about Broc.

"Broc should have returned by now," Ramsey said.

Isla looked from Ramsey to Hayden then to the head of the table where the MacLeods watched her. "What is the one place Deirdre feels safe, powerful?"

"Cairn Toul," Quinn answered.

Isla nodded. "I'm sure that is where she's at. She needs to build her army once again. She will gather any wyrran left alive there."

Lucan gathered Cara's hand in his and asked Isla, "I couldn't sleep last night and was thinking about Deirdre. Is there anyone else she can turn to for aid?"

Isla inwardly cringed at the thought of Dunmore. A man who craved power and immortality, he was always willing to do whatever Deirdre asked of him. "There is a man, a human man who Deirdre used in hunting Druids."

"Dunmore," Marcail said, her voice laced with malice. "The brute who hunted me."

Isla watched Marcail fiddle with the gold bands binding the many small braids. "Marcail is correct. Dunmore came to Deirdre when he was but a young lad. He had seen the wyrran, had seen one of the Warriors turn, and he followed them back to Cairn Toul."

"And Deirdre didn't kill him?" Lucan asked. "I cannot imagine a lad would have been beneficial to her."

Isla shrugged and looked down at the table. "Deirdre

isn't as complicated a person as you think she is. She wants power, and she wants to be adored."

Fallon blew a harsh breath. "So when Dunmore came to her, he bowed before her as if she was a goddess?"

"In a manner," Isla said and turned her face to Fallon. "He did exactly as she wanted. She brought him into the fold. At first he set about doing small things for her."

"Such as?" Quinn asked.

"Stealing. Murdering. Anything to prove his loyalty. It didn't take long before she would send him out with the wyrran to track down Druids. Dunmore was put in charge of those wyrran. Eventually, he became one of her most trusted."

Larena frowned. "Deirdre is all about magic. I still don't understand why a human man would appeal to her. Whether he worshipped her or not, he could only serve her for a few years."

"Maybe you're looking at it the wrong way," Hayden said. "Maybe this Dunmore was kept because he would be able to provide Deirdre with something."

"Like what?" Lucan asked. "What could he possibly do that a Warrior or even her wyrran could not?"

Ramsey leaned forward then. "Interact with others. She liked her Warriors to stay in their Warrior form. They couldn't walk into a village and talk to anyone."

Isla couldn't believe she had never thought of that. Of course Dunmore had always irritated her, so she'd stayed away from him as much as she could. "I think you're correct, Ramsey."

"I do, too," Hayden agreed. "It makes sense."

Fallon turned to Isla. "Did she ever send you into villages?"

"Nay." Isla licked her lips and tried not to fidget. "She had other things for me."

Arran spoke up from down the table. "How long are we going to wait before we go looking for Broc?"

"If he isn't back in a few days, I doubt there will be anything to look for," Isla said. "If Deirdre detects him, she will do anything in her power to capture him. Her anger will be fierce, and he'll be the first who feels her wrath."

Lucan swiped a hand down his face lined with worry and focused his gaze on her. "How long do you think we have before she attacks?"

"As I said before, I really don't know. She'll need a Druid's blood to help regain her lost power. If she hasn't already sent Dunmore after a Druid, she will soon."

The door to the castle suddenly opened and Broc strode inside. He looked exhausted, but none the worse for wear. He smiled at them and started toward the tables.

"Are those long faces for me?" he asked.

Ramsey rose and shook his head. "God's teeth, Broc. What took you so long?"

Broc held up a hand as others began to ask questions. He took a seat at the table and nodded to Larena, who handed him a goblet of water. He downed the entire goblet and wiped his mouth before he looked around the table. "Deirdre is at her mountain."

"As Isla suspected," Fallon said. "What else? Are there wyrran?"

Broc curled his lip. "The little bastards never seem to go away. There are more than I expected. They've been cleaning the mountain, but more disturbing than the wyrran is that Dunmore has returned."

Isla fisted her hands in her lap. She had hoped she'd been wrong, but it seems she knew Deirdre much better than she wanted.

"Again, just as Isla suspected." Fallon leaned back in

his chair and laced his fingers over his stomach. "Let me guess. They've gone after a Druid."

Broc nodded. "They have no idea where to find one, so they may be searching for a while."

Isla listened as Broc recounted everything he had heard regarding Dunmore's speech to the wyrran. If anyone could have gained entrance into the mountain without being detected, it was Broc. He was a formidable enemy, and she was glad he was aligned with the MacLeods.

Thinking of Cairn Toul made Isla remember Phelan. She wanted to ask Broc about him, but didn't want everyone to know. Once Cara brought Broc a plate of food, the other women rose to clean the table.

Isla hesitated. When only Quinn, Broc, Ramsey, and Hayden remained she knew she had to ask. She wished Hayden would leave, though. She didn't like him to know any more of her misdeeds, but there was no way around it.

"Broc, I need to speak with you about something."

He nodded and shoved a huge bite of bread in his mouth.

Isla's stomach wound into tight, hard knots. She was nervous, nervous about all of them discovering this dark secret of hers, but she had to know the answer. "Do you remember the doorway in the mountain that Deirdre forbade anyone enter?"

Broc paused in his chewing, his soft brown eyes regarding her. He swallowed and nodded. "I went there when the attack began. I heard something or someone roaring down there."

"There was nothing there when you went."

He set aside his food and regarded her with hard eyes. "What was down there, Isla?"

She swallowed past the lump in her throat. "A Warrior by the name of Phelan Stewart."

"What?" Broc placed his hands flat on the table, his gaze narrowed and dangerous.

Isla could see the other Warriors staring at her. Their presence only made this situation more uncomfortable, but she had already begun. She would end this. "Deirdre had him chained down there for . . . decades."

"How did he come to be there?" Quinn asked.

It became difficult to breathe. It always did when Isla thought of Phelan and what she had done to him. "I brought him there when he was just a small child."

FIFTEEN

Hayden never expected those words out of Isla's mouth. Even as they revolted him, one look at her angst-ridden face and he knew she regretted it.

"What happened?" he asked when no one else would.

She glanced at him, her ice-blue eyes wide and full of remorse. She seemed surprised he spoke. "Lavena had seen a vision of a great Warrior from the Stewart clan, one who could help Deirdre do amazing things."

Quinn leaned his forearms on the table. "What kind of things?"

Isla lifted a slim shoulder in a shrug. "Lavena never said. The other part of her vision, however, was one of her most clear. She described Phelan perfectly, as well as where he would be and his age. Deirdre thought it would be an ideal opportunity to raise the boy as she thought he should be."

"So that when she unbound his god he would pledge himself to her?" Ramsey finished.

Hayden fisted his hands. He hadn't spent near the time in Deirdre's mountain as some of the others, but even that small amount of time had left him with scars upon his soul that would never mend. He couldn't imagine a young boy being brought there.

His gaze swung to Isla. What would make a woman,

one who supposedly fought against the evil inside her, bring a young boy into Deirdre's care?

It didn't take long for him to find the answer. "Deirdre threatened your niece, didn't she?"

Isla looked away, but not before he saw the answer in her eyes. She nodded and blinked rapidly. "I had no choice but to find Phelan. Deirdre knew it would be folly to send Dunmore and the wyrran. She needed Phelan to come to her of his own free will."

"Isla," Broc said when she paused.

She blinked and looked around, as if she had been deep in her memories. "I had to trick Phelan to get him to leave his family. Deirdre had yet to turn Grania evil, and I thought I had a chance to gain her freedom. Phelan trusted me, and I delivered him into misery."

"Holy hell," Quinn murmured and rose to pace in front of the table. "What happened to him? If he was chained up, I gather he didn't trust Deirdre?"

Isla shook her head. She looked so desolate that Hayden found he wanted to go to her, to pull her against him and shelter her.

"Phelan blamed me," Isla said. "And rightly so. He fought Deirdre repeatedly. Nothing she did to him would break him. She starved him, beat him, and at one point killed him only to bring him back to life. And every time he refused to join her. She kept him separate from everyone, especially other Warriors. I was the only one besides Deirdre who ever saw him."

Broc put his elbows on the table and leaned his forehead on his hands. "When did she unbind his god?"

"When he was eighteen summers. I'd brought him to the mountain when he was only a lad of five," Isla explained.

Hayden's stomach churned as he thought of his fellow

Warrior. "How long after his god was unbound did she keep him chained?"

Isla wouldn't meet his eyes, and her face grew pale. "One hundred and fifty years."

"Dammit, Isla!" Broc roared as he rose to his feet. "How could you do that to one of us?"

If Hayden thought she would cower and cry, he was wrong. Rage filled her eyes, turning them cold and haunted. She stood slowly, her lips flattened as she glared at Broc.

"Aye, Broc, I regret bringing him there. I did everything I could to make sure he was spared many terrible things."

Broc's hands were fisted at his sides, his rage evident in the way his skin flashed from normal to indigo. "Did you bring him food, maybe? Or blankets? Is that what you consider sparing him?"

Hayden and Ramsey stood at the same time as Broc. Hayden wasn't sure if he should try and stop Broc or Isla from attacking the other, because at the rate things were going, someone was going to give into their rage.

"I brought him food and blankets," Isla said. "I took his tortures when I could, even angered Deirdre myself on many occasions so she would take her rage out on me instead of him. I was the one who released him during the MacLeods' attack."

Hayden was taken aback by her words. Would she never cease to shock him? She did things that continually contradicted her ways as a *drough*. Maybe she did have control over the evil.

"Why did you tell us all of this?" Hayden asked. "Where is Phelan now?"

Her face was weary as she briefly closed her eyes. "I don't know where he is. I freed him and told him to run. I told him if he ever needed anything to find the MacLeods, that they could be trusted."

"Do you think he believed you?"

"I doubt it. There is one more thing. Phelan's blood was special. It could heal anyone of anything. Deirdre drank his blood regularly to strengthen herself and her powers." She turned and left the castle before they could ask more.

Hayden wanted to go after her. He was supposed to be following her, after all. But there had been something so heartbreaking, so raw in her voice at the end that he'd been unable to chase after her just yet.

Once the door closed behind her, Broc threw his goblet across the hall and cursed. "I could have helped him. If I'd gotten to him before Isla, I could have brought him here."

"Nay," Hayden said. "He doesna trust anyone, and won't for some time. Nothing you said could have changed that."

"I agree," Ramsey added. "Phelan may be lost to all of us now. He might not have turned to Deirdre's side, but her evil warped him, I'm sure."

Quinn leaned his hands on Fallon's chair and shook his head. "To be kept separated from everyone and everything. I cannot imagine the loneliness. He's out in a world he knows nothing about. He needs us."

"You'll never find him," Hayden said.

Broc lifted a brow in defiance. "I can find him."

"And we will," Quinn said. "First, we make sure Dunmore and the wyrran do not find any Druids."

Ramsey rubbed his hands together, his gray eyes crinkling in the corners. "Ah, a battle. I'm ready for one."

Hayden was more than ready, but he knew he'd be left behind. This time. Soon enough the battle would come to MacLeod Castle, and he'd unleash every ounce of his hate and wrath onto Deirdre.

Quinn pushed off the chair. "I need to talk to my

brothers. How long do you need before you can leave again, Broc?"

"I can leave now," he answered.

Ramsey chuckled and slapped him on the back. "Aren't we all ready to leave immediately?"

"Rest," Quinn said. "You'll leave soon enough."

Hayden glanced at Quinn before he left the castle in search of Isla. She wasn't difficult to find. There were no other small black-haired Druids around.

He stood back and watched as she helped bring out the wreckage from the cottages. Though she didn't have the strength of a Warrior, she worked just as hard.

After a few moments, Hayden followed her into a cottage.

"Why did you tell us about Phelan?"

She paused as she lifted some debris in her arms. "I'm the reason he was in the mountain."

"Nay. Deirdre was the cause."

Isla blew out a breath. "I'm as much to blame, Hayden. I could have refused. I know the chance I took in telling all of you, but I had to. Phelan needs to be found. He needs to know there are good people in the world."

Everything he thought he knew about Isla because she was *drough* was slowly but surely being erased. He might not ever get past the fact she had turned *drough*, but he could appreciate that she wanted to make up for a past deed.

"I know what you think of me," she said as she tossed the pieces of broken wood out of the doorway.

Hayden raised a brow. "Didn't we already go through this? You cannot read my mind."

"Maybe not," she said. She bent and began picking up more broken wood. "But I know the anger and revulsion Broc so freely showed me was in you as well."

"I willna deny it. I feel for any man or woman being brought to Cairn Toul. Knowing it was just a small lad, it sickens me."

She had her back to him, but he saw the droop her in shoulders just the same. "You cannot think worse of me than I think of myself."

Hayden wanted to hate her, wanted to feel anything other than the attraction and lust that consumed him. But each time he was with her, every time she spoke, he learned more about her that cracked the mold he had fitted her with.

She, like them, was fighting Deirdre, only Isla was doing it in another way. Whereas Hayden and the other Warriors were freely battling her, Isla was trying to correct the deeds Deirdre forced on her.

Hayden sighed. As much as he hated to admit it, Deirdre did force Isla. If he had been in her place, he was sure he would have made many of the same choices she had.

"What will you do when Broc does find Phelan?" Hayden asked.

Isla wiped the sweat from her forehead before she retrieved more wood and tossed it outside. "I want to see that he finds a place he can call home. I'm hoping that will be MacLeod Castle."

"You think he will forgive you?"

She snorted and tried to lift a heavy piece of wood. Hayden took it from her and easily threw it in the pile outside the cottage.

Isla dusted her hands and shook her head. "I'm not a fool. Phelan has promised to kill me, and for what I did to him, he has every right."

Hayden didn't like the urge that welled up inside him to protect her. He didn't say anything as she moved onto the next cottage.

He stepped out of the cottage and found her working next to Larena. Hayden would get nothing more out of Isla for the moment. He could work while he digested the information she had given him.

Hayden had previously decided which cottage he wanted for his own. It had sustained the most damage, but it was set apart from the others. Isolated, just as he was. And for good reason.

Trees were already being cut and readied for when they began to rebuild for the second time. It would only be a few days before the first cottage went up.

Hayden worked tirelessly as he moved from cottage to cottage. There was nothing any of them could do until an attack came. Until then, they would ready the village.

Hours later with the sun high above them, Hayden realized Isla was no longer in the village. He lifted the water skin to his lips and let the fresh liquid flow down his throat.

The breeze from the sea helped to cool him, but nothing like a dip in the water would.

"We're done with the cleaning," Duncan said as he exited one of the cottages. "Three sustained minimal damage, five cottages needs structural work, and the rest need to be rebuilt."

Hayden nodded. "Good. Check with Lucan to see if we have what we need to either rebuild or work on the ones with structural damage. I know Fallon wants as many of these readied as we can get."

"Does he expect more Warriors?" Ian asked, and came to stand beside his twin.

Hayden was always amazed that they could look exactly alike. If their hair was cut alike, he'd never tell them apart. "Fallon likes to be prepared. If Galen and Logan find these Druids and convince them to return, they will sleep in the castle while we take the cottages."

Camdyn held out his hand and Hayden tossed him the water skin. "I'll sleep anywhere."

"We have slept anywhere," Ian said with a chuckle. "This rocky ground will be softer than the Pit."

Hayden had never seen the Pit in Deirdre's mountain, but he'd heard enough about it to know most never came out it alive. "Ian, find Lucan and report what we've done here."

"And where are you going?" Camdyn asked.

"I've got something else to tend to."

Duncan crossed his arms over his chest, a half smile on his lips. "Does that something have cold blue eyes?"

Hayden snorted disdainfully. "I'm going for a swim, Duncan, if you must know. The sea is big enough for both of us, but use another beach if you were thinking of doing the same thing. I doona want to be disturbed."

He turned and walked away before anyone could comment. Laughter and Ian teasing Duncan followed as Hayden strode away. He walked around the side of the castle to the path beyond Cara's garden.

Hayden knew he should be looking for Isla, but if he followed her everywhere she went, she would know what he was doing. He would give her a little time to herself, then he would seek her out.

Until then, he was going to enjoy a nice long swim.

Isla was glad she was allowed to find her own way around. No one followed her, no one asked where she was going. Did the MacLeods truly trust her?

She had a notion they might. A little. But if they were as intelligent as she thought they were, they would nevertheless be cautious regarding her. It was the practical thing to do, especially when pertaining to evil like Deirdre.

Isla found the path that lead to the beach beside Cara's

garden. It was steep, and a couple of times she nearly lost her footing, but the view was breathtaking.

The smell of the sea was invigorating, the feel of the spray as the waves crashed into the cliffs was stimulating, and the razorbill's calls that filled the air only added to the splendor.

She could stand where she was looking down at the churning blue sea and the white foam waves and be content for hours. Days even. The constant push and pull of the waves soothed her and eased the ache that made her muscles in her shoulders bunch with apprehension.

Isla made her way to the bottom, careful to watch her footing so she didn't break something on a loose rock. She'd heal, but it would still smart when it happened.

Once she was on the beach, she kicked off her shoes and tugged down her thick woolen hose. She stood just at the edge of the sea so that the waves rolled over her feet and wet the hem of her gown.

The water felt so delicious, so freeing that she lifted her gown to her knees and moved farther into the sea. It was cooler than she'd imagined, but the feel of the water tugging and pressing against her fed her magic in ways she never expected.

The sea was just as conductive as the earth to a Druid's magic. For the first time in centuries, Isla opened herself up to the pure magic, testing herself and the evil inside her.

Her chest expanded as joy and magic filled her, surrounding her until she was lost in it. Immersed. Entranced. Delighted.

Nothing had ever felt so right, so satisfying to her magic before. She swayed with the waves, became one with the wind. Her magic swelled within her like a bright light ready to burst from her chest.

In that moment, the evil inside her disappeared, hiding, but not gone forever.

Isla was so absorbed in the magic that it took a moment for her brain to register that something was in the water with her. She opened her eyes in time to see a man rise from amid the foaming waves like an avenging deity. He turned to face her, and Isla's breath caught in her throat.

She couldn't tear her eyes from Hayden, his blond hair slick against his head and falling past his shoulders. He was a striking silhouette against the bright sunlight and dark waters. Nothing but hard, lean muscle. And man.

Water ran in rivulets down his face, over his shoulders, and wound its way across his chest and abdomen to disappear back into the sea. He stood with his arms held away from his body, aggressive and commanding, as if he were ready for battle.

With the sun shining upon him, he looked like a god rising from the water, waiting to take his vengeance on anyone who dared to disturb his tranquility.

Isla tried to look away, but his body held her transfixed. She could see every muscle in his stomach, they were so defined. She wanted to run her fingers over them, to feel the power of his arms surround her.

He moved toward her, the sea lowering with each step, teasing her with more of his skin until he was bared, beautifully and stunningly naked. Her gaze traveled lower to his rod, thick and enlarged, as it jutted upward. She'd seen men before, but she'd never seen one like Hayden.

Her response was visceral. She forgot to breathe, forgot to think as her heart pounded erratically in her chest. Her reaction to Hayden was shocking and . . . wonderful. He finally halted so close to her she could lean forward and kiss his chest.

She remembered what it felt like to touch that hard

muscular body, to have him close, his heat surrounding her. And God help her, but she wanted it again. She was desperate to caress him, to feel like the woman she had always wanted to be.

"If you stay, I'm going to take the kiss denied me last eve."

Isla shivered, not from the cool water or the breeze, but from the absolute and thrilling truth of Hayden's words. Nothing could make her move now.

She would have her kiss, consequences be damned.

SIXTEEN

Hayden knew he was a fool. He should never have gotten near Isla, near her scent and her enchanting lips. But once he had, there was no turning back. He hadn't lied to her. If she didn't leave, he *would* kiss her.

And damn the consequences.

As soon as the magic, the seductive, lulling magic, had surrounded him in the sea, he'd known it was her. Isla's magic had a different feel to it than other Druids, stronger, steadier, more powerful.

With his powers he could have stayed under the water and swam away. She'd never have known he was there, but Hayden had risen out of the waves without a second thought.

For her.

He had to see her, had to touch her. And saints help him, he had to feel her.

Her gaze, hot and curious, had raked him from head to foot. Lust had taken hold of him with the first brush of her magic, but upon seeing her, watching the desire darken her eyes, his hunger had consumed him.

Swarmed him. Urged him. Impaled him.

Now, as she looked at him with a need that matched his own, Hayden knew he was lost, adrift in ice-blue eyes that haunted him. He couldn't turn away from her now if he tried, though it would be for the best.

Just one kiss, one small kiss. It would be sufficient to satisfy the yearning, the hunger enough to fill the void inside him. One kiss wouldn't harm anything.

With his decision made, Hayden didn't hesitate. He speared his fingers through her sleek midnight locks and dragged her against him. A small gasp tore from her lips and her hands came up against his chest, to push him away or hold herself up, he didn't know.

And didn't care.

A breath rushed past her lips as she stared up at him, waiting. Already he had lingered too long. This longing, this craving that rode him was bottomless and uncontrollable. So much so that he didn't think to even try and deny it once he had hold of Isla.

He bent his head and placed his lips over hers. The instant they touched, Hayden felt her magic again, this time blended with passion and desire.

It struck him full in the chest. Sunk deep into his skin, to the soul he thought had long ago forsaken him.

He pulled back, startled. He shouldn't have felt even that with only a quick kiss. What would he feel if he licked her lips or delved his tongue into her mouth to truly taste her?

He searched her gaze, saw the amazement and pleasure in her depths and wanted more. Needed more.

If Hayden thought he had yearned before, it was nothing to what flooded through him now. Raw. Primal. Undeniable. It was desire unlike anything he'd ever felt before, rushing through his veins, blinding him to anything but Isla.

He pulled her against his chest, crushing her breasts against him so he could feel every inch of her. He sucked in a breath when her small hands gently, shockingly rousing, caressed his abdomen. Her eyes were wide and luminous as she stared up at him with a mixture of wonder and longing. A heady blend for any man.

She glanced at her hands, as if she had just noticed she caressed him. She swallowed, the pulse beating rapidly at her throat, and skimmed her hands up to his shoulders. Her touch reverent, exciting. And he wanted more.

Hayden tried to give her time to touch him, but need rode him hard. He tilted her face to him and wrapped both arms around her as he kissed her once more. This time he lingered, learning her texture, her taste.

He ran his tongue over her lips, and when she parted them, he swept inside her mouth to lay claim. To conquer and capture.

Hayden groaned at the exquisite taste of her, drowned in desire that swirled around them. She was like mead, sweet and flavorful. And he had to have more.

Hayden angled his mouth over Isla's, his tongue dancing with hers as he cinched her tighter against him, his arms locking her in place so he could feel her lush, feminine curves. Her hands slid around his neck while her nails gently grazed his scalp and sank into his wet hair.

He felt her give into the kiss, felt her passion surge and manifest. When she kissed him back as flagrantly as he'd kissed her, it left him reeling and needing more. Always more.

Molten desire ensnared him and lured him deeper into the kiss, into Isla's sweet mouth and sumptuous body. Turning away wasn't an option now, even though he knew he should.

He teased, he coaxed. He burned. The kiss turned heated and frantic as his passion grew with every touch of her tongue against his.

Unable to keep his hands from her, Hayden learned the feel of her sweet body from her small waist he was sure his hands could span to her ripe breasts.

He cupped a breast, marveling at the weight of it, how

it swelled in his hand. His cock jumped when her nipple tightened, the small bud straining into his palm hard and wanting.

Just as he was.

Hayden moaned into her mouth, a mixture of ravenous desire and satisfied male as her back bowed, her body pushing her breast into his hand.

Her fingers spasmed in his hair as he kneaded her breast. Her soft cry was like molten desire as it shot through him straight to his groin. He let his fingers circle her nipple, felt her body tremble.

He let the anticipation build as he got closer and closer to the hard bud. When he finally let his fingers close over her nipple, to expertly tease and pleasure, she moaned softly. He lingered, rolling the tip between his fingers before squeezing lightly.

When she rubbed her body against his, Hayden gloried in the feel of her, in the soft femininity that held him enthralled. He shook with desire. Never had he wanted a woman so. Never had he dreamed he could feel such yearning, such an ache for anyone.

Hayden was stunned by the ardor that blazed within Isla. She, the Druid who always kept her emotions in check, seemed to break out of her shell with his kiss, with his touch.

And Hayden enjoyed it. Maybe too much.

His hands smoothed down her back to cup her bottom and bring her closer to him, to his cock that ached to feel more of her. Her sweet, soft groan when he brought her up against his erection made his knees weak and his longing swell until he was drowning in it. He hungered for her like he'd never hungered for a woman before.

When he began to contemplate laying her on the sand and rocks and cutting away her gown with his claws so he could sink into her wet heat, he knew it was time to end it. For now.

He would have her. It was inevitable now, now that he had tasted her, now that he knew the feel of her body.

Hayden reluctantly ended the kiss and looked down into Isla's dazed face. Her lips were damp and swollen from his kiss, making his balls tighten.

With her eyes half closed and desire smoldering in her ice-blue depths, Hayden knew he could have her right then and there. It wasn't the time or the place, though.

He slid his fingers into her long black locks and wound the length around his hand, holding her to him, locking her in place. She was too tempting by far.

She was on her tiptoes and still he had to bend to kiss her, to take her lips once more. He was powerless against his desire for her. As long as she was near, he had to touch her, to have her.

His body shook as he fought against his need to bury himself inside her slick, hot center. His control was slipping away like the sand with the tide.

"You should return to the castle." His voice sounded gruff even to his own ears.

Isla took a step away from him, her hands skimming his shoulders with her fingertips before falling to her sides. Grudgingly, half fearing he might never hold her again, Hayden released his hold on her hair and her body.

When she didn't speak, Hayden searched her face for clues as to what she was feeling. There was still desire there, still need, but she was quickly, and all too clearly, regaining her composure.

The man in him roared to remind her how he could make her forget again, how he could call forth her passion with just a kiss.

"We will finish this," he promised.

SEVENTEEN

Isla stood on the beach long after Hayden had strode away. She could still taste him, still feel him on her mouth and body. She licked her lips and shivered from the passion still inside her. For a moment, she contemplated following Hayden and kissing him again.

She looked down to find the hem of her gown soaked as the water swirled around her. The magic the sea had called forth had been unlike anything Isla had ever experienced. It was raw and pure, much like her need for Hayden.

Desire. Isla fisted her hands and turned her back to the sea. She ignored the jab of the smaller rocks as they bit into her feet. The large boulders called to her to sit and view the beauty of the coast, but she couldn't.

She had been careful to keep herself from befriending anyone lest Deirdre use them against her as she had with Grania and Lavena. Now, Isla found herself in a situation where she could see herself coming to like Hayden very much. Too much, in fact.

It wasn't a matter of *if* Deirdre regained her magic, it was *when*. When that time came, Deirdre would eventually find her, and Deirdre would use anything at her disposal against Isla. That included everyone at MacLeod Castle.

Isla looked up at the imposing structure of the castle built on the edge of the cliffs. Through destruction, fire, abandonment, and even isolation, the stones still stood proud and defiant. Much like the MacLeods themselves.

Could she find as much courage in herself? Did she dare?

Isla sat to put her stockings and shoes back on before she started up the path to the castle. She was halfway up when her foot slipped.

A hand grabbed her arm to stop her slide. Isla looked up to find Marcail smiling down at her.

"I think I found you at a good time," Marcail said.

Isla returned her smile and regained her footing. "Thank you. This path is dangerous. I'm surprised Quinn hasn't told you not to come down here."

"Oh, he has." Marcail shrugged, a twinkle in her eye. "But I saw you and wanted to speak with you."

Isla straightened and dusted off her hands. "About what?"

Marcail pointed to a section of the path that veered off to the left. "Cara told me about this path. Would you like to take a walk?"

"All right." Isla glanced at the castle. Whatever Marcail wanted to say, she wanted it done in private.

She followed Marcail for a ways down the path. It was several feet below the edge of the cliff, but Isla could tell that at one time it had been a well used trail.

"Quinn told me that they used to use this path to hunt when he was a lad," Marcail said. She looked over her shoulder and shrugged. "Cara used it when she ran away. She thought to leave so Deirdre wouldn't harm Lucan."

"Deirdre would have come for Lucan anyway."

Marcail paused and turned to face her. "I know that. I saw for myself the evil that Deirdre is. Larena saw a small part of it, but Sonya and Cara have only heard stories. I'd like to keep it that way."

"We all would." Isla had seen more horrors than anyone could comprehend, but she wasn't about to tell Marcail that.

Marcail lowered herself onto the ground and drew her knees up to her chest. Isla followed suit a moment later, and though her gaze was on the sea, she knew Marcail was troubled. It didn't take Isla long to realize what it was.

"You cannot recall the spell to bind the gods, can you?"

Marcail sighed and shook her head. "Those magical black flames Deirdre threw me in did something to my magic. Even after Quinn pulled me out, I nearly died."

"That fire was not meant to keep you alive like the blue flames for my sister. The flames Deirdre put you in were meant to keep you locked away from everyone. It would have killed you. Your magic protected you, but in doing so, you lost some of it."

"I lost nearly all of it. I wasn't a very strong Druid to begin with." Marcail smiled sadly. "My mother thought it was time we moved on from the old ways. When she died, I had lost years of valuable time in which to learn how to use and control my magic."

"What happened?"

"My grandmother was an especially powerful *mie*. She taught me as much as she could while she lived. It wasn't until I was in the Pit and fell in love with Quinn that I began to remember the spell."

Isla's mouth fell open. "You remembered it? Why didn't you use it?"

"I recalled parts of it. My grandmother had made it so I would never know the spell until I had fallen in love." Marcail dashed at her eyes to wipe away a tear. "When I went into the black flames, it took the spell. I've tried everything I know to remember it."

Isla reached over and put her hand atop Marcail's. She hadn't willingly touched anyone until she had come to

MacLeod Castle. Now, it seemed almost natural. "Has Sonya or Cara not been able to help you?"

"Cara is still learning her magic. She knows even less than I do, and Sonya has tried to help me. Nothing has helped."

"You want to know if I can do anything."

Marcail turned her unusual turquoise eyes to her and nodded. "You have powerful magic. Is there anything you can do?"

"I wish I could." She looked back out to the sea, unable to watch the hurt in Marcail's eyes. "Once your magic has been taken, you cannot retrieve it. The fact you have any left at all tells me that you had great magic inside you."

"And I lost it."

Isla stood and held out her hand to Marcail. "You did what you had to do to keep the spell from Deirdre. Do not discount your valor, Marcail. You did the right thing."

"Did I?" Marcail used Isla's hand and stood.

"Aye."

Marcail blew out a harsh breath and squeezed her eyes shut for a moment. "Tell that to the Warriors. They are still waiting on me to remember the spell."

"Does Quinn know you can't recall the spell?"

"Aye, and his brothers know."

"Then the others need to know as well. It is better that they not continue to hope."

Marcail looked at her with such sorrow that it nearly brought tears to Isla's own eyes.

"They know it's a possibility that the spell might have vanished forever. I just hate to disappoint any of them."

Isla knew all about disappointment. "They'll understand."

"Thank you anyway," Marcail said and began to retrace her steps back to the castle.

Isla lifted her sodden skirts and hurried after her. "Marcail. Wait. There is one thing you can do. I don't know if it will help, but since you are descended from powerful Druids, it just might."

"What is it?" Marcail asked, her face alight with hope as she swung toward Isla.

"Find whatever feeds your magic, be it the earth, trees, water, whatever. Go there and open yourself to the magic."

"That's what I did while in the Pit." Marcail's brow furrowed in concern. "I nearly lost myself in the magic."

Isla nodded. "There is a chance of that, aye. You need to have someone with you, someone who can pull you out if necessary. With the babe, you might not want to chance it now."

Marcail looked down as her hands cradled her stomach. "I don't want to hurt my child. Quinn has lost so much already, I couldn't bear to face him if something I did harmed our baby."

"Then wait," Isla advised. "A few months won't matter. Feed your magic until then. The babe inside you should help to strengthen the magic you lost."

"You mean the child will have magic?"

Isla shrugged. "I don't see why it wouldn't. Even with what happened in Cairn Toul, you still have magic."

Marcail laughed as tears began to spill down her face. "I feared there would be nothing for my child."

Isla wasn't so sure that would have been a bad thing. Magic in these times wasn't a positive, not with Deirdre and the Christians who feared anyone who believed other than they did. But Isla wasn't about to condemn Marcail's dreams for her unborn child. The world would do that soon enough.

Deirdre wanted to scream her frustration, but she couldn't. She floated as nothing more than a spirit, unable to do anything other than communicate with Dunmore and her wyrran. And even that exhausted her limited magic.

She had tried to contact Isla numerous times, but either the little bitch was dead or her magic was so inadequate that Isla could ignore her. Neither was good.

Deirdre needed Isla. If the MacLeods and their Warriors had not defeated her, Deirdre would know in an instant if Isla was dead or not.

Of course, if Deirdre had her full power restored, finding Isla dead or alive wouldn't be an issue. Now, Deirdre had to focus her wyrran on finding a Druid just so she could once more have a body.

Until then, if Isla was alive, she was free to do as she wished. Afterward . . . Deirdre smiled. Afterward, Isla would do as she commanded, and then Isla would pay with her life.

Deirdre floated from her chamber down the corridor to where she had found Grania lying dead in a pool of blood. Deirdre didn't know who had killed Grania, but she would discover who did it and flay the skin from their bodies.

Grania had begun as a test to see how far Deirdre could push Isla, but after several decades, the child had grown on Deirdre. They had spent much time together, and Deirdre had known then she would keep Grania with her always.

Now the child was gone from her, taken without so much as a blink.

Rage built inside Deirdre, feeding the evil and helping to restore her magic. She continued to nourish her anger. Every time she saw a dead Druid, a slain wyrran or Warrior, or her mountain destroyed, she thought of the MacLeods.

She had wanted the brothers to align with her. Now

she just wanted them and any Warrior who dared to ally with them destroyed.

The rest of the day crawled for Isla. Not even her earlier worry whether the pudding and pastries would taste good could help her sort through the jumble of emotions inside her.

It didn't hurt that Hayden was in the village helping to rebuild the cottages. At least she was saved from having to see him and remember their kiss.

That was until supper. It had been near impossible for her not to look at him, and whenever she did, his gaze was on her as well. It left her all too aware of him and what his kisses had done to her.

Her body warmed and her blood turned to fire. There was a peculiar, but pleasurable, feeling in the pit of her stomach. Her breathing was erratic, and Isla couldn't seem to think clearly.

She'd tried to leave the hall early, but everyone wanted to tell her how much they loved her pastries. It wasn't until she promised more that she was able to get away.

Now, as she paced her tower, she wondered if she should have stayed in the hall. Maybe she could have spoken with Hayden.

And said what?

She didn't know. It wasn't as if she had experience with this type of thing. It was all new to her, especially the longing, the everpresent, never-ending need he had set into motion since he came into her chamber and almost kissed her.

There had been times in the past when she had encountered a man who caught her interest, but she had never allowed herself to do anything about it. She was who she was, and that meant she had to be alone.

Isla sighed and reached for her comb. Brushing her hair had always helped to calm her. She sat on the edge of her bed and watched the light from her single candle dance on the opposite wall while she ran the comb through her hair.

She didn't know how long she sat like that before she caught a whiff of spice and woods.

Hayden.

His hand covered hers that held the comb. He took the comb from her and slowly, tenderly brushed her hair. He was gentle as he glided it from her head to the ends that fell to her waist.

"There is something compelling about watching a woman brush her hair."

Isla shivered at the sound of his deep, rich voice. "It is merely a chore."

"I think not. I think you get as much joy out of it as I do."

She licked her lips and tried not to think of his firm mouth that had kissed her into oblivion. She'd have done anything he asked of her after that kiss. And she feared that would never change.

"I want to finish what we began on the beach," he whispered near her ear.

Chills raced over her skin and her stomach fluttered with anticipation, with excitement. Isla turned to face him, afraid he was serious and terrified he wasn't.

The candlelight left much of his face in shadow, but she saw his black eyes. Even in the dim light she recognized the hunger, the yearning she glimpsed because it was the same within herself.

"I don't know if that's wise," she said. She had to keep him at a distance, if for no reason other than preserving her own sanity.

He smiled then, a knowing, seductive smile that lifted one side of his mouth and made her heart skip a beat. "It

most certainly isna wise, but I've tried to stay away. I cannot. Can you?"

Isla opened her mouth to deny it, but it would be lying
to herself and him. "Nay."

It was all the encouragement he needed. Hayden knelt
on the bed and pulled her, slowly, surely into his arms. As
soon as those bands of steel wrapped around her, Isla was
lost. Her own arms wound around his neck and into the
cool blond silk of his hair. It hung to his shoulders, thick
and golden, at complete odds with the darkness of his
eyes.

Those eyes watched her now. He studied her, gauging
her reaction. "Do you want this? Tell me the truth. I have
to know."

"Aye, Hayden. I want this." She wanted it like she had
wanted nothing else before.

Before the last word was out of her mouth his lips were
on hers. The kiss was passionate and fiery, intense and
consuming. With each stroke of his tongue on hers, she
felt her body sag against him, felt herself come alive.

Passion coiled low in her belly, urging her onward,
begging her to follow the desire that heated her blood and
pumped through her body.

Everything she was, everything she had been, and everything she wanted disappeared in Hayden's arms. He
made the world vanish, leaving just the two of them and
their passion that wouldn't be denied.

She tugged at the pin holding the tartan over his heart
while his hands gathered her skirts at her waist. There
was a whooshing sound as his kilt tumbled off him to the
floor. With his tartan at his feet, Isla tugged at his shirt,
wanting it gone so she could run her hands over his sun-
bronzed skin and the powerful muscles beneath.

"Take off your gown before I slice it off you," he ground

out as he jerked his saffron shirt over his head and tossed it aside.

Isla hurried to rid herself of her clothes, and when she looked up, Hayden stood by the bed watching her in all his naked glory.

She caught her breath, once more entranced by the utter perfection, the sheer beauty of Hayden. It was as if the gods had sculpted him themselves, fashioned him into the ultimate warrior, untamed and wild.

And the seamless combination of danger and excitement as a lover.

With a finger, Isla traced down his chest to his narrow waist and over his slim hips to his bulging thighs. She had never touched a man like this before, had never wanted to. Yet, she couldn't get enough of Hayden.

He knelt between her legs and took off first one shoe, then the other. Next, he reached up and began to roll down her stockings, all the while keeping his eyes locked with hers.

The promise of pleasure she saw in his dark depths made her desire settle deep within her and throb low and steady. Waiting for his kiss, waiting for his touch.

Isla shook with desire and the feel of Hayden's fingers lightly skimming her skin. He worked the stocking down slowly, as if he wanted to prolong the sweet torment of his touch.

She dropped her head back when he pulled off the first stocking and lifted her foot to place a kiss at her ankle. A moan escaped her when his hands reached up to her hips and caressed downward to her other stocking.

Isla's hips came off the bed when he came close to touching her sex. His fingers had teased the curls between her legs, tempting her with his touch, building her anticipation.

Her sex throbbed, eager for contact. For Hayden.

He took the same leisurely, sweet time he had on her first leg as he did on the second. This time, when he removed her stocking, he kissed her knee.

Isla fisted her hands in the blanket to help anchor her and the rioting sensations that flooded her body. She feared, yet craved, what came next. And when Hayden rose up to lean over her, she knew that whatever happened, she would never regret giving in to the passion he called forth. A passion that engulfed her.

EIGHTEEN

Hayden didn't think he had ever seen anything so exquisite, so breathtaking as the vision of Isla lying naked and wanting beneath him.

Her black locks were spread around her, her chest rising and falling rapidly, and her startling ice-blue eyes locked with his. She was aroused and ready. Waiting.

For him.

Her slender, curvy body had been taken straight from his dreams. He wanted to touch all of her, learn every nuance of her body in order to bring her pleasure so intense, so incredible she wouldn't be able to string two words together.

But where to begin first was the problem.

Unable to deny himself another taste, Hayden leaned down and kissed her. She eagerly opened for him, spurring his already burning lust to new heights, engulfing both of them in the reckless flames of desire.

Her hands, tentative and soft, touched his sides before moving up and over his back. In the wake of her touch, trails of heat lit his flesh.

Every touch, every sigh only brought him deeper under her spell. Only made him crave her, covet her ever more since the moment he had found her on Cairn Toul.

He shifted to his side and placed his hand on her hip as he deepened the kiss. She moaned into his mouth, impatient for more. Hayden glided his hand over the swell of her hip to the indent of her small waist up to her breast.

His thumb caressed the underside of Isla's breast before he cupped it. Her nipple was hard and straining, eager for his touch.

He wanted to go slow, to savor her, but need rode him hard. Coupled with Isla's growing passion, Hayden knew he would have to force himself not to lose control or he'd hurt her.

The fact he was kissing, caressing a *drough* didn't dampen his passion. He didn't stop to ask why, just accepted it for the moment. Later, he would allow himself to wonder how he could desire her as he did.

Hayden groaned when her nails scraped his back, sending chills over his skin. He'd never yearned, never hungered, never needed anyone as he did Isla in that moment.

He kissed down her neck to the valley between her breasts as he rolled her nipple between his fingers. She panted, soft moans of delight passing from her seductive lips.

His cock ached to be inside her, but he held himself in check. He wanted to taste more of her, learn more of her before he gave into his need.

Her back arched, a strangled cry fell from her lips when he pinched her nipple. Hayden smiled and wrapped his lips around the other nub. He swirled his tongue around it, teasing it, stroking it, until Isla whispered his name.

His name on her lips moved something inside him he had thought long dead. There was passion and wonder and joy in her voice.

Hayden could have suckled at her breasts for hours, but there was more of her to explore, more of her to enjoy yet. He lifted her hips to grind into her. The feel of her soft, supple body against him drove him mad with longing.

He could push into her now, sheath himself in her hot wetness, but he wanted her to scream his name first, to see her body bucking with a climax.

Then he would take her.

Slowly. Thoroughly. Savoring every moment.

Isla was mindless with desire. It raged through her body like a storm, overwhelming her with intense, fiery need. Her skin was extra sensitive and her blood burned in her veins. Every little touch, every caress from Hayden only stroked the flames within her.

Her breasts ached for more of his touch. She'd never felt anything like it before, and it had been amazing. The throbbing between her legs intensified, causing her to rub her hips against him. Heat consumed her, scorched her with passion.

Isla sucked in a shocked breath when Hayden shifted between her legs and held her thighs apart with his large hands. His black eyes rose to her, daring her to stop him as he leaned down and licked her sex.

She moaned, caught between the desire spilling through her and embarrassment that Hayden held her open for his view. The desire quickly won as Hayden's tongue expertly stroked her clitoris. Isla forgot to breathe as the pure, amazing pleasure pulled her under.

It was too much. The sensations racking her body were too pure, too powerful to take. Isla tried to get away, but Hayden held her hips firmly in his hands. Just when she thought it couldn't get more intense, the desire couldn't build any higher, her world shattered.

She cried out, Hayden's name on her lips as ecstasy unlike anything she'd ever known filled her, enveloped her. Even as her body calmed, she hungered for more.

Before she could take in a breath, Hayden was leaning over her, his hands beneath her back. He turned her, lifted her until she straddled his hips as he sat on the edge of the bed.

His arousal, hard and thick, lay between them. She wanted to touch him and stroke him as she had done her. She wanted to give him the same kind of pleasure, and she hoped he let her.

Isla cupped his face, running her hands over the rugged, chiseled features. She traced his wide lips with a finger, and was surprised when he pulled it into his mouth.

His wicked tongue sucked and licked her finger as his eyes blazed with desire. Isla knew it was the time to tell him she had never been touched by a man, but she feared Hayden wouldn't want her then. And she wasn't about to be denied now.

He looked at her as a woman, not a possession or *drough*. He saw her as she had longed to be seen. And he touched her as she had only dreamt about.

Hayden lightly wound his fingers around her wrist and pulled her finger from his mouth. He kissed her palm before flicking his tongue over the skin.

"Such passion," he whispered.

Isla shivered. This was a side of Hayden she had never thought to see, a side that touched her deeply all the way to her soul. It was a side she found she greatly enjoyed.

"I cannot wait any longer." He kissed her neck where her pulse pounded. "I have to have you."

Isla wound her arms around his neck. "Then take me."

His hands gripped her hips and raised her until she hovered over his cock. He moved her back and forth so that the tip of him teased her swollen, sensitive sex.

She dropped her head back and moaned at the pleasure. He slowly lowered her onto the head of his shaft. The feel of him large and imposing as he began to stretch her.

Alarm coursed through her. Isla opened her mouth to

tell him she was a virgin still, but before she could, he pushed inside her the same time he pulled her down.

Isla's gaze was locked with his. She saw his eyes widen in surprise, then his brow furrow in anger. Pain speared through her, but she refused to show any weakness, refused to cry out. He was huge, too huge for her.

"Why didn't you tell me you were untouched?" he demanded in a low voice filled with fury and disbelief.

Isla inwardly cringed at his harsh tone. "I thought you wouldn't want me."

He placed a hand alongside her face. "If I'd have known I wouldn't have hurt you. I would have gone slower, but I would still have wanted you."

She blinked, unsure of what to say. She was to blame for her pain. But by the look on his face she could tell he took the fault as his own.

"My lack of . . . experience doesn't matter?" she asked hesitantly.

He ran his thumb over her bottom lip before he kissed her soundly, completely. "Nay. Are you in pain?"

"It's beginning to ebb."

"Good," he said before he rocked her hips forward.

Isla bit her lip, expecting to feel more pain. Instead, heat flooded her body. The more she moved against him, the more her body wanted. She had thought him big, but now that her body had adjusted, he slid farther inside her, filling her even more.

"Aye," he murmured and kissed her neck just below her ear. "Open your body to me."

Isla was powerless to do anything but what he wanted. He moved her hips, slowly, lovingly while her body continued to adjust for him. When he was fully sheathed, he let out a low groan and covered her mouth with his. He kissed her deeply, leisurely.

"Move as you want," he instructed her.

For a moment Isla could only sit there, the feel of him inside her blocking out everything else. Isla rotated her hips and moved them front to back. The friction of their bodies had the flames of desire licking at her body once more.

She could feel her body building back up to what had occurred before her first climax. She wanted that again, wanted to feel it with Hayden inside her.

Isla held onto Hayden as her body began to spiral out of control. His arms locked around her, his breathing harsh and ragged as he thrust inside her.

He moaned and began to lift her up and down his rod. Isla could do nothing but experience the bliss of having him fill her time and again. His tempo increased and he went deeper, so deep he touched her womb.

Isla heard him whisper her name a heartbeat before his fingers dug into her back and he thrust inside her hard and fast. She could feel his cock pumping his seed inside her, and to her surprise, she peaked a second time.

Hayden held her against his chest, softly stroking her hair until she had come down. He was still inside her, holding her as tenderly as a lover would.

She dropped her head onto his shoulder and sighed. He lifted her off him and laid her on the bed before he rose and walked to the pitcher of water.

Isla watched as he poured water over a cloth and wrung it out. He sat beside her and spread her legs. It never occurred to her that she would need to be cleaned.

There were no words between them as he washed her blood and his seed first from her body, then his own. She expected him to leave then, to force some pretty words and go. Instead, he simply stared at her.

"You gave yourself to me," he said. "Why?"

Isla glanced away. How did she tell him he had called to her on a level she didn't understand? That she hadn't wanted to give in, but her body hadn't been her own?

"Is it wrong to wish to feel some happiness? Do I not deserve it?" she asked instead.

He reached out a finger and played with the ends of her hair. "I never said that. I'm simply wondering, why me?"

"You mean why you because you despise *drough*?"

"Aye."

Isla blew out a breath. "You saw me. Despite who and what I am, you saw me for me. I've had men lust after me. I've had men try to force themselves on me. But I've never had a man look at me with such desire or kiss me with such fire and hunger."

Silence descended upon them until finally Isla asked what she needed to know. "Why me? Why did you come to me if you hate what I am?"

"That is a question, isn't it?" he asked. "I'm not sure I can answer it."

She sat up and almost reached for him, but at the last moment decided against it. "You were tender with me, concerned even when you learned I was still a virgin. I thank you for that."

Hayden lifted a strand of her hair to his face and inhaled. "I think we've both made a muck of things."

"Whatever happens, I won't regret this night."

He dropped her hair and stood. Without another word he began to dress. Isla watched him, fascinated with every aspect that was Hayden.

When he finished he glanced at her and climbed onto the window. She waited to see his Warrior form, to know what color he would turn, but he melded into the shadows and then was gone.

NINETEEN

Hayden knew he was a fool. Even as he hurried away from Isla, he longed to return. It had stunned him to his very core to learn she had never been taken by a man. He'd been angry at her for not telling him, and angry at himself for being so rough with her.

But, by the saints, she was a passionate woman. She brought out a side of him he hadn't known he'd had.

Knowing he had been the first to lay claim to her spectacular body excited him, made him long for another taste of her.

Hayden climbed into his chamber from his window. He wished Logan was there, though he knew he wouldn't confide in his friend. What had happened between him and Isla was private.

Because you doona want others to know you gave into a drough.

Hayden wanted to deny it, but that was part of the reason. As much as he wanted to think Isla was different, she wasn't. She was a *drough*, had welcomed the evil into her. She might have pushed the evil aside for the moment, but the truth of the matter was that she had done terrible things.

He kicked off his boots and ran his hands down his face, weary to his core. He then lay back on the bed and threw an arm over his eyes.

No matter how hard he tried, sleep eluded him. He kept seeing Isla's beautiful face and amazing body in his mind's eye. He could still hear her moans, her soft cries of pleasure. She had screamed his name, just as he had wanted.

He should have stayed with her. If he had, he'd have taken her again. He had given her pleasure, that he knew. Her first sexual experience should have been with someone who cared about her, someone who would stand by her side.

He wasn't that man. Yet, as much as he regretted being with her, he wondered if he'd have the willpower to turn away from her the next time.

And he knew he wouldn't.

"Damn me," Hayden mumbled.

This couldn't be happening to him. When he'd found his parents, he'd vowed to them he'd find their killer and meet out his vengeance. As the strongest warrior of his clan he'd always been there to protect his family. He had never failed them until that night.

And with his family's death, Deirdre had come for him. So much had changed that night. Everything he had been had died along with his family.

Isla was up early and baking in the kitchens. She had managed a few hours sleep without the nightmares, her dreams instead filled with Hayden and his kisses. A very welcome reprieve, but one that made her realize everything she had missed out on while being in Cairn Toul.

She was sore, and every time she moved, it reminded her of a night she would never forget. Even now as she kneaded the dough for the bread she found herself thinking of Hayden.

Though nothing had changed, she saw the world with new eyes now. She had known what happened between a man and a woman, but to experience it herself, and with someone like Hayden, it gave her a new perspective.

Now she really understood the looks passed between lovers like Cara and Lucan, Marcail and Quinn, and Larena and Fallon. She recognized the secret smiles shared between them, and the small touches.

It should have been enough. Months ago it would have been enough. But now that Isla had seen what her life could have been, what it could be, she wanted more. She wanted what Cara, Marcail, and Larena had.

Isla's chances of ever finding that kind of happiness were slim, even if she did allow herself to get close to anyone. Yet the longing was still there. She feared it would now always be there.

"Up early again, I see," Cara said as she walked into the kitchens and began to get the morning meal ready.

Isla shrugged. "I used to spend most of my days in the kitchens baking. It seems natural still."

"Well, I know the men will enjoy it." Cara smiled and stuck her hands in the dough. "With Galen being gone for a while maybe now some of the others can get more food."

Isla grinned. "You baked Galen a loaf of bread just for himself, didn't you?"

"I did," Cara said with a chuckle. "He was like a young lad always begging for food. He would even come into the kitchen and try to steal food. He'll be sorry he missed your pastries."

"I'll bake him extra when he returns." Isla said the words without realizing she might not be around when Galen came back.

Cara paused in her kneading and glanced at Isla. "So you are planning to stay? I worried you might yet want to leave."

"You're not still thinking of leaving, are you, Isla?"

Marcail asked as she walked into the kitchen. "I thought you had decided to stay."

Isla exchanged a look with Cara. "I'm not leaving. Yet."

"Good," Marcail said as she stroked the fires of the ovens. "We're enjoying having another woman about."

Cara turned to Marcail. "How are you feeling this morn?"

As the two talked of Marcail's pregnancy and the sickness that came to her every morning, Isla felt a longing to share her problems as she used to with her sister. She had thought she didn't need anyone, but being around the women had changed Isla's views.

Larena paused beside Isla, her eyes full of concern. "Everything all right?"

Isla forced a smile and nodded. "Just thinking of my sister."

"You two were very close, then?" Marcail asked.

Isla thought back to the nights they would stay up talking, dreaming of when they would find husbands and have families of their own. Even after Lavena married, they had stayed close. "Aye."

"I wish I'd have had a sister," Cara said wistfully.

Larena walked around the work table and put her arm around Cara. "You do. You have all of us."

Marcail moved next to them and they pulled her in their hug. It was a touching moment, one that Isla felt she intruded upon.

"Aye," Cara said. "You are my sisters, just as Sonya and Isla are."

Isla knew she shouldn't be included, and that Cara was just being kind. Yet it felt nice. She smiled and kept her hands moving in the dough. The moment had touched a part of her heart that Isla thought long dead.

By the time she had set the dough to rising, she had

obtained control of her emotions again. Which was a good thing since the morning meal was under way and everyone was in the great hall.

Malcolm entered the castle and took his place at the farthest end of the table. He spoke only to Larena as he passed her, and then just briefly. Isla saw the hurt in Larena's eyes for her cousin.

Isla had seen such defeat in men before. Malcolm was alive, but he wasn't living. He merely existed until the time came for his death. Until then, he would walk about as nothing more than a shade of his former self.

As soon as Isla caught sight of Hayden she forgot all about Malcolm. Just seeing Hayden caused her heart to beat faster. She tried not to stare at him, but she couldn't help it. He was magnificent.

The fact he didn't spare her even a glance caused Isla to frown. She didn't expect him to get down on one knee and spout poetry, but they had shared something special.

Or had they? It had been extraordinary to her, but maybe to Hayden she was nothing more than someone to ease his need. If that was the case, he would treat her as he normally did.

However, as the meal progressed, Isla didn't feel his gaze on her once. She kept her own from straying to him, no matter how hard it became. Hayden had never sought her out, had never spoken to her unless he had a direct question, but he had watched her. Always his gaze had been on her.

Isla looked up to find Ramsey staring at her. His gray eyes seemed to notice all. If she didn't know he held no magic, she would think he was a Druid. It was the way he gazed at her, as if he could see inside her very soul. Her father used to look at her like that.

"You are troubled," Ramsey said.

Isla glanced around her, but everyone was deep in conversation and didn't hear him. "Of course I'm distressed. Deirdre isn't dead."

"There's more to it than that. It is not good for the soul to carry such burdens. You should share what is troubling you."

Isla found it difficult to breathe. Those had been her father's exact words to her on many occasions. Her father used to recite those words by ancient Druids whenever something bothered Isla or her sister.

Ramsey lifted a single black brow. "Do you not agree?"

"My father used to tell me that."

"Then he was a wise man. Did you listen to him?"

Isla slowly nodded.

Ramsey shrugged and bit into an oatcake. "Perhaps you will take my advice then."

She leaned forward so that her words would only reach him. "Did you have a Druid in your family?"

He paused and turned those steely gray eyes to her again. "Druids have walked this land since the beginning of time. We all have Druids in our ancestry."

"True enough." Isla straightened. Ramsey had said all the right words, but she knew there was more to his past than he was letting on.

Unable to help herself, Isla glanced at Hayden. He was turned with his back to her talking to Camdyn. She regretted looking as soon as she had done it.

When the meal was finished, Isla hurried out of the castle. She needed to be as far from Hayden as she could before she made a fool of herself.

"Isla, wait," Larena called from behind her.

Isla halted until Larena caught up with her.

Larena smiled, her eyes bright. "Where are you going?"

"I thought I would see if I could be of help in the village. I heard Quinn say most of the men were going to find more wood."

"Aye. We've already rebuilt the cottages once. I'm hoping this will be the last time, but somehow I know it won't. Not until Deirdre is dead."

Isla paused beside the first cottage. "I was here not long ago. Deirdre had dispatched me with the MacClures after she sent the wyrran to the village looking for Cara."

"Why were you with the MacClures?"

"When the MacLeod clan was destroyed, the Mac-Clures were the first to take their land. Deirdre saw them as a means to gain control. She offered them power, and the promise that if they ever needed her, she would aid them."

Larena crossed her arms over her chest as she listened. "Did Deirdre honor that vow?"

"Of course not. Just as she didn't honor her promise that no one would ever attack the MacClures."

"So she sent you with them—why?"

Isla looked around at the destroyed village. It had been a nice village, not as rich as some, but not as poor as others. "To see what I could learn and to make them believe she would help discover who had dared to kill their people."

"I see."

Isla ran her hand down the outside of the nearest cottage. "Even then I could sense Cara and her magic. I hated her for bringing me back to the MacLeod land."

"Back?" Larena's smoky blue eyes grew round. "You were here when the clan was murdered?"

To her everlasting shame. "Deirdre was as well. She made me watch. Not as it was being destroyed, but afterwards. We saw the brothers as they rode up and discovered what had happened. I despised anything to do with the Warriors, and anyone who caught Deirdre's attention.

It was unfair of me, I know. You Warriors didn't have a choice. Your god chose you."

"You didn't have a choice either. No Druid did," Larena said softly. "Why did you tell me this?"

"I'm not sure," Isla said. "I know Cara saw me that day, saw the look of hatred I gave her. Yet, she smiles at me and calls me sister."

Larena inhaled deeply and let her arms drop to her side. "Cara has an amazing heart. She cares for everyone and everything. Besides, if we're going to survive this war, we have to stand together."

"Divided we fall," Isla murmured.

"What was that?"

She shook her head. "Just something my father used to say."

Larena walked past her to the opposite side of the village and pushed open the door to the cottage. "This is where they brought Malcolm after he was attacked. I thought he would die that night, but he lived. And so have you. You have a new future now, Isla. Forget the past."

It was easier said than done. Isla turned when she heard footsteps and froze when she spotted Hayden walking beside Duncan. Both men spoke to Larena, but only Duncan looked Isla's way.

When Duncan halted beside her Isla wasn't sure what to expect. She assumed Hayden would as well, but he continued on, disappearing into a cottage to begin work she assumed.

"Duncan," she said when the Warrior simply gazed at her.

His brown eyes were hard as he stared. "I would ask you a question."

"Duncan," Larena warned.

Isla held up a hand to stop Larena. "Ask," she told Duncan.

"Why didn't you help us? Why didn't you battle Deirdre?" he demanded, his voice harsh and low. His anger evident with every word.

Isla folded her hands behind her back and took a deep breath. "I wish I could tell you that I did. I wish I could tell you that I've fought Deirdre from the moment she took us. But it would be a lie."

Duncan leaned down so that his face was inches from hers. "We could have defeated her for good that day."

"Nay, you couldn't have. I don't know if I would have helped you, Duncan. It doesn't matter since I was away from the mountain at the time, under Deirdre's control. By the time I arrived, the battle was nearly over. I released the ones I could."

"You could be lying."

She shrugged and looked away. "Believe what you will."

Isla held her breath, waiting for Duncan to demand more answers, but after a moment he walked away. She was surprised no one else had confronted her as Duncan had, and in a way she was glad he had. They all deserved answers, even if they didn't like what those answers were.

TWENTY

It took all of Hayden's control not to rush out and toss Duncan away from Isla. He shouldn't want to defend Isla, but he did.

Hayden cursed and placed his hands on the wall in front of him. He leaned forward and let his head drop. He hadn't needed to see the confrontation, not when his hearing was so excellent.

Isla's words echoed inside Hayden's head long after silence descended. What was she doing? Had she left the village? Did she now stand on the cliffs as she had done that first day?

"Fascinating."

Hayden whirled around to find Lucan leaning casually against the doorway. His arms were crossed over his chest and one ankle rested on the other.

"Tell me," Lucan said. "Do you watch her because you want to? Or because you were asked to?"

Hayden almost gave into the urge to walk over and punch him. "Because I was asked to."

"Hmm. Why the anger then?"

Hayden frowned. He had been turned away from Lucan, there was no way Lucan could have known the rage that boiled inside him.

Lucan raised a black brow and jerked his chin forward, his eyes lowering.

Hayden glanced down to find red claws extended from both hands. He'd never even felt them, never known his god had tried to break free.

"It is the way of a Highlander to want to protect and defend women," Lucan said. He lifted a shoulder nonchalantly, his gaze direct and forceful. "However, Isla can take care of herself."

"I know."

Lucan pushed away from the wall and twisted his lips wryly. "I think maybe you do. Odd how the need to safeguard, to shield doesn't leave with that knowledge."

Hayden stared at Lucan, wondering what he was getting at. There was no way anyone could know about his and Isla's night together. Hayden had been cautious not to even glance at Isla, but he always knew she was near. He smelled her, sensed her . . . felt her. It was disturbing, perplexing.

"Your point, MacLeod," Hayden said. He didn't want to talk anymore. He needed to see where Isla was. After all, the MacLeods had asked him to spy on her.

A faint grin passed over Lucan's face before he turned on his heel. "I've no point. Just talking."

Hayden didn't believe him for a moment. Lucan didn't seek someone out unless he wanted or needed something. What Lucan had wanted with him though was a mystery.

He didn't waste time thinking on it. With Lucan gone, Hayden could look for Isla. But did he really want to? Chances were he'd find her alone. Which meant he'd talk to her.

After what had happened between them, Hayden didn't think being that close to her was a good idea. It had been hell sitting with her in the great hall. She was so close, yet so far away.

All he'd been able to do was think about how her sweet body had come alive in his arms, how her skin had heated under his touch. Hayden had listened to Camdyn with half an ear, and many times he asked Camdyn to repeat something because he couldn't concentrate.

If that's how he acted with her in the same room with him, what would he do if she was next to him?

Hayden didn't want to find out. He'd given in to his urge to have her, but he couldn't do it again. He wouldn't give in again.

It had been the most glorious experience of his life, but she was a *drough*. She might not have been responsible for his family's death, but she was of the same origins. They were all the same. And if he believed that, he had tainted his family's memory.

Hayden rubbed his eyes with his thumb and forefinger. When had things gotten so complicated? How could one tiny woman disrupt his life so thoroughly and make him doubt everything?

He let out a sigh and once again wished Logan was there. Maybe his friend's jest could have chased away some of the melancholy.

Hayden squared his shoulders and looked around the cottage. There was much work to be done, work that would consume him and make him forget ice-blue eyes and silky, ebony hair.

He bent and scooped up a beam that had fallen from the roof. It was charred and useless for its former task, but it was still useable for other things.

Hayden walked it out of the cottage and tossed it aside before he went back inside to immerse himself in labor.

*　*　*

Isla let her head loll on the back of the wooden tub. Her muscles ached from the cleaning she had done of the cottages. It had occupied her mind, but always she knew Hayden was never far.

He hadn't spoken to her since he had left her tower the night before, and as far as she knew, he hadn't looked her way either.

She had half expected him to come to her defense when Duncan confronted her, but it just proved how little she knew Hayden. That they had kissed, had shared their bodies, did not mean anything to him.

And it shouldn't mean anything to her.

Isla finished washing and rose from the tub. She would have preferred to take a bath in the tower, but lugging the tub and the water up the long, winding steps would have taken too long. So she'd used Galen's empty chamber instead.

She stepped out of the cooling water and dried off before dressing. The castle was quiet as everyone settled in for the night, but for Isla, long, lonely hours awaited her.

With her hair still pinned atop her head, she exited the chamber and started toward the tower. She rounded a corner and found Broc blocking her path.

Ever since he had learned of her involvement with Phelan, he'd been angry. And rightly so. What she had done was wrong, and nothing she did would ever make up for it.

She paused several steps from him and waited. When he didn't speak, she knew she had to. "I understand your anger."

"Nay, you doona," he said over her. "I'm angry at you, aye, but I'm also angry at myself. I heard Phelan days before the attack. I knew it was a Warrior's howl, knew Deirdre had someone chained down those stairs, but I didn't go see for myself."

"You couldn't have freed him had you gone. Deirdre had bound the chains with magic. The only way to unlock Phelan's bonds was with a spell, a spell I memorized."

Broc turned his back to the wall and leaned against it, his chin to his chest. "There were many we could have helped through the years."

"Probably," Isla agreed. "We almost certainly would have been caught, though. Deirdre doesn't take kindly to betrayal. You would have been dead, and then who would have helped the MacLeods?"

He turned his head and grinned. "She suspected me always. I walked a fine line."

Isla could only imagine. There were many times she'd wanted to fight Deirdre, to try to save the many Druids she saw killed, but Lavena and Grania's life had been at stake.

Maybe she should have forfeited her sister and niece's lives years ago. She wondered if it would have changed anything.

"You won't have an easy time tracking Phelan," she told Broc. "He has a special power."

Broc turned so that only one shoulder rested against the wall. "Tell me."

"His god is Zelfor, the god of torment. Phelan is able to change the surroundings to suit whatever he wants."

"I doona understand."

"When I was with him he made that awful dark, dank prison of his vanish and put us in the Highlands with the sun shining and heather blooming around us."

Broc whistled. "That is a potent power. Why would Deirdre want to use him, though?"

"There were many plans that Deirdre had. Most I know nothing about. What I do know is her ultimate goal."

"To rule the world." Broc's lips twisted in a sneer. "She made that known to everyone."

"Find Phelan. I need to know that he is all right even if he doesn't return with you."

"I give you my oath that I will find him as soon as I'm able."

It was all Isla could ask for. "When do you leave?"

"Soon."

She nodded and moved past Broc and continued toward her tower. When she reached the top, she stepped into a dark chamber.

After she lit the candle, Isla looked around her tower. She kept her day filled so she wasn't able to let her mind wander, but with nighttime, she couldn't hold back her memories and thoughts.

Isla took off her shoes, stockings, and gown. She stood by the bed in her chemise and began to unpin her hair. It was the stir in the air that told her she wasn't alone anymore.

Her heart jumped at the thought that it might be Hayden. Who else had visited her in the dead of night?

She set the last pin on the table and turned to face her visitor. Her stomach fluttered like the wings of a bird as she stared at the imposing—and impressive—Warrior before her.

His skin was the deepest, darkest red. Hayden's eyes, usually as black as midnight, were the same crimson as his skin and claws. He didn't try to seal his lips over his fangs. At the top of his head, just through his blond hair, she saw the small scarlet horns and smoke that curled from their tips.

There was no desire in his red eyes, no kindness as she had seen the previous night. There was no revulsion as

when he had learned she was *drough*. What she saw reflected in his Warrior eyes was . . . resignation.

She shouldn't be surprised. She had asked him to end
her life. "Have you come to kill me?"

Hayden shook his head, his blond locks brushing his
shoulders.

Isla walked to him then. His saffron shirt was gone,
leaving him bare-chested. She longed to touch him, to run
her hands over the rippling muscles of his chest. It was
his lack of desire that held her hand.

"Why are you here, then?"

He glanced away from her, almost as if he couldn't
bring himself to answer her. "Does it matter?"

"It does."

He growled and took a step toward her, but Isla wasn't
cowed. She had seen more, experienced more than Hayden
could think to show her.

His hands locked around her arms painfully. She didn't
cry out or show him how he hurt her. As she searched his
eyes, his crimson Warrior eyes, she saw him warring with
himself on whether to thrust her away or not.

Isla decided for him. She raised her arms and pushed
at his chest, using just enough magic to propel him back
several steps.

"You don't want to be here, then don't. I didn't force
you into this tower," she said between clenched teeth. Her
anger rose with each beat of her heart. She didn't try to
tamp it down.

Instead, she unleashed it and let it soar within her.

Hayden bared his teeth and growled again. "Doona lie
to me, *drough*. I know the Druids have spells enough to
make a man lust after a woman."

Isla threw back her head and laugh. "Is that what you
think I've done? Have you so little experience with desire,

Hayden, that you cannot tell the difference between your wants and the urging of a spell?"

"As if a man could tell the difference."

"A man, nay. A Warrior? Most certainly."

His red eyes narrowed on her. "I shouldn't want you."

"And I shouldn't want you," she admitted.

Her rage disappeared as quickly as it had come. She couldn't deny the way her body responded to Hayden, and part of her didn't want to try. She just wanted his touch, his kiss, his body.

"Leave or stay, Hayden, but make your decision now."

TWENTY-ONE

Hayden knew he should leave. Hell, he should never have come to Isla's tower, but he hadn't been able to help himself. Thoughts of her, of their night together had given him no peace throughout the day.

He had thought to show her his Warrior form, to provoke her into rejecting him. Anything to break this hold she had over him.

She hadn't been afraid of him, though. Had in fact shown him her own anger. It had shocked him, as had the force of her magic when she pushed him away.

He was in way over his head, but there was nothing he could do about it.

Hayden took a step toward her. He nearly rejoiced when Isla's seductive lips turned up in a smile. How something so simple could move him, he didn't know. And didn't care.

She gave him a little shove. His knees hit the back of the bed and he sat heaving, impatient to touch her.

"Such a beautiful color," she murmured as she caressed up his arms and over his shoulders. "Crimson. The shade of desire."

Hayden could do nothing but sit while her hands stroked along his red skin. Her long nails teased his scalp as she sunk her fingers into his hair. And then those fingers wrapped around his horns.

His eyes flew open, lust filling him swiftly. Utterly. The force of it was powerful and addictive, the passion dizzying and beautiful. And the hunger . . . saints, the hunger clawed at him, demanded that he take her.

No one had ever touched his horns before. He was unprepared for his potent reaction or the longing that ripped through him sharp and true.

"This pleases you," Isla whispered seductively. She leaned forward and licked his earlobe, her warm breath skating across his skin.

Hayden tried to swallow, tried to keep his breathing steady, but all he could think about were Isla's hands on his horns, fondling and teasing him to such a degree that he nearly spilled his seed right then.

His climax swarmed him, intent on sucking him into the never-ending abyss of pleasure. But he wasn't ready. Not yet. He wanted Isla screaming with him, her body pulsing from her own orgasm.

He grabbed her wrists and jerked her hands away from his horns and the paralyzing pleasure her caress gave him. At the same time he turned them both and pinned her on the bed, her arms held over her head in his firm grip.

Careful not to cut her with his claws, he hovered over her. "How did you know touching my horns would do this to me?"

"I didn't. I've never seen horns such as yours, and I wanted to feel them."

She ground her hips against him then. Hayden's eyes closed and he moaned, thrusting against her as his desire only tamped down a moment ago, rushed to the surface. He wanted her right then, to lift her chemise and enter her with one push, deep and hard.

The need was so strong that Hayden shook with it. He had hurt her last time, he wouldn't do it again.

"You must stop," he ground out when she rubbed against him again. "I want you too desperately."

Isla lifted her head and placed her lips on his. Hayden jerked back, not wanting to harm her with his fangs.

"Cease, Hayden," she murmured. "You cannot hurt me."

But he knew he could. With just a thought he pushed his god back, waiting until the red faded from his skin before he spoke. "You doona know how you goad me," he said just before he kissed her.

Her chemise was thin and showed him the outline of her dark nipples, but it wasn't enough. He grabbed the neck of the delicate material and yanked it in half with barely a thought. Once she was bared to him, he feasted on her breasts.

They were small, but firm and delectable. Her nipples responded quickly to his mouth and tongue, becoming rigid nubs that drove her to trembling the more he licked and suckled them.

Her moans filled the tower and made him burn hotter, harder, made him hunger even more. Her skin tasted like snow, pure and delicious. How had he ever thought to stay away from her, to deny himself such a bounty?

Isla held onto Hayden's shoulders, her nails digging into his skin. He knew just where to touch, just how to touch to please her. She longed to caress his horns again, to see his nostrils flare and his body shiver.

It was heady, his reaction to her. She wanted more of it, more of him.

She gasped when his hand slipped between her legs and cupped her sex. She could feel the slick wetness of herself on his fingers as he parted her woman's lips and teased her flesh.

His fingers were gentle but insistent as they fondled

her, stroking the already bright flames of her desire higher, hotter.

Isla sucked in a breath when his finger rubbed over her clitoris, once, with the lightest of touches. Twice more he teased her, winding her into a fever pitch of need.

And want.

Her hips lifted from the bed, a cry on her lips, as he slid his finger inside her. Isla's body rejoiced at the contact, the feel of him within her.

He kissed her then, every ounce of his hunger, his craving in the way he laid claim to her. His finger began to move in and out of her in time with his tongue, caressing expertly.

His touch was easy and hard, delicate and rough. He gave no quarter as he fondled her, demanding that she take everything he offered and gave as much in return.

Isla was incapable of doing anything else. The pleasure was too intense, his touch too tender, but her body cried out for more, sought more the higher her desire built.

It coiled within her, building and building, winding her tighter and tighter.

Just as she thought she couldn't take any more, he joined a second finger with the first.

"Hayden," she murmured, her body moving on its own against his hand seeking the fulfillment that was just out of reach.

When he wouldn't let up on his exquisite torture, Isla reached between them and under his kilt to wrap her hand around his rigid cock. It was larger than she had thought, thick and hard as steel. Yet, the tip of him was soft as cream.

She moved her hand up and down his length and heard him hiss in a breath, felt his muscles stiffen. With her desire rising as quickly as the tide, she tried to hold it back the climax that was upon her.

But Hayden would have none of it.

He moved away from her long enough to jerk off his kilt with stiff movement, and then he loomed over her once more. "I can feel your magic every time you touch me. It makes me burn."

Isla had never known a Druid's magic to penetrate another as Hayden said hers did. Was that what seemed to connect them, what seemed to pull them together despite everything?

She soon forgot all about her magic and what it did to Hayden as he nudged her apart with his knee and positioned his erection at her opening.

His gaze locked on hers. He slid inside her slowly, steadily until he was sheathed fully, filling her perfectly. A soft, barely discernable sigh escaped him.

Isla lost herself in the black depths of Hayden's eyes. For just a moment, that half a heartbeat, she had seen inside him. It left her reeling, seeking more.

He shifted his hips, the friction jerking Isla out of her thoughts, her body reminding her of the pleasure that awaited her. She lifted her legs and wrapped them around his waist, bringing him even deeper.

He began to move with long, slow thrusts. Each glide of his cock inside her brought her closer and closer to her climax.

His tempo increased until he was driving into her hard and deep and fast. Hayden held her gaze, his black eyes smoldering with passion while his body filled her again and again.

"Come with me," he urged.

Isla was so close. She could feel the orgasm building, taking her higher and higher. And then she was flying. She screamed his name as her body jerked with the force of her climax.

Hayden continued to thrust, his hips pounding against hers until he let out a shout and buried his head in her neck as his own orgasm claimed him.

For long moments neither moved, their ragged, torn breaths the only sound in the tower. It took a long while before Isla's heart slowed. Even then, having Hayden atop her was delightful, incredible. She loved the feel of him, his thick muscles and wonderful heat.

He kept most of his weight on his forearms that rested on either side of her head. She let her legs fall open as Hayden raised his head.

Instead of leaving as she assumed he would, he pulled out of her and moved them so that their heads rested on the pillow. She turned toward him, just to soak up his warmth, and was surprised when he wrapped an arm around her.

Tears burned Isla's eyes. No man had ever held her so tenderly. For the rest of her life, however long that might be, she knew she would never again get into a bed without thinking of Hayden holding her.

She used her fingernail and lightly drew circles on his chest. She must have hit a ticklish spot on his side because he sucked in a breath sharply.

His hand closed over hers and he looked down at her with a smile. "No tickling."

Isla grinned. "But I love the feel of you. You're all hard muscle and smooth skin."

He snorted in response but released her hand. "And you're all womanly curves and silky softness."

She could hear the beat of his heart beneath her, feel his chest rise and fall with each breath. It lulled her, giving her a sense of tranquility that she hadn't had since before

Deirdre kidnapped her. It didn't even bother her that his hands skimmed over her scarred back.

"Do you like it here?"

She was surprised at his question. "I fear it's all a dream. That I'll wake back at Cairn Toul once again. The people here, their openness, their sincerity is difficult for me to accept sometimes."

"But you have."

She nodded against his chest. "I'm trying. I had given up hope. On the Druids, on Warriors, on life in general."

"That is certainly easy enough to do. I think all of us have done it at one point or another."

"What changed you?" she asked.

He was silent for a long moment. "After I escaped Cairn Toul I wandered continuously."

"Were you searching for something?"

"I suppose," he said with a lift of the shoulder she wasn't lying on. "One night, as I sat before a fire, I sensed someone. Wary as I was, I hid. He came toward the fire and looked to the exact spot in the tree I was hiding."

Isla smiled. "Who was it?"

"Galen. I knew instantly he was a Warrior."

"Yet you trusted him?"

Hayden snorted. "There is something about Galen that brings on that trust. I knew I would fight him if I had to, but it was soon clear he was nothing but a friend. A day later Ramsey joined us."

"So you three stayed together?" Isla was amazed at how Hayden had opened up to her, and she was eager to learn more about him.

"Off and on. We would separate, but always we would meet back up a few years later. One day on my way to meet them I stumbled across Logan."

When he paused, Isla lifted her head to look into his face. "What happened?"

Hayden's black eyes shifted to her. "He looked lost, as if he didn't know what to do with his life. I brought him with me to Galen and Ramsey. The hopelessness I had seen vanished eventually. He kept us laughing with his jests and teasing."

"You two are very close."

"He reminds me of my brother."

Isla returned her head to Hayden's shoulder. "I'm glad you found Logan. Everyone needs someone they can depend on."

"Aye." Hayden's fingers tangled in her hair as he pulled her tighter against him.

Isla's eyes drifted shut, but she didn't fight it. She would rest, just for a few hours in Hayden's arms. A few hours in heaven.

It was her last thought as sleep claimed her.

Hayden knew the moment Isla fell asleep. He was still stunned he had told her so much of himself. It hadn't been his intent. He had wanted to discover more about her.

He had told himself he would leave her once she was alseep, but now that the time had come, he was content to stay as he was. It would only mean trouble for him the next day, though.

The more he was around Isla, the more he gave into his desire to have her, he found it harder and harder to stay away. He tried to tell himself he hadn't spoken with her all day because he didn't want the others to speculate on anything, but the truth was he knew if he was near her, he would give into his desire and take her.

No matter who was around.

Everyone knew his hatred of *droughs*, yet the moment he had lifted Isla in his arms on Cairn Toul, he had wanted her. Only her. His ardor had dampened a bit when he'd learned she was *drough*, but that wasn't enough for him to keep his distance.

His body had been eased of its need, but his soul ached for what he was doing to his family's memory. What would they think of him if they could see him now?

Hayden stopped his mind before it continued down that path. The satisfaction he'd lain blissfully in was evaporating quickly, and he wasn't ready for that.

He cleared his mind of everything then. It didn't take long for the woman in his arms to fill his memory. Hayden closed his eyes and smiled as he recalled how she had once again screamed his name.

Every detail of their lovemaking replayed in his head. He had enjoyed his time with Isla, but he had to let her know that they could not continue as they were.

He must have fallen asleep because he awoke to Isla's hand on his cock, her caress sure and confident as she stroked him. Hayden groaned and thrust forward so that her hand slid down his hard length.

"Ah, you're finally awake," she whispered.

His brain wouldn't register any words in response. Her thumb smoothed over his arousal and smeared the drop of precum over the head of his cock. Her other hand cupped his balls and gently rolled them in her palm.

Hayden had never felt such pleasure, such blissful torment. Women had touched him before, but not like Isla. Not like this. She had a special touch. It was like her magic, extraordinary and vibrant.

It made his skin tingle and set his blood afire.

When she lowered her head, Hayden forgot to breathe. He was frozen, his limbs locked in place, his muscles tense. He watched, spellbound, as her lips hovered over his rod.

She glanced at him, her ice-blue eyes flashing with excitement and passion. It made his heart quicken its beat and his arousal to swell even more.

Isla smiled seductively, sensuously before her lips closed over the head of his cock and her mouth swallowed him.

Hayden's lips parted, breath filling his lungs as the heat, the wetness of Isla's mouth surrounded him. He was sinking, spiraling out of control with every lick of her tongue.

And he loved every moment of it.

"Isla," he whispered, his eyes rolling back in his head.

Hayden buried his hands in her hair, holding her head as he sank into her hot mouth. Her tongue licked him, her mouth sucked him, and all he could do was ride out the amazing, torturous pleasure.

Again and again her mouth slid up and down his arousal. He was lost in the pleasure, the elemental bliss of her lips on his cock.

No woman had ever freely taken him in hand. That Isla had did not go unnoticed by him. In truth, it only made him crave her more. If that was even possible.

It came to a point, much quicker than Hayden would have liked, that he knew if he didn't stop her, he would spill in her mouth. As much as that tempted him, he wanted inside her once more.

Hayden grabbed Isla's slim shoulders and tossed her onto her back. She reached for him again, but he rolled her onto her stomach and lifted her hips. He slid his fingers over her sex and found she was drenched and hotly aroused.

Just as he wanted her.

Just as he needed her.

He positioned himself at her entrance and thrust into

her from behind hard and quick. Isla moaned and threw back her head in abandon.

She was so tight, so hot, and he was already so primed to come that he feared he wouldn't be able to wait for her.

Isla panted, soft cries coming from her mouth every time he shifted his hips. He reached around so that his thumb found her clitoris, and he began to stroke her in slow, tight circles.

He rotated his hips, afraid to do more than that lest he peak too soon. The feel of his body rocking into her soft behind only built Hayden's desire to a staggering height.

Isla began to move back against him, matching him thrust for thrust. She held nothing back, gave him all of herself and more.

Hayden pumped inside, wanting to touch her soul, brand her so that she would think of no one but him. Want no one but him.

He wanted her to tremble for his touch, to dream of him. Just as he did for her. He didn't want to be this ravenous for Isla, but he was.

And he wanted to ensure she felt the same.

As passionate as Isla was, it wasn't long before she moved her hips back against him seeking more, her cries coming louder, her breath choppy and harsh.

"Hayden, please," she begged.

He kept his thumb teasing her as he began to move in and out of her core with long, hard thrusts. He closed his eyes and clenched his jaw at the feel of her heat, her slick wetness that pulled him in and nestled him deep inside her.

Dimly, he heard her shout, heard her cry out his name, but he was too lost in the passion, too lost in Isla.

When he felt the walls of her sex clench around him as she peaked, Hayden threw back his head and shouted her name as he finally gave in to his climax, finally gave in to her.

He rode the wave of the pleasure for what felt like eons, each shudder that wracked his body sending him spiraling anew, deeper inside Isla, closer to her than he had been to any woman before.

When he finally opened his eyes, he had never felt so calm, so content. So peaceful.

Hayden kissed her shoulder and rolled them to the side. She gave him a sleepy smile over her shoulder before she drifted off. Hayden knew better than to stay this time.

As much as he enjoyed tasting her body, he knew he had to leave. He couldn't chance staying, couldn't chance what would face him in the morning if he awoke beside her.

Couldn't chance finding her deeper in his psyche than she already was.

He rose from the bed and dressed, waiting until he knew for sure Isla wouldn't wake. He should talk to her now, tell her this was it, but what they had shared had been too special to ruin it with cruel, harsh words.

Tomorrow would be soon enough to crush whatever was budding between them.

Hayden leapt to the window and turned back to look at the bed one last time. Isla was on her side still, her long, thick hair spread around her like black silk. Her skin was flushed rosy and the moonlight illuminated the many vicious scars on her back, scars he hadn't noticed as he had held her.

She looked beautiful and tempting. Too tempting for him to risk sampling again.

TWENTY-TWO

Isla rolled onto her back and stretched, a smile on her lips. She was stunned to find the sun shining through her window. Had she slept, undisturbed those last few hours before dawn?

She turned her head and found Hayden gone. She swallowed past the lump of disappointment and sighed. His body might no longer be in the tower, but she could smell his woodsy spice scent on the linens.

Unable to help herself, Isla rolled onto his pillow and tucked it against her as she inhaled deeply. She wished he'd have been beside her when she awoke. It had been an amazing experience to caress him as he'd slept.

Isla had looked at him at her leisure. He was magnificent even in sleep, his power and strength evident despite his relaxed muscles. Her hands had stroked him from face to feet, had learned the feel of his lean, hard body.

She smiled as she recalled taking him in her mouth. He'd been surprised, to be sure, but it had soon turned to desire. Isla had never thought she would get enjoyment out of pleasuring a man. But then she had met Hayden.

Of all people, she should know how quickly life could change. Yet she had been unprepared for the passion Hayden stirred within her.

It would be so easy for her to allow herself to dream of a future with Hayden, but Isla had not lived five hundred years and not gained wisdom.

Her stomach rumbled as the smell of fresh-baked bread reached the tower. Though she could stay in bed all day and think of Hayden, there were things she needed to do.

She rose from the bed and glanced down at the ruined chemise. Thankfully she had another. Once she was dressed, she reached for her comb. Instead of leaving it free, she decided to braid her hair to help keep it out of her face while she worked.

Isla walked from the tower after she tied the thin strip of leather at the end of the braid. It felt odd not to have her hair around her, but it only got in the way.

When she reached the great hall, several Warriors were already there. In one glance she noticed Hayden wasn't among them. The MacLeod brothers, however, were.

They nodded in greeting as she passed on her way to the kitchen. She felt a tickle in her mind, something strange and new. And she didn't like it. It reminded her too much of Deirdre's invasion of her mind.

Isla paused and lifted a hand to her temple as she squeezed her eyes shut as pain began to build. She used her magic to push whoever—or whatever—was trying to get into her head out.

"Are you all right?" Broc asked.

She opened her eyes to find the hall spinning. She reached out to steady herself and locked onto a strong arm.

"Whoa," Broc said. "You need to sit."

"Nay." As quickly as the tickle had come, it was gone. Isla blinked her eyes open and released her hold on Broc's arm. "I'm all right. Just a little dizzy."

Fallon rose and walked to her. "Are you sure that's all? Maybe Sonya could help."

At the mention of the red-haired Druid, Isla saw Broc tense.

"I don't need to see Sonya. This has occurred before," she lied. "It's nothing."

She didn't want any of them to know she was disturbed and worried about what had just happened. The less everyone knew the better. At least until she had some answers of her own.

Broc looked over her shoulder and frowned. His fingers bit into her upper arm. She hadn't even realized he had hold of her until that moment.

She put her hand on his chest and smiled up at Broc. "Thank you. I need to help the others."

Isla glanced behind her to find Hayden standing at the entrance to the castle. He glared at Broc, murder in his eyes. Beside him, Arran looked puzzled and more than a little curious.

She ignored them all and walked into the kitchen. All four women were busy readying the morning meal. Sonya was the first to glance up. She smiled in greeting before she turned and reached into the ovens.

"There you are," Larena said. "We were worried you might not be feeling well."

Isla grabbed the ewer from Marcail's hand. "I slept."

"I'm glad you got some rest," Cara said as she cut into the bread.

Marcail tilted her head to the side, her braids falling into her face. "You do have the look of a woman well content."

Every eye in the kitchen shifted to her then. Isla forced herself to stay still and not fidget. She finally shrugged and said, "Sleep can do that."

Isla turned and retreated back into the great hall. At least no one there was eyeing her as if they knew she had been well pleasured last night.

The others followed her out of the kitchen, their hands filled with trenchers piled with food. She noticed Fallon, Camdyn, and Hayden missing, but didn't think much about it. The way the women kept looking at her made Isla more than a little uncomfortable.

Isla grabbed some bread and cheese intending to go to the beach. She was about to make her excuses when she heard shouting from above that drew her gaze.

Hayden's voice boomed above Fallon's and Camdyn's as he argued. Isla wasn't sure what was going on, but by the way Hayden's skin was turning red, she knew his rage was growing.

"If you want someone watching her, you do it," Hayden shouted. "I've got other things to do than spy on her."

Fallon glanced over the railing to the great hall below, his gaze landing on her. "Hayden," he warned.

Isla knew in an instant they were talking about her. Her skin turned clammy with fury and embarrassment. She couldn't take her eyes off Hayden's back as she willed him to look at her.

"It's not what you think," Lucan's voice reached her.

But Isla knew it was. They didn't trust her. She could understand that. Yet they had gone behind her back to have her watched.

She squared her shoulders and turned to the castle door. "I'm going for a walk."

"I'll come with you," Marcail said.

Isla speared her with a glance. "I'd rather be alone."

Marcail slowly sank back onto the bench, hurt in her turquoise eyes, but Isla didn't care. She had never felt such humiliation before in her life. Deirdre had done many things, but she had never made Isla feel as unwanted as a flea.

Isla walked into the bailey, then beneath the gatehouse.

She wanted to keep on walking and never look back at MacLeod Castle, but she had given her word to keep the shield up. She would not break that vow.

She turned and headed toward the village. There she would find her solace and something to take her mind off what Hayden had done and said.

Hayden knew Isla was in the hall even before Fallon looked down. He hadn't meant to let things get out of control. He had thought speaking with Fallon about it would solve everything. But Fallon had wanted him to continue watching Isla.

What Fallon didn't know was that Hayden couldn't chance it. Nothing Hayden said could change Fallon's mind. Finally, Hayden's control had broken and he'd let his ire get the better of him.

He hadn't wanted Isla to know. He certainly hadn't wanted her to hear him. Despite his good intentions, she had seen and heard all of it.

Hayden watched her walk from the hall, anger in every step. Her back rigid, her hands fisted, crushing the bread and cheese held there.

He almost went to her, almost took her in his arms and apologized.

"That wasn't well done, Hayden," Broc said from below.

Hayden sighed and leaned his hands on the railing. Camdyn walked away, but Fallon stayed.

"What is going on?" Fallon asked. "Did something happen between you and Isla?"

Aye. "Nay. I just doona want to be around her. I can't."

Fallon blew out a breath and clasped him on the shoulder. "I'll have another watch her, then."

Hayden should have felt relieved. He should have been overjoyed. Instead, he felt worse than a slug. How had his life gotten so messed up? When had things gotten complicated?

He used to be in control, used to make decisions easily and not change his mind or wonder if he was right. Now, all he did was second guess himself. Ever since he'd first seen Isla, dying on that cold mountainside, his life had been irrevocably altered.

And not for the best.

Hayden's appetite was gone, and the thought of sitting in the hall with some looking at him as if he was addled and others looking at him as if he were the bringer of doom, left him cold inside. He turned on his heel and looked for a window to climb out of.

There was only one place he could go where he knew he wouldn't be disturbed—one of the many caves.

Hayden easily reached the inaccessible holes in the cliffs thanks to his god. He stalked inside one of the shallow caves and ran a hand down his face. It was dark and clammy, just like his mood.

He'd gotten no rest after leaving Isla's bed. He had paced his chamber trying to find a way out of the situation he'd put himself in. The first step was to distance himself from Isla as much as he could. Which meant no longer watching her as the MacLeods had requested.

He'd gotten what he wanted, but he didn't like the empty feeling inside him now. He should feel relieved, happy not to have Isla as his responsibility anymore.

Why then did he have the insane urge to go and find her, to try and make her understand why he had said the things he had?

Hayden lowered himself to the floor at the cave's entrance and stared out at the sea. Waves rolled in, clashing with the boulders and sending spray shooting toward the sky. It was a constant battle the sea and land were in, and no matter how strong the land stood, the water eventually won.

If only Isla had been anyone but who she was. He could have enjoyed the passion they shared and not felt as if he dishonored his family. He wouldn't feel the need to push her away when all he wanted to do was pull her close and kiss her again.

Why did it have to be so difficult? It had been many decades since he had found a woman who intrigued him as Isla did. Why couldn't she have just been a normal woman?

Hayden knew part of Isla's appeal was her magic and how it affected him. He wanted to overlook it, overlook her, but he feared he wasn't strong enough.

Holding Isla in his arms, kissing her, caressing her . . . loving her had felt so right. As if his entire life had been building toward her, toward finding her and the moment he first kissed her.

He hated that something so right could be so wrong.

TWENTY-THREE

Deirdre felt her magic wane. She threw a fist in anger but it just went through the wall of her chamber. If only Dunmore and the wyrran would return with a Druid, she could be whole once more.

Her anger stemmed from more than that, though. She had tried to reach Isla. For a moment, Deirdre thought she might have succeeded, but the link vanished too soon.

With her magic so dimmed Deirdre wasn't sure if she was connecting with Isla or not. She had even sent a handful of wyrran to see if they could locate Isla.

If she'd somehow been captured Deirdre would make sure she was rescued, but Deirdre didn't think that was the case. Either Isla was dead, or she had tried to escape. With Grania and Lavena gone, there was nothing Deirdre could use to make Isla do as she wanted.

Deirdre had thought after five centuries Isla would have been swayed to her side, but the Druid was stronger than Deirdre had ever realized.

She had sought out Lavena for her skills in seeing the future, but the sister she should have bent to her will was Isla. Oh, Isla was a slave to her in more ways than one, but Isla still fought her.

Had Deirdre seen the signs of Isla's power sooner, she could have worked it so that Isla welcomed the evil inside her. Deirdre didn't think even Isla knew how great her magic was, and if Deirdre had her way, Isla never would.

Isla would be hers once again, and Deirdre would do whatever it took to have her.

Isla's braid fell over her shoulder and whacked her in the arm as she bent to pick up a broken ewer from the cottage floor. She tossed it through the open door and wiped the sweat from her forehead with the back of her hand.

She saw a shadow out of the corner of her eye and turned to the window. She had thrown the shutters open to let in the sun and breeze. Leaning an arm across the sill was Malcolm, Larena's cousin. Isla saw how he held his mangled right arm firmly against his side.

His face was haggard and he sported a mangy beard that hid most of his face, but even then Isla could see his handsomeness. A beard and scars did not hide his vibrant blue eyes or his hollowed cheeks and square jaw. His blond hair was darker than Hayden's and held more body to it. Malcolm had a lock that constantly fell over his forehead and tangled in his long eyelashes.

"Hello," she said when he simply stared at her.

"Why are you always alone?"

She raised a brow and chuckled. "You ask me that? You who stay by yourself most of the day."

His gaze moved around the cottage. There was a hard line to his lips, as if they were permanently twisted in a snarl. "You work as if you care what happens here."

"You don't think I do?"

"Why should you? You'll be gone soon enough."

Isla watched the sea breeze ruffle the hair about his shoulders. "And how would you know that?"

"Because we're the same." His gaze clashed and held

hers. "We're here because for now it's where we need to be. Soon, however, things will change and we will leave. It's in your eyes. Anyone who knows what to look for will see it."

She could only stand in muted astonishment. Was she so obvious? Of course, she had told the MacLeods she would leave, and Malcolm could have overheard the conversation.

"Does Larena know you plan to go away?" Isla asked.

Malcolm shoved the lock of hair back from his forehead. "I tried to tell her, but she willna listen. This is her home now."

"From what I understand, it's yours as well."

"I have no home," he stated flatly. "It was taken from me."

Isla knew where the conversation was heading. She decided to take the direct approach. "And you blame me."

Malcolm snorted and fisted his left hand. "You didna attack me. You didn't use claws to scar my face and body. You didn't make my arm useless."

"You're lucky to be alive, Malcolm. You should rejoice that Broc found you, and Sonya was able to heal you."

"I should, but I don't. They would have been better to let me die." He blew out a harsh breath. "Doona think I'm not grateful to them. Fallon has allowed me to stay and taken me in as one of his own."

"But you were to be laird," she finished for him. "Your life was taken from you."

"As yours was."

Isla looked away, unable to look into his haunted eyes another moment. In his gaze she saw the sadness, the anger, the bitterness that she carried within herself. And she ached for him because there was nothing anyone could do for Malcolm.

"What is between you and Hayden?" Malcolm asked.

Isla jerked her head toward him. "What do you mean?"

"I'm left alone, but that doesna mean I donna see things. I saw the kiss you two shared on the beach. It surprised me considering how much Hayden despises *droughs*."

She kicked at a broken table leg. "If there was ever anything between us, it is long gone now."

"I wonder," Malcolm murmured before he turned and left.

Isla shook her head and continued working. Hours went by before she heard someone say her name. She looked up to find Cara in the doorway of the cottage, a water skin in her outstretched hand.

"Thank you," Isla said as she took the water and drank deeply. She wiped her chin where water had dripped with the back of her hand and leaned against the door. She had worked nonstop for hours to occupy her mind, and it had worked just as she hoped.

Cara looked around the cottage. "You've been working hard."

"I cannot sit around doing nothing. I must keep busy." Now that she was idle, however, she found herself thinking about Hayden. Isla looked past Cara into the center of the village where the other Warriors gathered to rest.

She didn't see Hayden, but she was sure he wasn't far. No one had left the area since she had shielded it.

"He's not here," Cara said.

Isla glanced away hoping Cara wouldn't say more. She should have known better.

"We should have told you someone would be following you."

"Aye, you should have." Isla looked at Cara, wanting to be angry, but one look at Cara's honest, mahogany eyes, and Isla couldn't find it in herself.

Cara licked her lips and fiddled with the wine skin.

"Lucan and his brothers do trust you, but you admitted when Deirdre takes over, you are not yourself. They wanted to ensure everyone's safety in case that happened."

"I think they're doing the right thing. Had I been told, I would have understood."

Cara smiled, her face lighting up with joy. "I'm so glad. Why don't you come with me and Marcail? We're running low on herbs."

Isla had spent most of her five hundred years alone. Maybe it was time she made herself join others. "I would like that."

"Come then," Cara said and took her hand as she pulled her from the cottage. "It is time to have some fun."

As Isla followed her, she noticed that several Warriors watched them walk through the village. Isla wondered which of them was to follow her now.

Why had Hayden done it in the first place? And why did she even care?

They found Marcail waiting for them at the back of the village near the old convent. Cara slowed and glanced at the ruins.

"They took me in when no one else would," Cara said. "The nuns cared for many abandoned children."

Isla couldn't look at the convent. To think of the children who had died there made her sick to her stomach. She gave Cara a moment and moved to join Marcail.

"What herbs are we searching for?" Isla asked.

"None." Marcail laughed when Isla frowned. "I told Cara that to get her out of the castle. She's worse than Quinn in coddling me."

Isla chuckled at the devilment in Marcail's eyes. Behind them Cara blew out a breath and mumbled something about getting even.

Marcail linked her arms with Isla. "Don't get me wrong,

I like Quinn being concerned, but sometimes it can be . . . well," she with a shrug, "overwhelming."

"I can imagine." But Isla thought it would be nice to have someone worry about her like that.

Cara moved to Isla's other side. "Don't listen to her, Isla. Marcail loves that we fuss over her. It'll be the first child born in MacLeod Castle in three hundred years. We're all excited."

"Do you and Larena want children of your own?" Isla asked.

"Very much so," Cara said. "But not yet. Lucan . . . well, he doesn't want to have a god inside him when we have a child. I told him it didn't matter to me, but I conceded to his wishes. Larena has done the same for Fallon."

"They drink a concoction Sonya makes for them that's a mixture of herbs and magic."

Isla knew exactly what they were talking about. "I know the one. I helped my mother make batches of it for our village. Every family would take turns brewing it each month."

They reached the edge of Isla's shield and she held out her hands to stop them. "We cannot go farther."

"Then we'll walk around it," Marcail said with a smile.

Cara turned them to the right and they walked around the village toward the open expanse of land before the cliffs dropped off into the sea. It was a large distance. Enough that five other villages could have been placed there and still had room.

Isla listened to Cara and Marcail as they talked about baby names and their futures. It made Isla realize the huge void in her own life, an emptiness she now wanted to fill.

She immediately thought of Hayden. How could he be so tender, so loving during the night, but once the sun rose, he shunned her as if they hadn't shared the most delicious pleasure imaginable?

"What's making you frown?" Marcail asked. "I hope it isn't Hayden. I'm waiting to see him to give him an earful after what he did this morning. That was uncalled for."

Cara nodded vigorously. "He's been acting strange every since . . . well, ever since he brought Isla here."

Isla cringed. So she was the cause of his distress. Maybe it was better if she and Hayden kept their distance. It was obvious they weren't good for each other.

As irritated as she was, Isla didn't like the other two women being annoyed with him. "Hayden loathes *droughs*, and that's what I am. I can understand why he would be angry."

Both Marcail and Cara stared at her as if she'd grown horns. Which made Isla think of stroking Hayden's red horns, and how his eyes had burned with desire.

"If I didn't know better I'd think there was something between the two of you," Cara said.

Maybe it was the knowing look that passed between Marcail and Cara, but Isla had the distinct impression that they knew exactly what had happened between her and Hayden.

Isla opened her mouth to answer when she felt them. Wyrran. She halted and pushed Marcail behind her.

"Isla, what are you doing?" Cara said.

There was no mistaking the feel of black magic. Just as a *mie* could feel the magic of another *mie*, a *drough* always felt the presence of black magic.

Isla's blood iced with dread. They couldn't have found her so soon.

"Holy hell," Marcail said, using Quinn's favorite saying. "Am I seeing wyrran?"

Isla spotted the five yellow creatures as they walked

toward the edge of the shield. They were hunched over, their gazes searching, their long claws held in front of them.

Isla licked her lips and kept watch. "They cannot see us. They cannot hear us. We're safe."

"They came looking for you, didn't they?" Cara asked.

Isla wanted to lie, but she knew she couldn't. "They did."

There was a shout behind him. They turned and found Warriors racing toward them. Isla knew she had to stop them from killing the wyrran. If the wyrran didn't return to Deirdre, she would know Isla wasn't dead.

"Nay," Isla shouted and stepped in front of the approaching Warriors. "Stop. Please. You must stay in the shield."

But the Warriors continued toward her. They were turning as they ran, their skin and eyes changing colors as their claws and fangs lengthened.

"Stop," Isla tried once more.

When that didn't work, Isla knew she had to use her magic. She called it up inside her, let it build so that it would affect all the Warriors. She was about to release it through her palms, but she had taken too much time.

They were upon her before she could use her magic. Duncan was in the lead with his twin moving up quickly behind him. Ian went around Duncan and saw Isla too late.

There wasn't time for Isla to get out of the way, only time to brace for the collision. Ian's arms locked around her as they collided.

TWENTY-FOUR

From the cave, Hayden heard Isla's shouting, sending him to his feet immediately. He never hesitated, just knew he needed to get to her. He vaulted to the top of the cliffs before he could think twice and saw her standing solitary before Warriors running toward her.

He didn't think, just reacted. In an instant his god was released and Hayden was racing to her. He'd never run so fast in his life. His only thought was to protect.

No matter how fast he ran, no matter the powers of his god, he couldn't get to Isla in time to prevent Ian from barreling into her.

When Ian's body slammed her into the ground, Hayden roared his fury and launched himself at Ian. Hayden's claws sunk deep into Ian's back before he rolled and tossed Ian away from Isla.

Ian came to his feet with his knees bent and his arms held away from his body. Hayden raked his gaze over Ian's pale blue skin. He would have thought it would be Duncan attacking Isla, not Ian.

"You want a fight?" Ian asked as he stepped to his right. "I'll be the one to give it to you."

Hayden followed suit, his gaze trained on Ian and no one else. He smiled as his muscles readied for battle. He hadn't been known as the greatest warrior of his clan for nothing. Battle was in Hayden's blood, and it had nothing to do with his god.

He knew the instant Ian was going to attack by the shift in his shoulders. Hayden was ready for him. They clashed violently, brutally. Hayden grunted as Ian's claws scraped down his arm in deep grooves.

Blood gushed, and for a moment Hayden couldn't use his arm. But he began to heal almost at once. He pulled back his arm and slammed it into Ian's chest, his claws sinking deep.

Ian's pale blue Warrior eyes widened before he growled and punched Hayden in the kidneys. Hayden staggered backward, his claws breaking free of Ian. He growled and readied to attack again.

Before he and Ian could collide, they were surrounded by the others. Hayden fought against the hands holding him, eager to get back to tearing Ian apart. He and Ian never broke eye contact, never stopped fighting.

"Enough, Hayden," Lucan snarled.

But Hayden was beyond hearing. He was in kill mode, and he wouldn't stop until Ian was dead.

He watched as Ian's twin, Duncan, and Quinn tried to restrain Ian. Somehow Ian got an arm free, and then he was coming for Hayden.

Hayden stopped struggling, and instantly the hands holding him loosened. It was just what he wanted. He threw off his fellow Warriors and launched himself at Ian.

He would make Ian pay for harming Isla.

Pain exploded in Hayden as Ian's claws ripped through skin and muscles. But Hayden gave as good as he got. He would finish Ian if it was the last thing he did.

Isla could only stare in shocked horror at the image of Hayden in all his Warrior glory throwing Ian off her. She should have tried to get Hayden's attention then, to tell him Ian hadn't attacked her.

In fact, Ian had protected her when they'd fallen to the ground.

As soon as Hayden and Ian began to fight she knew there wasn't going to be a friendly ending. The Warriors surrounded the fighters, preventing Isla from seeing the battle.

She began to climb to her feet when she felt hands on either side of her. When she looked up she found Marcail and Cara.

"What just happened?" Cara asked.

Marcail swallowed, visibly shaken. "It looks like Hayden was protecting Isla. He must have thought Ian attacked her."

Isla would never get the image out of her head at Hayden's face twisted in anger, his claws outstretched as he launched himself at Ian.

Cara wrung her hands. "Someone needs to do something."

"They shouldn't be fighting against themselves," Isla said. "This is what Deirdre would want. To divide us."

Marcail patted Isla's arm. "Quinn and the others will see it's stopped. See? Even now they break them apart."

But Isla knew better. She'd seen that same look before that was in Hayden's eyes. Nothing would stop him until his opponent was dead.

A moment later, Hayden and Ian had both slipped free of their comrades and were at each other again. Isla couldn't take it any longer. Even if they hated her, she had to put a stop to it.

She stepped away from Cara and Marcail, ignoring their calls for her to get back. Every time Hayden's blood was spilled she cringed. Even knowing he wouldn't die didn't help.

"Step away," she said as she approached the men.

Arran glanced at her before he quickly moved to the side. Fallon came toward her and was about to say something when she held up a hand, never taking her eyes off Hayden and Ian.

"Don't. If you want this halted, you need to trust me."

Fallon swore softly. "All right."

Isla moved deeper through the men until she stood in the inner circle with Hayden and Ian. They were oblivious to her and everything around them. That would work to her advantage.

She had one chance to break them apart and get their attention. She prayed it was enough.

Isla called to her magic, felt it move and swirl within her. She splayed her fingers and held her hands above her stomach. The magic gathered at the center of her abdomen, growing and growing until she could barely contain it.

She held it as long as she could before she lifted her hands toward Hayden and Ian. The blast of magic that shot from her was so strong she had to take a step back to keep balanced.

Her magic held Hayden and Ian apart no matter how hard they fought. She glanced from one to the other, afraid at the savagery she saw in their eyes.

"Hayden," she called. When he didn't respond she tried again. "Hayden, look at me!"

Finally his red Warrior gaze shifted to her. "I need to finish this."

"It is finished."

"He attacked you!"

Isla never knew which Hayden she was going to be talking to. The one who wanted her in his arms, whose touch made her yearn for more. Or the man who couldn't stand the sight of her.

"What do you care?" she said, but didn't give him a chance to respond. "There are wyrran. Ian and the others were coming to battle them. I tried to prevent them."

Hayden's eyes narrowed on her, his jaw clenched. "Let me down. Now."

Isla knew Hayden would only go back to fighting Ian, and she couldn't have that. With a wave of her hand she pushed him through her shield. At the same time she released Ian who gave her a small nod.

"What have you done?" Lucan demanded.

Isla, however, was too busy watching Hayden to want to answer. If Deirdre had known how close to losing control Hayden was she would've set out to capture him in an instant. Hayden could lose himself in his god with the slightest of nudges.

Fallon stepped in front of her, blocking her gaze. "Answer, Lucan," he demanded.

"I'm trying to save him. None of you, especially Hayden, realize how close he is to losing it all. He's much closer than Quinn ever was."

She turned on her heel and started toward the castle. Hayden needed something to kill, and she'd given it to him. The wyrran.

Hayden stumbled backward at the force of Isla's magic. He felt her shield pass through him, knew she had tossed him out. The veil of anger and blood lust slowly fell away with the touch of her magic to leave him feeling lost and empty.

He looked around. The castle was there, he knew it was, but he couldn't see it. It looked as though the land was barren, no people, no buildings, and most certainly no castle.

There was a sound to his right and he turned his head and saw the wyrran. "God's blood," he murmured.

Everything Isla had told him was the truth. Why did she want the wyrran left alone? There had to be a reason. And even though every instinct inside him cried out to kill the evil creatures, he moved back through the shield instead.

"Hayden," Ramsey said as he took a step toward him.

Hayden looked at the men around him, the Warriors he called his brothers. His gaze landed on Ian and humiliation washed over him. He of all people knew better than to attack those that fought with him.

"Ian," he began.

Ian held up a hand to stop him. "There's no need."

But Hayden knew there was. "I'm sorry. I doona know what came over me."

Actually, he knew exactly what came over him—the need to defend Isla. It had been instinctual, primal, and so profound he had thought of nothing else.

Was he fighting his attraction to Isla based purely on his family's memory? Did his instincts know something he didn't? He'd never denied them before, had trusted them with his life, but now he questioned everything.

Isla did that to him. She twisted everything, turned everything about until he didn't know which way was up.

"Hayden?"

Ramsey's voice pulled him out of his thoughts. He looked into his friend's gray eyes and saw a wealth of wisdom there. Ramsey might be able to help him.

"I've only ever felt rage like that once before," Hayden lowered his voice so the others couldn't hear. He rubbed the back of his neck and glanced at the wyrran over his shoulder. "I never thought to feel it again."

Isla's shield was holding, preventing the wyrran from going forward or seeing anything inside. A few moments later, they turned and walked away.

Ramsey crossed his arms over his chest. "When your family was killed?"

Hayden nodded and closed his eyes. The memories of seeing his family slaughtered still haunted him.

"We're all balanced on the edge of a blade. Sometimes it's effortless to control what's inside us. Other times, it's impossible."

Hayden looked at Ramsey. "If only it were that simple."

"What else is going on? Is it Isla?"

It was most certainly Isla, but that was private. Whatever his feelings for Isla, he had to figure them out on his own. "Nay," he lied.

Ramsey lifted a black brow in question. "We all heard you this morn in the hall, yet you would kill one of your own to protect her? I think there's more than what you're telling me. I understand your need for privacy, but that is long gone now."

Hayden thought of Isla's alluring mouth, her sweet kisses, and her unmatched passion. He thought of how it felt to hold her warm body against him, how she could turn him ablaze with just one touch.

"It's . . . I cannot," Hayden finally said.

Ramsey dropped his arms and nodded. "I think I understand. Your hatred for *drough* has driven you all these one hundred and eighty years. The world is either good or evil to you, with no gray areas. Now that you've found one of those gray areas, you doona know what to do."

It wasn't quite so simple as that, yet Ramsey had a point. "Do you see the world as good or evil?"

"Nay. There is good in everyone just as there is evil in everyone. Look at us. We fight for the side of good, yet we have some of the greatest evil ever to walk the earth inside us. Are we good? Or are we evil? The same can, and should be applied, to Isla."

"Maybe," Hayden replied.

Ramsey sighed heavily. "You are fighting the very thing that is pulling you to her. You are fighting yourself, Hayden. If you aren't careful you will destroy her along with you. I admit the world would be much easier if we could categorize everything into black or white, but nothing is that simple or that uncomplicated."

Hayden's head began to pound. His world had changed with the death of his family and his god being unbound. He didn't want to go through that kind of upheaval again, yet that's exactly where he found himself.

He had nearly lost it all the first time. He wasn't sure he could survive a second.

TWENTY-FIVE

Isla spent the rest day in her tower too embarrassed by Hayden's dismissal of her earlier and too astonished by his battle with Ian. Over her.

She didn't want to speak to anyone, not after all that had happened. Marcail, Cara, Larena, and even Sonya had taken turns trying to coax her out of the tower. But Isla was content were she was.

She made herself eat the food left for her while she contemplated her options. It would be best if she left. She had known that from the very beginning.

It had been too tempting to be a part of the MacLeods, to be welcomed and offered friendship. She had made a terrible mistake, though.

Now that she had stayed and shielded the castle, she couldn't just leave. Already the wyrran had come looking, whether for her or just to check on the MacLeods, she didn't know. Not that it mattered. They had come, and it was only a matter of time before more were sent.

There were plenty of Warriors who could defend the castle. They would survive, and with Deirdre's forces cut back, they could gain the upper hand for awhile.

But then Isla thought of the women, of Marcail's child growing in her womb. How could she leave them now?

They had become her friends, sisters even. To abandon them now would be heartless.

And when Deirdre gains strength and takes over your mind?

Isla knew that was a possibility. The longer it took Deirdre to find a Druid the better off Isla would be. And then there was the chance that the artifact—and the Druids—Logan and Galen had set off to find might know something that could help Isla dissolve her tie with Deirdre forever.

The sun had long set when Isla finally ventured from the tower. She paused at the landing that overlooked the great hall, thankful she didn't spot Hayden. Only the Mac-Leods and their wives were in the hall. The men were seated in the chairs before the empty hearth, and their wives were in their laps.

Isla took a deep breath to steady herself and descended the stairs. As soon as they caught sight of her, their conversation ceased.

"We were getting worried," Cara said. Her arm was around Lucan's neck, her fingers running over his thick gold torc.

Isla stopped when she was in front of them. "I would speak with you all."

Marcail bit her lip, her anxiety great. "You're not leaving, are you?"

"Nay." Not yet anyway.

"What is it?" Fallon asked. "If it's what happened today, I will talk with Hayden."

She shook her head. "Leave Hayden out of it."

"I doona understand." Lucan sat his goblet on the floor near the chair. "After what Hayden did this morning, then attacking Ian. I would think you would want something done."

"Leave Hayden out of it," she repeated. "What I have to discuss with you doesn't involve him."

"All right. What is it?" Quinn asked.

Isla drew in a deep breath. "I would have your word that someone, not one of the women, follow me always. Let it be someone you trust, someone who will do the right thing when the time comes."

Larena's head cocked to the side and she rose from Fallon's lap. She walked behind his chair and rested her arm across the back. "And that right thing would be?"

"Killing me."

The silence was deafening, but Isla expected it. The MacLeods and their women, everyone at the castle actually, saw everyone else as family. You didn't ask family to kill you.

Fallon sat forward, his brow furrowed with a mixture of outrage and confusion. "I think you had better explain."

"The wyrran have come. If they are dead—"

"Hayden left them alone," Quinn said.

Isla nodded, trying to hide her surprise. She had wondered how Hayden reacted to being outside the shield. He hadn't come to her, though she knew he wouldn't. "They will report back to Deirdre that they found nothing."

"You don't think they'll tell her the castle has disappeared?" Cara asked.

"They aren't that intelligent. They will answer her question. Deirdre doesn't know where I am, and the chances of me ending up here won't be something she thinks about. Thus far. So, she won't ask the wyrran."

Quinn said, "Are you sure of that?"

"As sure as I can be," Isla answered. "I spent five hundred years with her."

Lucan's mouth twisted. "I doona know. Deirdre can be secretive."

"There's no doubt she kept most things from me, but I know the wyrran. And I know that she's sure I've run away. She'll assume you would never trust me, so would either kill me or turn me away."

"How long do we have before she figures out you're here?" Fallon asked.

Isla shifted her feet and shrugged. "She'll have her full power as soon as a Druid is brought to her for sacrifice. She'll find me soon after."

"She's thinned the Druids significantly," Marcail said. "There aren't many left, and the ones that are keep hidden to avoid detection."

"She no longer has my sister to aid her," Isla said. "It could take months, but it could take as little as a few days. I would err on the side of caution."

Quinn nodded in agreement. "So what do you propose?"

"I cannot leave now that my shield is in place. There are Warriors aplenty to stave off an attack, and the more Druids you have to protect, the more likely one will be taken. My shield will keep everyone safe that much longer.

"Not to mention I am curious to see if Galen and Logan find anything that could help me. The chances are slim, but if anything could, it would be artifacts that could harm Deirdre."

Fallon glanced at Larena behind him before he asked, "And where does your death come in?"

"I don't want to continue as I am. If Deirdre gains her power before Galen returns, or if the artifact cannot help me, I would rather die than be put in a position where Deirdre controls me to get to any of you."

"Nay," Marcail said. "You are strong, Isla. You've fought her and the evil. You can continue to fight her."

Isla remembered when she had looked at the world as

Marcail did. That was long ago now, long ago and lost forever. "I fought her for Lavena and Grania. Lavena is gone, and Grania tried to kill me when I attempted to take her from the mountain. The dagger she had . . . I tried . . ."

"It was an accident," Quinn said. "No one blames you."

She swallowed and pressed on. "I survived and plotted and watched the years pass by for them. Deirdre has no hold over me now. Is it too much to ask that my wishes be granted?"

"It isn't," Lucan said and stroked Cara's cheek before she moved to stand beside him. "We just want to find another way."

"There isn't one. I would have found it in five centuries."

Fallon rose to his feet and put his hands on his hips. "I would rather you ask us to deliver Deirdre's head to you, but I give you my word I will do as you ask, just as I have before."

"As will I," Lucan said and straightened to stand beside his brother.

Quinn set Marcail from his lap. He stood and let out a ragged breath. "You have my vow as well."

"You've the promise of us three," Fallon said. "We will see to it that the others know."

She bowed her head in gratitude. "Deirdre has been right to fear you three. You will be her downfall."

Larena walked around the chair to Fallon's side. "Do you have a preference to who guards you?"

"Whoever you see fit."

"We saw Hayden as that man," Quinn said.

Isla looked to the floor. If she was to stay, she would have to become used to seeing Hayden daily. And that was going to be more difficult than battling Deirdre. "You didn't make a wise choice."

"I disagree," Fallon said. "I was there when he found you on Cairn Toul."

"He wanted someone to protect. That isn't me."

Lucan huffed. "And this morning? What do you call that? Every one of us saw him strike Ian. Because he thought you were in danger."

"You would have to speak to Hayden on that. I have no idea why he did what he did. I'm . . . he doesn't like to be around me." By the saints, it was almost impossible to say. Each time became harder and harder. "Respect Hayden's and my wishes on this as well."

Fallon watched Isla walk out of the castle. He waited until the door closed behind her before he said, "Hayden may not like to be around her, but he needs her."

"You saw that as well?" Lucan asked. "It's obvious to any who look."

Quinn shook his head. "I saw them kiss on the beach. It wasn't a simple kiss either, but one of . . ."

"Passion and longing," Cara finished for him. "Why are they denying it?"

Larena laid her head on Fallon's shoulder. "He's denying it. She's just trying to hold herself together in the face of what he's done."

"He would have killed Ian for her." Fallon kissed Larena's forehead. "I've fought beside Hayden. I've seen how deadly he can be, but today? That was something different."

"Like it was his woman's life at stake," Quinn said. "I would kill for Marcail, especially if I thought she was in peril."

Lucan met Fallon's gaze. "We all would for our women."

Fallon glanced at the door again. He wished there was a way to help Hayden and Isla. "Who do we assign to watch her?"

"Guard her," Larena corrected. "We're guarding a dear friend, Fallon."

He smiled into her smoky blue eyes. "Who do we ask to guard her, love?"

"Ian," Marcail suddenly said.

Fallon jerked his gaze to his sister-in-law. "Have you lost your mind, Marcail? After he and Hayden nearly killed each other?"

Cara laughed then. "Ah, but Fallon, that's the point."

Fallon looked from Lucan to Quinn as the realization came to him. "Ian it is then. This should prove interesting to say the least."

"Very interesting," Quinn said.

Isla kept to the shadows of the bailey. Warriors guarded the castle at all times. That hadn't changed even with her shield in place.

She hadn't wanted to spend the night in the tower with her memories of Hayden. It had been hard enough the few hours she had stayed during the day.

But on the off chance Hayden did come to her again, she couldn't be there. She wouldn't be able to turn him away, and for her sanity she had to do just that. She longed to feel his touch and taste his kisses. He was her greatest weakness, a weakness she could ill afford.

She also couldn't handle another night in his tender arms and then feel his distance and contempt in the light of day. It was destroying her as nothing else had. Hayden had more power over her than Deirdre had ever thought to have.

It terrified Isla, but it also made her realize just how her feelings for Hayden had grown. It was a dangerous game they played. Hayden had said it the first time, but only Isla knew just how true those words were.

She made it to the village without being detected. She walked from cottage to cottage, using the shadows, until she found one set away from the others. It was just what she was looking for.

It was where she would stay for the night. Alone with her memories. And her dreams.

TWENTY-SIX

Hayden fought against venturing to the tower for as long as he could. He told himself he was just going to wander the castle as he did many nights. He liked to scale the outside, to get different vantage points than others.

Somehow he wasn't surprised when he reached Isla's tower that he found himself at her window. He tried not to look inside, and yet, he did just that.

Hayden expected to see Isla in bed, or maybe combing her hair. What he didn't foresee was an empty tower. He frowned, wondering where she was, wondering if she was safe.

His gaze swept the round chamber before he jumped from the window. He shouldn't be in there, but he couldn't help himself. And with Isla gone, it gave him the excuse he needed to be in her domain.

Her snow and wild pansy scent teased his senses. He glanced at the large bed, remembering taking her, making her his.

His cock thickened just recalling Isla with her black hair spread around her and her lovely lips parted on a scream as she peaked.

He recalled her small waist, the flare of her hips, her trim thighs parted so he could see her black curls that hid

her sex. She had been stunning, one of the most beautiful
sights he had ever seen.

Hayden ran his hand over the pillow. He sank onto the
bed and laid back. It was folly, but he would stay until he
heard her on the stairs. She'd never know he was there,
but he would know that she was all right.

He hadn't asked if she was injured from earlier. He'd
been so enraged at Ian that his only thought had been to
kill. It had come upon him quickly, consuming him.

The bloodlust had been the most severe he had ever
felt. After the first time when his family had been killed,
he'd made sure to keep himself under tight control. Normally that wasn't a problem. Why it should be now didn't
make sense to him.

In the deepest recesses of his soul, he knew it had to do
with Isla, yet he wasn't ready to admit that even to himself.

He threw an arm over his eyes and let himself doze.
His superior hearing would alert him to Isla's approach.

Isla nestled herself in a corner of the cottage. For hours
she stared into the darkness trying to think of nothing and
failing. Her thoughts returned to Hayden time and again,
of the passion he brought out in her, of the desire his presence caused her.

She had kept herself alone, not befriending anyone
in Cairn Toul. Now, she was surrounded by those who
wanted to be her companion. It would—had been—so
easy to let down her guard and allow herself to be friends.

But more had happened. Hayden had happened, and
Isla hadn't been prepared for what he did to her body
much less her heart. He touched a part of her no one else
had, and her heart and soul trembled because of it.

Her chest still ached at seeing him so close to the edge

while he had been fighting Ian. What she had witnessed that day she was sure is what had occurred with the original Warriors who had fought the Romans.

If Hayden went over the edge, he'd never be able to pull himself back to the man he was. Hayden was needed by the MacLeods. He was a warrior whose loyalty would never waiver, a warrior who would fight to the death. A warrior who would give his own life so that others would survive.

Isla's mind was full of Hayden. She couldn't get him out of her thoughts no matter what she did, just as her body couldn't forget what it felt like to have his hands on her. She rubbed the heel of her hands into her eyes and gritted her teeth.

It felt so good to close her eyes. She was so tired. All she wanted to do was to sleep. Not the naps she gave into, but a deep, dreamless sleep that would permit her to feel refreshed and ready to face anything.

She dropped her head back against the wall and closed her eyes. The sun would be up in just a few hours. Time enough for her to have one of her short naps, just enough to regain her strength, but not long enough for the nightmares to take hold.

Hayden came awake with a start, jerking upright in the bed and glancing around him. Dawn streaked the sky pink and purple and brought him to awareness.

He'd fallen asleep in Isla's bed, slept better than he had in weeks. More disturbing than that was that Isla had never returned to her chamber.

Hayden leapt from the bed. In three strides he was at the window. With barely a thought he jumped up, his hands on either side of the windowsill. His gaze scanned the castle surroundings. Everything seemed normal.

He knew Isla's shield was still in place since he could feel her magic. It wasn't as strong as when she herself wielded it, but there was a distinct feel to the shield's magic. So much so that Hayden would know her magic anywhere.

His thoughts turned to finding her. He vaulted from the window. The wind howled around him as he held his arms out to his side and waited to alight on the battlements below.

He landed with his knees bent and his head down. Hayden didn't pause before he straightened and turned to the door that led inside the castle.

Hayden rarely slept in his own chamber, so it wouldn't be odd for anyone to see him enter the great hall from the battlements.

Hayden paused at the landing and peered down into the hall. The MacLeods were present, as was Ramsey, Camdyn, Arran, and Duncan. Malcolm, Broc, and Ian were missing, though.

He was hungry, but Hayden couldn't concentrate on food when Isla was nowhere to be found. It was ridiculous, this need of his to find her, to know that she was all right and unharmed. He wasn't the one following Isla anymore.

That stopped him in his tracks. Had the MacLeods given that duty to someone else? Hayden fisted his hands. It was a thought, one that wouldn't go away even as the moments passed. Despite his curiosity, his most pressing concern was finding Isla.

He knew she wasn't in danger. No one at MacLeod Castle would harm her, and even if they did, she would survive. *Unless they take her head. As she asked you to do.*

Hayden turned on his heel and began his search in the castle. It would have been easier to ask someone, anyone if they had seen her, but that would mean they knew he was looking for her.

It would be better if he kept this to himself so he wouldn't have to answer any questions he wasn't yet ready to face himself.

It didn't take him long to conclude she wasn't in the castle. He even walked through Cara's garden and peered into the kitchens, but Isla wasn't there.

He looked on the beach next. The sun had risen higher, its golden light brightening the sky and glinting off the water. The sea beckoned, urging him to her shores. A swim would help chase away his dark mood, help to calm his anxiety. First, he needed to find Isla.

Hayden turned his attention to the village. He was half-way there when he saw Ian walking with purpose toward the back of the village, to the very cottage Hayden had picked for himself.

He halted, something telling Hayden to wait, to be patient and he would find what he needed. It was just a few moments later that Isla walked from the cottage, Ian behind her.

The twin laughed at something Isla said. Isla herself had a small smile on her face, something Hayden had seen so rarely. It wasn't until that moment that he realized he hadn't heard her laugh.

That caused his chest to constrict and his lungs to seize up, but it was nothing compared to the annoyance that rose up in him. Isla had a new watcher now—Ian.

And Hayden didn't like it.

Isla heard the laughter, the shrill, evil laughter that was Deirdre's alone. She knew before she opened her eyes she was in Cairn Toul.

The smell of malevolence and death surrounded her. Evil lived and breathed in the depths of the mountain. It was as if the very stones gave birth to the wickedness that seeped into the ground.

Or was it that the mountain hid a doorway into hell itself?

Isla shivered. She didn't want to open her eyes. She had been taken from Cairn Toul. Hayden had carried her broken and bloodied body away. She was at MacLeod Castle. Safe. For a while anyway.

What had happened?

She forced open her eyes and nearly gave in to the urge to weep when she saw her familiar and hated chamber in Cairn Toul. The plain stone walls, the small bed, the single chair.

"Nay," she whispered. "Nay."

Deirdre's face appeared before her. It was so sheer Isla could see through it, but there was no mistaking the white hair and eyes. There was emptiness in Deirdre's gaze, emptiness and rage.

Isla waited for her to speak, waited to hear that Deirdre planned to torture her yet again. Or maybe, finally, give her death.

But Deirdre didn't speak. She just stared at Isla with those cold, cruel eyes.

"Isla."

She came awake with a start, her heart pounding so loud she feared it might burst from her chest. Her hands were braced on the wall at either side of her as her body shook.

"Isla?"

She looked up to find Ian standing over her. His brow was puckered and his brown eyes watched her with worry and a hint of alarm.

It took her a moment to realize she was in the cottage on MacLeod land. It had been a dream. As soon as Isla recognized that she breathed a sigh of relief and dropped her head into her hands. She couldn't stop trembling, though. It had all been so real.

The sound of Ian moving and bending next to her filled the silence. "Bad dreams?"

"Always," she said. She raised her head and tried to steady her heart. Nightmares had plagued her ever since Deirdre had taken them captive. But this one had been different.

"I thought you were given the north tower as yours?" Ian asked.

"I was. I came out here last night to think, and I must have fallen asleep."

The way Ian watched her she knew he didn't believe a word she said, but he didn't press the issue. He straightened and held out his hand. "It is time to break our fast."

She took his hand and let him pull her to her feet. Her body ached from being in the same position for so long, but anything was better than her nightmare. She led the way out of the cottage surprised to find the sun higher than she anticipated.

"Fallon asked that I escort you from now on. That is, if it's all right with you."

She glanced up at him and smiled, the urge to tease overtaking her. "I think you're the perfect person. After all, you have already attacked me."

He threw back his head and laughed heartily. Isla inhaled the fresh Highland sea air, grateful that she was no longer at Cairn Toul.

"I didn't see you in time," Ian said when he stopped chuckling. "I was focused on the wyrran."

"I know." And she did. She didn't hold it against him. "Are you in favor of being my shadow?"

He shrugged. "I'm not averse to it, if that's what you mean."

"Did Fallon tell you everything?"

Ian glanced at her, no hint of laughter on his face. "He

told me you requested death if Deirdre does take your mind."

She halted and turned to face him. "You'll know if it happens. The pain is overwhelming. I have a few moments before she takes over where I know what's going on. You'll have to do it as soon as I tell you."

"I understand."

"Good." She let out a sigh.

They had begun walking again when Ian asked, "How does Hayden feel about me taking his place?"

The mention of Hayden brought back the ache that had been with her most of the night. "I'm confident he could care less."

"I'm not so sure. You didn't see his face when he attacked me."

"I saw it," she interrupted him. She'd seen it all too well.

TWENTY-SEVEN

Deirdre gasped as the last of her energy vanished. She'd had Isla! If only she'd been able to talk to her. Deirdre didn't know where Isla was yet, but it would only be a matter of time before she found her.

The use of her magic to try and contact Isla had been great, and Deirdre would pay for it for several days to come. She'd been trying for hours, and then finally she'd located Isla.

Only to lose her a moment later.

"If I had my full magic, Isla would be mine again," Deirdre said to herself.

Deirdre knew she should have waited until Dunmore returned with a Druid, but she'd had to know if Isla was dead. Now that she knew her greatest weapon was still alive, once Deirdre's magic had been restored she could rain down her wrath on the MacLeods and all who were loyal to them.

Before she could begin to plan on exactly how she would rip each MacLeod apart, five wyrran walked into her chamber. Deirdre motioned to them with unseen hands, but somehow the creatures saw her.

They halted before her, their yellow eyes lifted to where her face would be if she had a body. She smiled down at them. She still recalled the first wyrran she created. It had been the most lovely, frightening thing she had ever seen. They still were.

And they were hers. No one else could rule them. Only her.

"What did you find?" she asked them inside their minds.

They shook their hairless heads, their thin lips peeled back over the mouthful of large teeth.

"You didn't see Isla?"

Again, a shake of their heads.

Deirdre had known Isla wouldn't be with the Mac-Leods. Where she was, though, was another concern, but one Deirdre would hopefully discover soon.

It didn't matter how far Isla had traveled. Deirdre would summon her back to her side, and Isla would have no choice but to do as commanded. There was nothing Isla could do to break the connection Deirdre shared with her.

Oh, Deirdre knew Isla had tried several times, but nothing could stop Deirdre's magic. It was too strong and backed by *diabhul* himself.

Deirdre waved the wyrran away. She had planning to do. By the time Dunmore arrived with her Druid sacrifice, Deirdre would have everything set in place for her revenge.

She'd been a fool to think she could convince the Mac-Leods to align with her. With their deaths she would get some satisfaction. She would also have their women, women they had kept from Deirdre's use.

No more would she allow anyone to go against her in such a fashion. From now on, death awaited anyone who did not ally with her or who betrayed her.

Deirdre smiled. Nothing could stop her now.

Hayden waded into the sea and dove into an oncoming wave. As soon as the water engulfed him, he felt the solace of it. It soothed, it caressed, it cradled.

He swam far from shore, fighting against the currents that had swept weaker men to their deaths. He knew the instant he swam through Isla's shield. Her magic sang around him for a moment, blinding him with desire that left his body renewed and his cock aching, and then was gone.

Hayden came up for air once he passed through the shield. The wondrous feel of Isla's magic had faded once he was through the shield. He found he missed it, missed the way it hummed around him and tantalized his body. Just as before when he turned and looked, there was no castle atop the cliffs.

He gulped in a lungful of air and dove straight down in an effort to forget Isla and how she had complicated his life. He dove lower than he'd ever gone before. The water crackled in his ears and the pressure pushed against him, but still he continued.

When he could go no farther, he swam out to the side, lazily surveying the sights. He let his eyes take in the murky depths of the sea and the life that lived below the surface. Fish of all sizes and colors. Seaweed that swayed with the currents. Dolphins playing in the distance, and even some seals.

With his god he was able to hold his breath much longer than a mortal man. There were times Hayden had wished he could breathe under water. He chuckled, bubbles exploding past his lips to rise to the surface.

He remembered as a young lad his mother telling him stories about the mermaids who lived in the sea. Even then Hayden had wished he could live under the surface.

Mermaids or not, it was a completely different world than the one on land.

Hayden knew he should be helping the others rebuilding the cottages, but he couldn't chance running into Isla just yet. He needed to get himself under control or he just might start another fight with Ian.

As much as he hated to admit it, it was the cold hard pit of jealousy that iced his veins when he thought of Ian with Isla. It was ridiculous, this resentment, but as his mother used to say: "You cannot help the way you feel, Hayden."

He wished he could change his feelings on the matter, and with some solitude and control, Hayden could.

When he could hold his breath no longer, he surged to the surface. He shook his head to get the hair from his eyes. Already he felt better. Water had always done that for him.

So did being in Isla's arms.

Hayden cursed and slapped his hand atop the water. Just when he thought he had some semblance of control, he'd think of Isla.

He needed a longer swim, he surmised. But no matter how deep he dove, no matter how far he swam, the image of Isla's ice-blue eyes and her long, straight black hair would not leave him. Just as the feel of her body, the slick passage of her sex as he thrust inside her, wouldn't let him forget.

Hayden finally gave up. No amount of denial on his part would erase his feelings for Isla. And they were feelings, strong feelings.

Now that he had hurt her horribly he realized just how deep his feelings went. The things he had done, the things he had said no small apology could remove.

What was worse was that Hayden feared she might never forgive him.

With a deep sigh he started back to shore. When he came to Isla's shield he paused in the middle of it. His skin tingled with the magic, and his senses, already enhanced, seemed to surge to new heights.

It baffled him how he could be affected by her magic so. Neither Sonya's, nor Cara's, nor Marcail's did anything to him. He felt their magic surely as any Warrior did, but not in the way he did with Isla's.

Hayden entered the shield and caught sight of the great MacLeod Castle. It was imposing in its grandeur, striking in its design.

The pale stone that made up the castle, four towers, the sawtooth merlons and crenels, and the massive gatehouse had seen much, yet still the stones stood intact, even if some were crumbling, waiting to give shelter to those who sought it.

Hayden stepped onto shore and tilted his head all the way back to see the castle. His home now. His family. Why then did he feel like the outsider?

Isla paused with her hands deep in the earth of Cara's garden. She sank her fingers into the ground to till it up before she planted the new seed.

She didn't know how she would feel having Ian with her at all times, but so far it was working out all right. He gave her space, but she knew he was always near, always watching. Just as with now he stood off to the side.

Isla wanted to ask him how he fared since Deirdre's torture of him. It was obvious his twin, Duncan, was having a difficult time of it. Of course, it might be worse for Duncan since he had been helpless to do anything for Ian.

She should have helped Ian. She should have done so many other things, but she'd been a coward. Marcail called her strong, but Isla knew the truth. It was fear that kept her from going against Deirdre, even when she knew Grania and Lavena were lost to her forever. Isla still hadn't had the courage to break way.

If anyone could have given her freedom it would have

been Phelan. He hated her enough that had she asked, she knew he would have taken her head. It would have ended everything.

But she wouldn't have tasted passion. She wouldn't have had Hayden.

Isla snorted. As if she'd ever had Hayden. Hayden was no one's. He was a loner, a man who wanted and needed no one. How had she come to find herself wanting him so desperately?

She moved to the next spot and sunk her hands into the dirt. Her mother's magic had been greatest when she was next to the earth as Isla was now.

Isla had always found it amazing that each Druid found that special connection in different places with different things.

She had offered to help Cara to stay out of the village and therefore away from Hayden. She wasn't ready to see him yet. She wasn't sure she'd ever be ready to see him again. He stirred feelings too deep, made her long for things she couldn't have.

Every time Isla was near him she could think of nothing but him. For her own sanity, she decided against her present course of action.

If Ian, Cara, or anyone else suspected why she was in the garden, no one said a word. Which Isla was eternally grateful.

"You're a natural," Cara said with glee as she inspected Isla's work.

Isla shrugged and rubbed her cheek against her shoulder. "My mother's magic was like yours. She found her greatest pleasure in the earth. She thought mine might be like hers, so she often had me with her."

"I wish my mother had stayed alive so I could have learned the Druid ways as you did."

Isla sat back on her heels and turned her face up to the sun. "Spells are learned, Cara, but who you are, the magic that makes you a Druid, has always been inside you, guiding you. You just needed to learn to listen to it."

"Ah, but listening to it when for nearly a score of years I didn't isn't as easy as you might think."

Isla smiled and looked at Cara. "Nay, I cannot imagine it is. You seem to be coming along nicely."

"I have help," Cara said with a wink. "I'm also a quick learner."

"That certainly comes in handy." Isla rose and dusted off her hands after planting the last seed.

Cara's head cocked to the side, her dark brown eyes gazing thoughtfully at Isla. "Where is the source of your magic? The place where you feel its power the most?"

In all her five hundred or so years Isla had never found that source. Until she had stepped into the sea at Mac-Leod Castle. She recalled that day with clarity. How her magic had sharpened, how everything had seemed to come together in a rightness and calmness that surprised even her.

"The sea," she answered. "It's the sea."

"Then it's a good thing we live next to it, aye?" Cara said with a grin. "You don't happen to hear the trees talk like Sonya, do you?"

Isla shook her head. "I've heard of Druids being able to do that. It's a rare gift Sonya has."

"So is her healing. I've come to truly understand how wonderful the Druids are. And to think Deirdre is killing them."

Isla removed the dirt under her fingernails on one hand with the fingernail of her other. "For every Druid Deirdre kills, one turns from our ways. We are a dying breed, Cara. I fear that one day none of us will exist at all."

"What will Deirdre do for power once all the Druids are dead? Won't she need them still?"

"It was a question I posed to her as well. I thought if she realized how quickly she was killing them that she might allow more to live."

Cara's nose wrinkled in distaste. "That's not what happened is it?"

"Nay. Deirdre explained to me that it was her goal to slay all the Druids. I would be the last to be killed."

"Why?" Cara asked and threw her hands up. "I don't understand."

"If there are no Druids, no one would be able to challenge her."

Cara rolled her eyes. "No one has yet. What makes her think there would ever come a time that it happened?"

"The *droughs* might be more powerful alone, Cara, but if a group of *mies* ever got together and focused their power against Deirdre they could destroy her. Or they could have. We're past that now, I believe."

"There are too few of us left," Cara said sadly.

"Once Deirdre has consumed the magic of every Druid, she will be unstoppable."

Ian leaned a shoulder against the kitchen wall and snorted. "And here I thought she was already unstoppable. We couldn't kill her."

Isla looked from Cara to Ian and back again. "But we did slow her down. If that can be done to her, there has to be a way to kill her."

TWENTY-EIGHT

Isla hoped she was right. Deirdre had more power than any Druid had thought imaginable. Not even the *droughs* had expected her to gain that kind of powerful black magic.

Isla had seen for herself the envy other *droughs* had of Deirdre. In the early years the *droughs* could have easily destroyed Deirdre, but their fatal flaw was that they never worked with other Druids. So they had allowed Deirdre's power to grow.

The *mies* had expected the *droughs* to take care of Deirdre. And when that didn't occurr the *mies,* who should have banded together and killed Deirdre, decided to hide instead.

Isla couldn't blame either side. She wondered if the decision had been hers to make what she would have done. She'd like to think she would stand up to Deirdre, but she had failed to do that in the past.

Ian and Cara's conversation turned to the other Druids, but Isla caught sight of something more interesting emerging from the sea.

She moved toward the edge of the cliff and the path that led to the beach. Her eyes were fastened on Hayden. Her mouth went dry and her heart quickened at the sight of his stunning body, the hard muscles, the bronze skin.

He was perfectly made, perfectly beautiful. A man any woman would want in her bed. She had felt his mouth, his hands on her skin, knew how they could tease her.

She had held his rod in her hands, felt it fill her, knew the joy of having him thrust inside her. She had touched his muscles, felt them flex beneath her hand, knew the places on his body that brought him to his knees.

Isla drew in a shaky breath as her nipples hardened just thinking of Hayden. She folded her arms at her waist and watched him shake the water from his fair locks.

He stood nude, unabashed in his body. Her eyes drank him in, ever hungry for more.

"The longing on your face tells me there is most definitely something between you and Hayden."

Isla stiffened when Ian walked up beside her. She glanced at Ian to see him twirl a long stem of grass between his teeth. She thought to lie to him again but decided against it. It wouldn't do her any good.

"I doona know him well," Ian continued. "But what I do know of Hayden is that he often reacts before he thinks. He's the kind of man you want by your side in a battle, the kind who would never leave a friend behind."

"He is all of that."

"Like any Warrior I know, his past holds him. It is why he acts the way he does, why he chooses to be alone."

Isla cut her eyes to Ian. "Are you defending him?"

His face scrunched up. "Nay. I'm merely pointing out that what he said in the hall the other morning might have been done rashly."

"It wasn't."

Though she wanted to believe it was. Her heart hurt the more she watched Hayden on the beach. He tugged his saffron shirt over his head and reached for his kilt.

"Hayden's hatred for *droughs* goes very deep. He has

every right to detest us. It was *droughs* who killed his family."

Ian shrugged. "I'm not so sure you should include yourself as a *drough*. You battled the evil inside you and won."

She turned to face Ian then, no longer able to look at Hayden without feeling as if a hole was in her chest. "I am what I am, Ian. Nothing can change that, no matter how I wish it otherwise."

"Sonya took your Demon's Kiss and you never asked for it back."

"What does that prove?" she asked in frustration. "It was empty anyway."

Ian's jaw clenched and his nostrils flared. "Do you want us to treat you as a *drough*? Do you want us to think every word out of your mouth is a lie?"

"What I want is irrelevant. The simple truth is I am a *drough*."

"If you were really a *drough* the evil would have overtaken you centuries ago. Do you deny that?"

Isla sighed. She wasn't sure why she was arguing with Ian. She didn't want to be a *drough*, and certainly didn't want others to think of her as one. Yet, she was, and she had the scars on her wrists to prove she went through the ceremony.

"Have you killed people?" Ian asked.

Isla frowned as she looked into his soft brown eyes. "You know I have."

"Nay. Have *you* killed anyone? I'm not talking being under Deirdre's control, I'm talking about you making the decision, you taking a weapon, and you ending another's life."

She swallowed and thought of her niece. "Nay."

"Well, I have. Many of them. It doesn't matter that they were Warriors and we're at war. They were men first and foremost. I took their lives. I watched the life drain from their bodies."

Isla shook her head and smiled. This was an argument she wouldn't win. No matter what she said, Ian would have a defense for her. It was something a friend or family member would do, not a stranger who barely knew her.

She scratched at her cheek, befuddled at why Ian would go to such lengths. "Why do you care what I think of myself?"

Ian reached his hand out and gently ran his thumb over her cheek where she'd just scratched. "Because you're an asset to this clan, and we need you. If you're confident in yourself and your magic, then I suspect it will be more difficult for Deirdre to prey on you."

"Am I interrupting something?"

Isla's heart fluttered as she heard Hayden's voice behind her. Ian's warm gaze moved over her head, a cocky smile on his lips.

"Not at all," Ian said. "Isla had a smudge of dirt on her face. I was merely removing it."

Hayden wanted to toss Ian off the cliff. The way he'd had his hand on Isla's face, as if he were caressing her as a lover, had sent a spurt of rage and jealousy through Hayden.

Hayden had told himself to walk on or even turn back and leap to the top of the cliffs, but he'd been unable to help himself.

Isla turned to look at him. The smudge of dirt was still on her left cheek. Hayden glanced down to see the dirt beneath her fingernails and on her hands.

Her hair was pulled back in another thick braid and flyaways caught in the sea breeze tangled around her face and into her eyelashes. He longed to pull her against him and block the wind from her as he bent and took her lips in a kiss.

He wanted it so desperately that Hayden found himself stepping toward her. And if Ian hadn't been there, he might have done just that.

"Did you enjoy your swim?" Ian asked him.

Hayden forced his gaze from Isla's lovely face to Ian's. "I did."

Silence stretched between the three of them. Hayden didn't want to walk away, but he didn't know what to say to Isla, especially not with Ian around. It was obvious something was going on between the two of them.

Hayden hated to think it hadn't taken Isla long to replace him in her bed.

You're the one that spurned her.

She could have at least waited a few days. She hadn't waited a single night. And that's what needled under Hayden's skin.

He felt the tips of his fangs hit his tongue, a telltale sign his anger had risen, that his god was breaking free.

It was Isla who broke the silence. She stepped toward him, anger flashing in her ice-blue eyes. "Get hold of yourself, Hayden. You're closer to the edge than you comprehend. The MacLeods need you. Every innocent person of this world needs you to fight against Deirdre. You cannot help anyone if you lose yourself to your god."

He was so taken aback by her fury that he could only stare at her. He blinked as she turned on her heel, and then she was striding away.

Ian rubbed his jaw and slid his gaze to Hayden. "She's right. We do need you. Both of you can deny what's between you, but it's obvious to everyone."

"Just as its obvious she's turned her attention to you." As soon as it was out of his mouth Hayden regretted the words. It wasn't Ian's fault. Isla was a beautiful, alluring woman. If she turned her attention to a man, he'd be hard-pressed to deny her.

Ian's face went hard as he looked Hayden up and down. "You know nothing. You're blind to everything, Hayden, and that will be your downfall."

Hayden waited until Ian had followed Isla before he scrubbed a hand down his face. Complicated now defined his life. And he hated it. He preferred simple. Everything was easier that way.

He glanced at Isla's retreating back before she turned the corner and disappeared from view. Ian was right behind her, his long strides eating up the distance.

Every time Hayden saw Isla now, Ian was with her. Ian didn't hide in the shadows as Hayden had done. Ian stood beside her, not caring what the others thought of him.

Maybe Hayden should have done the same. He snorted. That wasn't like him. What he did was his business. No one else needed to know.

Once again Hayden wished Logan was there. This was the time Logan would say something clever, something that would make Hayden laugh and forget what he was upset about.

But Logan wasn't there and memories of Isla wouldn't loosen their hold.

TWENTY-NINE

Dunmore jerked on the reins, making his horse skid to a stop. It had taken more time than he'd liked, but he'd found the man he'd been searching for. Peter was one of those men others trusted. Maybe it was his kind face or his mild manner, but people told Peter things, secret things.

In the past Peter had been willing to share that information with Dunmore. For a price. Everyone had a price, and Dunmore had found Peter's easily enough.

If there was anyone who knew where more Druids were, it would be Peter.

Dunmore swung down from his mount and looked around. The wyrran were keeping themselves hidden, waiting for the time he would call for them. He faced the small, rundown cottage and lifted his lip in revulsion.

Peter had either been kicked out of his village, or he was trying to run from something. Dunmore chuckled to himself. Peter was most likely running from him, but it had done Peter little good.

The blacksmith at the village some twenty leagues away had given Dunmore the location. It had taken a few broken fingers and a broken nose, but Dunmore had gotten what he wanted.

"Peter, come out," Dunmore called. "I know you're in there. You doona want to make me come in for you."

A moment later the door creaked open and Peter stuck his head out. His mousy brown hair was tangled and matted around his face. He was thin, more thin than usual, as if he hadn't eaten a proper meal in weeks. Months even.

"Dunmore?" Peter said, his voice low and his eyes scanning the area chaotically.

Dunmore put his hands on his hips. "What's got you so afraid?"

"Some people in the village found out what I was tellin' ye. They didna like it much and banished me."

"And the coin I'd given you?"

Peter shrugged and opened the door wider. He didn't step outside, but he straightened to his full height. "I lost it while I fought for my life."

"I didna figure it would take people long to realize you weren't the kindhearted man you pretended to be. What would they care that you told me about the Druids?"

Peter folded his arms over his chest and shivered. "I . . . I didna know until they told me."

"Told you what?" Dunmore asked and took a menacing step toward Peter. Something was wrong, but he cared little of Peter's trouble. All he wanted was answers so he could find a Druid and return it to Deirdre.

"At one time my village had been occupied by Druids," Peter said softly. He wiped at his nose and blew out a deep breath. "They used to come often and heal the sick. They would assist the harvests to grow in bad years as well."

"So?"

"The more I told ye where the Druids were, the fewer of them came. The sick stayed sick. Bad harvests didn't grow. The village went from thriving to dying in a matter of decades."

Dunmore laughed and dropped his hands. "Just what

I wanted to hear. You were doing your duty, Peter. And were rewarded handsomely."

Peter's gaze dropped to the ground and he turned away. Dunmore was no fool. Something else had happened.

"I need the location of at least one Druid, Peter. I'll take you with me as a reward this time. You can live in the mountain with us and rejoice in our victories. No more hunger, no more cold nights."

Peter shook his head so vigorously that he nearly toppled over. "Nay. I cannot."

"Cannot or will not?" Dunmore demanded. "You were willing before. So what if the village tossed you out? I will give you all that you dream."

Peter stepped into his hut and slammed the door. "They'll kill me," he screamed through the wooden door. "The Druids saved me as a child from a fever that took me two brothers. They saved me, and I betrayed them."

"What you doona want to do is betray me now, Peter." Dunmore ground his teeth together. He'd have to beat more information out of someone today. Not that he minded. He had always found great pleasure is bringing others pain.

"Go away," Peter yelled. "I willna tell ye anything else."

Dunmore walked to the cottage. He kicked open the door and stepped over the threshold. He scanned the small hut with one glance. It reeked of urine and something rotting.

Peter was huddled in a corner shaking. Dunmore grabbed him by the collar and jerked him forward. Peter was tall but weighed nothing, so it was easy for Dunmore to haul him outside.

Dunmore tossed Peter to the ground and smiled when he heard Peter wince and curl onto his side. "I'm just beginning, Peter. You've seen me beat others to death before. Doona think I'll spare you."

"What ye'll do to me is nothing compared to what the others will do."

Dunmore was growing tired of this. "What others? The Druids? They're running for their lives, Peter. They doona have time to worry of your stinking flesh."

"Nay. They keep watch on me."

Dunmore motioned with his hand to tell the wyrran to take a look around and bring back anyone they found. If there was someone out there the wyrran would find them. Until then, he'd get what he needed from Peter.

An hour later Peter was dead. Dunmore cursed and kicked him in the gut. Peter had been so malnourished that with the first punch Dunmore had broken his ribs. No matter what Dunmore did to him or promised him, Peter would tell him nothing.

Dunmore growled his annoyance. He would not fail Deirdre, not now, not when she needed him.

The wyrran returned, their big yellow eyes watching him soberly. They were empty-handed as well. Peter had been terrified for nothing. And Dunmore didn't have a location on a Druid.

He grabbed the reins to his horse and jumped onto his back. He didn't have time to waste. He'd return to all the places where he'd found Druids before. There had to be one foolish enough to think they were safe.

As Dunmore rode away with the wyrran behind him, he never saw the falcon that watched from high in the trees.

Hayden bristled as he watched Ian and Isla enter the great hall deep in conversation. Once again Isla said something to make Ian chuckle, which only angered Hayden all the more.

He had been the one to awaken Isla's passion. He had

been the first one to taste her decadent body. Yet she had never tried to make him smile.

You never gave her reason to.

Hayden growled, hating his conscience at that moment.

"If looks could kill," Camdyn mumbled from beside him.

Hayden glanced at the Warrior. "What's that suppose to mean?"

"It means exactly what he said," Malcolm said.

Hayden glared at the only mortal man at MacLeod Castle. He respected Malcolm for putting his life on the line for their cause, but he didn't like anyone poking their nose in his business.

Duncan smiled, clearly enjoying Hayden's distress. "Are you envious of my brother, Hayden? I didna think you could get away from that *drough* fast enough."

"She has a name," Hayden ground out.

Duncan snorted derisively. "What do you care?"

Hayden stood as Ian walked to his brother's side. Hayden knew he couldn't sit across from Ian and not punch him. He could smell Isla's snow and wild pansy scent on Ian, and it sent Hayden's blood to boiling.

He strode from the great hall and didn't look back. He'd eat later once the evening meal was over. Besides, someone needed to keep watch over the castle.

Hayden settled himself on the battlements near one of the crumbling merlons and tried to clear his thoughts. Fallon had taken most of the guards off rotating duty, and the castle was down to just a few. Isla's shield allowed them to do things other than stand watch.

He gazed at the sky with its vibrant colors of orange and bronze and purple as the sun descended. Pinpricks of light began to show in the darkening sky as the moon awoke and took her place in the heavens.

It was Hayden's favorite time of day. The world was going to sleep while a different world began to awaken. There was a moment between when the sun set and night took over where everything was gray and quiet.

It was usually a peaceful time, but once again all Hayden could think about was Isla and the turmoil that was now his life.

How he could want someone so fiercely who was everything he hated? It didn't seem right that fate should give him something like this when he was doing everything he could to stop evil from taking over the world.

Maybe it was his punishment for killing so many *droughs*. He hadn't murdered them, though. He had given them a fair chance at defeating him, and with their magic, many had nearly succeeded. But it was his need for vengeance that drove him onward.

How many years had he walked Scotland searching for *droughs*? He hadn't ever stopped to wonder if they had families. All he had been concerned about was the evil inside them.

Looking back, he wondered if he'd done the right thing. What if he'd killed Isla on one of his many rampages? He'd never have known the feel of her lush body or enticing lips. His emotions wouldn't be tied in knots right now either.

He turned and lifted his face to Isla's tower. He'd see the light from her window whenever she lit the candle. He intended to have a few words with her.

If he hadn't felt the obstruction of her hymen himself he'd think she'd been lying about being with other men. But he had pierced that barrier, had seen her blood with his own eyes.

You claimed her. She's yours to do with as you please.

Hayden knew that wasn't true, but that didn't stop him from wanting to confront her, to lay claim to her body once more despite how wrong it was. He'd never had the need to take a woman regardless of the consequences, regardless of who she was. It alarmed him, but his hunger for her overshadowed everything else.

The castle door opened and drew his attention. He watched as Fallon, Lucan, and Quinn walked into the bailey. They stopped in the center and faced each other, their faces solemn and set.

"I'll go hunting tomorrow," Quinn said.

Fallon nodded. "Take Duncan with you. I think he may need a bit of time away."

"I agree. His anger at what happened to Ian hasn't diminished as I'd hoped it would. It's only been a few days, but I'm worried."

"Talk to him," Lucan said. "Have Ian talk to him as well. The last thing we need is two Warriors on the edge."

Fallon crossed his arms over his chest and shifted feet. "I agree that Hayden has always been a wee bit intense in battle, but we all are. Just because he became angry at Ian doesn't mean anything."

"It means a lot," Quinn said, his voice sounding weary.

"Hayden's problem is Isla. We all know that." Lucan looked from Fallon to Quinn.

Fallon lifted a shoulder. "If Isla has her way, Hayden willna have a problem for long."

"Ah, doona start," Quinn said and ran a hand through his dark hair. "It's all Marcail will talk about. She's not happy we pledged to do as Isla asked. She thinks there has to be another way."

"If there was another way, Isla would have found it," Lucan pointed out.

Fallon held up a hand when Quinn began to speak. "You aren't saying anything we didn't say to Isla, Quinn. She asked for our pledge and we gave it. All we can do now is pray that Deirdre stays in her weakened state and that Logan and Galen find the artifact."

"And that it somehow works to break Deirdre's hold," Quinn added.

Lucan sighed. "Aye. It's no wonder Isla feels as if the odds are stacked against her. They are."

"At least Ian is proving to be someone she can talk to," Fallon said. "She needs someone she can lean on, even if she doesn't realize that's what she's doing."

"Marcail made a good choice." Lucan smiled at his brothers.

Quinn turned back to the castle. "Speaking of my wife, she said Isla made more of those pastries. Marcail has a sweet tooth, it seems."

Fallon slapped Quinn on the back as they started toward the castle steps. "You just want to make sure you have your share of pastries before Marcail eats them all."

"I think she is going to give Galen a run for his money on the food around here," Lucan said with a laugh before they entered the castle.

Hayden blew out a breath as his mind struggled to process all that he'd heard. Just what had Isla made the brothers promise? He feared he already knew what it was, and he'd be damned if he let anyone take her head.

It seemed an eternity before he saw the flicker of light from her window. Hayden didn't hesitate to unleash his god and vault onto the side of the castle. He climbed his way up to the tower and stood in her window.

He paused, content to watch her without her notice. She looked miserable and exhausted. She looked lonely.

Hayden no longer concerned himself with the feelings that always arose when he saw Isla or thought of her. There was nothing he could do to stop them. He could try to act against them, but stopping them had proved futile.

She turned then and spotted him. "I'm not in the mood, Hayden. Please go away."

He ignored her and jumped through the window. He landed softly. "What did you ask of the MacLeods?"

Isla rolled her eyes and began to unbraid her hair. "That's none of your concern. Please leave."

"Not until you tell me what I want to know."

"You'll be waiting a long time then."

Irritation filled him. He'd asked a simple question. Why couldn't she answer it? "You want them to kill you, don't you?"

She lifted a shoulder in a half-hearted shrug. "What difference does it make?"

"It makes a difference."

Her gaze jerked to his, and she narrowed her eyes. "Is that so? It seems that I remember quite plainly how you said you couldn't stand to be near me. In front of everyone in the hall. What I do with my life is no concern of yours."

"Just tell me. Please." He hated to beg, but the need to know exactly what she had asked of the MacLeods drove him.

"Oh," she stormed and threw up her hands. "Fine, Hayden. Aye, I did make the MacLeods vow to take my head."

"Why?"

"Would you rather be the one to kill me? I'm sure they won't mind if you step in for them. You'll know when Deirdre has control of me, so don't hesitate to do your duty."

"Stop!" he bellowed. He stared at her, his jaw clenched tight as he fought the fury inside him, fury at her for turning to the MacLeods. "That's not what I meant, and you know it. Now tell me why, Isla."

She blew out a breath and glared at him. "Because I don't want to live like this anymore. When Deirdre does find me, my death needs to be quick before she can cause me to hurt anyone else."

"You really want this?"

"Do I want to die? Nay, but neither do I want to live in constant fear of hurting the people who I call friends."

That made Hayden remember Ian and what brought him to her to begin with. The thought that she now shared her bed with Ian soured his stomach. "I suppose that includes Ian."

"It does," she answered without hesitation.

"It didn't take you long to replace me in your bed, did it?"

Her ice-blue eyes went wide with shock and then anger. She took two steps and slapped him hard across the face.

Hayden hadn't predicted that. His cheek stung, and he knew if he looked in a mirror there would be an imprint of her hand. He jerked his head around to give her a piece of his mind when she raised her hand to hit him again.

He captured it before she could connect it to his face a second time. To his surprise she raised the other, which he easily caught. "Not a good idea, Isla," he ground out as he pushed her back against the wall until she was trapped.

"You're an arse, Hayden."

"Maybe, but at least I give my lovers a day before moving someone else into my bed."

"You know nothing. Nothing. You speculate and assume."

"I know what I see."

Her chest rose and fell with each heavy breath, anger coming off her in waves. Her beautiful ice-blue eyes were bitter and hard as she glared daggers at him.

He realized then just how close to her he was. He

could feel her heat, her softness, and the passion coiled tightly within her.

And it was his undoing.

He tried to look anywhere but her eyes. It was only her fury that kept him from kissing her. He'd be damned if he'd make that mistake again and get caught up in her body, forgetting everyone and everything.

THIRTY

Isla couldn't believe Hayden would actually think Ian was her lover. She had never dared to slap anyone before. As soon as her hand had connected with his face, the need to hit him again had been too powerful to resist.

It had released something inside her, released the anger that had built.

But Hayden had been too quick. He'd ensnared both her wrists and trapped her against the wall. The cool stone to her back, and his warm body at her front.

It took less than a heartbeat for her indignation to turn to searing desire. She didn't want to feel anything for Hayden, especially after he had embarrassed her so, but her body refused to listen.

Hayden's face was breaths from hers. She stared into his fathomless black depths and knew she was his, knew resisting would only cause herself more heartache. There was no getting away, and she wasn't sure she wanted to.

Aye, he had hurt her. Terribly. But what he made her feel, how he made her come alive whenever he was around, was beautiful and like a dream come true.

It was something Isla never thought to experience for herself, yet here it was, right in front of her. Could she—should she—walk away?

Hayden seemed to understand at that moment that

something had changed. His gaze searched her face, and he leaned down as if to kiss her when suddenly he began to pull back.

Isla wanted Hayden, wanted all the distrust and anger that came with him. Without a second thought she rose up on her toes and placed her lips on his.

He jerked and stood motionless. Isla kissed him again, and this time Hayden came out of his stupor. His mouth greedily devoured hers in a kiss that left her breathless and aching for more.

His lips were firm yet gentle, demanding yet seeking. His tongue swept into her mouth and stole her breath—and her soul. His kiss was urgent, passion-filled, and seductive.

It never entered her mind not to give all of herself in return. She opened her body, opened her heart and dove into the seductive passion she knew awaited her in Hayden's arms.

She wanted her arms around his neck, to feel the slide of his silken hair through her fingers, but he still held her wrists. Imprisoned, trapped by his solid body.

The feel of his hot, hard shaft against her stomach sent flutters of excitement through her. Her blood turned to fire and heat settled between her legs, throbbing and insistent.

His hands flattened against her palms for a moment before he threaded his fingers with hers. Connecting them, uniting them on the basest of levels.

Yet Isla couldn't help but feel as if an invisible thread wove them together, binding them in ways only they would be able to detect.

Hayden moaned deep in his throat and leaned his body against hers. She wanted to wrap her hands around his arousal again, to feel the steely strength of his cock as she brought him pleasure. She wanted to take him into her mouth until he came, until he shouted her name.

His hands caressed down her arms to her sides then to her back where he crushed her to his chest, locking her tightly against him, as he turned them away from the wall. He bent her over his arm as his mouth traced a hot, wet trail from her jaw down her neck.

One moment they were standing, and the next Isla was on her back on the bed. She stared up at Hayden as he looked down at her. His black eyes watched her with a measure of lust and wonder. Unable to stop herself, Isla ran a thumb over his wide lips.

He turned his head into her hand and kissed her palm. Achingly tender, lovingly gentle.

The yearning she saw in his eyes made her heart leap into her throat. How could someone who hated her so much want her so desperately? She didn't understand it, and at the moment, none of it mattered.

He made her feel adored, treasured, beautiful. Wild and awakened. Erotic and aroused.

As soon as he reached for the pin holding his kilt, Isla jumped from the bed and began to jerk off her clothes. They couldn't come off fast enough. She heard a rip and knew she would have to mend her gown later but didn't care.

The feel of Hayden's large hand on her back sent chills running over her skin. He smoothed her hair out of the way and kissed her shoulder. She shivered as his fingers traced her scars.

Her heart caught in her throat. Her back was repulsive, vile. She didn't know if she could stand to have him look at it as he was, but she couldn't move.

"You're beautiful."

Her eyes clouded with tears. No one but her father had ever called her pretty. To hear it from Hayden, now, filled her with emotions raw and intense that left her exposed, afraid.

Isla turned to face him, uncaring if he saw the tears or not. He sank to the bed, and she knelt in front of him. She cupped her hands on either side of his face and let him see how much his words meant.

She had no experience with what was happening to her. She wasn't sure if she should say something or keep it locked away to look at later in the quiet of her dreams.

Hayden took the decision from her when he kissed her again softly, gently at first, then the fire took them both. The kiss deepened, pulling them both into the flames of passion. His kiss demanded everything of her, and she eagerly, easily gave it to him.

His hands were everywhere. He teased, he caressed, he tempted. Every place he touched burned for more of him, more of what they were together.

He laid her on the bed and straddled her hips while his mane of golden locks framed a face filled with desire so fierce, so searing that it stole her breath.

His hand stroked her jaw and neck before he splayed his fingers and slid his hand down between her breasts to her stomach.

Isla trembled with a need so great she didn't think it would ever be quenched. Hayden bent forward as his body moved to cover hers. She loved the feel of him atop her, loved the way his skin moved over hers.

Her hands roamed his shoulders and neck before her fingers plunged into his cool, clean locks. She held onto him then as he began weaving his seductive passion around her.

Hayden cupped her breasts in each hand and smiled devilishly at her before he captured a nipple in his mouth. Isla gasped as she felt him suck at the tiny nub before giving it a gentle nibble.

She tried to watch him, but she was caught on a wave of passion as dark and promising as Hayden's midnight eyes. Desire turned her blood molten, her body yielding and eager.

His lips drew back so she could see her nipple caught in his teeth. He tugged, giving just enough pressure with his teeth that pleasure speared through her body to center at her sex, making it throb to feel him deep inside her, moving and filling her.

With Isla, Hayden found he always wanted more. Nothing was ever enough. He couldn't kiss her enough, touch her enough, or desire her enough. He couldn't know her body enough, pleasure her enough, or claim her enough.

He loved watching the play of emotions cross her face as he fondled her. She was so responsive to his every touch that it made it easy for him to discover what pleased her most.

Hayden wanted to spend hours feasting at her breasts, but when Isla's hand reached between them and stroked his aching cock, he couldn't wait another moment to be inside her.

He rose over her, his hands braced on either side of her head. He let her guide him to her opening and felt the slick moisture there, the heady heat of her waiting for him. She was more than ready for him. And he couldn't linger another moment.

As soon as the tip of him was inside her, he thrust his hips forward, hard and fast, burying himself deep. The feel of her hot, tight walls surrounding him was the most wonderful, the most soul-awakening sensation.

He didn't want to think about what she was anymore. He didn't want to see his dead family anymore. All he wanted, all he craved, was the woman in his arms.

When she wrapped her legs around his waist and locked her ankles together it only spurred Hayden's need.

He tried to keep his pace slow to prolong the exquisite torture, but Isla wanted none of that.

He matched her tempo, his hard, deep thrusts filling her, stretching her time and again. He felt her body stiffening, felt the desire growing quickly and knew she was close.

His hips bucked, seeking to drive deeper into her, to give the same pleasure, the same ecstasy she gave him.

"Hayden," she screamed and raked her nails down his back. Her back arched, her head thrown back as she peaked.

He watched in awe as her body trembled beneath him as pleasure overtook her. As her stunning ice-blue eyes opened and focused on him. In her depths he saw pleasure, aye, but he also saw something deeper, something more profound.

Before he could wonder at it, he found himself reaching his own orgasm. Her hands smoothed over his back as he plunged inside her once more and gave himself over to the climax.

His arms shook as he struggled to hold himself up while he was carried on the wave of pleasure so intense, so driving that he knew he'd never be the same again.

Hayden let himself drown in her eyes, wondering what had just happened and afraid to ask. He lowered his forehead to hers and shared a satisfied smile. Her hands, however, never stopped touching him.

It wasn't long before it became difficult to keep his eyes open. He rolled onto his back and pulled her with him. He didn't question his need to keep her near, just gave in to it as he had everything else that night. She cuddled in the crook of his arm, her head on his chest and her hand over his heart.

She fit perfectly against him, as if she had been made just for him.

The last thing Hayden thought before he fell asleep was how right it felt to be with Isla.

Isla woke with the light of dawn filtering through her window. She was on her side facing where Hayden had been. The spot was empty now. She tried not to let his absence ruin the glow of their wondrous night, but it was difficult. The only evidence of him was the hollow in the pillow where his head had been.

She was disappointed. She had thought he might stay the night, but she should have known better. Isla ran her hand over the pillow and wondered when Hayden had left.

How would he act when she saw him later? Would there be contempt now? She sat up, clutching the linens to her chest. That's when her gaze landed on Hayden sitting in the chair studying her.

"You thought I left," he said.

She nodded.

His mouth twisted wryly. "It would have been the easiest thing to do. I couldn't, though."

Her stomach fell to her feet. Whatever was to come, she knew it wouldn't be good. "Why?"

He leaned forward so that his forearms rested on his knees. His head dropped for a moment before he raised it to look at her. "I came here last night to understand why you had asked the MacLeods to kill you. I also wanted to know why you had turned to Ian so quickly."

"I never took Ian to my bed," she inserted hastily.

His gaze bore into hers, searching for the truth. He must have found it because he gave a single nod of his head.

"What happens now?" she asked.

"I doona know. I've never been so befuddled in my life, Isla." He slapped his hand on his thigh before he rose to his feet and paced in front of the bed. "I've never had difficulty making decisions before. And I doona like it."

She knew what his dilemma was, but it was nothing she could help him with. "I am what I am, Hayden. I'm sorry for it. I should have been stronger, I know. Instead, I became a *drough*."

"For your family." He paused and turned to her. "Do you believe I think you weak?"

Isla shrugged and drew her knees to her chest. "It's what I think of myself."

"I would have done anything to save my family. Anything. You did what you had to do."

His eyes glittered with intensity. She knew in that moment that he would, in fact, do whatever it took for his family. And right now, everyone at MacLeod Castle was that family.

Everyone except her.

"What's the reason you are so confused?" She knew the answer, but she wanted him to say it.

Hayden blew out a ragged breath and looked away. "You know the reason."

"Say it."

"Why? You know it."

Isla would not relent in this. He had to admit it to her, to himself. "Say. It."

He jerked his head to her, his nostrils flaring and his face set in hard lines. "All right. You're a *drough*. I loathe *droughs*. I vowed to my family I would kill them all, especially the one responsible for their deaths."

Finally. She had wanted to hear him say it, but now that he had, she wished he hadn't. He hated the very thing she was. How could they continue on in any sort of fashion? Not even the night they had shared when she was sure he had opened himself to her had done anything to change that.

The simple answer was that they couldn't.

He blew out a harsh breath. "I had always protected my family. I was the one they looked to, and I failed them. I wasn't there to fight off the *drough*."

She wanted to tell him it wasn't his fault, but she knew he wouldn't listen. It was easier to blame oneself than see the truth that nothing could have prevented what happened to his family.

"I have one question for you," she said. "If you had known I was a *drough* when you found me on Cairn Toul, would you have left me there?"

His muscle worked in his jaw as he clenched it. "Without a second thought."

At least he told her the truth. It may not be what she wanted or needed to hear, but it was the truth.

"Then I got to know you. The attraction between us began the instant I found you on Cairn Toul. I tried to deny it, tried to ignore it. But I cannot deny or ignore you."

His words were a balm to her soul. Yet she saw the torment in his black eyes, saw how he suffered from her presence. He might desire her, but he still didn't like her. "I will be gone soon, and your life can return to the way it was."

"Do you mean dead or gone?"

Isla had already decided that either way she would ask the MacLeods to take her head. She hadn't lied last night. She was tired of living this life. "Does it matter?"

He looked away and she smiled ruefully. "Ah. I see. You want to make sure I'm dead so there will be one less *drough* around."

"That's not what I said."

"You didn't have to say it. I saw it on your face."

He face mottled with fury as he faced her. "Doona put words in my mouth."

"So you don't think Scotland would be better with one less *drough*?"

"Isla. Enough."

She rose from the bed, still holding the linen sheet against her. "All I'm asking for is the truth. Is that so much to ask? You've been honest with me until now. How is this different?"

He only stared at her in response.

"You have every right to hate *droughs*. They took your family from you in the most heinous way. *Droughs* are evil. The ceremony is meant to bind them with wickedness. Everything a *drough* does, everything a *drough* says is steeped in malice."

"I know," he ground out through clenched teeth.

Isla raised a brow. "So *droughs* need to be killed?"

"Aye," Hayden finally admitted.

She dragged in a shallow breath. That had hurt far more than she anticipated. "Will you make sure I'm dead? The MacLeods gave me their vow, but I know they don't really want to do the deed. Ian is the same. I know there is only one man here who would make sure it's done."

Hayden turned his back to her. "I couldna do it when I first discovered you were *drough*. What makes you think I can do it now after sharing your bed?"

"Because you know how important it is that Deirdre not be able to control me."

"You must think me some kind of monster with no heart."

Isla sighed and stepped closer to him. She raised her hand to place it on his back, intent on offering him comfort. At the last moment she changed her mind and dropped her arm.

"Nay, Hayden. I think you're a man who is loyal to a fault. I think you're the type of man who wants to save everyone. I think you're the type of man who will honor a vow, no matter how difficult it may be."

Hayden turned to face her. "Do you intend to have everyone's pledge at the castle to kill you?"

"If I must. It's the right thing to do."

"Is it?"

"Of course."

He snorted and shook his head. "I will give you my word to end your life, but I will do it when I think the time has come. Not when you wish it."

"If that was the case, Hayden, I would ask that you kill me now."

Her words startled him. His brow furrowed deeply. "You think you have no other choice?"

"I know I don't. I've lived five centuries in an evil mountain surrounded by the darkest kind of cruelty. I've been alone for so long, and I don't want to spend another day like that."

"You aren't alone. Not here."

"I have nothing to live for."

"And if you did have something?" he asked. "Would you fight Deirdre?"

She laughed though there was no humor in it. She turned away before he could see the tears that filled her eyes. She was more alone than ever before.

After having Hayden, after getting a glimpse of what life could be like with him, nothing could ever replace that. "What would I have to live for? Deirdre's demise? That can be accomplished without me."

"Live for me."

Isla's lungs seized, her breath refusing to leave her body. She was afraid to turn around, afraid to look into Hayden's eyes and see him mocking her.

Did she have the strength to fight Deirdre? Could she

stand against something so evil? For Hayden she would walk through Hell itself.

Silence stretch endlessly before she glanced over her shoulder to give Hayden his answer, to tell him she would live for him.

Somehow she wasn't surprised to find Hayden had left.

THIRTY-ONE

Hayden stared at his morning meal without seeing it. He wasn't hungry, not even after having missed the previous evening meal.

His mind whirled with the conversation he'd had with Isla. Hayden had woken early, but had been unable to leave her. He'd sat instead and just watched her.

He didn't think he had ever watched another person sleep before. It was a new experience, and one that mesmerized him.

She had lain there looking so tempting and beautiful that it was easy to forget she was a *drough*. The small smile on her lips when she'd awoken had made his heart quicken, but the grin vanished when she'd found him gone from the bed.

Then she had asked for answers he hadn't wanted to give, had been afraid to give. The more he'd said, the harder it became. He had hurt her. She had tried to hide it, but his words had cut her deeply.

But no more deeply than her telling him she knew he would kill her.

He hadn't known where the words had come from when he asked, urged her to live for him. As soon as they had been spoken, he knew he could never kill her.

The words had been spoken from the depths of his soul,

and as the silence had stretched in the tower, he realized she either couldn't or wouldn't answer him.

Not that he blamed her. So he had left before he heard her response. The things he had said to her, the things he had done were atrocious. He didn't deserve anything for acting like such a beast.

Hayden rested an elbow on the table and put his hand over his face. Everyone ignored him, which was just what he wanted. He picked up bits of discussion here and there but nothing he wanted to contribute to.

He both hoped and dreaded to see Isla. After what had happened last eve and that morning, he wasn't sure how he would react upon facing her. Not to mention seeing Ian with her.

She smiled for Ian, laughed for Ian. How Hayden hated the boil of envy that caused him.

"You look like death," Malcolm said as he glanced up from his trencher.

Hayden rubbed the back of his neck. "You mean I look like you?"

A ghost of a smile touched Malcolm's lips. "Aye. This doesna happen to have anything to do with the beautiful Isla, does it?"

Hayden looked away, but Malcolm must have gotten his answer because he shook his head.

"I thought as much," Malcolm mumbled.

"Why do you say that?"

Malcolm shrugged his left shoulder. "It isna hard to see there is a deep connection between the two of you. She's lonely and hurting. You're confused and angry. There's an easy solution."

"What might that be?" Hayden couldn't help but ask. If someone had an answer, he wanted it.

"Forget she's a *drough*. She was forced to do the

ceremony, and she beat back her evil. In my mind, that makes her the strongest *mie* I've ever encountered."

"She's a *drough*, but not the same type that I've hunted and killed. That, I already figured out."

"I certainly don't think she's a *drough* so I'm glad you've gotten it all sorted out."

The sarcasm in Malcolm's voice made Hayden grin. "You think I mock you?"

"I think until you truly face what Isla means to you, you willna be able to see clearly."

Hayden gave Malcolm a nod before he rose and strode from the castle. There was work to be done, and it was just what he needed to sort through his thoughts.

Deirdre grew impatient the longer Dunmore was gone. She knew Druids were scarce across Scotland, but he should have been able to find one. That's all she needed, one insignificant Druid who she could sacrifice and gain the magic.

But it was taking too long. She'd tried to connect with Isla again, and had been unsuccessful. It left Deirdre drained of what little magic she had as well as weak. She hated it.

"I need my magic now," she seethed.

For nearly a thousand years she had been the strongest Druid ever to walk the earth. Now, she was no better than what her sister had been.

Deirdre wished she could have seen Laria's death. Had her sister lived to a ripe old age, bent and wrinkled? Or had she been taken while she was still young?

Deirdre had looked for her not long after she made Cairn Toul what it was, but Laria hadn't been found. Laria had no magic, so to sacrifice her would have just been for pleasure. It had been a touchy subject with her parents. As twins, their magic should have been shared, but Deirdre had gotten all of it and Laria none.

"I need my magic!" Deirdre screamed.

But her scream went unheard by all except the wyrran in the mountain. Others used to tremble when she spoke. How could this have happened to her?

The Warriors shouldn't have been able to harm her, but somehow something had happened that prevented her from fending off their attacks.

She would figure out what it was so that it never occurred again. She would not be put in this situation a second time.

Though Deirdre was nothing more than an invisible, floating mist, she still felt as if she had a body. She moved her arms, shifted her legs, and turned her head.

So when she sensed something in the chamber with her, something that wasn't a wyrran, she turned and watched in awe as the black cloud poured up from between two stones to surround her.

"Deirdre, Deirdre, Deirdre. Why are you ranting so?" the hard, deep, cold voice asked. The voice was soft, almost mellow, but she knew it could turn vicious in a heartbeat.

"My magic is gone."

The voice in the cloud laughed coldly, its evil evident. "Of course it hasn't. You can speak to your wyrran, and even Dunmore. Do you think that is done without magic?"

"Nay," she said. "But that is nothing to the magic I had."

The cloud was so thick she couldn't see out of it. She knew what it was, or rather who. It was *diabhul*, the Devil, the very being who had given her everything. She served him willingly, and he was the only thing she feared.

"I warned you about taking the Druids too soon.

Dunmore is having difficulty finding one for you. It could take weeks. Months even."

Deirdre cringed. That wasn't what she wanted to hear. "I will kill Dunmore if he fails me."

The cloud laughed again. "Ah, but you are an insatiable one. Do you think your revenge cannot wait? The MacLeods will still be there."

"I need Isla."

"I wondered when you would get to her. Be careful there, Deirdre. I warned you that Isla was stronger than you realized. Making her turn *drough* was not a good idea."

But Deirdre wasn't worried. "She's mine to control. There is no way for her to break the connection between us. As long as she's alive, she's mine."

"Hmmm," the cloud said. "I don't think you can still control her."

"Why do you say that?"

"She's with the MacLeods."

Deirdre stilled. She knew he would never lie to her. "She cannot escape me."

"Your anger is fierce, Deirdre. Feed off of it, nurture it. You will have vengeance and what better way to begin than inside MacLeod Castle? Use Isla to kill the Druids. Then let the Warriors kill Isla."

"Aye," Deirdre agreed. "Can you assist me?"

There was a moment of silence before the cloud began to thin and disappear back into the rocks. "You will have your wish, but I will expect something in return."

"Anything you want."

"I'll let you know what that is later. For now, grow your magic."

Deirdre instantly felt stronger. She waved a hand in front of her face and actually saw her fingers instead of nothing as before.

She concentrated on Isla, letting her fury build until it consumed her. Her magic increased enough that she could see herself in the mirror.

Deirdre wasn't whole yet. She could see through her body, but she was close, so close.

She would have Isla and her vengeance. And once Isla was back in Cairn Toul, Deirdre would punish her again and again until her anger was appeased.

It could take centuries, but Deirdre would have the time. There was nothing that could stop her now.

Isla put a hand to her forehead. The headache had begun not long after the morning meal as a dull ache and had only increased as the day progressed. No matter what Isla did, nothing would relieve the throbbing.

"What is wrong?" Ian asked from beside her.

Isla raised her head and forced a smile. "My head aches."

"Still?"

She saw the worry in his eyes. "I'm just concerned about everything. I'll be fine."

"Have you asked Sonya to heal you?"

Isla wouldn't ask for help unless the pain became unbearable. She raised a brow and went back to sweeping out the cottage. "If I don't feel better by the time we're done here I'll go to Sonya."

"Why doona I believe you?"

She smiled in spite of her pain.

"Does your head ache often?"

"Nay. In fact, this is my second since arriving here."

Ian scratched his whiskered jaw. "And before?"

"None like this." Her head always ached before Deirdre took control, but this felt different. Still. Could it be Deirdre?

Her blood turned to ice. It couldn't be happening already. If Deirdre had her magic, she could have easily gotten control of Isla's mind.

Isla's shield would have dimmed Deirdre's magic, but not enough to prevent it. Unless Deirdre was still very weak. None of which boded well for them.

If Deirdre was strong enough to cause Isla's head to hurt, then it was only a matter of time—a very short time—before Deirdre was strong enough to take over completely.

Isla dropped the broom and started out the cottage door. She had to tell the MacLeods. She took two steps outside before she ground to a sudden halt.

The sun blinded her and increased her agony until she could hardly breathe. She doubled over and bit her lip to keep from crying out. She reached out her hand for the cottage to help guide her when strong, familiar hands took hold of her.

"I've got you," Hayden said.

Isla had never been more relieved to be lifted in his arms. She wound her arm around his neck and buried her face in his shoulder.

"What happened?" he asked.

There were footsteps and then she heard Ian say, "It's her head."

"It hurts," Isla whispered. "The sun hurts my eyes."

Hayden rubbed his check on top of her head. "I'll get you somewhere safe. Trust me."

It never entered her mind not to. As long as Hayden was near, she knew she was safe.

THIRTY-TWO

Hayden hated the taste of fear in his mouth. It was made worse because he could see the hurt etched on Isla's face. She kept her emotions in check, so to show anything she must be in a terrible amount of pain.

Her hands held onto him tightly while she kept her head buried in his neck. Her body was tense, and she was much too pale.

He wished they had already been at the castle or that he could jump as Fallon did from one place to another without so much as a thought.

The walk to the castle was taking longer than Hayden wanted. At first he had taken long strides, but it must have jarred Isla because he heard her gasp in pain a few times. Hayden had shortened his steps while he tried to dodge any rocks that he might trip over.

Hayden could feel Ian's presence behind him. He didn't care. It allowed him to hold Isla while Ian could talk to the others and let them know what was going on. All Hayden wanted to do was get Isla somewhere dark so the sun would no longer harm her eyes and her head.

"We're almost there," he murmured. "Just a little farther, and I'll have you in your tower."

Her only response was a light pressure from her fingers on his neck. Hayden had never felt so powerless. He didn't know what was wrong or how to help Isla, but he would find a way.

Out of nowhere Broc landed beside Hayden and folded his massive wings behind him. "What happened?"

"I'm not sure," Hayden answered.

Behind him Ian said, "She complained about her head aching, and when she walked into the sun it seemed to grow worse."

"Sonya can help her," Broc said. "Sonya can heal anything."

Hayden had seen Sonya's magic, but he had his doubts. Especially if this had anything to do with Deirdre. "Let's hope you're right."

"I'll alert Sonya and the others." With that Broc leapt into the air and flew to the castle.

Isla moaned softly. "I'll be all right. I just need to get out of the sun."

Hayden didn't bother to answer her. She might think she would be fine, but he would make sure of it. He didn't stop and wonder why he would go to the ends of the earth to help Isla, he only knew that he would.

He'd seen her in pain, and all that mattered was her. All that would ever matter was Isla.

By the time he reached the bailey, Lucan and Fallon were waiting for him. Hayden walked to Fallon, ready to beg him to use his power.

"Ready?" Fallon asked a moment before he placed a hand on Hayden's shoulder.

In a blink the three of them were in the tower. Hayden felt Isla relax against him. He was about to lay her on the bed when he paused. Sunlight fell from her window and bathed the bed in light.

"I'll take care of it," Broc said.

Hayden hadn't even realized Broc was in the chamber.

He watched Broc take a blanket and fly to the window. Broc's wings held him suspended as he closed the shutters and draped the blanket over them to block out all the light.

Isla lifted her head a little and sighed. Though Hayden was loath to release her, he knew she needed to be on the bed so Sonya could try to help.

As Hayden was laying Isla down, she lifted her head and whispered, "Do not let Marcail near me. She might try to take the pain, and I would not have her or her unborn child harmed in any way."

"I promise," Hayden said and looked into her eyes still clouded with pain. "Now allow Sonya to help."

Hayden took a step back and then another. He had to force himself to give Sonya and Cara room to move, but it was difficult when all he wanted to do was hold Isla and try to make her better.

It wasn't long before Quinn and Marcail arrived in the tower. As soon as Hayden saw Marcail start toward the bed, he grabbed hold of her arm.

"I can help," Marcail told him when she tried to jerk her arm free and couldn't.

"Hayden," Quinn threatened behind him.

Hayden looked from one to the other. "I promised Isla I wouldn't allow Marcail near her. Isla is afraid Marcail might try to help her, and she willna have you or the babe hurt."

Marcail sighed, and then gave a small nod. "All right. I'll stay back, but if they need me, don't try to stop me again."

Hayden returned his attention the bed. Isla was curled onto her side with her back to him, her lips pressed into a tight line and her face even paler than before.

Sonya was bent over her, talking quietly. Every so often Hayden would see Isla's lips move in answer.

He was a Warrior. Immortal. With powers from an ancient god that could not be rivaled. But he couldn't help Isla. He hated the feeling, the frustration of being able to do nothing.

Hayden allowed his claws to lengthen and fisted his hands. His claws sank into his skin and he felt the blood run between his fingers. But it did nothing to help the turmoil inside him.

"Sonya will help her," Fallon said. "Give her time."

Hayden glanced at the eldest MacLeod. "And if she cannot? What if no one can help Isla?"

"Then we will figure something out."

"You think this is Deirdre, don't you?"

Fallon's jaw clenched before he gave a small jerk of his head. "It's a possibility."

Hayden didn't want to hear it, even if he knew it could be the truth. He couldn't lose Isla. He wouldn't lose her.

"You will not kill her," Hayden heard himself say. "If it is to be done, I will do it."

Fallon raised a dark brow in question. "I gave her my word."

"So did I just last night. I will do it." It would kill him, but he would be the one to give her the freedom she yearned for.

"Are you sure you'll be able to?" Fallon asked.

It would be the hardest thing Hayden had ever done, but he owed Isla at least that. "Aye."

"So be it."

Fallon walked away, but Hayden wasn't left alone for long. Broc crossed his arms over his chest, his gaze on the bed just as Hayden's was.

"Your blood is dripping on the floor," Broc said as if he were speaking of the weather. "I'm sure Isla willna approve."

Hayden unclenched his fists. "How is it we can do anything but stop the pain of others?"

"I have no answer for you. I'm just thankful we have a Druid with strong healing magic. Without Sonya we'd have already lost Malcolm, Larena, Quinn, and Marcail."

Hayden looked down at his palms that were already healed. "I've taken so many lives without a second thought."

"They were Warriors and wyrran of Deirdre's, Hayden. That doesn't count."

"Doesn't it?" he asked. "I've spilled so much blood. And the *droughs* I killed? Who am I to ask that someone be spared?"

Broc inhaled a deep breath. "What right does anyone have, yet everyone asks. If Isla can be helped, she's at the right place."

Hayden prayed he was right. His stomach churned each time he thought about having to take Isla's head. How many *droughs* had he killed? He'd lost count, it was so many.

"Have you finally admitted to yourself that you care for Isla?" Broc asked.

Hayden glanced over to find Broc's dark brown gaze on him. "Has it been that obvious?"

"To everyone."

"Aye, I've admitted it to myself. And now, to you."

"Does Isla know?"

Hayden shook his head. "Things have a way of getting out of control when I'm around her. She spins me about so that I cannot get my bearings."

"Ah," was all Broc said understanding laced through that one sound.

"I never wanted this."

"Those who seek it rarely find it. It's those who doona want it that it comes to them easily."

Hayden thought on Broc's words long after the Warrior had departed the tower.

Isla just wanted to be left alone. Now that she was out of the sun she could try and turn her mind to other things to help with the pain.

"Tell me where it hurts?" Sonya coaxed.

Isla would rather ignore her, but Sonya was persistent. She wouldn't leave until she had attempted to help Isla. "It began in my temples and now has gone down into my neck."

Sonya's cool fingers lifted Isla's braid and softly rubbed the back of her neck. "Does your head ache often?"

"Nay."

"But it does happen?"

Isla didn't want anyone to guess that Deirdre was the cause of it. Isla wasn't even sure herself, which is why she wanted to be left alone to think about it. "Occasionally."

"I'm going to try and heal you now," Sonya said.

Isla kept her eyes squeezed shut. Even without the sunlight, the candles that blazed to allow the others to see caused her head to throb more.

Every time someone so much as bumped the bed she had to bite back a moan of pain. She didn't want anyone, especially Hayden, to see just how badly she hurt.

Sonya's magic began to flow over Isla, the feel of it beautiful and sweet. It was strong and pure. Isla felt as if tree limbs were softly brushing over her, soothing her. It was an illusion of Sonya's magic that only other Druids would be able to detect, but it was lovely and did help to calm her.

It was just a moment later that Isla felt more magic. This time it was earthy and like a root that coiled around her giving healing energy. Cara, Isla realized.

Together the Druids did their best to take away the ache in Isla's head, but they could only manage to diminish it somewhat. It was enough that Isla was able to open her eyes, though.

"Save your magic," she told Sonya and Cara. "I just need to rest."

Isla heard Hayden bark Marcail's name. A moment later Marcail knelt beside the bed, her head even with Isla's. "Nay," Isla said. "Don't."

"Shh," Marcail whispered. "I won't take away the pain, though I would if you would allow me."

"It might harm your child."

Marcail smiled, a smile full of love and wisdom. "I feel my child's magic already. I don't think it would hurt the babe."

"Nay," she said again.

"As I thought you would say. If you won't let me take the pain, there is something you could try. Your have more magic than any of us here, so if anyone can do this, you can."

Isla felt a cool cloth on her forehead. "What is it?"

"When I do take someone's emotions, I have to let my magic surround me. If I don't, the emotions could very well kill me."

"I knew it," Isla heard Quinn grind out from somewhere in the tower.

Marcail didn't break eye contact with Isla. "Call your magic and let it fill you, let it protect you."

"And you think this will make the pain stop?"

"It helps to lessen my illness when I take emotions."

It was worth a try at least. "Can you have everyone leave?"

"Of course." Marcail rose to her feet. "Isla needs to be alone."

Cara wiped Isla's face once more. "I'll be back in a wee bit to check on you."

Isla smiled and let her eyes shut.

"I'm not leaving," Hayden said tightly.

Elation swept through Isla. His presence comforted her as nothing else could. She caught Cara's hand before she could leave. "He can stay."

Cara's smile was slow as it spread across her face. "Fallon. Quinn. Leave Hayden. Isla has asked that he be allowed to stay."

Cara's fingers squeezed Isla's for a moment before she walked away. It wasn't long before the door closed. Isla had her back to the door so she didn't know where Hayden was, and she feared turning over would cause more pain.

"None of it helped, did it?"

His voice was warm, deep, and soft as it drifted to her. "A little."

She wanted to feel his arms around her again, to have his strength surround her. It had felt so good to be carried by him. Hayden had sheltered her from the sun and protected her as much as he could. He might say he didn't care, but she knew he did. Deep down, he did.

And that was the problem. He did care. For a *drough*. Though he wanted to despise her, to shun her, she had heard the worry in his voice, felt the tenderness in his hands.

If she died right then, it all would have been enough. She had known the warmth of a skilled lover, the gentleness of a fierce Warrior. And it had all been for her alone.

Isla's heart swelled with the knowledge.

THIRTY-THREE

Isla wanted Hayden beside her. She wanted to feel his touch, his warmth. As if he had heard her silent plea, he loomed beside the bed staring down her.

"What can I do?" he asked.

"Hold me."

His brow puckered. "I doona want to hurt you."

"Your touch soothes, Hayden. I need you."

She didn't have to tell him twice. He kicked off his boots before he gently removed her shoes. He walked around the bed and crawled in behind her.

Isla sighed contentedly when he molded his body to hers. His warm breath fanned her neck, and he laid his arm next to hers as it draped her stomach.

"Is it Deirdre?" he asked.

"I'm not sure." And she didn't lie. "Before, when Deirdre would take over, the pain was blinding, but it never lasted long."

His fingers intertwined with hers. "So this is different. A result of Deirdre's loss of magic?"

"She didn't lose all her magic. You need to remember that. But, aye, it could be."

"Your shield? Would that hinder her?"

"If her magic was weak it could distort it."

He sighed and tightened his arm around her. "I want to help."

"You are. More than you know." She thought of Grania, of how her niece had died, and she found she wanted to tell Hayden. "I've something to tell you."

"What?"

"You know the little girl Fallon found in Cairn Toul?" She felt his head nod. "Aye. That was Grania."

"It was. While Deirdre was occupied fighting you, I went to Grania. I had already seen Lavena and knew nothing could help her, but I thought I could take Grania away."

His hand smoothed the hair away from the side of her face. "What happened?"

"She fought me. She had a dagger and tried to use it. She called Deirdre her mother."

"Deirdre corrupted her," Hayden murmured.

"Aye. I knew it then, but I couldn't give up. I tried to take the dagger away from her, but we slipped. Somehow, she fell on the weapon. She was dead by the time I realized what had happened."

His fingers with hers and gave her a slight squeeze. "It was an accident."

"I still killed her."

"And she's better off where she is. Deirdre no longer has control of her."

Isla knew he was right. She was glad he had listened to her. "I want to try what Marcail suggested. Sonya and Cara were able to lessen the pain."

"But it still hurts," he finished for her. "I can see it in your eyes and the way you hold your body. I would see it gone, Isla. Just tell me what you need."

He'd given her more than she could have ever thought

to want, and now he was offering her even more. "Don't leave me until I'm finished."

"I willna leave. As long as you need or want me, I'll be here for you."

The way he said it, with such conviction, Isla had no choice but to believe him. Finally he was giving her the words she needed, now, when it was most likely too late. "Thank you."

He kissed her neck. "Come. Let loose your magic so you can rid yourself of this pain."

Isla settled more comfortably against him and let out a deep breath. She found herself more relaxed with Hayden next to her, and that gave her the courage she needed to turn to her magic.

She then focused on her magic, channeling all that she was, all that she yearned for toward building her magic. It was difficult to push past the throbbing of her head. At times she lost her grip on her magic, but she continued to concentrate.

Once she had a firm grasp on her magic, she easily centered it and brought it around her. She could feel the pulse of her magic and hear the call of the ancient Druids, the ones who first settled Scotland so many centuries ago.

The pounding of her head grew more intense the further Isla called to her magic. She refused to give up, though. She thought of her mother, how she had smiled and told Isla her magic could do anything.

Isla hadn't believed her, had never believed. But now, she was determined to make it so.

Dimly, Isla could hear what sounded like drums beating a steady, seductive beat. It calmed her breathing, slowed her heart . . . and fed her magic.

Her magic engulfed her like a warm blanket. It held

her, but she didn't feel trapped. It eased her, comforted her. It was like a cloud she floated upon with nothing anchoring her to the ground.

It was then Isla realized the pain had receded to a muted ache. She became aware of how Hayden's fingers caressed her arm and the feel of his arousal pressed against her back. She heard his shallow breaths and felt the heat of his skin.

"Your magic does this to me," he whispered. "It pulls me, lures me to you. I want more of it, and more of you. It makes me wild, makes me want to claim you fiercely and repeatedly."

She didn't know what to say. She had never heard of magic affecting anyone like it did Hayden. Knowing she affected him so sent a thrill of anticipation and desire racing along her skin.

Isla carefully turned in his arms until she faced him. His black eyes were drowsy with desire, but they watched her closely while cocooned in his arms.

"Did it work?" he asked. "Your eyes are brighter, and your skin almost glows."

"The ache isn't gone, but it is lessened enough that I can tolerate the hurt."

He ran the back of his fingers across her jaw as his brow furrowed. "I doona ever want to see you in such agony again."

As much as she didn't want to talk about it, Isla knew she had to prepare Hayden. "There is a very good chance it was Deirdre. If it was, it means it's only a matter of time before she takes control."

"You can fight her."

He said it with such authority that for a moment Isla almost believed him. But she knew the truth, and he needed to know it as well. "I've tried in the past."

"You were alone then. Here you have friends who will help you, Druids who can add their magic to yours. You have me. I don't want to kill you, Isla."

She briefly closed her eyes and prayed it wouldn't come to that. "You took care of me today when I needed someone. I want to thank you."

Without giving him time to reply, Isla reached under his kilt and took his hard shaft in her hands. His length and thickness always took her breath away. Every time he entered her she was stretched and filled to aching awareness, and she could never get enough of him.

Isla pushed Hayden to his back and leaned forward to take him in her mouth. She wrapped her lips around his tip and slowly eased her mouth around his thickness. His moan, low and tortured, caused her to smile.

When she could get no more of him in her mouth, she wrapped her hands at the base of him and began to move her head up and down his rod. She loved the taste of him, salty and all male.

His hands fisted in the sheets as his hips rose to meet her each time her head came down. Isla glanced at him to find his neck stiff with tension, his lips parted as his harsh breathing filled the tower.

"Isla," he moaned. "You're killing me."

Just what she wanted to hear. She was about to settle more comfortably when his hands closed around her arms and jerked her up and over him.

"Nay," he said and nipped at her lips. "I want to be inside you when I come. I want to feel your walls clenching around me, milking me of my seed."

He pulled her head down for a kiss, a slow kiss filled with passion and promise. Yearning and need. Excitement and hope.

Hayden bunched her skirts in his hands. He wanted to

rip the gown from her body so he could feast his gaze upon her luscious curves and silken skin. Instead he broke the kiss long enough to pull her gown and chemise from her to toss it to the floor.

He leaned up on his elbows after Isla had unfastened the pin of his kilt. Together they got his shirt and tartan removed and piled next to her clothes.

Hayden reached for her, but before he could, she once more had her mouth on his cock. He groaned in ecstasy, surrendered to the pleasure.

He grabbed Isla's legs and turned her so that she was lying on his chest, her legs on either side of his head. Her sex was bared for him in all its glistening beauty.

While her hot mouth continued to pleasure him, Hayden buried a finger deep inside her as his tongue swirled around her clitoris. Isla's moan, deep and long, only served to push his desire higher, only fueled the deep raging need he had for her.

Every time he touched Isla, every time the desire took him, the connection between them strengthened, intensified. He had been a fool to not see it sooner, but his eyes were opened now. And he was going to prove to Isla he could be the man she needed.

He could feel her body tightening, her moans coming quicker. Hayden had much more planned for them. He didn't want her peaking too soon.

Hayden shifted them so he was on top, and then turned so he could kiss her. He gave in when Isla pushed on his chest and she rolled him onto his back.

The sensual, loving smile she gave him as she bent to lick his stomach made Hayden's heart skip a beat. Up his chest she kissed and licked until he thought he would burst from need.

Hayden, at the point of no return, situated Isla so that

she straddled him. He grabbed her by the waist and tilted her forward so that her breasts were even with his mouth. He flicked out his tongue and let it move back and forth over the tiny nub until it strained toward him, glistening and pebble hard.

He shifted to her other breast and repeated his teasing until her breaths came in short gasps and small cries of desire fell from her lips.

Isla's hips ground into him, her sweet sex, already wet and ready, grazed his aching cock repeatedly, sending him further and further toward the ecstasy that awaited him.

When he could take no more of the exquisite torture, he reached down and guided himself into her. She gasped, her eyes rolling back in her head with a pleasure-filled moan. Hayden, with his hands still locked on her hips, pushed her down on his length as he slanted his hips to thrust inside her.

Once he was sheathed to the hilt, he removed the binding of her braid. He worked his hands through her long, thick locks and let them slide over his arms.

He found her watching him, a warm smile on her face. He would thank Marcail later for her idea. Right now, he was just happy to see the pain erased from Isla's face.

To his surprise Isla sat up and braced her hands on his chest. She rotated her hips, sending bolts of desire straight to his shaft and through his body. He cupped her breasts, rolling her taut nipples in his fingers.

She cried out, her hips bucking faster. With her head dropped back and her hair grazing his legs, Isla was the most beautiful sight Hayden had ever seen, or ever would see.

He'd been a fool to think he could ignore her or his need for her. Her passion, allure, and magic stirred something deep and primitive inside him. And he found he quite liked it.

Hayden smiled as he thought about how lovely she looked when she peaked. Her face and body flushed with fulfillment. It was a heady sight, one he needed to see. Now.

He put his thumb in his mouth to wet it, then placed it on her sex with his fingers splayed over her stomach. Her nails dug into his chest at the first contact of his finger on her clitoris.

Her head lifted and her ice-blue eyes locked with his. He held her gaze as he ran his thumb around her with just enough pressure.

Isla's lips parted, her breathing hitched and her hips rocked back and forth, enticing him to his own climax. But Hayden wasn't about to go. Not yet.

She jerked and he felt her sex squeezing his cock as she peaked, her lips parted and rapture covering her face. Hayden kept teasing her clitoris to prolong her pleasure.

He smiled when she screamed his name and her nails drew blood. It was all he needed. His hand fit on her hips again as he lifted her so he could thrust hard and fast inside her.

His orgasm came quickly, engulfing him in the abyss of pleasure. He gave another plunge and felt his seed pour hot and quick inside her.

Isla fell forward on his chest, her face turned to the side. A fine sheen of sweat covered them both, and the only sound was their ragged breaths filling the chamber.

Hayden caressed down her hair and over her back. He was tired of running from Isla and this thing between them. It might never work, but how would he know if he didn't try?

For himself and Isla, he had to try. He just hoped she

was receptive to the idea. After everything he had done to her, he deserved for Isla to tell him to go away. And he would if that was her wish.

Hayden looked up at the window and saw light coming from the sides of the blanket. It was still daylight, but Isla needed rest. He also wanted to make sure the ache was gone from her head for good.

He couldn't stop the niggling worry that it was Deirdre. Isla had said it was different than usual, but he had seen the fear in her eyes. He had once vowed to protect her, and he would do just that.

Whatever happened to Isla, he would make sure he was with her from now on. She wouldn't have to face Deirdre alone. He would help her fight the evil, even if it meant sacrificing his own life.

"Sleep," he whispered. "I'll be here when you wake."

She murmured something he didn't understand. Hayden smiled. She'd already been half asleep.

And for the first time in years, Hayden let himself slip into a deep, dreamless slumber.

THIRTY-FOUR

Deirdre grinned as she looked at herself in the mirror. Almost whole again. And her magic was back. She closed her eyes and thought of Isla. The traitorous bitch was in league with the MacLeods, and it was time Isla remembered who ruled her.

To Deirdre's surprise there was a barrier around MacLeod Castle. It was strong, too. There was only one who might have that kind of magic—Isla.

That only fueled Deirdre's ire. It took her more time than she'd like to admit to build her magic enough to penetrate the shield.

And that's when she found Isla.

Deirdre laughed and rubbed her hands together in anticipation. It was going to be too easy.

"I'm coming for you, Isla."

There was blood everywhere. It coated the walls, the blankets, and the bed. Isla looked down at her hands to find it on her as well.

She gagged and tried to jump from the bed. Her feet tangled in the covers and she landed hard, her head hitting the floor with a thud and pain exploding in her body.

Isla propped herself up on her hands and kicked with

her feet until her legs were free. She was naked, her body streaked with thick, red blood.

Though her mind told her not to, she looked to the bed. There was Hayden, strong, commanding Hayden, now lying dead in a pool of his own blood.

His midnight eyes were turned to her. There was no life left in them, but she still saw the accusation, the betrayal in their depths.

Tears blurred her vision before trailing down her cheek. How could this have happened? How could Deirdre have taken over and she not known it?

"Nay," Isla said. "Nay!"

The castle was eerily quiet. Too quiet. Were the others dead as well? Was she to blame?

Isla stumbled to the bed, her feet numb with shock. She reached out a trembling hand and stroked a lock of Hayden's fair hair from his forehead.

Her heart stopped as she realized she had seen his face before. The same blood, the same black stare. It had been so long ago, but it was the first time she had ever came to herself after Deirdre had sent her on a mission.

"Dear Lord," Isla murmured. "I'm the one that killed Hayden's family. I'm the *drough* he's been searching for."

Unable to look at the man who had stolen her heart, the man she had betrayed, Isla turned and raced to the door. She started down the winding steps and tripped. A scream tore from her throat as she pitched forward and began to fall . . .

Isla gasped and sat up in the bed. Her heart hammered and sweat coated her body. She glanced at her hands, but there was no blood.

She was afraid of what she might find, but she had to know if she had killed Hayden. She turned her head to find him on his side facing her. His face was relaxed, his lips slightly parted as he slumbered.

Isla lightly caressed his hollowed cheek. She needed to tell him what she had done to his family. Everything they had bridged would be ripped apart, but he had a right to know. He'd spent years searching for the *drough* who had destroyed his family.

He had given her hope and a reason to continue on, and now she would repay that with a truth that would tear him apart. A lone tear trailed down her face. She hurriedly wiped it away.

She couldn't carry around this truth with her, as tempting as it was to do. Especially when she knew it had been Deirdre who had given her that awful dream. It was what Deirdre planned for her, but Isla wouldn't be a willing accomplice.

The MacLeods and other Warriors were strong. She knew Hayden would protect the Druids with his life, and she would help as much as she could.

Isla would do as Hayden suggested and fight Deirdre's command. She would make certain she was far enough away from MacLeod Castle not to harm anyone.

Though her heart tore in two, she rose silently from the bed and began to dress. She tried not to think of the joy and wonder she had found in Hayden's arms, of the love and hope he had unlocked inside her.

Love. Her stomach fell to her feet and her breath locked in her lungs. By the saints, she *loved* him. The knowledge made her heart swell. She had probably loved him from the moment she opened her eyes in the great hall and found him staring at her.

Why after all these centuries had she finally found happiness but was about to lose it all? If she thought there was time, she would wake him and have him carry out his vow. But she knew he would fight her and that would give Deirdre more time than Isla could allow.

Isla didn't want to wake the MacLeods either. It was better if she departed and did so immediately. Too much was at stake. These people had become her friends, her family. And Hayden . . . she never wanted to hurt him again. She'd done enough of that already.

She wished there was another way out of her tower. She didn't want to encounter anyone, but she didn't have a choice. After checking the space between the blanket and the window, Isla saw it was dark outside. Just what she needed.

With one last longing look at Hayden, she turned and went to the door. It opened without a sound. She closed it softly behind her and started down the stairs.

Every step that took her farther from Hayden was like a dagger to her heart. She couldn't stop the tears from flowing, and didn't even try. Her hatred for Deirdre began to burn brightly, causing her magic to swim around her.

Deirdre had now taken everything from Isla. If it was the last thing Isla did, she would make Deirdre regret ever bringing her to Cairn Toul.

Isla walked to the great hall without seeing anyone. She paused on the landing and looked around to make sure no one was about. If she had to, she would use her magic to make her escape. Too many lives depended upon her leaving the castle.

It was as if the castle held its breath with her as she reached the last step and hurried across the hall and out the castle door.

She pressed her back against the door once it closed behind her and searched the battlements. Even with her shield in place Hayden had kept Warriors on guard.

The gate was closed, and even though she could get through the small door in the massive gate, it might bring too much attention to her. Instead, Isla turned left to the postern door in the castle wall that was hidden between the blacksmith's shop and the chapel.

The shadows were her constant companions as she made her way toward the door. The latch was stuck from years of not being used, but eventually Isla got it unlocked. The door creaked loudly, the sound like a blast in the silence of the night.

She halted, her eyes glancing around her to see if anyone had heard. No one shouted for her to stop. She opened the door just wide enough that she could slip through, and then hastily shut it.

Hayden would find it unlocked. He would know that's how she left, but by then she would be long gone and too far away for him to find her.

Isla lifted her skirts in her hand so she could lengthen her strides as she ran. When she was far enough away from the castle, she turned and let her gaze search the towers, battlements, and the other places the Warriors liked to hide.

She saw slight movement on top of the main castle. Without a second's hesitation, Isla raised her hand and chanted the spell that would make the Warrior forget he saw her—at least for a while.

Isla was sure there was another Warrior, but time wasn't on her side. She raced to the village and then skidded to a halt in the center.

She looked toward the forests, then to the mountains in the distance. She didn't know when Hayden would awaken, but she did know the Warriors moved too fast for her to gain any distance on them. Then there was Broc.

There had to be some place she could go that they wouldn't think to look.

Isla turned and looked at the sea. The perfect solution. She thought of the beach near the castle, but the last thing she wanted was to be near the castle again and chance being seen.

Then she recalled Cara telling her about another beach the villagers used to use when they fished. Isla once more lifted her skirts and ran as fast as her legs would carry her.

Thick, angry clouds blocked the moon, creating an ominous feeling over the land. There was no scent of rain in the air, only black magic.

Deirdre.

"You always did like to show off," Isla murmured as she ran.

She reached the edge of the cliff and found the path that led to the beach. It wasn't as steep as the one at the castle, but it was treacherous just the same.

Isla navigated the path easily enough and started for the water. Her skirts would hamper her as she swam. She began to undress when she saw the small boat.

Could she be so lucky?

Isla rushed to it. It was turned over and completely out of the water. It took all of her strength, and considerable amount of time, just to flip it right side up. She wiped the sweat from her face with her sleeve and gave a mighty push.

It seemed to take an eternity before the rowboat began to move, and when it did, it was in small increments. But Isla eventually got it in the water.

She found two oars and threw them in the boat as she held on to the side. The water churned around her, soaking her skirts and weighing her down.

Isla didn't fight the water. She opened her magic and felt it grow, felt it seep through her skin. She would need her magic, all of it. After two tries, she finally made it inside the boat.

She cast a glance at the sky. If anyone looked up they would think a storm was about to break, and there was. Just not the kind everyone expected.

After taking up the oars she began to row. It didn't take long for Isla's arms to begin to tire, but she kept rowing as fast as she could. She couldn't get away from the coast, and the castle, fast enough.

That's when she remembered her shield. It was extended as far as her power would take it. There was no way to make it larger and expand to where she wanted to be. She would keep it in place until she passed the barrier. Her only hope was that Deirdre wouldn't send her wyrran to attack the castle once the shield came down.

The waves began to grow bigger, pushing her back toward the beach, but Isla kept rowing. She gritted her teeth and used her feet to give her added leverage as she moved the oars.

Isla knew the moment she passed through her shield. The barrier charged around her for a moment before disappearing altogether. She blinked through a new wave of tears and a heart that continued to break for Hayden. She rowed herself farther and farther from the castle, farther and farther away from the only man she had ever loved.

Pain exploded in her head, more ferocious than anything she had felt before.

"You fool," Deirdre's voice screamed in her head. "How dare you betray me? You will know the full extent of my wrath. Once I'm done with you, you'll beg me for death, but first, you will kill everyone at that castle."

Isla wanted to grab her head, to curl up in a ball as the throbbing continued. But she thought of Hayden, of what Deirdre had made her do to his family, and Isla kept rowing.

"Nay!" Isla screamed into the churning waves. "Get out of my head, Deirdre. I won't kill anyone else for you."

"Oh, you will," Deirdre said with a laugh. "You will kill them all!"

In the next instant lightning split the sky. Isla cringed, for she knew the lightning came from Deirdre. Isla could feel Deirdre's black magic spread over the water.

Isla wouldn't give up fighting, though. She would do it for Hayden, for the friendship she'd been offered by those at the castle. It was the least she could do for them. Deirdre would eventually win, but Isla wanted to give everyone enough time to prepare.

The lightning grew closer and closer, its booms louder and louder. Isla had seen Deirdre use her magic this way only once, and the outcome had been disturbing and brutal. Isla knew she would fare no better.

The first strike of the lightning made Isla drop the oars as her body froze amid the torment and blistering heat that scalded her skin. She screamed and crumpled over while Deirdre commanded her to return to the castle and kill.

Deirdre's magic wasn't as strong as before, but even in Deirdre's weakened state Isla had a difficult time keeping her from taking her mind. It was only the thought of Hayden that made Isla reach for the oars once more.

Hayden knew something was wrong as soon as he opened his eyes. He reached a hand over to Isla's side of the bed and found it cool to the touch. She had been gone for some time.

He threw back the covers and jumped from the bed. As he reached for his clothes, something strong and magical passed through him.

Isla's magic.

Her shield was gone. Which meant . . . she was gone.

Something inside Hayden snapped. Broke. The strange and new and glorious emotions he had let into himself just the day before crushed and left him . . . shattered.

He threw back his head and let out a roar that seemed to go on forever. Time stood still as his mind and heart raged. His god broke free, but Hayden didn't stop him. Hayden would never stop him now, not with Isla gone.

THIRTY-FIVE

Fallon's eyes flew open with the first crash. He sat up and looked over at Larena who was leaning on her elbow staring at him.

"What was that?" she asked.

Fallon shook his head the same time the second crash came. And then the howl. Whatever it was, it wasn't good.

"Get the Druids to safety," Fallon told her as he leapt out of bed and tugged on his breeches.

Larena was right behind him as he raced from his chamber. Fallon followed the roars to Isla's tower.

"Ah, shite," Lucan said as he came to stand beside Fallon.

Quinn joined soon after. "We need to get up there."

"Let me," Broc said.

Fallon looked over his shoulder to find Camdyn, Ian, Duncan, Arran, Ramsey, and Malcolm behind him. "I think it's going to take all of us."

"I'll go through the window," Broc said.

Fallon started up the stars, each crash, each bellow getting louder and more violent. When he reached the door, something smashed into it, splintering the wood.

Quinn kicked in the door, and all Fallon could do was stare in stunned silence. Hayden was nude, his god free as he raked his red claws down the stone walls.

The bed had been sliced in half, the linens ripped to shreds. Hayden had thrown the table at the door, and it now lay splintered on the floor.

"Holy hell," Quinn murmured. "She's gone."

Fallon had never seen a man so anguished, so devastated. "We've got to get him calmed down."

Hayden suddenly turned to the doorway. The red eyes of his god flashed with anger and sorrow. "Isla's gone, Fallon. She left. She left me."

Lucan took a step into the room, and Hayden picked up the chair and threw it at him. Fallon didn't waste another moment.

"We need to get him under control. It's going to take all of us!" he bellowed over Hayden's roar.

At that moment Broc busted through the window. Hayden swung toward him, his fangs bared. Fallon used that distraction to rush into the tower and wrap his arms around Hayden's shoulders.

Hayden fought like a wild man, hitting and clawing and snapping with his fangs. It took all ten of them, even Malcolm, to subdue Hayden. Even then he fought them. Fallon knew Hayden would continue until he was dead, and he wasn't about to lose a Warrior and a good friend.

Fallon wrapped a leg around Hayden's and tripped him. They all fell to the floor. Hayden had fallen face down with the weight of them, his breathing ragged and hoarse.

"Listen to me, Hayden," Fallon said through his own harsh breaths. "You doona know that she's gone."

Hayden groaned in misery and turned his head to the side. "The shield is gone. I felt her magic leave."

Fallon's gaze met Quinn's. This was bad. Very bad. There was only one reason Isla would have left.

"Deirdre," Quinn murmured.

"We can find Isla," Lucan told Hayden. "We can find her and protect her."

"She wants me to take her head," Hayden said, not hearing Lucan. "How can I do that? I gave her my word. I promised her I wouldna let Deirdre hurt her anymore."

Fallon jerked him. "Then help us. We're going to need you, Hayden. Isla needs you. Protect her as I know you can."

A moment later Hayden nodded and his red skin faded away as he once more took control of his body. Fallon motioned for the others to back away. He was the last to rise from Hayden.

"Where would she go?" Camdyn asked.

Hayden moved to his hands and knees before climbing to his feet. "As far from the castle as she could."

"I'll find her," Broc said. "She couldna have gone far."

"Far enough," Hayden murmured as he lifted the bits of linens and blankets to look for his clothes.

Fallon walked to the door. "We'll wait for you downstairs."

Hayden's chest ached. It felt as if his heart had been clawed out. He'd known there was a chance Isla would one day leave, but he hadn't expected it so soon. He should have known with her aching head the day before.

He looked about the tower, disgusted with himself at the destruction he'd caused. He'd destroyed Isla's things. Once he found her, he'd make it up to her.

If you find her. And if you find her in time.

Hayden didn't want to think like that, but he knew he had no choice. He left off his shirt and hurried to put on his kilt. He wrapped the ends of the kilt around his waist and hurried to the hall.

No sooner had Hayden stepped from the stairs than Broc burst into the castle.

"Hayden!" Broc called. "Come with me. Now."

He didn't hesitate to follow Broc. He heard the others moving behind him, knew they would follow. Hayden raced from the castle and in one leap, vaulted over the gatehouse. He kept Broc's flying form in his vision at all times.

It was the lightning that drew Hayden's attention. It seemed to be centered over the sea, in almost the exact same place every time. Lightning didn't react that way.

"Unless magic is involved," he whispered to himself.

Hayden found Broc hovering at the edge of the cliffs to a beach he'd seen only once.

"Down," Broc said.

Hayden jumped to the bottom. He landed smoothly and straightened. There was a sound behind him. He turned to find Quinn, Arran, Ian, and Duncan.

"We're here to help," Ian said. "Anything you need."

"I need Isla."

Broc dropped from the sky in a smooth movement and pointed out to see. "She's there, Hayden. In the boat."

Arran swore beneath his breath. "And I suppose the lightning is Deirdre?"

"Aye," Hayden mumbled. "Have you seen this before, Broc?"

The winged Warrior turned his face away. "Once. It wasna a pretty sight."

"But Isla is immortal like us. She heals."

"Which will only cause her more pain."

Hayden clenched his hands in aggravation. "What can we do? We need to get her away from Deirdre."

"If that's even possible," Duncan said.

Hayden hated that he was right. If only Logan was there. Logan had control over water. He could have Isla back on the beach in a matter of moments.

"I'm going to swim to her," Hayden said and pulled off his boots. "I willa let her suffer this alone."

"You'll likely die," Arran said.

Nothing mattered without Isla. His life had been dull and gray, somber and empty. She had given him light and opened his heart. She had given him everything. He could do nothing less. "Then so be it."

"Let me try," Broc said before he flew into the air.

Hayden waited and watched as Broc flew to Isla. Broc landed in the boat, and almost immediately, a bolt of lightning slammed into him.

It threw Broc out of the boat and into the water. Still, the Warrior didn't give up. He tried again, but each time he neared the small vessel, more lightning would strike.

"Enough," Hayden said. He had given Broc his try, but if anyone was going to save Isla, it was him.

He strode toward the beach and removed his kilt. He'd swum the sea often enough to know its currents. Hayden dove into the water and started swimming with strong, sure strokes. He kept sight of the boat, but he saw nothing of Isla. He prayed she was in the bottom of the boat and not in the water somewhere.

The lightning began to hit more often, and it was striking near him as well as the boat. He swam fast enough that it was difficult for Deirdre to determine where he would be.

Finally, Hayden dove down deep and swam long distances beneath the water to confuse Deirdre. He stayed underneath the water until he saw the boat. Once he was beneath the boat, he surfaced.

He wiped the water from his eyes and moved behind the boat to push it toward shore. Hayden hadn't gone very far when both Ian and Duncan's heads popped out of the water.

"What are you doing?" Hayden demanded.

"Fishing," Duncan said with a roll of his eyes.

Ian shook his head, a wry smile on his lips. "What do you think we're doing, Hayden."

"You'll get yourself killed." Hayden didn't mind risking his own life, but no one else should.

Duncan moved to Hayden's left and put his hands on the boat. "We are all of us family. This is what families do."

Hayden was too speechless to do more than follow as the twins began to push the small vessel. They hadn't gone very far when Deirdre's lightning struck Hayden.

He cursed, his body frozen for several moments as her black magic ran through him. It left his entire body feeling as if he was roasting over a fire, not to mention he feared his head might explode.

"Hayden?" Ian called.

"I'm all right," Hayden bit out. His pain was nothing compared to what Deirdre was doing to Isla. "Keep pushing."

A moment later the lightning hit the boat, sending them flying backward. Hayden heard Isla cry out, the sound tearing at his soul. It was all he needed to spur him faster.

"Hurry," he called to the twins.

Hayden couldn't remember ever swimming so fast. Even with the continued lightning strikes in and around the boat, Hayden never stopped. He couldn't. Isla needed him. He ignored the pain of the lightning and focused everything on getting Isla to the others.

It wasn't until Broc and the others came to the boat that Hayden realized he had reached shore. He pushed Ian out of the way and looked in the boat to see Isla on her side, her arms over her head while her body shuddered in agony.

"Isla," he whispered and lifted her in his arms.

She struggled against him, weak though it was. "Nay,

Hayden. I need to stay away. Leave me be. I don't want to hurt you."

"You cannot hurt me."

She turned her tear-streaked face to him, her gaze filled with such remorse that it broke his heart. "But I have," she said and shook again. "God forgive me, but I have. I knew you looked familiar, but it wasn't until tonight that I remembered."

"Stop," Hayden said. He didn't want her to say anything else. "It doesn't matter."

She cried harder, the tears raining down her cheeks. "It does."

"Hayden," Broc yelled. "The lightning is striking us. We need to get away."

Isla pushed at Hayden's chest, her face wreathed in anguish. "Let me go."

"Nay," he said. "Fight this. Fight her, Isla. I know you can."

She shook her head. "I'm not strong enough. Let me go."

"I willna."

Her lips thinned, and he knew she was about to tell him her great secret. Before he could stop her she said, "I'm the *drough* that killed your family."

He shut his eyes as her words sank into his mind. He expected to feel anger, betrayal, and even want her death. Instead, all he wanted to do was care for her, to protect her and cherish her. The past was over, his family long dead, and he had killed many *droughs* in his need for revenge.

Yet somehow, he wasn't surprised to find it was her. It saddened him, but he knew she had been under Deirdre's control. It wasn't Isla's fault anymore than it had been any of the *droughs* that he'd killed over the years. "I know. It doesna matter. Please. I need you."

"Hayden," she said and put her head against his chest.

She was giving up. His beautiful, brave, courageous Isla was giving up. He couldn't allow her to do that. She had to know he would stand beside her, that he would shout to the world that she was his.

Before he could utter a word the lightning struck them. Hayden would have taken all the pain onto himself if he could have. It killed him to hear Isla scream, her body wracked with convulsions.

"You willna have her!" Hayden shouted to the sky. "Isla is no longer yours to command!"

Isla suddenly went limp in his arms. He knew the more Deirdre used her black magic the more Isla's magic waned. Hayden knelt half on the beach, half in the water with Isla in his arms, silently praying that she lived.

He shook her gently until her eyes opened and focused on him. "I'm here to help you fight her," he said. "I will stand by you no matter what. I was an utter fool before. It wasn't until I awoke to find you gone that I realized how desperately I need you in my life."

"Shh," Isla said and placed a finger over his lips. "It's all right. I'm not afraid to die. If you cannot take my head, one of the others will. Deirdre wants me to kill all of you, and I cannot hold her off much longer. I thought I was stronger, but I'm not."

"Nay!" he bellowed. "No one is going to kill you. I willna let them. You are mine, Isla. I need you. I love you."

As soon as he'd said the words he knew they were true, had always been true. Without Isla, he was nothing.

Isla couldn't have heard Hayden correctly. Her expression must have told him as much because he smiled and stroked her face with his hand.

"I love you," he said again, his eyes portraying the truth

for her to see. "You're a powerful Druid, Isla. I know you can defeat Deirdre. Live. Live for me. Live for us."

She had claimed to have nothing to live for, but Hayden had just given her the best reason of all. Hope blossomed in her heart and spread its healing through her body.

Lightning hit the beach near them and out of the corner of her eye she saw one of the Warriors fall to his knees. Deirdre's power was growing each time she struck someone, especially Isla. It was as if Deirdre was feeding off Isla's magic and pain. And maybe she was.

Could Isla do as Hayden asked and fight? Did she dare try? She knew she had to do it for him.

Just as she was about to rise lightning struck her again. The pain was unbearable. Her body boiled, her blood thickened and slowed in her veins. She could hardly move her arms and legs, and always there was Deirdre's voice commanding her to kill, waiting for Isla to grow weak enough that Deirdre could take over.

And then Hayden's lips pressed to Isla's.

Isla wrapped her arms around him and held on as if her life depended upon it—because it did. She felt the water lapping at her feet. She called to her magic and let the water feed it, grow it, until it swarmed around her.

"Kill them all!" Deirdre's voice shouted in her head. "You cannot win, and the longer you fight me the more you will suffer, the more they will suffer."

Fear tried to take hold of Isla, but she concentrated on her magic, on the feel of its purity and influence, and Hayden's love. It grew and grew and grew until Isla felt the power of her magic.

That's when she used her magic and shoved at Deirdre in her head. To Isla's surprise, she felt Deirdre's hold on her wane a sliver. It wasn't much, but it was something.

Isla did it again and again, each time gaining more ground on Deirdre.

Hayden never lifted his lips from hers. He kept her locked against his chest, giving her all of him that she needed. And Isla refused to let him down.

She kept shoving at Deirdre until at last there was a loud snapping sound in Isla's head. A scream tore from her lips and her body stiffened as her head fell back.

Isla could feel Deirdre trying to maintain her power, but whatever Isla had done worked. There just needed one more bout of magic to break Deirdre's hold forever.

Isla turned her head to Hayden and looked into his black eyes. "I love you."

She heard Deirdre scream's of rage, her threat of death, and then she was gone.

The only sounds to break the silence were the waves and someone cursing. Isla couldn't stop shaking. She'd thought for sure her life was over.

She'd wanted to rejoice at hearing Hayden's voice, but with Deirdre commanding her to kill everyone at the castle, Isla hadn't wanted him near her for fear she would break under Deirdre's magic and kill him.

"I'm sorry," she said. "I'm so sorry for your family."

His large hands rubbed her back as he brought her against him. "It wasn't your fault. The blame lies with Deirdre. All of this is Deirdre's fault."

"Are either of you hurt?" Broc asked.

Isla shook her head, and Hayden answered, "Nay."

"Good. Is she gone, Isla?"

Isla turned her head so she could see Broc and the others. "She's gone from my mind. For good, I think."

Broc smiled and opened his large wings. "I think Hayden can get you back to the castle. We'll report this to Fallon and Lucan and the others."

Quinn was the last to leave. He gave them a smile and a nod of his head before he turned on his heel and started up the path.

Isla swallowed, suddenly nervous now that they were alone. She slowly rose from Hayden's arms and staggered to the sea. Once there, she let her magic rebuild her strength.

She felt Hayden behind her and shivered when his hands rested on her shoulders before skimming down her arms.

"You said you loved me." His voice held an odd note, almost as if he was afraid to say it.

"Aye."

"After everything I've done and said to you, how can you?"

She turned in his arms to face him. "Because of who you are. How could I not fall in love with you? And you? Do you still care for me despite what I've done?"

"I mourn the loss of my family. I want revenge for their murder, but I will get that vengeance when Deirdre is dead. You give me strength. You alone make me see the good in the world. I would be nothing without you."

She felt tears sting her eyes again. He brushed away one that escaped to land on her cheek before he kissed her.

Isla rose up on her toes and wrapped her arms around his neck as he deepened the kiss. Their laughter mingled with the dawn as he lifted her and spun them about before falling into the water.

Somehow, some way, Isla had beaten Deirdre. But that's not what she celebrated. Isla celebrated Hayden and the love they had found.

EPILOGUE

Hayden couldn't stop smiling. He had almost lost everything for the second time in his life, but he had managed to keep it all. Most especially Isla.

Now, as they sat in the great hall with the others laughing and talking, Hayden looked around at his new family. And the love of his life.

"Are you happy?" he asked Isla.

She turned her ice-blue eyes to him and smiled radiantly. "I've never been happier. I never thought it was possible. Not for me."

Though there was still much to do and the war still raged around them, the castle had been rejoicing the entire day. After Deirdre's attack on Isla, and Isla's triumph, it was cause for merriment.

More importantly was the fact Hayden no longer thought about Isla being a *drough*. She was his, and that's all that he needed.

"What happens now?" Isla asked.

He threaded his fingers in hers. "We're together. That's all I need."

"I don't know if I'm still immortal."

"Then we'll take special care of you," he promised. "I will always take care of you."

She leaned her head on his shoulder and sighed. "We've such a difficult path ahead of us."

"We'll face it together."

"Together," she repeated and looked up at him.

Hayden cleared his throat and glanced around. He was a private man, so he didn't want everyone to overhear what he was about to say.

"Hayden?" Isla asked.

He lifted her hand to lips and kissed her knuckles. "I doona deserve you, but I won't let you go. I never thought I would find myself in this position, Isla, but I have a question for you."

"What is it?"

"Will you marry me?"

She swallowed and blinked rapidly. "Aye, Hayden Campbell, I'd be most delighted to be your wife."

There was a loud cheer in the great hall as Hayden pulled her into his arms. He should have known everyone could hear them, but he didn't care.

The well wishes came, each Warrior stopping beside them. The MacLeods and their wives were last.

"You two are perfect for each other," Marcail said after she gave Isla a hug.

Quinn laughed and clasped arms with Hayden. "Congratulations. I told you when you found the right woman your life would be complicated, but in a good way."

Hayden smiled down at Isla. "A very good way."

Cara reached for one of Isla's hands. "Let's rejoice. It's not every day we get to have a wedding."

"It sure seems that way," Lucan said.

Larena shrugged and glanced at Fallon. "Maybe we should see if we can tempt a priest to come live here. After all, there might be more weddings."

There was a loud snort from Duncan. "Doona be speaking for us, Larena MacLeod. I'm content just as I am."

Hayden and Quinn shared a smile, for they knew better than the others what could come when a man least expected it.

Deirdre's scream of rage filled the mountain and seeped through the cracks to fill the air. Animals scurried away in fear and dread, because the evil that grew in Cairn Toul just became stronger.

Somewhere not far away a Warrior lifted his head as he heard the scream. A slow smile spread over his face as he realized just where that scream had come from.

He changed his direction and headed back to Cairn Toul.

Tomorrow Reaghan planned to leave the only home she had ever known.

The small village went about its daily life, unaware, and uncaring, of the turmoil that ripped through one of their own. Reaghan didn't want to leave. She was a part of the land and the village.

Yet how could she ignore the insistence of her own feelings?

It was true the Druids who had left the village over the years were never seen from again, but there was an exciting world out there. At the same time she yearned to see the world for herself and to experience it—all of it, she also feared leaving.

She didn't know what was out there. Though she knew who was out there—Dierdre.

Not to mention the only men left in their dwindling group tottered about, barely able to stand on their own. Neither of them would be fit choices for a husband. Besides, they were already married.

Reaghan wanted . . . more of a life, more *in* her life than what she had. It wasn't that she was unhappy with the Druids. In fact, she was very content. But the part that wanted and needed more wouldn't be denied.

The ache, the need to see and experience more had

grown in the past six months to the point that she could no longer push it aside. It was as if her future was right in front of her and she had only to reach out and grab it.

Every time Reaghan had tried to talk to Mairi about it, the elder had been quick to point out why the village needed her.

Mairi and the other elders meant well, but Reaghan had to make this decision on her own. It would likely tear her in two, but she had to leave. There was something out there for her to do; she just didn't know what it was yet.

Then there was the parchment Reaghan had come upon in Mairi's chest by accident. It had been so old the edges had crumbled when her fingers touched them. The words, though faded, had been in Gaelic—a language Reaghan had never read before, but somehow she had recognized the words. Had understood them.

But that surprise had faded to nothing when she'd read her name and discovered she wasn't from Loch Awe but instead came from a group of Druids on Foinaven Mountain.

There had been so many questions running through her mind. Her head had swum with suspicion and supposition. Mairi had been like a mother to her. She wanted to give the elder a chance to explain things.

As usual, Mairi had given evasive answers. And Reaghan couldn't handle that. For some reason Mairi and the other elders thought they had to lie to her about her past. But why? What was so awful?

Regardless of what it was, Reaghan wanted the truth.

Reaghan had put the parchment with her own things and begun to plan to find the Druids and home, where she belonged. It was as good a place as any to begin, and maybe it would halt the persistent feeling inside her that there would be something for her to do.

On the morrow Reaghan would depart the safe haven she had known for ten years and strike out on her own in a world she didn't know.

Tomorrow, everything would change. For better or worse. She was fearful, but eager. Nervous, but exhilarated. It was the start of a new life, one she intended to seize with both hands and make the most of. Whatever the outcome.

She had dreams she wanted to fulfill like anyone else. And she didn't want much. She wanted to be happy, to find a man whom she could share her life with and start a family with. She wanted children to fill her days with laughter and memories.

The pounding began at the base of her neck and worked its way up to her temples, increasing with each beat of her heart. She didn't know why her head had begun to ache the past month as it had, and she feared there was no cure for it.

She put a hand to her forehead, the coolness against her skin giving some relief, but not nearly enough. Reaghan tried to hide a grimace of pain as she turned away, but Mairi's brown eyes were sharp, despite her age.

"You're hurting again, child. You need to rest."

The soft, comforting hands which had helped heal Reaghan from the fever so long ago took hold of her arms now and guided her to her cottage.

Not that the structure could be called a cottage. The Druids had moved around Loch Awe for years until the young ones began to go away, leaving only the older Druids and a few others who didn't want to abandon the beauty and safety of the loch. That's when the Druids had decided to make a permanent village, hundreds of years ago, hidden away from the world by magic, blending into the surroundings.

Reaghan leaned her hand against the trunk of the giant oak that stood in the middle of her home. All the Druids used what nature supplied them with to craft their homes. Many travelers had walked past their village and had never seen it. Partly because their homes blended with the forest, but also because of their magic—limited though it was.

"Sit," Mairi ordered, her voice brooking no argument.

Reaghan allowed the old woman to push her down into a chair. The throbbing of her head always began slowly, building with intensity. And each day when it came, it grew worse, lasted longer. Reaghan would be weak for hours afterwards, her body not her own.

Something wasn't right. Reaghan knew it in the marrow of her bones. But no matter who or what she asked, no one had any answers. Maybe the headaches were connected to the fever Mairi had saved her from, and no one wanted to tell her.

"I'll be fine," Reaghan said and took the cool, wet cloth Mairi handed her. She put it to her forehead and sighed. Just speaking made her head pound worse. The ache was so terrible she couldn't clamp her teeth together.

Years could have passed as Reaghan endured the pain, concentrating on keeping her stomach from souring. Just as suddenly as the ache had come on, it disappeared. For long moments Reaghan didn't move, afraid her head would begin to hammer again. Her body was weak, and all she wanted to do was lie down and sleep.

Finally, she dropped the cloth and raised her head. "It is gone."

"For now," Mairi murmured. Her eyes, filled with concern, dropped to the table as she tapped the wood with a fingernail. "How bad was this one?"

"I was able to handle the pain."

Mairi smiled sadly and cupped Reaghan's cheek. "My darling girl, that is not what I asked."

"It was worse than the one from yesterday."

Mairi lowered her hand and looked away, but not before Reaghan saw the resignation in her old brown eyes.

"You know what is happening to me, don't you?" Reaghan asked.

Mairi released a long breath. "Reaghan, sometimes it is best if you don't know the answers to all your questions."

It was too much. Reaghan stood and moved around Mairi, needing to be alone. Her body was weak, but she couldn't stay with the elder a moment longer. She needed some time alone. "I'm going to go for a walk."

"You do understand we need you, don't you, Reaghan? Our numbers decline more each year. I fear that one day I will be the only one left."

Reaghan's heart clenched in her chest as Mairi's words made her pause near the door. She understood the panic which ran through the village as their numbers declined. "What will be, will be," she said without turning around.

She didn't slow once she left her cottage and walked out of what the remaining twenty-three Druids called a village. Reaghan didn't stop, not even when the only child, Braden, called to her to pick berries with him.

Reaghan felt as if she were slowly going daft. There was much more going on than just the aches in her head. Her dreams had been filled with images she couldn't explain but felt she had seen with her own eyes. People. Places. Events. All of which she knew she hadn't experienced, yet she knew she had. Somehow.

It was illogical. She had never left Loch Awe, so how could she have seen the magnificent castle on the cliffs, or the mountain peak where, she somehow knew, evil was bred?

Reaghan paused beside a pine, her hand upon the rough bark, and took a deep breath. The sunlight filtered through the overhanging branches and leaves to make vivid, interesting designs on the ground she'd always found fascinating. But not today. The smell of pine, of decaying leaves, and a hint of some sweet flower did not calm her as it usually did.

The anxiety inside her only grew with each day, filling her so that she could barely close her eyes at night. There was a part of her which screamed to leave post-haste before . . . before *what*, she didn't know, only that something was going to happen.

She knew she was safe with the Druids. They might not answer her questions, but they had shown her only love and friendship since she had awoken from the fever.

There was safety in the village. Reaghan knew of Deirdre, knew how the *drough* hunted other Druids. Yet Reaghan wanted to know where she had come from. There might be family still on Foinaven Mountain.

Reaghan shook her head and swallowed past the painful lump in her throat at the thought of leaving Loch Awe and the Druids.

Her thoughts ground to a halt when she heard the keening call of the falcon. It wasn't so much the peregrine itself as the feeling that went with the bird of prey, as if it called to her, *for* her.

There was magic with the bird, of that Reaghan was sure. She didn't know how or why, only that it was.

Reaghan watched the magnificent bird fly over the loch before swooping into the trees. Falcons were majestic birds, and the peregrine was the fastest of them all. It moved with artistry and grace, precision and deadly intent.

The bird landed on a thick branch high in a tree not far from Reaghan, folding its wings against its sleek body.

She could have sworn the bird's sharp eyes turned to her as its blackish colored head cocked to the side.

Reaghan was disappointed. She would have preferred to watch the bird fly. She could have pretended she was the falcon, and the vast expanse of sky her only prison.

With a sigh she lowered her gaze and stilled. Two men stood below her at the shore of the loch. Her fingers dug into the bark of the pine tree as her heart raced frantically and her stomach dropped to her feet like a stone.

Their gazes moved slowly, as if they searched for something—or someone. She stood inside the magical confines of the village. As long as she stayed within the border, the men would never see her. Why that filled her with regret, she wasn't sure.

"We've been searching for four hours," one mumbled.

The blond nodded. "I well know. I'm no' about to give up, though."

A glance at their different kilts told her they weren't from the same clan. Travelers, maybe? What were such handsome men doing at Loch Awe, unless they were on their way to MacIntosh Castle? And what could they be looking for?

Many times she had watched such travelers and yearned to speak to them. What could it hurt? She was leaving on the morrow once she gathered the rest of her items. What better way to test what awaited her than by speaking to strangers near the safety of the village?

And if they are from Deirdre? She would step back into the magic barrier and watch as the men, confused, looked for her.

Her decision made, Reaghan took the step which put her outside the magic. The men, as one, turned their heads to her. They stared at her, silent and intent.

She didn't worry about the men seeing the village. Yet.

For the moment, they seemed satisfied to observe her. The men looked affable enough, but Reaghan knew better than to trust on appearances alone. Everyone hid something.

"Hello," the one closest to her said.

His voice was rich and smooth, friendly. The sound of it made her blood quicken, making her want to hear more. He had thick, dark blond hair that was tied in a loose queue at the back of his neck.

Even from the twenty or so paces he stood apart from her, she could see the vibrant cobalt blue of his eyes. The way he watched her, studied her, made gooseflesh rise on her skin as awareness skidded around her, through her.

He stood with his arms to his side, seemingly at ease, belying the corded muscles she glimpsed in his arms and chest. There was a predatory elegance about him, a ravenous warrior that told Reaghan he could—and would—defend what was his. To the death.

Unable to help herself, Reaghan let her gaze run over his chiseled face. His forehead was high, his brows thin and golden. His cheeks were hollowed, his chin hard, and his jaw squared. That jaw was shadowed with a beard, making him appear more interesting, more dangerous.

More enticing.

Reaghan tried to swallow, tried to think of anything but the very male, very appealing stranger before her. She knew she was being rude in not answering him as she looked her fill, but how could she not? He was everything a Highland warrior should be.

His lips tilted ever so slightly in a smile, as if he knew what was going through her mind. Reaghan wanted to move closer to him, to touch his skin and run her hands through his hair.

She yearned to feel the strength of him, to have his

muscles move beneath her hand. She longed to run her fingertip over his wide lips, to look deeper into his stunning blue eyes.

Her blood pounded in her ears like a drum in her chest the more she thought about touching him, of learning him.

It was as if for the first time in her life she was truly alive. Sounds she hadn't paid attention to before filled her ears, scents she hadn't noticed before swirled around her, and the colors of the forest and loch seemed more brilliant, more effervescent than usual.

All because of one man.

She inhaled a shaky breath and pulled her scattered longings back inside her. She would look at her reaction to the man later in the privacy of her own cottage when his cobalt gaze wasn't on her, reading her every emotion.

"Hello," she finally replied. She knew the elders wouldn't approve, but it had been so long since she had seen anyone other than those in her village, especially men of marriageable age.

"Do you live around here?" the other man asked.

Reaghan regretfully shifted her gaze from the first man to the second. His wavy brown hair hung freely about his shoulders. His smile was wider, more teasing, but she saw darkness lurked in his hazel eyes, a darkness he tried valiantly to hide. He was the same height as the first, with the same build, though he was leaner.

She licked her lips, wariness stealing over her for the first time, crushing her newfound excitement. She didn't know these men, didn't know where they had come from or what they wanted. Was this fear what she would experience once she left the village? "Many live on Loch Awe."

"My name is Galen Shaw," the first man said. His words were unhurried, casual. "My friend is Logan Hamilton."

Just knowing his name eased some of Reaghan's trepidation. She was just a step away from safety and Druids who would come running, their magic—inadequate though it was—at the ready. It gave her the courage to ask, "And what brings you to our loch, Galen Shaw?"

He grinned, sending ripples of perception through her as the corners of his eyes crinkled. "We're looking for Druids."

"Druids?" Reaghan's heart fluttered like a butterfly caught in a net. So that's what they'd meant when they said they'd been searching for hours.

Gazing at Galen's handsome body made it difficult to breathe, to think, but the mention of Druids nearly choked her. No one spoke of Druids. "You realize there are no more Druids? Those who claimed the old ways were burned as pagans."

Logan moved until he was even with Galen and gave her a teasing wink. "Aye, my lady, but we know the truth. Druids are most certainly around, and it's verra important we speak to one."

She wondered what they would do if she told them she was a Druid. It was the truth, though she held no magic of her own. Such was the way when Druid blood was diluted with those who had no magic. It was what was slowly becoming of her people, one reason they fought so brashly to keep her among them.

"I'm afraid you gentlemen are wrong. There haven't been Druids around here in centuries."

"We have proof," Galen said.

This was getting interesting. Maybe too interesting. Reaghan knew she ought to send the men away, but she was having too much fun. Besides, she liked the way her body and senses came alive with Galen. It was peculiar and terrifying, but breathtaking at the same time. "What proof?"

"Another Druid sent us."

Galen pulled out a rolled parchment from his kilt and spread it out for her to see. Reaghan recognized it as a drawing of the loch. Her gaze jerked to his blue eyes to find him watching her closely.

"That only proves someone has been to the loch and can draw."

"True enough. Except it was a Druid who told us we could find the village of Druids here," he said, and pointed to the spot on the map where her village sat.

Reaghan didn't know what to say. Her fellow Druids had long thought there were no more of them out in the world, that they were the last. The parchment Reaghan found the other day proved there had been other Druids, but there was no evidence those Druids still existed.

She wanted to know. She had to know. If there were more Druids, she was going to find them.

"Reaghan."

Startled, she turned her head to find Odara, one of three elders, to her left. Odara stood like a soldier with her stooped shoulders back and her head held high. She was only able to look down at the men because of her advantage on the slope.

"These men claim to be searching for a Druid village," Reaghan told her.

Galen nodded and again pointed to the location on the map. "A Druid sent us. Isla promised we would find a Druid village."

For long moments Odara silently measured the men, her gaze moving from, first, Galen, then to Logan.

It was Logan who finally spoke. "We can feel your magic. We know we've found the Druids."

Reaghan's blood drummed deafeningly in her ears as his words sank in. They could feel the magic of the Druids?

Who were these men? And what did they want with Druids? She suddenly began to doubt her wisdom in talking to them. Had she just put everyone in terrible danger?

"Please," Galen said. "We would like to talk to the elders. It's extremely important."

Odara sighed and clasped her hands in front of her. "Do you expect me to take your word for it, young man? That you can feel magic?"

Logan coughed to cover his laughter as Galen sent him a warning glare. Reaghan couldn't take her eyes off them. It was fascinating to watch how they interacted with each other. The young men of her village had long departed, so this was all new to her.

"Young man?" she heard Logan say in a choked whisper.

She had no idea why Logan would find that amusing, but obviously he did.

"I do not lie," Galen told Odara. "We're here in an effort to fight Deirdre."

At the mention of the name, Odara sucked in a breath, her hands shaking. Her gaze darted around, as if at any moment, Deirdre would jump from behind a tree. "What do you know of her?"

"Too much," Logan muttered angrily.

Those two words, laced with such revulsion and a hint of anxiety, were enough to make Reaghan believe them. It wasn't just the words, though. She had always been able to tell when someone was lying to her, if she could look them in the eye. Galen and Logan weren't lying. About any of it.

Reaghan was more intrigued than ever. She had heard stories of Deirdre before, the *drough* who wanted to rule the world. It was one of the reasons her village was hidden, why they were wary of strangers.

"Odara, I think we should listen to them," Reaghan whispered.

She let out a deep breath and nodded her silver head as she looked to Galen and Logan. "Stay with Reaghan. I will return."

Once Odara walked away, Reaghan opened her mouth to begin asking the men many, various questions. She wanted to know as much as she could before the elders returned and seized the men's attention.

"It was your magic we felt."

Galen's words halted any questions Reaghan had thought to ask. "You're mistaken. I have no magic."

The falcon gave a loud cry above them, its shrill call echoing around the forest and loch. Reaghan paid the bird little heed. She was too shaken by Galen's words. She wished it had been her magic he had sensed, but she knew first-hand there was no magic to speak of inside her.

A pity that. She would have liked to be a part of whatever Galen and Logan had come to her village for. To be a part of something meaningful, something which changed the world, appealed to her in ways she had never expected.

It wouldn't matter anyway. As much as the men captivated Reaghan, once the other women spotted the new arrivals, she would be forgotten. And that was best, especially since she was about to leave for her own adventure.

It was all working out perfectly. Mairi and the other elders would be occupied with Galen and Logan, leaving Reaghan free to depart without any fuss. Reaghan didn't like the prospect of a long farewell.

"We're never mistaken," Logan said, voice breaking into her thoughts.

Galen's brilliant blue eyes held hers. She was caught, trapped in his gaze, and she found she didn't mind at all. "Your magic is very strong. You just don't know it yet."